The Deposition

A Novel

Scott Wellinger

The Deposition

A Novel
by Scott Wellinger

World Wide Publishing Group
New York   Los Angeles   London   Toronto

Jacket design by Jason Goodchild

Printed in the United States of America

10 9 8 7 6 5 4 3 2 1

ISBN: 978-0-9861514-8-4   (Ebook)
ISBN: 978-0-9861514-9-1   (Print)

For LW~

I told it my way.

Thank You.

Epigraph

"There's already a verdict to that nature, sir.

I'm not going to answer that question again."

~ Casey Anthony during her 2014 deposition

Chapter 1

May 15, 2015

4:00 PM

The Trial

THIS WAS THE MOMENT THAT EVERYONE WAS waiting for. Pay dirt as it were. New Yorkers had been on the edge of their collective seats since the trial began, reenergized daily since the murder first hit the news nearly a year ago.

In the age of social media and terrorist plots and mass shootings, the murder of a forty-one year old white lady from Manhattan doesn't garner the same level of national attention. The waning attention span of the general public often narrows the news cycle to a pithy and often unedited one-liner. The army of people running in the presidential race—especially on the Republican side—filled the gaps between police shootings and the nut jobs who shoot up night clubs and schools. Generally, there was little room nor prolific interest in the murder of an affluential socialite on the upper west side beyond the blurb on page six, the parenthetical on the Huffington Post, or the two minutes squeezed into the C-block on the nightly news.

But not this story. Hunt Media was forcing this story down the throats of the New York elites, the bridge and tunnel crowd, as well as the nation at large. The media mogul was imposing the conversation because it was one of theirs that was slain. Rather than scroll or swipe or turn a page or turn the channel, New Yorkers were eating it up.

Since the murder, the presidential race for the White House had now become battle royale in earnest, though the election was still more than a year away. The press never tired of the candidates squabbling about sophomoric tweets, fitness for the job, a bridge that was closed, whether one of the candidates was actually Canadian, a lack of a platform, socialism, and ill-conceived emails sent on a private server. Through the unpresidential-like noise, New York along with the rest of the nation, relished the distraction and waited with bated breath as the jury entered the courtroom, rumored to be fortified with a verdict. Finally. This was it.

If one of the most wealthy and recognizable women in New York wasn't safe, who was? As the jury filled the box, ears were bent to hear the words everyone wanted to hear. "GUILTY".

Television cameras focused on the jury, the judge, the defendant and the attorneys as usual since the trial began. Sketch artists and reporters and bloggers and the ilk had pads and recorders and touchscreen devices at the ready to broadcast to the world what the twelve New Yorkers who comprised the jury had decided regarding the guilt or innocence of the accused. It had been a long month in wait. And it all was coming to a climax. After four weeks of legal volleying back-and-forth, of the posturing, of testimony, the opening and closing statements, at long last closure in the form of a verdict was forthcoming.

The defendant and his basketball-sized legal team stood as instructed by the judge. None looked worried, nor had they appeared to be over the course of the excruciatingly long trial. Every angle, every facial expression, every jot on a yellow legal pad, every whisper from one person to another at the defense table was captured and analyzed to the spoon-fed public. If the defendant had been worried, he hadn't shown it then or now.

The commentators all agreed that the defendant looked smug, bordering on arrogant, though he never spoke a word. He hadn't bothered to testify at his own trial, exercising his right to confront and question his accusers without subjecting himself to questions from the prosecution. He was innocent until proven guilty, though all agreed that he'd murdered his famous, astronomically wealthy, and beautiful wife. Stoic meant heartless in the eyes of those that purported to know these things. Had he shown more emotion as testimony was heard, the commentators might have accused him of being excitable and quick to violence, and therefore guilty. There had to be something to the case, however. Innocent people aren't brought to trial for murder. Husbands killed their wives all the time, sometimes for the insurance money, which in those cases paled in comparison to the enormity of the Hunt estate. He must be guilty, and his lack of empathy was the added proof to substantiate the people of New York's claim.

He hadn't, however. He hadn't shown the slightest of emotion. Each day the man accused of killing his wife sat in the courtroom with his lawyers devoid of visible sentiment and nary a hair out of place. His three-piece designer suits were flawless. His wire-framed eyeglasses hadn't so much as a smudge or piece of lint on the lenses. He sat upright—perfect posture for a month—with a blank stare as witness after witness took the stand to hammer in another nail.

And now it was time to hear the guilty verdict.

Doctor Linus Hampton, law professor at Columbia University on 116th Street just ten miles to the west, watched as the jury handed a piece of paper to the court officer who then gave it to Judge Carl Schriber. His Honor took a page from the Hampton playbook, supplying no indication of how he felt about what he'd just read on the form, and quickly gave it back to the court officer who then handed the document back to the madam foreperson. She, the court officer, the defendant, and the team at his defense table were the only people in the courtroom on their feet, save for the standing room only crowd in the back. All of the Hunt Media outlets will have another top story to broadcast to the public along with the Dzhokhar Tsarnaev trial and Tom Brady's suspension appeal across the street. The rest of the media elite would follow suit.

"In the matter of People V. Hampton, has the jury come to a unanimous decision?" His Honor asked.

"We have."

"For the top count of Murder in the First Degree, what say you?"

11

The middle-aged, female foreperson read the sheet of paper unfolded in front of her rather than look at the judge, the defendant, or a camera. "We find the defendant .... Not guilty."

The gallery exploded with voices and flashes.

Schriber swung his gavel like he was attempting to pound a three-inch nail into hardwood. The sound failed to quiet the commotion. "QUIET!" He waited a few beats while the gallery slowly regained composure before continuing. "For the lesser-included charge of Assault With A Deadly Weapon, what say you?"

"We find the defendant not guilty."

The crowd rumbled again but not with the same fervor as the verdict regarding the top murder count.

"And for the charge of Hindering Prosecution, how does the jury find?"

"We find the defendant not guilty."

"So be it. I thank the jury for its service." Schriber turned to the defendant. "Linus Hampton, your bail and passport will be reimbursed to you, your ankle monitor will be removed forthwith, and you will then be free to go." His Honor then looked to his far right and spoke to the court stenographer. "That concludes the matter of the People of the State and County of New York V. Linus Fredrick Hampton. The jury is free to go. Good day."

More than two hours later, the sea of reporters looking for a soundbite to make the evening news—or more immediately the social media outlets looking to be the first to post something along with the hashtag 'HamptonInnocent'—were still congregated at the base of the courthouse stairs. They lay in wait clogging up the pedestrian traffic in Foley Square, looking up at the massive columns, for the man acquitted and his legal counsel to leave the courthouse. Finally, after two hours of standing in the unseasonably warm sun, Hampton and his lead attorney, William Reid, appeared at the top of the stairs as anticipated. The beat reporters, who's job was to routinely cover the courthouse, knew to keep to the bottom of the stairs. Those who were unusually present for the now infamous verdict were reminded where to wait by the ample police presence that acted as a human barricade. All shouted questions to the still far-off men who hadn't as yet completely descended the concrete stairs below the engraved words on the building, 'THE TRUE ADMINISTRATION OF JUSTICE IS THE FIRMEST PILLAR OF GOOD GOVERNMENT'.

Neither man said a word. Hampton, as always, remained stoic. William Reid Esquire had a grin from ear to ear as he approached and stopped a few feet in front of the mob. Reid resembled an older Don Cheadle yet was said to be more akin to Johnnie Cochran without the rhymes or facial hair. A press conference was about to take place and everyone present knew it. This is what they'd been baking in the sun for. Both men made the frothing press wait a bit longer.

A small faction of the media scurried away from the mob toward the two prosecutors from the District Attorney's Office who were attempting to sneak away from the spotlight. Assistant District Attorneys Michael Hardison and Judy Kemp looked content to retreat with tail between legs, abashed to lick their wounds away from prying eyes with scotch in-hand. They'd just lost a landmark case and were understandably less than keen on having their noses rubbed in it. A dozen or so of the reporters split off from the masses to corner them.

Questions like "How do you feel about the decision?" and "Do you think justice was served?" were bellowed out as the frenzied press rushed toward the prosecutors.

Hardison reluctantly responded without breaking stride. "Obviously we don't think the jury made the right decision. We felt we had a strong case, with more than ample evidence to support the charges brought against Mister Hampton. We're disappointed with the outcome. A wealthy man got away with murder because he could afford a legal team and a mouthpiece like Reid Williams. That is all."

Another question was shouted. "So you were out-lawyered?"

"No further comment," Hardison said as he pushed through the eager dozen, trying to forge a path for his female co-counsel to follow. The small crowd dispersed quickly when Reid began his delayed speech a hundred feet away. The offshoot group rushed back to the mob on the opposite side of the stairs to hear him.

"Was justice carried out?" a reporter shouted above the din of other questions. That was the question the attorney was going to focus on.

"It is a great day in America when the system works. An innocent man had his day in court and a jury saw through the conjecture and the lies. But no, justice was not 'carried out'. True justice will occur when the real murderer is made to account for his actions. We clearly showed during the trial who the person the police and the overzealous District Attorney should have prosecuted. And should be the one being prosecuted this very day.

14

Maybe now, after this colossal waste of time and taxpayer dollars, maybe now the District Attorney will exact justice on the true perpetrator of this horrific crime. Professor Hampton is a respected member of Columbia University, of New York society, and he can put his terrible tragedy behind him if and when the actual murderer is held accountable for his crime. His beautiful wife of eleven years was murdered just one year ago, and my client was never afforded the opportunity to grieve. He couldn't. Because the police and the overzealous District Attorney's Office had their sights set on him. In their zeal for a conviction, they let the real killer go—"

"—Do you think the police will reopen the investigation to find the real murderer?" another reporter shouted from the crowd.

"You'll have to take that up with ADA Hardison or his boss, District Attorney Cyrus Vance. What I am saying is that my client hasn't been able to piece his life back together after this terrible event because he was forced to defend his very life, his very freedom, while the real perpetrator of this horrific crime was free to do it again. For a year now, this murderer has been free to move about this city, if he's even still in this city at all. The full resources of New York County were used to prosecute the wrong man at the taxpayers expense, at the behest of the very powerful and influential Hunt Family. All that time and money spent to harass and vilify the wrong man because the District Attorney was too afraid to be in the crosshairs of the powerful Hunt family. Hundreds of thousands of dollars wasted. Maybe the DA should send Hunt Media the bill since they're obviously so content to remain in the hip pocket of the Hunt empire. But either way, will the District Attorney do it all again? We certainly hope so. The taxpayers of the City, State, and County of New York should *DEMAND* it. My client needs closure. The system needs finality. While we stand here in front of the building where justice and the system of jurisprudence in Manhattan is executed every day, a murderer is still free. That is unacceptable. So I will answer the first question posed. While the system worked, justice did not prevail. Thank you. That is all for now."

Chapter 2
February 5, 2016
3:00 PM
Preparedness

THE OFFICES OF REID, WEINSTEIN, HANLEY & Wood, located on Manhattan's Upper East Side—specifically on First and East Seventy-Seventh—took up floors eighteen through twenty-two of the skyscraper on the fourteen-hundred block of First Street. The glass and granite building looked like every other skyscraper in New York, in Hampton's mind. The large revolving door in the center of the front facade spun slowly yet constantly as those with business therein came and went. The two glass satellite doors to each side of the ever-spinning carousel weren't in use, as the signs more than insinuated that they were for emergency egress only.

Hampton's Caesium Blue, five-liter supercharged Jaguar XJ came to a stop directly in front of the building. He waited for his driver to exit and open the rear passenger-side door for him. In truth, Hampton hated having a driver, but parking in the city was the stuff of nightmares. The ability to go from point A to point B without the need of public transport was in his mind less a

17

luxury and more of an essential. Drivers, by nature, were morons. Their only skill was knowing how to get from said point A to B. This was no skill. Every immigrant who made their way to New York could figure out that avenues run north-south and streets run east-west. Numbers are universal in every language, a GPS is needed as much as an abacus. Any idiot can follow sequential numbers and find the desired block. Any kindergartener can navigate through Manhattan, any foreigner can become a cabbie, and any idiot with a grasp of the English language can be a personal driver. Look at Lyft and Uber for Christ's sake. Drivers were simpletons with no ambition. His latest was no different.

Linus had been through countless drivers over the years; all were white, and all were fluent in English, he presumed. None understood that he never wanted to hear one word from their lips, however. An attempt at small-talk would put them in the unemployment line posthaste. Hampton's only requirements were that his drivers be punctual, navigate the city properly—avoiding the heaviest of traffic wherever possible affording him the ability to be punctual—and to keep bloody quiet. Yet they always cocked it up. Male. Female. No matter. This one, Daniel, had been with him nearly two weeks and would soon break the record for longest tenure.

The rear door of the Jag opened at the curb. Hampton exited his flash sedan and immediately smoothed out the nonexistent wrinkles on his pristine Kiton dark blue suit, fastening the top button on his suit jacket as a final flourish. He'd forgone an overcoat as the milder than average, forty-four degree day made one unnecessary. Linus looked to his feet as he smoothed a non-wrinkle from his slacks, noticing the shallow puddle formed from the melting snow which had pooled in a depressed area on the sidewalk. He further noticed that Daniel had parked exactly in front of it. Had the driver pulled ahead a few feet or stopped a few feet sooner, Hampton wouldn't now be standing in a shallow puddle risking the soiling of his Bontoni loafers. *One demerit*, he made mental note. As the driver closed the Jaguar door behind him and handed him the thin Maxwell Scott attaché case from the boot, he broke the cardinal rule.

"Should I circle the block or should I park somewhere and wait for your call?" Daniel asked.

Maybe the sod won't break that record after all. Linus made another mental note to call the temp service to have this one sacked and another in his place tomorrow morning. "I'll call when and if I require your service," he said without tone or expression.

All parties entering the building housing RWH&W have to go through security prior to moving further into the lobby, to the building receptionist-slash-greeter, up the stairs for those wanting a bit of exercise, or to the bank of elevators along the far wall. Skyscrapers in New York are always a rather tall target for a terrorist of one sort or another, September Eleventh had taught us as much. Hundreds if not thousands of people entering the building at First and East Seventy-Seventh were forced through a wide scanner—slash—gate each day, usually without breaking stride. De rigueur. A way of life in Manhattan. People walked through the contraption shoulder—to—shoulder. No exceptions.

Save for Linus Hampton of course.

This was not his first time entering the building, each previous time he'd forgone the protocols and it was his expectation that this day be no different. Hampton had visited often during the criminal trial, and had resumed the frequency since filing the current civil matter. Each time he entered through the side door, circumnavigating the security protocol. His civil attorney, Miranda Wood, who shared the letterhead of his legal firm, was waiting for him in the lobby as he entered through the seldom used door, guiding him around the security team. No scanners or state-of-the-art x-ray system for Hampton. Employees and visitors of one of the many offices held in the First Street skyscraper walked through the wide security gate, side—by—side, without breaking stride, every day, with nary a second thought. Not Professor Linus Hampton, however. He was neither pedestrian nor workaday. Beyond being lumped in with the plebeians, Hampton's objections were constitutional. Unlawful search and seizure. His protestations were vocal to the point of rubicon and so his eschewing of normal protocol was forever waived.

The security team was more than familiar with the RWH&W client, had received their orders, and therefore unaffected by the circumnavigation. Hampton was allowed to join his lawyer, Miranda Wood—who acquiesced to the security measures when going to work each day like everyone else—unimpeded. The two walked toward the bank of elevators with nary a word or glance at one another.

The staff at Reid, Weinstein, Hanley & Wood made a ridiculous fuss over him on the twenty-second floor as he and Miranda made way toward the conference room. He was asked no less than ten times between elevator and conference room if he required a specific refreshment. A latte, sparkling water, hot tea, finger sandwiches, and a bowl of fresh fruit were a few of the offerings made to the law firm's client. Each and every encounter feigned pure bliss in seeing him again. If one was forced to be immersed in a legal entanglement, RWH&W was the best possible way to go through it. While he found the entire charade obnoxious, he was secretly just as chuffed about it. With the amount of money he'd spent in attorney's fees over the past two years, they should offer him every flourish one could think up. And they did. The criminal trial had cost him nearly four million. God only knew how much this civil matter was going to bleed him.

Hampton accepted a Perrier with lime from a green-eyed brunette as he took a seat at the large conference room table across from Miranda Wood. He made sure the fabric of suit was taut so as not to form wrinkles as he sat.

Miranda checked her appearance in the glass as she walked toward her seat. Appearances were very important to her client. He'd made it plain to her on numerous occasions. It was clear she was making hers a priority just then. Hampton liked that though he noticed a small chip on the right high heel of his lawyer's Jimmy Choos. Had it been anything more pressing than a pre-dep conference, he might have made mention of it. On the conference room table in front of where she took her seat, Miranda had a laptop and documents laid out in preparation for the meeting.

"Thank you for meeting with me. Monday's deposition has to go well if we are to prevail at trial," she said to Hampton as she took her seat. The comely

21

subordinate who'd delivered the Perrier closed the blinds and the conference room door behind her as she exited.

"This will never go to trial, but I do understand your desire to pad the billable hours," he said sitting posture-perfect as always.

"Meeting now to go over what will happen on Monday isn't about billable hours, Linus," the shapely civil litigator said as she leaned in toward him from her seat on the other side of the table. "It's about ensuring that this case moves forward, not backward. Capstone's attorneys are going to try and trip you up, get a look at our case-in-chief and lay out how they will present theirs at trial. This is important. Vital."

Hampton shook his head slightly before removing his glasses. His right hand pinched the bridge of his nose with thumb and forefinger, eyes closed as if by doing so he could make the idiocy vanish.

"Have you forgotten that I am a professor of law at the most prestigious law school on the planet? I know what a deposition is, and this case is never going to trial."

"One of."

"I beg pardon?"

"One of the most prestigious schools. You said 'the most'. I went to Yale. I'd like to think that my hard work wasn't wasted. That neither the diploma I proudly hang in my office nor the years I've devoted to make partner were all for naught."

He dropped the hand that pinched his nose, the wire-framed glasses immediately replaced to their designed post. "Agree to disagree. I didn't mean to offend."

"Yes you did. Also you don't teach there anymore. You were mandated to take a sabbatical from Columbia, remember?"

The muscles in Hampton's jaw twitched. His eyes burned into his attorney's. An unprecedented loss of control. A relative temper-tantrum.

Miranda sighed and put up her hands in surrender. She recognized his anger and put hers aside. He was the firm's client. *HER* client. "I apologize. We've started badly. But Linus, you would be well-advised to take this more seriously. There is a great deal of money at stake."

"Two hundred million dollars, give or take. I am well aware. It is, after all, my money, isn't it?"

"Not yet it isn't. And if your deposition goes poorly, it never will be."

"My wife was murdered. Two years ago. Capstone holds the entirety of her estate in escrow. All of our assets. Those wankers have not paid one cent of the monies, have they?"

"Lest we forget you were accused of her murder, which you cannot financially benefit from."

"I was acquitted, Miranda. Why is that so difficult for you or anyone else to fathom?"

"The fact that you were acquitted is something they are going to fight tooth-and-nail in order to avoid releasing the money and assets bequeathed to you in Ellen's Will. Their claim is that you got away with murder. Capstone is going to try this case all over again. Public opinion is on their side. The opinion is that you got away with murder."

"By public opinion you mean the rubbish the Hunts continue to spin. That gag order hasn't done much in the way of slowing them down has it? What am I paying you for? And since when have I cared what the bloody mob thinks?" he asked.

"That 'bloody mob' is our jury pool."

"I'm aware."

"If they win? Forget the Will. Her family will have a rock-solid case of their own and the Hunts have more money than everyone in my entire firm combined. That penthouse apartment that you own? The beach villa on Tortola? Your bank accounts? All seized. Everything up to and including those designer suits of yours will be gone, Linus. You will have no job, no home, no money, and nowhere to hide."

"I would still have my job. I am a tenured professor," Hampton said.

"They pay you to not show up. You are persona non-grata. Are we calling that a job, now? They've taken your books off the shelves in the library and at the bookstore. Columbia has all-but erased any trace that you once taught there. I'm sorry to have to be so blunt with you, but it seems to be the only way I can make this sink-in. We need to go over what is going to happen on Monday, okay? Can we start over? We need to go over every possibility, every permutation of what Capstone's lawyers are going to sling at you. The deposition is going to be filmed and steno-graphed. If their attorneys can't hang you with your own words, they'll do it with your body language. The last communication from their office indicated that there will be two lawyers at the dep. Studying your every move. They'll use the slightest thing, the smallest of misstatements or missteps, to kill you at trial."

"I'm suing *them*, Miranda. They should be the ones on the defensive. That is the very definition of defendant, isn't it? Yale didn't teach you that?"

"Yale taught me that pompous and smug assholes lose juries."

"Asshole? Aren't we the firebrand?"

Her face blushed. "I was illustrating how they might perceive you. You know how I feel about you. Misunderstood."

"Yes, quite. What say you let me worry about my perceived demeanor? I've hired a braintrust for no other purpose than outward appearances so you just focus on the dep, yes?"

Miranda sighed. "I am, Linus. That's why we're here. They can and will ask you whatever they want. I can object, just to get it on the record, but you'll still have to answer the question whether we like it or not."

"For the final time .... I understand how a deposition works. I am a legal scholar. My legal opinions are quite sought after."

"Really? Fine. Have it your way. Doctor Hampton, did you kill your wife?" Miranda sat back in her chair, folding her arms below her ample breasts.

He sat in quiet, staring at her. His head slightly tilted. An unprecedented departure from his perfect posture for the second time in the meeting.

"That is what they'll ask you. That will be the kindest of things that they will ask you, Linus. And you'll have to answer."

"No, Miranda, I do not."

25

Chapter 3

February 8, 2016

9:00 AM

Capstone's Army

THE DEPOSITION WAS SCHEDULED TO TAKE PLACE
at a neutral location. While the offices of Reid, Weinstein,
Hanley & Wood provided several conference rooms on the
various floors of their offices, each with ample space, it was
considered bad form to make the attorneys representing
Capstone walk into the proverbial lion's den. Going to the
New York headquarters of the life insurance and financial
services superpower across Midtown, or the offices of the
firm representing their interests, was also out of the
question. Linus Hampton brought about the lawsuit
against Capstone, their legal team called the dep and
would be asking all of the questions, however. An ad hoc
office space and conference suite was booked for Monday,
February 8. The space in Midtown would be the equivalent
of Switzerland. Neutral ground.

New York had many such spaces designed for those
that required occasional office or meeting amenities
without the need of an astronomical Manhattan monthly

lease for said space. For a few thousand dollars, premium space and staffing could be rented out by the hour. A bit more for the full day. Or, for the price of a luxury automobile, the space could be rented for the week. Many small-time businesses used the ad hoc spaces established throughout the city to make them appear more substantial to those with whom they'd invited to take a meeting. The staff at these facilities would in many cases get a rough script to follow in order to legitimize the farce. The staff would often give the appearance that the space was occupied full-time by the very temporary and often meager enterprises which rented it. Receptionists greeted those that exited the elevator with whatever name the leasing party wanted and phones were answered as scripted. Signs were made. Stationary with letterhead and the ilk were provided.

This particular ad hoc space provided an upscale Manhattan address for snail mail and couriers to use. Also in this case, the space was leased by a large, legitimate firm to provide neutral ground for an adversarial meeting to take place.

The moment the elevator doors opened on the twenty-fifth floor, Linus and Miranda were looking out of the conveyance into a sterile, open space. The wall-hangings were sparse and generic, though expensive in appearance. The Aspen-gray tiled walls and white faux-marble floor did nothing to provide warmth despite the brightness. Lighted wall sconces and hanging pendant lights added layers of light where none was needed. Windows lined the north side of building, casting more than ample light into each of the glass conference rooms. None of the shades were drawn in the bank of rooms, natural light bled into the reception area, shining off of the bright surfaces.

Behind the reception desk was a large space for a sign or logo, yet none was present at the moment. On this day, there were no fledgling companies looking to bolster their appearance. The entirety of the space was rented by the firm representing the civil defendants. Attendees would be said legal firm, their staff, the plaintiff Professor Linus Hampton, and his attorney Miranda Wood.

The receptionist stood and nodded at two of her coworkers who immediately moved toward the elevator as Miranda and her client exited it. She said, "Welcome" or something but Hampton hadn't quite heard. He looked her over from head to waist—as that all that he could see of her with the desk in the way—immediately assessing that she was an aspiring model. Or actress. Probably an actress. The city was filled with pretty woman that fancied themselves actresses. This one was raven-haired with brown eyes. He decided to pay her no further mind as her two assistants approached.

The two other probable-wannabe-actresses that the raven-haired receptionist nodded toward began helping them with their coats. He'd needed a coat today. The mid-thirties temperature felt like low twenties with the wind gust-ups. He let the Asian one take the London Fog double-breasted long woolen overcoat off his shoulders and immediately didn't like the way she was handling the garment. Nor the way her ginger colleague handled his attorney's Burberry after clumsily moving around Miranda's rolling briefcase. The Asian handed the red-head Hampton's coat who haphazardly threw it over her arm with Miranda's and carried both coats off to some unknown location. He didn't like that. He wasn't sure if his facial expression or body language betrayed him, and at that precise moment he didn't care. As always, he tried to remain stoic and unreadable yet the carelessness with which the designer garments were being handled irritated him to his very core.

Miranda didn't seem to care.

The Asian then led them to their room for the day, stopping in front, opening her arm toward the conference room in lieu of pointing. Two people who he rightfully assumed were the Capstone attorneys were already within, accompanied by a stenographer and a videographer with their respective apparatuses.

The male attorney was middle-aged, tall with a light freckled complexion and oversized eyeballs. He had very little hair and the little remaining was fine and thin. His suit was off the rack and atrocious in Linus's estimation. The man's proximity to his female colleague indicated to Hampton that he was a close-talker, and physically projecting his dominance. *Only weak men feel the need to exude superiority over women*, he thought. By appearances, this was not a worthy adversary.

The man's female co-counsel was of middle-eastern descent. Her skin was a caramel brown and her frame was petite nearing the point of unhealthy in Linus's view. Frail. *It takes a big man indeed to push around such a slight woman.* Her thick black hair with brown highlights seemed almost too heavy for her head. Hampton's own wrists were larger than this woman's neck. She would have been very pretty but would need to gain weight to contend for a modeling career. One look at

29

her and Hampton knew he could physically crush her, as he was sure many men had thought—including the one in the conference room with her at the very moment. Hampton decided then that she was the stronger of the two attorneys. She'd likely been pushed around her entire life because she looked weak. She was in his way, which was unfortunate for her as he decided then that he would be forced to professionally ruin her.

The woman moving around the stenotype machine was the antithesis of the middle-eastern attorney. She was pasty-white and as round as she was tall. The same thickness of hair on the on male attorney's head resided on this woman's upper-lip. Hampton noticed the three muffins on a plate on the conference room table in front of her. She was just a stenographer anyway, present only to record the proceeding. She too was no threat.

The young man behind the camera still had spots. Linus wondered if he'd graduated high school as yet, let alone university. As he stared at the young man's pronounced Adam's apple, Hampton imagined him to have a squeaky, prepubescent voice and hoped he wouldn't have to hear him speak. It didn't take an MBA or better to run a bloody camera, neither did it require a voice.

"Capstone's army," he mumbled to himself. Nobody seemed to hear him. "Time to feast."

"May I offer you some coffee, muffins, or scones? We also have freshly cut fruit-bowls and Greek yogurt if you would prefer," the Asian would-be actress asked.

"Coffee please," Miranda said.

"Tea. Earl Grey with lemon," Linus requested, his eyes never leaving the room in which he was about to enter. "I shan't be needing any food, I'm about to devour my morning meal."

The runner either didn't know what to make of him or didn't know what to say, so she bravely retreated to collect the requested refreshments.

"Linus, was that necessary?" Miranda whispered.

"I was merely stating a fact. I'm going to make a meal of those clowns," he said nodding toward the conference room.

"It's that attitude that has me concerned. You are not likable. I don't say that to be insulting, I say it because you are off-putting and I'm trying to help you."

"I'm quite self-aware."

Miranda was about to say something but thought the better of it. Instead, she walked into the conference room with her rolling briefcase that resembled luggage in tow. Hampton followed.

"Good morning. I'm Miranda Wood representing Linus Hampton. I assume since the camera is pointed in this direction, that we will be sitting over here?" The camera was pointed away from the windows at the far end of the conference room table from the door. Behind the camera, the Ichabod Crane-looking operator was checking levels. Behind him was the Trump Tower building. Between and below the two buildings, the traffic on Fifth Street fought the daily fight. Harry Winston was open for business far below their feet on the first floor.

"Yes. Good morning. I'm Michael Kettering and this is co-counsel Roya Dressner. We represent Capstone, naturally. The deposition will be reported by Nicole Wheeler and recorded by Dominic Howerton," the attorney said as he pointed to each of them. "If you would like to see their credentials—"

"—I would," Hampton said.

"He means I would," Miranda offered.

Nicole stood behind her stenotype machine, extending her short arm to show her credentials. She had the necessary RPR and CRR certifications. Howerton moved from behind his camera to do the same. Each had also signed NDAs, meaning that they were forbidden to discuss what was about to transpire to anyone.

Miranda began to unpack her suitcase-like conveyance which housed her laptop and a ream of legal documents in various file-folders.

"Please have a seat," Kettering said as he pointed to the chair the camera was pointed toward. Hampton made no bid to sit. Nicole sat to Hampton's right, Roya's immediate left, followed by Roya herself with her folders and such, then the camera and the operator, then Michael with his sea of documents, and finally around to Miranda who sat to Hampton's immediate left. Ample space separated the countering parties as each needed space to stack their respective piles of folders and documents. Somewhere in Central Park, a tree wept.

"I'll sit when this begins," Hampton said. "This charade is going to consume an entire day—"

"—Seven hours," Wood interjected. "Rule 30, section D-1. 'Unless otherwise stipulated or ordered by the court, a deposition is limited to 1 day of 7 hours.' So unless you intentionally delay the proceeding ...."

"—I'm not opposed to seeing a judge about more time," Kettering said. "If we need it. Or cut it short if we don't."

"Rule 30 allows for one, seven-hour day," Hampton said. "I doubt you'll win a motion for more time, but I do take your point, Miranda. I should have been more precise. Slightly less than *ONE-THIRD OF AN ENTIRE DAY* is going to be spent in that bloody chair. I will sit when and only when this charade begins."

Just then the coffee and tea arrived. It was placed on the table in front of the corresponding party and the Asian woman left as quickly as she'd entered, closing the door behind her.

Roya began to move about the room, drawing the vertical shades hanging on the glass walls closed so as not to be able to see out or into the conference room.

"This doesn't have to be antagonistic," Kettering offered. "We're only doing our job."

"Oh but it does. You are impeding my lifestyle, my way of life. Withholding what is rightfully mine."

"I am not doing anything. I—I should say Roya and I —are simply litigators hired to represent Capstone in defense of the lawsuit you filed against them. The insurance and financial institution whom you are suing has the right to defend itself. Let's not make this personal."

"We both know that this is quite personal indeed. My wife was murdered. We both had Wills and insurance policies in the event that one of us should die, so the other could continue to live a lifestyle in which we had become accustom, albeit without the other. Your client doesn't want to release the money and properties from escrow because the sum is quite substantial."

"They don't want to pay—"

33

"—This is all off the record," Miranda interjected.

"Nobody is recording this and yes this is off the record," Michael said as he looked around the room. "And as I was saying, our client is refusing to pay the person who is responsible for said murder."

"I was acquitted in an exhaustive criminal trial. You may remember. A month of very public probing a year ago."

"Civil court has a different standard."

"The people clamoring for tort reform have a point. I'm saying this as a lawyer," Linus said. "As a lawyer I can see their point. Very telling."

"Be that as it may .... "

"Be that as it may, I loathe you in ways that are unquantifiable."

Miranda stood. "Okay. That's enough of these ad hominem attacks. We have a long day ahead of us." Her voice was curt yet somewhere between laying down the law and talking a jumper away from the edge of a cliff.

There was a pregnant pause as the temperature of the room cooled. Kettering nodded to his co-counsel and the two people who would be witnessing and recording the proceedings. As he sat down in his chair, retrieving a few documents from a folder, he said while reading, "Then we are on the record. Good Morning Mister Hampton. Thank you for coming. My name is Michael Kettering and this is Roya Dressner. We are attorneys for Pompeneau, Ferris & Kline, the firm representing the Defendants, Capstone Insurance and Finance, in their defense of the claim you have asserted against them, alleging that they are in breach of contract by withholding probate funds and assets. Do you understand that?"

Linus took his chair, sitting in his usual stoic posture, his default. "Yes."

"I am obliged to go over some ground rules so you understand how today is going to go. I may use the words Capstone or Defendants or The Board or Our Clients or CIF to collectively refer to all of the parties you have named in your lawsuit. Is that okay?"

"Yes."

"The purpose of this deposition, the reason we have called you here today, is to ask you questions bearing on your assertion against Capstone and to ascertain your full position. The transcript of this deposition can and likely will be read or referred to as a cross-reference to your position when this case be litigated in court. You will answer truthfully, right?"

"Yes."

Hampton was then sworn in by Roya Dressner. No bible was offered or a hand solemnly raised. He simply was asked if he would tell the truth under penalty of perjury charges before the proceeding continued.

After Linus said that he would, Kettering continued. "If at any point during the questioning you would like to take a break, please inform either your attorney, Roya, or myself. I or she will then finish the line of questioning, you will be required to answer, then we will break. Okay?"

"Yes."

"Also, please let us finish our question before you respond so that the court reporter can transcribe everything that is being said. Okay?"

"Yes."

"If you don't understand a question that has been asked of you, please let us know. Is that fair?"

"Yes."

"Okay," Kettering said as he continued to read off of some form or checklist hidden by the folder which enveloped it. "If at some point you realize that an earlier answer you gave was inaccurate or incomplete, please tell us that you want to correct or supplement your earlier answer and we will allow you to do so. Do you understand?"

"Yes."

"We also ask that you answer with verbal responses so that the court reporter can record your response. While we will have the video, the video will not be allowed to be shown in court, it is for internal use in determining our course of action. The court reporter can't take down a nod or gesture or 'uh-huh'. Do you understand that?"

Linus removed his glasses, pinching the top of his nose. He paused in that position before cleaning the lenses of his glasses with the kerchief from his breast pocket and returning the glasses to his face. "Yes," he said in a calm tone while refolding the kerchief and returning it to the pocket of his jacket.

"Are you currently under the influence of alcohol or drugs or can you think of any reason that you cannot testify completely, accurately, and truthfully here today?"

"No."

"Okay. Then with formalities out of the way, let's begin."

Chapter 4

February 8, 2016

9:30 AM

And So It Begins...

KETTERING CLOSED THE FOLDER CONTAINING THE
documents outlining the procedure and legal formalities
he was reading from and set it aside. He then leaned in
toward the center of the table, looking to his left.
Howerton moved the camera to take the back of the
middle-aged attorney's balding head out of the shot and
retook his own chair just behind the device.

"So, Mister Hampton. May I call you Linus?"

"If you wish. However, it is *DOCTOR* Hampton."

"Mm-hm. Linus .... Did you kill your wife?"

"Objection," Miranda said.

"You can't object," Roya interjected. "This is our
deposition."

"I was noting it for the record."

Kettering continued. "Your objection is noted.
Linus, I repeat, did you kill your wife?"

Hampton took a sip of his tea before responding.
"Taking your queen out a bit early, wouldn't you say?"

37

"You don't get to ask questions, but you do have to answer mine."

A rare smile. It was pained and showed no teeth though it was clear that is what he wanted to show. It could be inferred from the cold stare of Hampton's eyes. "As I have said, repeatedly, I was accused and acquitted of the ridiculous charge," he said with no tone.

"That doesn't really answer the question, but we'll come back to that. I will remind you that you have to answer these questions, Sir. This is your lawsuit and our clients have the right to defend their position. You responded to this deposition as part of the process which, as an attorney, you must have known would come from your assertion. If you don't want to answer these questions, rescind your assertions and drop the lawsuit."

Neither Hampton nor his attorney said a word.

"Okay, then I'll continue by stepping back before we move forward. Your wife was Ellen Hunt, correct?"

"Yes."

"As in the Hunt Corporation?"

"Her father, yes."

"As in Hunt Media? Hunt Communications? Hunt Investments and list goes on?"

"Yes. I believe you know all of this since twenty or so percent of Capstone is owned by the Hunt Corporation under one umbrella or another. Hunt. Your client."

Kettering quickly peeked into another folder. "At last we checked, the Hunt Corporation is worth approximately twenty-eight BILLION dollars."

"Was that a question?"

"Sorry, yes. Is that information accurate?"

"Thereabouts. As far as I know. You know the market fluctuates."

"I understand. Give or take. But who is going to quibble over a few million, give or take, when the pot is in the billions, right?"

"You'd be surprised. And a few million is a bit different than quibbling over a few quid, isn't it?"

"Quid? I can't help but notice that you use British terms frequently. Constantly, actually, but I don't detect even a hint of a British accent. You're not British, are you? According to our records you were born right here in New York. Mount Sinai. Your father was from Brooklyn and your mother from Long Island. Why the British terminology?"

"Objection."

"Noted. Mister Hampton?"

"Well, they invented the language, didn't they? As a litigator you know that language is important. What people say has meaning and should be held accountable for it."

"And you don't think that we speak English?"

"Proper English? No. Eight of the signatories to the Declaration of Independence were British. A more perfect legal document one would have difficulty in finding. Shakespeare. Dickens. Tolkien. Rowling if you prefer someone a bit more modern. Agatha bloody Christie. The list goes on and on. Churchill. Darwin. On this side of the pond we consider language to be whatever you can cram into one hundred forty characters, and if you can't, use a bleeding emoji. No, I do not think *WE* speak proper English."

He'd begun to show a tone with his last statement. He caught himself, arched his back and seemed to reset as Kettering moved to the next question.

"Your wife was from New York. Midtown. Hunt Tower. The building with all of the triangles on it."

"Was that a question?"

"Excuse me, I didn't add an inflection on the end of my sentence. I now know you're a stickler for language, so let me try again. Your wife was from New York? Midtown? Hunt Tower? The building with all of the triangles on it?"

"Yes. Very droll."

"Is that why you killed her? Because as rich as she was, she wasn't British? You want to be British, don't you?"

"Objection," Miranda interjected again for the record. "That question is absurd."

"Noted," Roya said to Nicole Wheeler who was taking this all down on her machine to be transcribed later.

"You want to be a Brit. But you're not. You never even went to school in England. Why is that? They wouldn't take you?"

"Objection. This is already getting out of hand. Ad hominem attacks won't be tolerated."

"My apologies," Kettering said in a softer tone. "We can come back to that if it makes you feel better. I'll ask an easier question. Linus, how long were you married into the fourteenth wealthiest family in the United States?"

"Eleven years."

"How did you meet?"

"We were set-up. A friend of a friend."

40

"Hm. How is it that you knew people in the same circles? I mean she was a Manhattan socialite and you, forgive me, were not in her league."

"I don't understand the question."

"Before you met her, you were upper middle-class. She was born into substantial wealth. Old money. The Hunt family has owned newspapers since the print-press was invented. Now they have a television news division, a cable and internet provider company, expanding their newspaper and magazine division when everybody else is going out of business, and many, many other businesses and holdings. Don't they even have a majority share of a jet engine company?"

"Yes. I believe so."

"What don't they own, right?"

"What is your point?"

"How is it that you happened to know anyone in Ellen Hunt's social circles?"

"I knew someone who was in charge of the Met Gala. The Hunt family makes a large contribution to that event every year, and therefore invited to attend. We met at the Gala."

"Simon Barteau, correct?"

"Correct."

"The same Simon Barteau that is now serving a prison sentence for embezzling from that very charity, correct?"

"Objection."

"Noted," Roya said reflexively.

"Correct?"

"Yes, but that hasn't a thing to do with me."

"You just said that he was your friend."

Hampton took off his glasses and cleaned the lenses again. "I believe I said he was a friend of a friend, shall we have Miss Rounder read it back to you?"

"Wheeler," Nicole said.

"Excuse me?"

"My last name is Wheeler," Nicole said.

Roya raised her hand, first turning to Hampton then to Nicole. "Stop. We are off the record. Please don't speak to the stenographer, and please don't speak to the respondent. We are back on the record."

Hampton picked up where he left off. "Shall we have the *STENOGRAPHER* read back my answer?"

"That won't be necessary and let's get back on track. I ask the questions, you answer them." Kettering paused to collect himself. "How long did you date before getting married?"

"Two years."

"And you were married for eleven?"

"I believe I already answered that."

"You did. Will you answer it again?"

"No."

"If you don't answer my questions, I will have to notify the court that you didn't comply with the notice for the deposition and that will all-but ensure that you lose your civil suit against our clients."

"Objection. You can't threaten him."

"I'm not threatening, I'm merely stating a fact."

Hampton sighed but offered no tone. "Notify whom you must, old-boy. I've answered your question. It's on the record. You get to ask me a question once, and attain that answer. You can then probe the veracity of that answer at a trial. That is what a deposition is for. Do you have any other questions for me or do you not need the remaining ...." Hampton looked at his TAG Heuer watch. "....Six hours and five minutes you've been allotted for this farce?"

Miranda kicked Linus under the table and gave him a look that left little doubt as to her meaning. She wanted him to behave. Fortunately is was not caught on camera as only Hampton was in view.

"You teach law at Columbia, correct?" Roya asked as a way of moving on. She appeared to want to take over.

"Correct."

"I'm sure you've heard the expression, 'Those that can't do, teach.'" Kettering added.

"Hell hath no fury like the second-rate," Hampton said, again without tone.

"Couldn't cut it as a lawyer?"

"Objection."

"Noted."

"I scored a 398 on the UBE and was admitted to the New York Bar first department. I've tried cases before the Supreme Court for the New York Defense league, overturning two wrongful convictions. Not only can I *CUT IT* as a lawyer, I happen to be an exceptional one, indeed. My legal opinions are so widely sought, I am forced to choose which I can be bothered to offer."

Kettering shrugged. "And so you teach."

"You speak to me as if we are peers. I am without peer."

"Am I to understand that you think that you are better than me? We're both attorneys." Kettering leaned

43

across the table toward Hampton and continued, "Or is it that you believe that you are better than everyone?"

"I am without peer should be quite self-explanatory, but I should say that this rubbish I'm being subjected to proves the point. As for my profession, *OUR* profession as you say, you fare no better. Unless of course your aim is to be a cartoon character. You are a litigator, not a criminal lawyer."

"And you teach."

"I do. Another area in which I excel. In fact, I am teaching you as we speak. You cannot hope to prevail here, for which you will likely learn from your ineptitude. I reiterate, I am without peer."

"This is getting out of hand," Miranda said. Across the table, Roya seemed to agree.

"If you're so preeminent in the field of law, why not represent yourself in both your criminal and now your civil matter?" Kettering asked ignoring the two female attorneys.

"Objection."

"I very much wanted to. It was told to me about a hundred different ways that representing myself would look terrible to a jury of my so-called peers. That a person with money who doesn't afford himself a legal team looks suspicious. Sorted. Odd. Odd doesn't sit well with juries determining guilt or innocence of murder," Hampton said. "As it turns out, I've been more than adequately served by my lawyers. That's why we are here, isn't it? Because you feel as though I got away with murder? That I bought a verdict?"

"You're not allowed to ask me questions," Kettering said, "But I do. I do believe that the reason you got away with murder is because you had a very competent, very high-profile, and very expensive legal team. But that is small-beer compared to what this case is about and why we're here today."

"Small-beer? You think getting away with murder is a shrug?"

"No, I certainly do not. But unless you're a moron you're not going to kill anyone else. You'd never get away with it twice. So while what you've done makes me sick, you're not likely to be a danger to anyone else. Profiting from your actions? Well .... There's a special place in hell. A two hundred million dollar payout for a murder you committed? It's repugnant. And it would stand the life insurance industry on its head."

"Objection. You haven't asked a question in quite some time and now seem to be testifying."

Hampton added, "Do you get a percentage of every dollar you save Capstone from having to pay me?"

"Stop asking me questions."

"Insurance companies, in aggregate, consume mass wealth from others on the premise that tragedy will ultimately befall them, and when that time does come, said companies do anything and everything in their power to withhold payment. Please refrain from crying poverty and rattling your tin cup."

"Maybe I should take over the questioning for a little while," Roya offered. After a few beats it was apparent that no one objected. After a short time shuffling some of her papers, she changed tack.

"You found your wife on the night of her murder, correct?" Roya asked the question in a softer, more stable tone. A cooler head.

"Yes."

"Can you relive that night for us two years ago?"

"It's on the criminal record," Hampton said.

"We weren't a party to the criminal trial. This is a civil matter. Can you please go over it again? As painful as it may be, we need you to tell us what happened. Again. In your own words."

"Very well."

Chapter 5
April 18, 2014
9:30 PM
The Night Of

IT HAD BEEN A LONG DAY, EVEN AS FRIDAYS GO.
The final day of the workweek inevitably moves slower than the other four days. The clock simply doesn't seem to move to the end of the workday very quickly. Seconds seem like hours. The weekend will never begin. Inevitably someone impedes one from leaving for the two short days of respite needed to recharge for another week. Hampton often wondered it was like that in England. They seemed to relish free time much more on the other side of the Atlantic. More time was given for holiday. Someone who is recharged is much more productive than a person who is worked to the bone. The Brits had a pension for the quality of life, he reckoned.

In New York, there was always an additional demand on Hampton's valuable time. And always on a Friday. An adjunct needing some guidance. A Teacher's Assistant asking how to grade something subjective. A student who needs a bit more time than scheduled for

47

office hours. An Associate Professor feeling the need to blather on about this or that. The New York Defense League simply will not take no for an answer that the case that was cocked up ten years ago will not be reversed no matter what ingenious legal argument Hampton made. There was always someone with their needy hand out.

All he'd wanted all day Friday was to go home and watch the Chelsea - Manchester United fixture from earlier in the day. While he was standing in front a class of future law degrees, Manchester United had taken the pitch at Stamford Bridge for a day game. He'd recorded it so as to watch the football match on his ninety-inch flat screen, with a Stella Artois in hand, the moment he arrived home. His wife, Ellen, would be off doing her own thing as usual, affording him the time and space needed enjoy the match. The weekend would begin with his beloved Red Devils, led by Rooney, give a good thrashing to The Blues.

But of course it hadn't gone as planned.

One of Professor Hampton's sycophant students had been watching the game on his phone or tablet or something while he was teaching the class about how the Necessity Defense in People v. McVeigh might have resulted in a different verdict because 'Imminent' doesn't necessarily mean 'Immediate'. While Doctor Hampton was instructing on how he would have better defended the man responsible for the Oklahoma City Bombing, as a justifiable response to his governments's crimes at Waco, his suck-up student was watching what Americans call soccer. When the class had ended, said student spoiled Hampton's plans for later by telling the result on the way out of the theatre.

"Sorry about Man-U, Professor. Six - zero."

"It's six - nil and thank you very much for dashing my plans for later. Did I ask you for the result? No, I did not. I didn't ask you because it is my job to teach you law, not to engage you in any other interaction. If you want to impress me, do better in my class," Hampton said.

Then came all of the road-blocks and emergencies that couldn't wait until Monday. A buxom student all but offered her body in order to get a grade changed. Hampton wondered if that sort of behavior ever worked. After disposing of that situation, the New York Defense League needed to speak with him urgently. His assistant didn't have the ability to take a message or the wherewithal to forward the call to his mobile for the car ride home. Upon the completion of the phone call, said assistant needed a letter of recommendation in an effort to attain an open position in the Dean's Office. While the position had been posted for weeks, she'd let the request for the letter go to the final minute and was now urgently dumped into his lap.

It was near nine o'clock by the time he was able to call his driver du jour to pull the car around. The driver was caught in heavy traffic on Broadway and would be there as quickly as he was able, he'd said. Hampton told him not to bother, that he would just walk the one mile home to the corner of West One-Tenth and Amsterdam. He also made a mental note to sack the new driver on only his second day on the job.

The walk home was as miserable as his day had gone. What was a beautiful sixty-three degree April day had turned into a windy, frigid, forty-six degree night and he wasn't dressed for it. His Prada loafers weren't meant

49

for power-walking and his Maxwell Scott attaché case was growing heavier by the step.

By the time he arrived at his building, a bluish-gray mirrored skyscraper, he was gelid and knackered. The doorman greeted him with some tripe as he held open the front door under the canopy, but Hampton paid him no mind. The elevator took forever to open as did the journey up the shaft to his penthouse on the forty-fourth floor. It was 9:20 PM. He specifically remembered the time because he'd looked at his luxury wristwatch when waiting for the damnable elevator to arrive in the lobby.

The elevator opened to a large vestibule. There was only one door as there was only one apartment on the entire top floor of the building. He'd once asked his wife why the need for a front door to their apartment, when the elevator could simply act as the door? She prattled on about the extra security measure of a locking front door and the second elevator, the service elevator, on the other side of the building which stopped on the floor just below them. Hampton never understood the argument because no one could get up to their floor without either a keycard or a security-code authorization from someone either on the main floor or from inside the apartment. Anyone coming up the service elevator would still have to be let in through the stairway door next to the main elevator.

Now, even in the vestibule before entering his home, he could hear the loud music. His wife liked pop music and often took up VIP rooms at trending Manhattan night clubs. DJs knew his wife by sight as well as name. Hell, everyone in Manhattan knew her name. It wasn't a scene until she or Paris Hilton or a Kardashian visiting from Los Angeles or some other top-tier celebrity arrived. Ellen

Hunt was very well-known in those circles. Often caught by the paparazzi, it was not unusual to see his wife getting out of a car or leaving a club on some tabloid paper or television program. The couple had shared a laugh once over the fact that one of the tabloids that shot a candid photo of her out on the town was actually owned by her family. Odd that.

Linus didn't recognize the music just then. He and his wife didn't share the same taste in music. What she called "chunes", he called knobby clanging. Hampton's tastes ran toward the classics. Real music. Actual classical music. What was playing so loud as to be heard in the vestibule on that night he would later learn was an extended house version of *Sleeping With A Friend* by the Neon Trees.

The music was near-deafening when he opened his front door. An unusual event to be sure. Ellen might have played her music that loudly when he wasn't around, but definitely not when he was home or expected to be at any moment. He again looked at his watch. 9:30. He was supposed to be home hours ago. She was expected to be at some late dinner or social event just then. On a Friday night, she would leave that gathering to then have her photo taken at some new or trending club into the wee hours of the morning. It was unusual for her to be home before 2:00 AM on weekend nights, much less now.

She must still be getting ready to go out, he thought.

Hampton set down his satchel just inside the front door and walked the thirty or so paces to the McIntosh stereo system centrally located by the bar. He turned it down to nary a whisper. In comparison to its original volume, it was practically turned off.

"Ellen," he called looking upward to aid in projecting his voice. They had twenty-foot high ceilings but not a second floor, his voice echoed but received no other response other than his own reverberations. "Is the volume set so high really necessary? You can isolate the music to whatever room you're in, love," he said after a time.

"Love" repeated a few times but again there was no response.

Since he was already at the bar, he decided to open a much needed and well-deserved Stella Artois. He made it a point to not drink during the week, and only moderately on the weekends or holidays. Never hard alcohol. Hampton felt the need to control everything around him. Alcohol deadened the senses and dulled the wits. After a sip he again called out to Ellen. "Hello?"

Nothing.

"Are you here?"

Silence save for the very faint and barely audible music that may or may not have even been on a different song.

Maybe she's not even here. Why would she leave the music on at such a level if she went out? And all of the lights on? Odd that.

Hampton set his bottle of beer down on the bar-top and moved into the apartment in earnest. They were in the process of being renovated. Ellen had the need to redesign the place every few years. This year it was Modern Minimalist which meant exponentially more modifications than a new coat of paint and a few new fixtures. Modern Minimalist meant geometric shapes and clean lines through the use of glossy metals, glass, stone, and plastic. The entirety of the space had been undergoing remodeling for the past six months and there was no end in sight. For someone who was obsessive about tidiness, everything having a proper place, this current situation was the stuff of nightmares. He moved around plastic curtains and drop cloths which were fastened in place to reduce the dust from the sheetrock, metal, stone, and wood being cut on a daily basis. He slowly moved past sawhorses used as makeshift work tables, work-lights, saws, and other tools as he made his way further into the enormous apartment.

Just then his two Maltese Terriers came toward him from around a two-by-four'd corner sheathed in semi-clear plastic. They were normally excited to see him. Rooney and Tom, named after Wayne Rooney and Tom Cleverley of Hampton's beloved football club, were normally quite spritely, playful, and loving. Not just then. Nor were they white. They were matted, pink, and whimpering.

Hampton squatted down. Tom begged away while Rooney timidly came near. *Blood. They're covered in blood.* He stood and quickly moved through the house struggling to get a sense of his own residence even through the clear plastic walls.

There, in the bedroom, lying face-down on the plastic-lined floor, was Ellen. She wasn't moving. Her body was contorted into an unnatural position. Hampton didn't know if the lacy bra, panties, and leggings were pink or if they were once white and currently stained in blood like his dogs. He went to her and knew she was dead at first touch. She was cold. His wife was dead in her own apartment, in her underwear, and left to bleed out onto the plastic. He noticed her auburn hair was wet on the back of her skull. Pieces of brain and bone were tangled within those wet locks.

As he stood to take out his cell phone to call 9-1-1, he noticed the ball peen hammer no more than fifteen feet away. There was blood and bone and a few strands of hair on the rounded bevel. The hammer had been tossed after the macabre deed had been done as indicated by the smeared blood and bunched plastic leading up to and around where the tool now rested. Hampton took a few steps back from his wife's corpse and dialed for help. He nearly slipped and fell on the slick plastic, the coagulating blood making the surface that much more slippery. He'd stepped in her blood. Blood was on his hands from when he touched Rooney.

As Hampton spoke to the 9-1-1 operator on his cell phone, he backed out of his apartment and waited for the police to arrive in the unnecessary vestibule.

This is the story Doctor Linus Hampton told the police on the scene. This is the same story the professor told the detectives who later questioned him at the police station. It's what he told his entire criminal and civil legal teams about the night of the murder. And the story Hampton now told at his deposition.

Chapter 6
February 8, 2016
11:15 AM
Suite Music

ROYA DRESSNER WAS STILL CONDUCTING THE
interview by the time Linus Hampton had run through his
account of what occurred on April 18, 2014.   Michael
Kettering had been content to let a calmer, cooler litigator
take over for the time being. He let her gain some sort of
rapport with the plaintiff. She had the feminine touch.

It wasn't how they'd originally drawn up the
deposition, of that Hampton was certain. Kettering had an
ego. A chauvinist. A slight woman handle him? Never.
But Kettering's temper had gotten the better of him and it
was now time for them to play the good-cop, bad-cop game.
He imagined that the two attorneys thought that the game
was going well. Roya seemed to enjoy playing the good-
cop.

"And it was at this point that the police investigation
began?"

"I would argue that the investigation never truly began. To this very minute the person who murdered Ellen has not been held to account."

"In your opinion."

"Isn't that why I'm here? For my opinion?"

"Mister Hampton, you're here to give sworn testimony, to the best of your knowledge, so that we may determine a course of action and to know what you will say in a civil court in front of a judge and jury, when the time comes. You know that."

"It's not opinion that the killer is still free since I'm the only person ever indicted and tried for it. *To the best of my knowledge* I am innocent of that crime."

"Says you," Kettering interjected.

"Says twelve members of a jury. Unanimously."

"Of your peers."

"We've been over that."

"You really are a piece of work, aren't you Hampton?"

"This Hobbesian Trap you seem to favor gives you away."

"A what?"

"Come now, Mister Kettering. Hobbesian Trap. You're afraid I'll launch preemptive strikes, and you'd like to beat me to the punch."

"May I continue?" Dressner asked. "Again, this is when the police investigation began?"

Hampton removed his eyeglasses, cleaned the nonexistent grime off them with his kerchief again, and pinched his nose before replacing them. "I realize that you are just a civil lawyer, Miss Dressner, but police don't begin

56

investigations until there is a crime. Until then, there was no body, no murder, and no crime. Yes, this is when the investigation supposedly began because I had just called the police to inform them that my wife was dead. Right then. When I found her." Hampton gave no to tone through his sarcasm, almost robotic. Ever reticent.

"And did they bring you to the station for questioning 'right then'?"

"You know the answer to these questions. This was all testified to at the criminal trial, on the record. I'm sure you've read the transcript in its entirety at least once."

"We're going to go over it all again. In our context. Please answer the question."

"No."

"Did the detectives at the scene," Dressner opened another file, "Brock and Gamble question you?"

"Procter and Gamble?"

"Brock and Gamble. Do I have misinformation? I have the two New York City homicide detective's names as Brock and Gamble."

"I call them Procter and Gamble. Have you ever heard of the company?"

"Yes. They make personal grooming and hygiene products, don't they?"

"You've never met them."

"The detectives? No."

"Indeed. That's why you don't get the quip."

Kettering leaned in again. "I didn't know you had a sense of humor."

"Oh, I'm a joke machine."

Dressner continued ignoring the interruption. "Did detectives Brock and Gamble question you at the scene?

This is going to take longer than it needs to if I have to ask every question twice," Roya said with both audible and visible frustration from both her side and the opposing.

"Yes. Briefly. I was upset as you can imagine. After a few questions Proctor and Gamble let me leave to find solace in a hotel. They assured me that there would be follow-up questions when I felt up to it."

Kettering sneered. "I'm sure you were beside yourself. Look at you now. You can hardly control your emotions."

"Mike," Dressner said before continuing. "He does have a point, though, Linus. The recording of the 9-1-1 call is unemotional to put it mildly."

"I was in shock."

"It didn't sound like shock. Those aren't my words, those are the words of the 9-1-1 technician that testified at your criminal trial. It was matter-of-fact. You, quote, 'might as well have been calling a cab.' End-quote. The police corroborated that statement."

"I don't call cabs."

"I believe the technician was illustrating her point. You didn't appear to be upset by your wife's murder then, according her testimony. A person who handles 9-1-1 calls for a living found that odd. Quite frankly, you don't appear to be upset by your wife's murder even now."

"People grieve differently," Hampton said. "I am a deeply private person. I simply wanted to go someplace where I could do just that without judgement."

"The hotel," Kettering said.

"Yes."

"We will get to that," Roya said with a raised hand. "But first, you say that you were upset. The DD5s, the police reports the detectives turned in—"

"—I know what a DD5 is—

"—Said that …. And I quote …. 'He couldn't have looked more distraught if his goldfish had just died.' What do you say to that?"

"As I just said. People grieve and show emotion differently. I assure you that I was in a terrible state."

"Uh-huh. So you then left to check into a hotel?"

"My apartment was a crime scene. Scientists and investigators were combing over the entire place with chemicals and UV lights so I wasn't allowed to stay there. They even commandeered my dogs as they had blood evidence in their fur and under their nails. My poor dogs have been quite traumatized since."

Kettering rolled his eyes but said nothing. Roya pressed on. "Which hotel?"

"The Mandarin Oriental. It's nearby. Columbus Circle by the Park."

"Suite five thousand at the Mandarin Oriental New York on the fiftieth floor of the Time Warner Center, correct?"

"Yes."

"You had just seen the body of your very beautiful, very famous, and now dead wife. You'd been questioned, albeit briefly, by two New York City homicide detectives. The first thing you do is check into a thirty-three hundred square-foot, three-bedroom penthouse space? We had one of our interns dig into your hotel bill and go up there. She said she had to see for herself what thirty-grand a night looks like. Thirty-grand a night for a hotel room?"

59

"A hotel suite."

"Fine, a suite.   It had a full dining room and a kitchen worthy of a Michelin-starred chef.   You were so distraught after finding your wife of eleven years beaten to death with a hammer, after calling 9-1-1 and dealing with two homicide detectives, that you had the presence of mind to request a turntable with access to an extensive record collection by New York's Academy Records?"

"The Mandarin has some sort of arrangement with them."

"That's your explanation?   'They have an arrangement'?   You might want to clarify that statement, so I'll ask again.   Your wife is brutally murdered and the first thing you do is go out and get one of—if not THE best—hotel *suite* in all of Manhattan?"

"It wasn't the first thing I did, no."

"Oh, that's right.   You went on a hundred-thousand-dollar shopping spree first," Dressner said with a tone that now mimicked Kettering's.

"I needed clothing.   I wasn't allowed to have mine at that moment.   They were in my closet being tagged as evidence."

"That's some wardrobe."

"I needed some toiletries as well."

"Maybe Procter and Gamble could have helped you out."

Hampton gave a fake smile with no teeth.

"Forgive me but I am really and truly struggling here," she continued.   "You'd just found your wife, your half-naked wife, brutally murdered—"

"—Isn't that both redundant and obvious?"

"Excuse me?"

"When is a murder not brutal?"

"Miranda, can you get your client under control?" Roya asked of her counterpart.

"Linus ...."

"Apologies, Miranda. But she's taken a page from Mister Kettering here. They have swapped roles, or they've abandoned the good cop—bad cop routine entirely."

Roya ignored the comment from the respondent and continued her line of questioning as if there'd been no pause. "Your celebrity wife has just been murdered and you are so upset that you blow a hundred grand on a shopping spree and book a luxurious suite at another thirty-thousand a night?"

"The Mandarin gives discounts if you stay for an extended period of time."

"Even still. How long have you lived there now?"

"Objection."

"I didn't know how long I was going to be displaced from my home, or if I even wanted to go back to it. In the event that I could sell it, the renovations were going to have to be finished. I was in for an extended period of time without a home in any respect."

"It looks to me to be more of a celebration."

"Looks can be deceiving."

"Not to any sane person," Kettering interjected. "I mean, if my wife had just been killed, my first thought wouldn't be to go buy some new duds, book an expensive suite overlooking Central Park, and request special access to some rare vinyl records. I don't think *anybody* would.

61

And your explanation is that 'P*eople grieve differently*'?"

"Objection."

Hampton turned back to Roya. "Plenty of sane people turn to music when they are sad, don't they Miss Dressner?"

"Not in five-thousand-dollar tailored suits and a well beyond lavish hotel room, no. Not plenty of people. No."

"As I said, I am without peer."

"I am beginning to agree."

"Objection."

"Noted. Do you want to amend or clarify your statement for the record? Because I'm about to move on and you've just said that after finding your wife dead, you went shopping and checked into Shangri-La. Your wife is a celebrity. You have the press in your lobby and the police are everywhere. The homicide detectives have questioned you and told you there's more coming, and you go out and buy some new suits and listen to some rare Elvis records?"

"Elvis? No. I've told you what happened, unabridged with no amendments forthcoming."

"Have it your way. So when were you interviewed by the detectives?"

"That night. As I've said."

"Excuse me. The follow-up interview. When was the official interview?"

"Ten days later in the suite that you're so fascinated with."

"And what became of that?"

"Procter and Gamble took on a tone that quite resembles your own."

"I meant what became of the interview?"

"What began as a quote-unquote '*Informal and procedural interview*' became an onslaught of accusations and innuendo."

"And what became of the interview?"

"After the barrage, Procter and Gamble—"

"—Brock and Gamble—"

"—Left my home."

"Your suite."

"Yes. My temporary home."

"After you insisted that they leave."

"Yes."

"And did you leave with them?"

"No."

"You weren't placed under arrest?"

"No. Not at that time."

"When did that come about?"

"A few days later."

"At Columbia."

"At Columbia. In front of my students"

Chapter 7

May 1, 2014

2:00 PM

Malice Aforethought

PROFESSOR HAMPTON UNFAILINGLY BEGAN HIS classes on time. He was very fastidious in that way, among a slew of other idiosyncrasies. Everything had a place and an order, punctuality was of great consequence, and above all—look the part.

Students were often late, and though said tardiness was not called attention to, those students didn't often pass his class. Every now and again the professor would recite the rule he'd made during the first class of every semester, "Fifteen minutes early is on time, on time is late." Those who would pass his class inevitably understood and heeded the credo, those that didn't, didn't pass. Hampton felt that the students who were as pedantic as he, need not be burdened with having to stop his valuable lecture for someone who was not as diligent with their studies. So he made no mention of the stragglers, only the occasional recitation and mental notes of which students had better things to do than get to his class on time. Punishment would come in the form of a failing grade. One was better off skipping the class entirely and getting the lecture notes from a classmate than to walk into the lecture hall even one minute after the start of Professor Hampton's class.

On that Thursday, the class was teemed with young law students and was teetering on the verge of being standing room only in the stadium-style lecture hall. An infamous Hampton final exam was looming the following week. It was important to sort out as much information about the final as possible. Unlike other professors at Columbia, Hampton didn't keep past exams on file in the library for students to use as a guide. Every student who had taken a Hampton course could tell you, however, that acing his exam was as likely as becoming the first lawyer-astronaut. Though the students would make the attempt at a masterful result, the practical hope was that each student would score better than their counterparts so as to benefit from the grading curve.

Hampton paced back and forth while lecturing his students down in the front of the class, wearing his usual haute couture three-piece designer suit. Today's ensemble was a not-quite black Armani with sterling gray pinstripes. A microphone was attached to his lapel so the students sitting far above and in the back row could hear his lecture. Not his favorite flourish, but it was necessary else he would be forced to shout out his entire lecture. He looked the part despite his recent personal turmoil. Linus Hampton's personal rule number one.

"From the queue of students outside my office during office hours, the incessant emails, and the feedback I am getting from my TAs, the lot of you are struggling with our case study of People v. Rheinhold. Therefore, we will take a remedial step backward in an effort to move some of you forward," Hampton said as he turned toward his laptop with the notes being projected on the large screen above his head. Those in the back of the mid-sized theatre could follow along without having to strain to see a chalk or dry-erase board, and could hear his voice through the PA. system. The blueish LED light from the laptop glared off his spotless eyeglasses. "It amazes me how crowded the class is just before the final, and no other time throughout the semester. For those that don't attend my class regularly, you will now learn that a portion of the final will charge you with finding an alternate defense than the one presented at Rheinhold's trial. This *WILL* be on the final so I suggest those that are still wading through the muck and the mire get to solid ground by taking copious notes or gleaning as much knowledge as possible from a student who has."

Stopping Hampton's train of thought by shouting out a question or raising a hand was an exercise in futility, as the disruptions were ignored with the same fervor as a tardy arrival.

"Let us forget for a moment about the actual case of People v. Rheinhold and focus on another, easier hypothetical, shall we? Let us study a scenario with Bonnie and Clyde. If you are unfamiliar with the bank robbing bandits of old, might I suggest seeking an education at a learning annex or community college rather than Columbia.

"By way of example, Bonnie and Clyde do what they do and rob a bank. Clyde shoots and kills the armed guard

66

during a confrontation inside the bank. What is Clyde charged with?"

A group of students mumble, "First Degree Murder."

"Why not Felony Murder?" Hampton asked. "He did, after all, kill the guard while committing a felonious act."

No one raised a hand.

"You, in the front row. I believe you were one of the brave mumblers. Why not Felony Murder?"

The young woman sheepishly replied, "It could be included in a lesser charge but in this case, Clyde walked into a bank—"

"—I never said he walked into the bank, Miss."

"....Entered the bank armed with a gun," she corrected herself after a pause. "The guard being shot was an inevitable result of bringing the weapon into the bank to commit a felony with Malice Aforethought."

"Very good, there is hope for you yet. Make note that, A: I never said he carried the gun into the bank. He could have wrestled it away from the armed guard, but if one is a professional bank robber, it's not likely Clyde went into the bank unarmed. B: She refrained from using the ambiguous term 'premeditated'. First Degree Murder is the correct charge because Clyde planned the crime and any other foreseeable crimes that result, in this case the murder, is part of the same set of events. Bonnie, if she goes into the bank with Clyde, even if she does nothing and is present for the sole purpose of moral support, can and would be charged with the same crime of First Degree Murder.

"Alternately, let us now assume that Bonnie is waiting out in a getaway vehicle. Nobody is killed inside the bank, fortunately, and when Clyde gets into the getaway vehicle, as Bonnie speeds away, she accidentally hits and kills a pedestrian who crossed their path as she speeds away. Both Bonnie and Clyde are charged with what?"

"Felony Murder," many in the room softly said in unison.

"Correct, because they accidentally killed the pedestrian while committing another, in this case separate, felony. While the robbery was with Malice Aforethought, they hadn't planned on killing a pedestrian who crossed their getaway path. What about Bonnie, who is waiting in the getaway vehicle? What if she didn't know what Clyde was going to do inside the bank?"

No one raised a hand, nor did anyone speak. A few unintelligible grumbles could be heard from the back.

"If the prosecutor is unable to prove beyond a reasonable doubt that she knew why she was parked in a running vehicle outside a bank, Bonnie's crime in killing the pedestrian is reduced to Vehicular Manslaughter. Now, how do the scenarios I've just provided relate to the seemingly monumental task of mounting an alternate defense in People v. Rheinhold? Do not answer that now, answer it on the final and remember that your position must be supported by case law. I will warn you, if any of you use the hypotheticals I've just given you regarding Bonnie & Clyde, I will instantly stop reading your final and fail you. I don't even want either of the two bandits mentioned. I hope I've made myself clear."

Just then, Detectives Brock and Gamble entered the lecture hall. Gamble had his handcuffs out, readying them for the next wearer.

"If you you've come to audit the class, gentlemen, please note that the class has already started and I abhor tardiness," Hampton said, the microphone picking up his every syllable. Of course it was plain to see that they weren't there for the education; which is why he then removed the microphone from his lapel and the wireless pack from inside his suit jacket, wrapping the cord haphazardly and setting the device next to his laptop.

Gamble walked toward Hampton. "Linus Hampton, we would like you to come with us, we have some questions for you regarding the murder of your wife, Ellen Hunt."

"Now? I am in the middle of class."

"Are you refusing to come with us?"

"Yes."

"We thought you might," Brock said. "You are now under arrest for hindering prosecution and are being detained as a person of interest in the murder of Ellen Hunt."

Gamble fitted Hampton with the handcuffs as Brock read the suspect his Miranda rights.

"As you know, Professor, you have the right to remain silent. Anything you do or say can be used against you in a court of law. You have the right to an attorney, even though you are one. In the event that you cannot afford an attorney other than yourself, one will be appointed to you by the court. Any questions?"

Hampton remained silent, as was his right. There was no emotion on his face as per usual. He held his head up high as he was escorted out of the lecture hall. His students, on the other hand, were flabbergasted, rife with a gamut of emotions.

At the police station, Hampton was questioned by Brock and Gamble for more than ninety minutes before both the Assistant District Attorney, Judy Kemp, and Hampton's lawyer, William Reid, arrived simultaneously.

"Why are you questioning my client outside the presence of an attorney?" Reid asked as he entered the interrogation room. "Shame on you detectives. Nothing he has said is admissible."

"He hasn't said anything," Brock said. "He just keeps pinching his nose and cleaning his glasses."

"Good. I would like a moment with my client please. Alone. And please turn off the listening monitor."

Brock and Gamble joined ADA Kemp in the anteroom on the other side of the two-way mirror to confer while Hampton and his lawyer did likewise inside the interrogation room. Everyone reconvened after the twenty-minute attorney-client conference.

"My client maintains his innocence and would like to be released immediately," Reid said to everyone in the room but focused on Kemp. "He is still grieving the tragedy that took place upon his wife and cannot attain any sense of closure until the police apprehend the actual murderer. Her body hasn't even been released for him to cremate, as was her wish. He can't go back to his home because it's still considered a crime-scene, his dogs are still being housed by animal control, and after today's stunt it will be awkward—to say the least—going back to his job at Columbia University. This is textbook harassment. Why are you harassing my client?"

70

"Harassing?" ADA Kemp said with exaggerated astonishment. "It's been three weeks since the murder occurred."

"My point exactly. You haven't even finished examining the body let alone had time to exhaust all possible suspects because you have focused on one. My client. How many more possible tests could you perform on his beloved pets that haven't already been done? What's stronger than harassment? Malicious Harassment?"

"Your client had means, motive, and opportunity. He has no alibi and there is more than ample evidence to support the charge," Kemp said.

"You call the blood on his shoes evidence? He found her, for God's sake. Of course he stepped in her blood after seeing her and running to her to determine whether she was alive and in need of immediate medical assistance. As for the alibi, he walked home. He walked twenty blocks. Two million people live in Manhattan, not many have cars. Had he known he needed an alibi, I'm sure he would have struck up a conversation. "

"Did you stop into a bodega for a pack of gum or a bottle of water, Mister Hampton? Can anybody corroborate your story?"

"Not that I recall. And it's Doctor Hampton," Linus said after a look and a nod from his attorney acknowledging that he could answer.

Kemp continued. "I've pulled your cell records as well as the calls to and out of your office phone. You told these two detectives in your hotel suite that you called your driver and he was caught in traffic across town, so you decided to walk home. We have no record of that

71

phone call nor has anyone come forward saying that they saw you walk home that night."

"Keep looking."

"I even went so far as to speak with your assistant. She said that she couldn't have held you up because she left early that Friday. She also said that she never asked you for a recommendation because she didn't think you'd give her one."

"A disgruntled employee is somewhat less than reliable."

"Be that as it may, we've prosecuted cases with much less evidence," Kemp said with a shrug of her shoulders.

William Reid interjected, "Maybe, but this one you will lose. He didn't kill his wife. His very beautiful and very famous wife. Save yourself the time, energy, money, and embarrassment. Let him go."

"Your client is smug, Mister Reid, and he refuses to answer any of our questions. When he doesn't answer our questions, we have no choice but to draw our own conclusions from the evidence. Would he now like to answer our questions, in the presence of his attorney? Because if not, he's going to spend the night in The Tombs."

"He has answered your questions and will be happy to continue," Reid said. "But first some ground rules. This is all off the record. This is just an informal fact-finding discussion. Nothing he says can be used in court. No cameras, no recorders."

"That's not how this is going to work, Counselor," Kemp said. "Our investigation, our rules."

"Then I believe we have a stand-off. My client doesn't have to speak with you. He is willing to if and only if it is off the record."

"I'm not deaf. I understood what you said. The answer is no. He complies or we arrest him for murder and send him to The Tombs for arraignment tomorrow. I would think he would want to speak with us. The newspapers are camped outside his hotel and the university. The press has not been kind, and he's already been tried in the court of public opinion. Why not make a statement and get this all behind him? As you said, to grieve."

Reid looked to his client. The two men looked each other in the eye. The communication was clear without saying a word. Reid nodded and Linus Hampton began his version of events.

Over the course of the next three hours, Hampton told and retold his story six times. Each telling was matter-of-fact, with the same lack of emotion. Cameras recorded him as did digital recorders. To the Assistant District Attorney and detectives Brock and Gamble, this was a cold-blooded killer if ever there was one, and they treated him as such.

Chapter 8

May 1, 2014

10:00 PM

The Tombs

MANHATTAN'S DETENTION COMPLEX AT 125
White Street is where the city's pretrial detainees are held
to save on both the personnel and transportation expenses
of shipping accused felons back and forth from Rikers
Island. Every time an inmate who is held without bail—
either because they were denied or couldn't afford
whatever bail was set at the arraignment hearing—has to
be transported back and forth to and from the courthouse
for one reason or another. These inmates are transported
by officers working for the Department of Corrections.
Sometimes these trips occur often, sometimes months
span between court appearances depending on how speedy
the trial is progressing. Both the municipal jail,
nicknamed The Tombs, and the maximum security prison
known as Rikers are overcrowded and are rife with
scandals and abuses; however, one is generally a preamble
to the other in the event that the accused becomes
convicted.

The nickname has lasted from the time the building, originally known as the Halls of Justice, was built back in 1838 in the architectural style of Egyptian Revival. The name has endured—despite now being two buildings—for the reasons that the granite building itself has undergone little in the way of cosmetic upgrades. The Egyptian style remains and the interior of The Tombs is as dark, dank, and dreary as the day it was built.

The two buildings, set on opposing sides of White Street, have a combined capacity of nine hundred people. The revolving daily inmate headcount is roughly eleven hundred. Many inmates who are awaiting trial aren't afforded a cot much less a cell. Those not assigned a cell with at least one cellmate are forced to fight for a place to sleep in the open common area below the tiers. Not that sleep would come. The easiest way to get at someone who is not in the relative safety of a cell is when the lights go out. The HSU was ill-equipped to handle the number of injuries inmates sustained at the hands of other inmates or even the Correctional Officers. Men who were beaten, broken, and bloody often went with wounds untreated. Because snitching was the cardinal of all sins, rarely was the aggressor ever held to account.

Prior to detectives Brock and Gamble going to Columbia University to bring Linus Hampton in for questioning, Assistant District Attorney Judy Kemp was seeking an indictment in front of a Grand Jury, presenting evidence to sixteen of the twenty-three members called for month-long Grand Jury duty.

The five-foot-eleven Assistant District Attorney had the physique to go with her reputation for ruthlessness. Big-boned is how most would describe her. Mannish is how others described her. Judy had never been—nor would she ever be—thin. Kemp played racquetball a minimum of three mornings per week and carried the frame of a short Tight-end. Her sexuality was always inferred by her haircut and size, yet those who judged her did so incorrectly. Judy Kemp wore the chip on her shoulder and took out her rage on every suspect she brought before a judge.

Hampton, as predicted, would refuse to go to with the detectives, which is why he was placed under arrest. He was in her sights and she would go after him with the ruthlessness that had earned her both the position of Assistant District Attorney and her reputation.

By the time Hampton was brought in to the police station and processed for Hindering Prosecution, the Grand Jury had handed ADA Kemp a murder indictment.

No matter what Linus, in the presence of his attorney, had said to Kemp or the detectives at the police station, he was going to be arraigned for trial. Kemp had the indictment in her briefcase the entire time Hampton was being questioned. A fact that neither Reid nor Hampton were aware of. If they'd been informed about Kemp convening a Grand Jury and their decision to indict, Hampton would have exercised his right to remain silent since he was going to go to The Tombs anyway. His interview with the police wouldn't help him, only hurt him. Regardless of the outcome of the interview, Hampton was going to be held for a Friday morning arraignment.

After going over his story on the record, ad nauseam, he was placed under arrest for the murder of his wife, added to the hindering prosecution charge that was given to him in the lecture hall. Because it was too late in

76

the day on Thursday to get an arraignment hearing, Hampton was brought to The Tombs. Kemp had planned it that way from the start.

Seven other men were handcuffed and chained to the inside of the bus over to White Street, none could take their eyes of the man in the black three-piece suit. He didn't belong. None of the other seasoned criminals had to ask if this was his first time in a bus or the first time going to The Tombs. They didn't have to. No matter how stoic the suit tried to look, it was clear that he was scared. Somebody was going to make a meal out of him.

Once off the bus, Hampton was shoved against a wall in line with others, his restraints were taken off so he could strip off all of his clothes. His faced showed the first clear sign of emotion when his suit was haphazardly shoved into a large, clear bag. Hampton's name was then scribbled on the bag with a black Sharpie marker. No time was taken to fold his clothes. Nor would the Corrections Officer allow him to fold them. Instead, he was bent over and a man with a white glove felt under his scrotum and dug a finger inside his rectum. Hampton then turned and opened his mouth. The same corrections officer looked around the inside of his mouth and Linus had all he could do not to vomit. When the search was over, Linus Hampton became #963476. He was given a t-shirt, jumpsuit, socks, and Bobos for his feet. None of the garments looked new. The guards watched him dress and brought him further into the jail for processing.

After fingerprinting and signing the form listing all of the belongings he'd come in with, Hampton was brought to a holding cell where he was finally corralled and escorted to where he would spend the night.

The solid sliding metal door opened to a large space the size of a gymnasium. To his immediate left was a glass booth where uniformed men stood within, watching over the incarcerated men who were now screaming at him. Cells lined the walls to the left and right on two tiers. The center of the space was filled with two rows of cots.

The screams and taunts from the inmates became objects thrown at him. "I would like to be put into protective custody," Hampton said to the CO who'd escorted him into pod.

"Ain't you the fuckin' funny one. Find a spot and park your ass. Try not to get fucked-up," the Corrections Officer said as he left him and walked toward the glass observation area. "Number 963476 - Hampton," he said to his colleagues inside the glass booth. "Best keep an eye on him or he ain't gonna make it."

"Suicide watch?" Hampton heard the CO inside the glass say through the tinny speaker.

"Fifty-fifty. Odds are he's gonna get fucked up. Asked to be PC'd but he's going back on the bus for arraignment first thing."

"What'd he do?"

"Murder. Ellen Hunt."

"No shit? Him?"

"None."

"He don't look the type."

"How long you been doin' this? What does 'the type' look like?"

"Fair enough. Still, maybe we should put him in PC. He's gonna need a safe spot when he gets back anyway."

"Guy checked in a fuckin' AMEX Black at property. If he's rollin' with that in his wallet, he'll make bail."

"The Ellen Hunt murder? You think he'll get bail?"

"Worry about that tomorrow, I guess," the officer outside the glass said as he looked at his plastic watch. "He's only got like six hours until we gotta get him on the bus back to arraignment. I'd let it ride. Just keep an eye out if ya can."

Hampton didn't make a move to go anywhere while the conversation between corrections officers took place. He stood where he was, assessing the situation he now found himself in. This was not his first time going to a jail or prison. He'd interviewed inmates many times in such places. Never in the depths of the facility, however. He'd conducted the meetings in conference rooms or visiting areas inside the prison, never in general population. Hampton had never even seen a place like this. Of course he'd heard the stories, none had done this justice. Prisons weren't supposed to be fun. Stories don't prepare a person for when it happens to them, however. And the entire cell block had just heard the CO announce that he was wealthy. AMEX Black credit cards don't have a credit limit. Every two-bit hustler knows that. Fear enveloped him, though he consciously tried not to show it.

This is what hell must look like, he thought. He looked at his wrist where his watch normally lived, then at a clock with a metal cage over it above the glass room. Almost midnight. *Don't these people sleep?* His arraignment hearing would be at 9:00. Nine hours. He had to survive nine hours with no end of people who would look to get a nice payday in exchange for not beating him to death.

Hampton removed his glasses and tried to clean them, but he had no kerchief. The jumpsuit he was given and now wore had the same texture as sandpaper. He thought twice about cleaning his lenses and replaced his fragile glasses on his face upon realization that he wouldn't be able to.

Another look at the clock on the wall. A full minute had not yet passed.

He was thankful that he'd been arrested on a Thursday instead of a Friday. Hampton wasn't sure he would survive an entire weekend in that place. He definitely wouldn't survive if he was denied bail at his arraignment tomorrow morning. He might not even survive the night.

Hide your fear, he told himself. *One step at a time. You just have to survive tonight.*

Chapter 9

May 2, 2014

9:00 AM

The Arraignment

SHOVING PEOPLE AROUND AND BEATING ON *everyone in sight is just what these people do,* Hampton was thinking when he was pushed toward the defendant's table. He'd been waiting in the concrete hallway outside the courtroom with the seven other men he'd gone to The Tombs with and a few more that he hadn't.

After a hellish night the likes of which he'd never so much as dreamt, he was transported from The Tombs back to the courthouse for his appearance. Upon arrival he was incarcerated in a large cell with nearly a dozen other accused criminals all with similar business before a judge. After three hours in the tank in the bowels of the courthouse, Hampton was then corralled into the hallway outside the courtroom with his docket number. The wait in the hallway was another eternity.

All of a sudden, the court officer grabbed him by the lapel and shoved him out of the hallway and into the courtroom.   The gallery was packed.   Cameras were everywhere.   Reporters were everywhere.   His docket number, name, and accused crimes, were called aloud by the court officer.

"Docket number 153726. Linus Fredrick Hampton. Murder in the First Degree, Assault with a Deadly Weapon, and Hindering Prosecution."

Hampton was still in his jumpsuit, hands and feet bound as he shuffled over to the table. Dried blood stained the shoulders and front of the garment.

His attorney, William Reid, met him at the table. The counselor would normally have had to struggle to compete in terms of couture, but not on this day.   Reid could have been wearing a track suit instead of his current attire and still been tonier than his client.

"What in the hell happened to you?" Reid asked in horror and not softly.

"I fell."

"Into a wood-chipper? Look at your face."

"I guess that's why they don't give us mirrors."

"I want names and details—"

"—How does the defendant plea?" The judge, who looked exactly like Wilford Brimley, asked over the din of noise in the courtroom. The gallery was abustle with side conversations. "Quiet! Or I'll clear the courtroom." He sounded just like the no-nonsense old guy in the old Quaker Oats commercials in addition to imitating the actor's image. The judge might as well of said, *It's the right thing to do and the tasty way to do it*' to complete the emulation.

82

"William Reid for the defendant Linus Hampton, Your Honor. My client pleads not-guilty."

"Where do the People stand on bail, Miss Kemp?" the arraignment judge said as he turned toward her.

Judy Kemp was behind a podium on the opposite side of the courtroom. Her pant-suit did little to give her even the smallest hint of femininity. In fact, it did the opposite. The padding inside her jacket accentuated her wide shoulders. "Given the nature of the crime and almost limitless means at the defendant's disposal, The People request remand."

Reid was incensed. "Your Honor .... These charges are preposterous. My client has lost his very high profile wife at the hands of some killer who still roams free. The DA's office has seen fit to vilify him without a scintilla of proof, only conjecture and a strained set of circum—"

"—Save it for the trial, counselor. This is an arraignment hearing."

"Where can he go? The press is tracking his every move. The murder has been on the television, in print, on social media .... And now that my client has been arrested, do we think that is going to diminish?" Reid turned and pointed toward the cameras in the back of the courtroom, but continued to speak to the judge. "I think not. It stands to reason that it will only get worse. So I ask again, Judge, where can he go?"

"I don't think we should give him the opportunity to find out," Kemp said.

"Your Honor, look at my client. He spent less than ten hours in jail and he's already been beaten to a pulp. He's obviously a target. Incarcerating him would be a death sentence."

"The People would agree to Protective Custody."

"Please.   Linus Hampton is a member of the New York Bar Association, a respected professor at Columbia University as well as a revered member of Manhattan society at large.   The man has never had so much as a parking ticket. He wants nothing more than to get on with a speedy trial and to try to put not only the death of his wife but these ridiculous charges behind him."

"First Degree Murder, Judge.   The charge alone warrants the denial of bail in any amount," Kemp interjected matter-of-factly.

The elderly judge with coke-bottle glasses and a thick mustache looked at the files on the clipboard in front of him and then at the defendant. "I've heard enough out of both of you. Bail is set at five million—"

"—Your Honor!" ADA Kemp bellowed.

"—Cash or bond."

"Judge."

"I've heard enough, Miss Kemp.   He's not going anywhere."

"We will post that this morning," Reid said.

"I'm not finished," Brimley's doppelgänger said.   "I am going to cover my backside and order that Mister Hampton surrender his passport and be fitted for an ankle monitor.   Other than teaching his classes, meet with his attorney, or with court approval, he is to remain in his home under house arrest."

"That's just my point, Your Honor.   The defendant has no home." Kemp pointed at Hampton while making her case.

"My client has no home because the police have not, nor have any immediate plans to, release his residence

84

from their custody as a crime scene. He has moved into a suite at the Mandarin Oriental and will reside there in such time as he is free to move back into his apartment, all traces of the murder are removed, and/or the renovations being done are complete and the residence is deemed livable."

"Then for the purposes of this hearing, his home will be considered his suite at the Mandarin Oriental. Miss Kemp, if you want the defendant confined to his former place of residence, you best get on the police to release the apartment back into his possession so he can get it cleaned up. Next case."

"Your Honor, one more item," Reid said.

"Pushing your luck, aren't you, counselor?"

"I prepared a brief. I want a gag order issued."

"Freedom of the Press," Kemp argued. "The public has an unassailable right to know about the progress of the case."

"Or to corrupt the jury pool, if the DA's machinations go so far as to warrant a trial. With every passing hour, the rhetoric about my client becomes exponentially more viral. We are going to move to have a speedy trial but even so the damage will be irredeemable. His celebrity wife was murdered and they are now accusing my client of the vicious crime. How is he supposed to get a fair trial?"

"The People vehemently oppose a gag order. His in-laws are the Hunts. Hunt Media. Mister Reid will have unfettered access to spin this case in any way he chooses and The People will have no remedy."

"The gag order works both ways, Your Honor."

The judge scratched his head. "Better to be safe than sorry. A gag order is in place forthwith. Outside the courtroom. All proceedings inside a courtroom are fair game. No press conferences until this is resolved."

"Your Honor—"

"Your Honor—"

"Are you both unhappy?" he asked from his chair behind the bench. "Good. I must be doing the right thing. Can we move on now? Next case."

Reid turned to Hampton. "Hang tight. I'll have you out of here in two hours."

Chapter 10

February 8, 2016

11:45 AM

The Quip Is No Joke

ROYA DRESSNER SAT BACK IN HER CHAIR FOR a moment after hearing Linus Hampton tell his story for seemingly the thousand-and-tenth time. She reviewed the contents of one of her folders containing the transcript from the arraignment hearing on May 2, 2014. The story he'd just told under oath, in front of a camera and stenographer, was consistent with the files she had in front of her. Roya looked to her right at Michael Kettering who shrugged.

"And you were released and under house arrest shortly after that hearing, correct?" she asked turning back to her respondent.

"Yes. For the moment I was safe from the sword of Damocles," Hampton said.

Kettering leaned in. "There you go again with your .... way. Acting all superior."

"Because I have the benefit of a classical education? Shall I explain for you, the camera, and for the record what the sword of Damocles is?"

"Yes."

"No," Roya interjected. "But you can testify as to if this was when you learned that you would no longer be required to teach your classes at Columbia, Professor."

"That evening, yes. The media coverage was quite extensive, despite the gag order. Everything that took place at the arraignment was tweeted, in print, and on every bloody television station. The Dean—"

"—Your boss?" Kettering interrupted.

"I don't have a boss, per se. I am the department chair, he is Dean of the School of Law."

"So he is your equal?"

"Objection," Miranda Wood offered.

"As I've said, I have no eq—"

"—Can we move on?" Roya asked. "Finish your thought please. The Dean?"

"Called me to inform me that with the attention my predicament was garnering, and the pressure he was receiving from students and parents of students who were paying tuitions, that it would be best if I sort out my situation outside of the university."

"You were fired?"

"I have tenure. I was not sacked, I was officially taking a leave. With pay."

"I see," Roya said. She opened another folder. "And if I have my sequence of events correct, you then filed a writ of Habeas Corpus, pro se."

"I am a lawyer and I now had the time."

"Why not let your lawyer file it?"

"I believe I answered that."

"How did it go?" Kettering asked.

"There was a criminal trial, so it is quite obvious, even for you I would imagine, how it went."

"You lost the motion?" Kettering probed further.

"Are you a troglodyte? The writ required that I be brought before a judge to determine if there was enough evidence to support a trial, and if not, that the issue be dropped with prejudice," Hampton explained.

"Which of course there was. You were indicted."

"A Grand Jury would indict a bowl of broth, it doesn't mean there's any meat to it."

Kettering shook his head. "I'll ask again, how did it go?"

"There was a media circus and I was the only suspect. Judge Schriber was unwilling to grant the writ. If it had been proven that I was guilty of Ellen's murder at some future point, I could not be retried. Jeopardy would be attached."

"How did it feel to lose the motion?"

"I've lost other motions. Motions are tertiary compared to the trial as a whole. I was now focused on the trial since the onslaught at every level was devoted on seeing me put to the cross."

"You poor thing."

"Objection. Is that necessary?" Miranda asked in a bit of a huff.

"I believe I'll take over, Mike," Roya said. She briefly looked through a folder before setting it aside. "So when did you hire a private investigator?"

"Wednesday. I spent the remainder of that Tuesday after the Habeas Corpus motion researching who best to hire for the task at hand. I set a meeting for Wednesday. I hired him subsequent to that meeting."

"You hired a private investigator even though you had a legal team with an army of investigators on their payroll? A payroll afforded by the enormous amounts of money Reid, Weinstein, Hanley & Wood were and are still charging you by the billable hour?"

"Objection."

"You can't object to that, Miranda. He has to answer."

"I just did. My fees and those of my firm are not relevant."

"Seriously?"

"Our firm charges what we deserve, given our historical performance. We charge what the market will bear."

Roya rolled her eyes. "Said the attorney on the letterhead. Please answer the question Doctor Hampton. Do you need me to ask the question again?"

"No, I have a brain and yes I hired an outside investigator."

"Why?"

"I'm not the sort to do nothing and claim to be out of ideas. I was charged with murdering my wife. I thought it best not to sit on my hands and wait for my life to be in ruins. Diligence is the mother of luck."

"Emmanuel Alvarez. That's the name of the outside investigator you hired?"

"Another job outsourced," Kettering offered though no one in the room responded to it. He slunk back into silence at the lack of reaction and the realization that his outburst was on the record.

"Yes."

"You say that you interviewed him and hired him, but you knew him didn't you?"

"Yes."

"Because you'd used him before?"

"Yes."

"Then why the 'research' as you put it and the subsequent interview?"

"I called it a meeting."

"So you did. Can you answer the question?"

"He had a different name when I'd hired him in the past."

"To do what?"

"Look into the background of a student who claimed that I had used her for sex in a quid pro quo. Pay to play. Sex for grades."

"Objection. Prior acts are not relevant here," Wood said.

"It's a deposition, Miranda. He has to answer."

"You haven't asked a question, Roya. You just put on record that he was accused of a separate crime that has no bearing on this case."

"Goes to credibility. He said he interviewed a man he already knew."

"Are you suggesting that I cut a wide swath through the student body?" Hampton asked.

"I'm saying that it would be understandable given your position, looks, and wealth. So I'll ask the question your lawyer doesn't want me to ask. Didn't you already know this investigator, Emmanuel Alvarez, from a past investigation in which you'd hired him to investigate a woman—excuse me student—who claimed that you offered to improve her grade in your class if she had sex with you?"

"Yes, though I was unaware that I knew him because he changed his name when he was married. He is gay and took his partner's last name, Alvarez. As for the student, she was sub-par and looking to attain a law degree with sex. I shutter to think what she was willing to do to pass the bar exam."

Roya leaned in toward Hampton and his lawyer. "Let's start with your first statement. He didn't change his first name, did he? How many Emmanuels to you know?"

"He goes by Manny."

"How many Mannys do you know?"

"Manny."

"Was that a joke?"

"That was a quip. I don't tell jokes."

"What's the difference?"

"A priest, a rabbi, and an Imam walk into a bar. That is a joke. Did you really depose me to explain the difference between a witty rejoinder and a joke?"

"Maybe it's time for a break," Miranda offered.

"As soon as I finish this line of questioning," Roya said. "So you hired this Manny, that you didn't know you knew, to investigate your wife's murder or how best to defend you against being charged with murder?"

"Objection."

"One in the same. If I didn't do it, someone else did. The real monster, at that time, had proven illusive."

"And it was this Manny Alvarez that came up with the idea to go after the contractor? Or was it your legal team?"

"My investigator. Ellen was, after all, having an affair with him. They'd known each other in preparatory school. What you will probably consider high school. He knew her in the biblical sense. The reason he was hired for the job, as it turns out."

"This was not your late wife's first affair, was it?"

"My late wife was made of weaker seed."

"Because she was a woman?"

"Don't be absurd," Hampton said. "Because she was infinitely less resolved in her decisions and actions."

"Like the affair."

"Shall we label that Exhibit A?"

"We're up to Exhibit J thus far, and accusing him of the crime, clears you. Correct?"

"His fingerprints were on the weapon."

"You were having construction done on your luxury apartment. It was his ball-peen hammer. Of course his fingerprints were on it."

"His blood as well."

"Let her ask the question, Linus. You don't need to respond," Miranda said leaning in toward her client.

"Contractors get cuts on their hands and bleed on their tools," Roya said. "But funny that YOUR fingerprints were on the hammer as well."

"It seems you are as good at telling jokes as I am."

"Linus, Please. Make her ask the question."

"Why were your fingerprints on the murder weapon?"

"My, OUR, entire apartment was being renovated. He left his tools strewn about. It seems that penetrating my wife was far more important than tidying up after himself. I had occasion to move them out of the way."

"And murder your wife with it?"

"What say we take that break?"

"One more minute, Doctor Hampton. First, answer, for the record, the following please …. When did you really hire Manny Alvarez, and when did you really find out about her latest affair?"

"As I told you. After I was accused and released on house arrest pending trial, I hired Manny Alvarez."

"Because if you hired him before hand, that would give you a pretty strong motive to kill her, wouldn't it?"

"She'd had other affairs. I didn't murder her after those, did I?"

"Maybe this was the final straw. Tell me, what would you have gotten in terms of a settlement if you had divorced her, due to her infidelity?"

"Twenty million."

"Even if SHE cheated on YOU?"

"The Hunts protected their money in an iron-clad prenup."

"Iron-clad? Aren't you a brilliant lawyer?"

"My wife got the better of it, didn't she? The Hunts are vastly wealthy."

"So it would be much more profitable for you in the event that she died?" Roya asked with a hint of a tone.

"Yes, though we had an open marriage."

"You had affairs as well?"

Miranda stood up. "We are going to insist on that break now."

"Just answer my last question please."

"We asked for a break twenty questions ago, and again ten questions after that. We are going off the record and taking a break. Right now."

Roya nodded to her partner, to the camera man, and to the stenographer. "We are off the record. Let's take fifteen minutes."

Chapter 11
May 11, 2015
2:20 PM
Hammer Down

DOUG HART SAT ON THE WITNESS STAND,
rivulets of perspiration formed on his forehead, the thin
mist glistening in the fluorescent light inside the
courtroom.   He was clearly uncomfortable with being
called to the stand to testify as he sat in his seat below His
Honor.

Hart was notified weeks in advance of the trial by
subpoena.   The door to the waiting room outside the
courtroom opened after Reid told Judge Schriber he'd be
calling his first witness, Doug Hart, to the stand. Hart was
escorted to the stand by a court officer.   He looked more
timid with each step closer to his chair near Judge
Schriber. By the time he was sworn in—to tell the truth
and nothing but the truth—the collar on his oxford shirt
was wet and sticking to his neck.

William Reid, Esquire called Hart to the stand and
was going to ruin him. The witness knew it. The entire

96

courtroom knew it. "This will likely be the defense's only witness," he'd said. "Though we reserve the right to call rebuttal witnesses."

To this point in the trial, Reid's strategy was to discredit every witness the prosecution produced. Each witness was dissected until their testimony was suspect at the very least. Since Hart was the only witness on the defense's list, the case would hang on his testimony.

Reid had vigorously cross-examined all of the prosecution's witnesses throughout the trial thus far to create reasonable doubt. To create the notion that the unlikable person ADAs Hardison and Kemp had spent two full weeks demonizing, the man on trial for the murder of Ellen Hunt, wasn't the person who committed the crime. Decades of experience had given Reid the knowledge, however, that all the reasonable doubt in the world wouldn't add up to an acquittal unless the jury had an alternate person to point a finger at.

Doug Hart, the contractor with whom Linus Hampton's wife was having an affair prior to her murder, needed to be that person.

With the amount of fidgeting and sweating going on without even the first question raised, Reid felt very good about the way this examination would go. The defense attorney hadn't even rose from his seat to ask the first question and the witness was doing his work for him. The discomfort worked in the defense's favor, so Reid milked the moment.

After asking His Honor if he could approach the witness, Reid took the silk kerchief from his breast pocket and handed it to the witness. "You look nervous, Mister Hart. Please. Take this for your brow."

"Thank you," he said as he took it from Reid. "You can call me Doug. My father was Mister Hart."

Reid smiled. His pure white teeth seemed to give more light to the room. "Let's get started then. You are the construction worker that was hired to renovate the home of my client, Linus Hampton, and his late wife, Ellen Hunt, correct?"

"Contractor. Yes."

"How did you get the job?"

"I don't get it."

"Did you bid on it? Respond to a request on Angie's List? Craig's List? Help Wanted? How did you come to get the job?"

"I knew Ellen."

"I see. Wait. No I don't. How did, no offense, a construction worker," Reid pointed to the witness on the stand, "Know one of the wealthiest, most famous women in Manhattan? I mean before getting the contract to do the renovations."

"From school."

"You went to Princeton?"

"No. Prep School."

"Ah. Wait. No, I'm sorry. You still have me at a loss. How did you, a construction worker—"

"—I'm a contractor—"

"—Go to a private preparatory school, Chapin, one of the most exclusive schools in the country? The same school the Hunt family, one of the wealthiest families in the history of the United States, sent their only daughter?"

"'Cuz my parents sent me there too."

"Enrollment in Chapin, back when Ellen went there, was more than fifty-thousand dollars per year. Times four

98

years unless you graduate early. It's a legacy school. Roughly a quarter of a million dollars over the course of four years for high school. How did your parents swing that? Did either of them attend Chapin? Or were you on scholarship?"

"No. I mean yes. I wasn't on scholarship. My family has money. My father went there. So I went there."

"Your father?"

"Mister Hart."

"Very funny. Did you get good grades, Doug?"

"I graduated."

Reid looked to Judge Schriber. "Your Honor, permission to treat the witness as hostile?"

"Granted."

"This is how the process works, Doug. I ask the questions, you answer the questions I ask as truthfully as possible. Now, I didn't ask if you graduated, I asked if you received good grades. There is a distinction."

"No, I didn't get good grades. I'm not book-smart. But I'm not stupid."

"I didn't say you were. Are you a thin-skinned person, Doug? You take offense where none was meant."

"Objection," ADA Hardison said as he slid his chair out from under him and stood. "He's badgering the witness."

"It's his witness," Scriber said, "and the witness has been deemed hostile. Overruled."

"You don't have to answer that, Doug," Reid said. "But you must be a bit of a disappointment. Your father runs a hedge fund, correct?"

"Yes."

"And you, you're a laborer."

"I own my own business."

"For which he gave you the start-up money," Reid said with a nod. "Fair enough. What are father's for, right?"

"Objection."

"Withdrawn. I have to ask though, Doug, how does an underachiever get to know ELLEN HUNT, even back then?"

"Our last names are close. Hunt. Hart. We were next to each other on the same lists, same classes, standing on lines. We ran into each other a lot."

"And you were the bad-boy, right?"

"I don't know what you mean."

"Sure you do, but I'll admit that was a leading question. We have't established that you were bad yet. Were you ever reprimanded for having drugs?"

"What the hell? No."

"I have a report from Chapin where you were caught with marijuana and LSD in your locker. The principal at the time didn't think it wise to get the police involved and smear the Hart name. Your family had a good name at one time and so you received only the proverbial wrap on the knuckles. Do you remember that?"

"Now I do. Yeah."

"That your family had a good name or you remember the incident?"

"The incident."

Reid nodded again. "And that was the one you got caught for. So, a rich girl can have anything she wants, so she goes for the thing she's not supposed to have. You were an outsider attending an insider school. You were the bad-boy ladies man, were you not?"

"I had girlfriends if that's what you mean."

"Ellen Hunt being one of them?"

"Yeah. Yes."

"So you admit that you and she had a relationship back then?"

"I wouldn't call it a relationship."

"What would you call it?"

"I think the kids call it a 'Netflix and chill' nowadays. We called it a 'booty call' back then."

"Underage sex?"

"Yeah. Consensual."

"Was it? Weren't you accused of Statutory Rape?"

"Objection. Prior bad acts and he was a minor at the time," Hardison said while quickly getting to his feet.

"Sustained. The jury will disregard," Schriber instructed.

Reid continued. "So you ran into Ellen Hunt at some point later in life. What, if anything, did she say to you?"

"That my name came up and what I did for a living and the timing was cool because she needed some work done on her apartment."

"So she wanted to hire you?"

"Something like that."

"I need you to be more specific, Doug."

"She wanted more than just the renovations."

"Come now, don't be shy. She wanted sex, again without the relationship, and she thought the best way to do it was to hire you to renovate her apartment?"

"Objection."

"Withdrawn. Let's take a step back. How exactly did you reconnect?"

"She called me. Out of the blue."

101

"And that is when she said that your name came up?"

"Yeah."

"What else, if anything, did she say?"

"Objection." Hardison stood. "Hearsay."

"Direct conversation, Your Honor," Reid said.

"I'll allow it, subject to connection."

Reid turned back to the witness. "Please answer the question. Do you need me to remind you what it was?"

"No, I got it. She said she got my number from a friend. I get a lot of referrals. I do good work."

"I'm sure you do. I'm sure all of your clients are very satisfied with your service."

"Objection."

"Is that when she hired you?" Reid continued without waiting for a ruling from the judge. Schriber made no attempt at making one either, he simply waived his hand.

"No. She said she wanted to meet up. She wanted me to look at her place."

"And have sex?"

"No. Not then. I walked through the apartment, looked at the architectural drawings, and listened to her ideas. She said she wanted me to start within the week. That's when she hired me."

"And did you?"

"Yes."

"And you began having sex with her—"

"—Objection."

"Sustained. Move on counselor."

"Yes, Your Honor. This construction and renovations business of yours, do you often have affairs with your clients?"

"Objection."

"For the last time, move on Mister Reid."

"Yes Sir. My apologies. Do you have a crew? Other laborers in your business?"

"Yes."

"How many?"

"Depends on the job. Up to ten on each crew. I have up to ten on a job. I have two jobs going on right now, five on the one I have in the Bronx."

"Have? You have a crew working my client's project now?"

"No. I haven't been asked to finish the job yet."

"Do you expect to be?"

"I'm under contract," Hart shrugged. "I get paid either way."

"That's not what I asked you. Do you expect to be called back to the project when this trial is over?"

"Probly not."

"Why is that?"

"'Cuz I was bang .... Sleeping with his wife."

"I think your right."

"Objection. The defense is testifying." Hardison was on his feet again. "Where are we going with this, Your Honor? None of this is relevant."

"I'm getting there, if I can be afforded some latitude."

"Quickly," Schriber bellowed.

Reid turned and quickly restarted his examination. "How many laborers besides yourself did you have on the Hunt job?"

"Just me."

"So you could have sex without an audience?"

Hardison was on his feet but Reid withdrew the question before the ADA could object. Reid moved on without skipping a beat. "Did I hear you correctly when you said that you have up to ten employees per job? Times however many jobs you have going simultaneously?"

"Workers. Not employees."

"Day workers."

"Right."

"Why is that, so you don't have to pay for benefits?"

"Partly."

"And the other part is that all but one of your 'workers' are illegal, correct?"

"Their paperwork looks legit," Hart said before wiping his saturated forehead again with Reid's kerchief. Hart was panting like he'd been on a treadmill. The silk was now so wet that the sweat beaded off the lowest corner, dripping onto the ledge in front of him. "I don't have permanent workers 'cuz I don't know if I'll have steady work for them from one job to the next."

"But you *DO* know their paperwork is not 'legit', correct? You keep one white guy as a foreman on each crew to make things look good or to warn the illegal workers to scatter when Immigration or OSHA comes calling, correct?"

Hart looked to the judge and then to the ADAs at the prosecution table. No help was forthcoming. The courtroom held in silence while waiting for the witness's response.

"I'll tell you what, Doug. You don't have to answer that. I'll cut you a break. I'm not your lawyer, but if I were I would tell you to plead the Fifth. You're not legally obligated to say anything that would incriminate yourself in a crime, especially an ongoing one. But I think that you're non-response tells us, tells the jury, all that we need to know.

"So, lets change tack. Did you kill Ellen Hunt?"

Hardison was on his feet. "Your Honor may we approach?"

Schriber motioned the attorneys from both sides toward him on the bench. He covered the microphone in front of him with his left hand while the prosecutor spoke in a loud whisper.

"Judge, there is only one place Mister Reid can be going with this."

"I'm allowed to offer an alternate theory of the crime."

"Yes, but a plausible one. I would like Your Honor to direct the defense to provide proof of what they are about to allege and until he does, I want Your Honor to instruct the jury to disregard his last question."

"I don't have to prove that Mister Hart committed the murder," Reid said.

"No, but you can't just throw out incredible theories like a martian did it," Hardison said.

"Credibility is for a jury to decide. If they think a martian did it, they can't in good conscience convict my client."

"Your Honor?"

Scriber took a deep breath. "Mister Reid, do you have any evidence to support the road you're going down? Mister Hardison is right, once you ring the bell he cannot unring it."

"I do, Sir. If you allow me to continue ...."

"Very well. But I'm warning you, if at the end of this examination there is nothing to support your allegations about the witness, I'll be forced to declare a mistrial. No jury instruction will suffice, and I'll cite you for contempt. Do I make myself clear, Mister Reid?"

"Abundantly." Kemp and Hardison returned to their seats, Reid turned back toward the witness. "Where were we? Oh yes, Doug .... Did you kill Ellen Hunt?"

Hart's mouth gaped open but no words escaped.

"Right. Right. That pesky Fifth Amendment thing I was just speaking about. Fair enough. The night of the murder, you were working on the apartment, meaning having sex with the victim—as usual—when she said something that made you mad. You were sort-of living the life that you could of had after prep school if you'd had a real relationship with Ellen Hunt. You saw the apartment, the lifestyle, and you played pretend. In your mind you were with her. She was yours. Rich. Beautiful. Famous. And then she said something, or did something that put you in your place. She was wearing lingerie and she made you feel cheap, just like she did in the old days. So you snapped. You grabbed the nearest hammer, YOUR hammer, and brained her."

"Objection." Hardison was incensed. "Your Honor, the defense is testifying again. I want his entire statement stricken from the record and sanctions—"

"Withdrawn."

"—Not good enough," Hardison said.

"Mister Hardison, sit down. Mister Reid—"

"Just allow me a few more questions—"

"—You'd better get there quickly. You've been warned."

"Yes Your Honor. Doug, are you testi-lying today to save yourself from being prosecuted for the murder of Ellen Hunt?"

"NO. GOD NO." Hart was visibly shaking in his seat.

"Why should we believe you? Why should any of these people believe you? You cheat the government by not paying payroll taxes. You cheat the community by hiring illegal workers instead of local, skilled workers. You cheat your illegal workers by not paying them market wages or health benefits. You cheated my client by not doing the job you were hired to do and literally were the one who was cheating with his wife in his marital bed. You expect us to believe that you didn't up the ante to murder? Why would any reasonable person believe you?"

"Because I didn't do it."

"Ellen was in the house, alone with you."

"I left hours before it happened."

"Says you. But you can't account for your whereabouts can you?"

"I was in a bar."

"In a bar. The woman you were having an affair with was dressed for sex and you were in a bar that nobody can remember seeing you in?"

"I was there."

"We talked to the bartender at ...." Reid went to the defense table to look at his notes, then turned back to the witness. ".... Decker's Tavern. We spoke to all of the employees there. None could say with any certainty that you were there that night. You're a regular, but none of the staff remembers seeing you. We spoke to twenty-seven regular patrons. Nothing there either. How is that possible, Doug? How is it that you were in a public bar but nobody remembers you being there on April eighteen, two-thousand-fourteen, the night Ellen Hunt was murdered?"

"It's a dive bar. People drink. Heavily. I can't help it if nobody remembers me."

"Really? That's what you'll have us believe? She was dressed for you, Doug. It was your hammer that was used to kill her. Your DNA was in the bed. Your DNA under her fingernails. You had motive. You had opportunity. And the hammer was the means. Again, it was YOUR hammer."

"I left the hammer there. I left all of my tools there so I wouldn't have to carry them up and down the elevator every day."

"The main elevator?"

"No. I use the service elevator."

"Cameras?"

"No."

"Doorman?"

"No."

"You had a key?"

"Key code. Ellen gave me a code."

"So you could come and go as you please?"

Hart shrugged.

"You have to answer so the young lady here can type your answer for the record."

"Yeah, I guess. Only the code keypad was broke. You could punch in anything, or nothing, then hit pound and it would unlock the vestibule to the service elevator."

"You don't say. So you could have left ten minutes after the murder or hours before like you claim and there would be no record?"

"Uh. Well. No. I don't know. Look, I left before she was dead, okay? Anyway, I used the main elevator that day. I didn't have any tools, I wasn't dirty .... So I used the main elevator."

"So you say."

"It's true."

"So you admit that you were there on the day that Ellen Hunt was murdered?"

"Yeah. I never denied that. But not at the time she was killed. I ordered lunch. It was delivered to the apartment. I was there, but I left."

"After you killed her?"

"No. She was killed later."

"How do you know that?"

"She was alive when I left. Plus it was on the news."

"Despite the gag order?"

"I don't know about any gag order."

"So how long after you left was she killed?"

"I don't know exactly. How could I know that? I don't know what to tell ya. I went out the main elevator and that was the last I saw her."

"You know that for a fact? You specifically remember that day, of all days, that you used the main elevator down to the main lobby and out the front door? Instead of the service elevator?"

"Yeah. Yes."

"Picked the right day to use the main elevator, huh?"

"Objection."

"Withdrawn."

"The doorman didn't see you. The attendant in the lobby didn't see you. A nine hundred square foot lobby and nobody saw you leave. My investigators have been through a hundred hours of CCTV footage and the camera didn't capture you leaving."

"And I wasn't in the apartment," Hart said and pointed to Hampton at the defense table. "I wasn't there when he showed up. I wasn't in there when the cops showed up. Obviously. I wasn't there."

"Which doesn't prove that you didn't leave after you crushed Ellen Hunt's skull in with your hammer either."

"Objection."

"Overruled."

"Could you have used the service entrance, in and out on the day of the murder and gone undetected?"

"No."

"No? You just said that the keypad was broken. You went up the service elevator, brained her to death and left the same way you came, right?"

Hart looked at the judge. No help was forthcoming. Hart then looked toward the prosecutor's table. No help there either. Then, finally, at the jury who were transfixed on him. Sweat was dripping off the end of his nose and jawline.

Reid broke the crisp silence. "Best not answer that one either, Doug. That pesky Fifth Amendment thing. No further questions at this time. I reserve the right to reexamine the witness."

Schriber looked down from his chair at the witness. "The testimony of the witness will be admitted for the record. The prosecution's objection is overruled. Mister Hart, do you need a break before the prosecution cross-examines you?"

Hart wiped his face again before taking an enormous gulp of water from the glass on the ledge. "No. I'm good. Let's get this over-with."

Hardison was already out of his chair and approaching the witness. "Did you kill Ellen Hunt?"

"NO."

"There are no time stamps on your fingerprints, nor the blood on the hammer, nor your semen in the bed, nor skin under Ellen Hunt's fingernails are there?"

William Reid's chair behind the defense table had not yet taken all of his weight before the attorney was back on his feet. "Objection. The witness is not an expert in forensics."

"Sustained."

"How do you explain your skin under her fingernails?"

"She scratched my back when we were, ya know, intimate."

"So you could have had sex with the victim a day or a week before the murder and your DNA would still be under her fingernails, correct?"

Reid stood up. "Objection. Speculation."

"Sustained."

Hardison shrugged. There was nothing he could do for Hart, not that he was interested in it. He'd made his point and therefore his cross-examination concluded. "I have no other questions for this witness."

Chapter 12
February 8, 2016
12:00 PM
Colossal Waste

OUTSIDE THE AD HOC CONFERENCE ROOM, Miranda Wood and her client were taking up a corner in the reception-slash-waiting area. Plush chairs and a matching sofa decorated the enclave but none were being used at present. The two stood in the middle of the area during the short break the attorneys for Capstone afforded them to take some refreshment, and to perform a body function in the rest room if necessary. Their mission, however, was to regroup. No refreshments or bathroom breaks. Miranda needed to confer with her client.

"Linus, you can't let them bait you. You're walking right into some of their traps. This Kettering asshole has a real hard-on for you."

"Pity he's not my type."

"I'm being serious," she pushed. "Don't let them rattle you."

"I look rattled, do I?"

Miranda bobbed her head about as if it were on a spring. "It's tough to tell with you."

"I assure you I'm quite steady on my feet. In fact, I have them right where I want them."

"Where is that? Winning?"

"Complacent. They *think* they're winning."

"I don't disagree with them, Linus. The standard isn't very high in civil court. Unlike criminal court, they don't have to prove that you did it. They just have to convince a jury that you might have and therefore shouldn't profit from it."

"You couldn't convince twelve people—who don't have the wherewithal to get out of jury duty by the by—that water is wet," he said as he cleaned the lenses of glasses.

"I find it ironic that you teach a subject that you have such distain for."

"That is not the correct use of the overused term ironic, nor is it *surreal*. I don't have distain for the legal system, nor am I quixotic. My distain is for the uninformed public who preside over the fate of others. The mob is getting dumber by the day and nobody gives a bloody fuck."

"You might want to keep that thought to yourself and your voice down."

"This is never going to a civil trial, Miranda."

"This is absolutely going to a trial, *Linus*. There is no way that Capstone is going to pay you what is equal to the GDP of some small countries. At least not without one hell of a fight."

"I abhor the fact that you are my lawyer and quite apparently playing the other side. If you're not fit or up for it, it is past time to inform that you can't be bothered."

"And I *abhor* that you're so cocky about this."

"What you call cocky, I call confidence. With the education that I'm giving you, Miranda, you should be paying me."

"When you lose this case, you might need the income."

"Very droll. Shall we return to my supposed ruining?"

"I think we have to. Kettering is waiving us to go back in," Miranda said as she raised a hand to one half of Capstone's counsel in acknowledgement. Hampton turned toward Kettering then back to his lawyer who was still speaking. "Just take a deep breath before responding. Give me a chance to get an objection on the record."

"It's a deposition," he said. "Objections are pointless. Just sit and be trained."

"My objections are not pointless. If the objections are on the record, Linus, I can argue each one in motion hearings which may eliminate the questions and your answers at trial—"

"—I grow weary from repeating myself. This is not going to a trial. This is an exercise in futility on their part. Custer's last stand, if you like. There is no nuance here. I was accused and acquitted of murdering my wife. They can re-litigate all they like, Capstone *WILL* pay."

Miranda Wood shook her head with eyes closed. She took a deep breath. "Let's go back in there."

Back inside and on the record, Kettering wasted no time in attempting a kill-shot before Roya Dressner could utter a sound. "You've claimed your innocence before, during, and since your criminal trial. If you're innocent of murder, why offer a plea deal with the prosecutor?"

"Objection."

"Answer the question please."

"As usual Kettering you have your facts mottled."

"Do I?" He opened a folder, producing another document to be marked in to evidence. Once the stenographer fastened a sticker marking it 'Exhibit L', Kettering slid it in front of Hampton. "Do you recognize this?" The document was an unsigned plea arrangement in criminal term."

"I do."

"So if you didn't kill your wife, why offer to take a deal for a reduced prison sentence?"

"The document is unsigned. I didn't take any deal."

"But why offer one? Why even entertain the idea if you didn't do it?"

"It was not my offer, it was proffered by New York District Attorney, Cyrus Vance. ADAs Hardison and Kemp called the meeting to discuss Vance's proposed deal with my criminal lawyer, William Reid, and myself. The notion was rejected before I'd laid eyes on the document. The meeting was yet another colossal waste of time and money."

Kettering nodded in understanding. "Yet there had to be a small part of you that wanted to take the deal. Ten years for Man-One is a sight better than life for Murder-One, no?"

"Any sentence is repugnant and a legal anathema when one is innocent of the crime he or she is accused of."

"Then why take the meeting?"

"I was under the impression that the ridiculous charges were going to be dropped, not a proposed reduction. As I said, it was a rather colossal waste."

"And yet?"

Linus leaned in toward the center of the conference room table, breaking his starched posture for the first time on camera. "And yet what? Out with it man."

"And yet your lawyer took the meeting. Why would the great William Reid, Johnny Cochran's brother from another mother, even consider it unless ...."

"Objection."

Hampton retook his stoic position. "My lawyer is paid to listen to all options. If there was a deal on the table, he has the legal responsibility to listen to it and present it to me. Canons of Ethics. You mightn't be familiar with the concept. The deal was rejected. Even for you that must cut and dried. Not signed. Never entered for the record. It was a proposal that was rejected the moment it was communicated to me. I don't know how to say it more plain. I know it's your job to make something from nothing, create a universal truth from an imaginary grain, but Jesus bloody wept. You've pulled on the wrong thread man. I can assure you, however, that if this document is the rack with which you are hanging your legal hat, best not bother. You'll embarrass yourself."

"Thank you for your legal advise, Linus—"

"—Doctor Hampton. My students call me Doctor Hampton. Or Professor Hampton."

"We aren't in your class," Kettering said. "Nor are we your students."

"And yet I'm schooling you."

"Here we go again," Roya interrupted. "Michael. Please?"

Kettering didn't respond, not that he was given a chance. Roya Dressner took up the questioning. "We've been calling you Linus or Mister Hampton thus far in the deposition, are you now informing us that your preference is now Doctor Hampton?"

"I am"

"Your preference is noted. Let's get back on point," Roya said. "So you refused a plea deal, which is your right, and you continued to proclaim your innocence."

"Was that a question?"

"Sorry. Yes, *Doctor* Hampton, it was. Through the police interrogation, the arrest, the house arrest, the denied requests for interviews and the press hammering on you despite the gag order, you continued to proclaim your innocence?"

"Yes."

"You never thought about throwing in the towel? A deal would have made it all go away. The press would have made another meal of it for a day or two—a week tops—and you would be quietly serving a reduced sentence on Rikers Island. You never thought about taking the deal?"

"Objection. Asked and answered."

"No. Not once did I entertain the notion of a deal of any kind. I am innocent. Innocent people don't contemplate prison sentences for crimes they didn't

117

commit.   I'm afraid I don't know how to say it any differently."

"Ten years is better than the rest of your life."

"There must be an echo in here. I was *ACQUITTED*. You are as dense as he is."

"Linus let her ask the question," Miranda said.

"If I have to keep reminding her to ask a bloody a question, making her repeat this twattle in the proper form, we'll be here until Saint Crispin's Day."

"When is that?"

"My point."

"Can we get back on track please?" Roya asked. "You were acquitted, yes. But no other suspects have been arrested and the case has been closed by the DA's office. Their position is that you got away with murder. Sorry. You got away with murder?"

"No. I was acquitted by a jury because there weren't any facts to support the charges against me. Then or now. Yet I'm being tried again."

"For the record, Doctor Hampton, you are not being tried again.   Double Jeopardy prevents you from being tried for the same crime or set of crimes twice. This is a civil matter."

"Thank you for the unnecessary clarification."

"A civil matter that you brought about."

"Objection."

"YOU are suing US," she continued.

"I'm suing Capstone, not you personally. Though the thought has merit."

"Linus." Miranda gave him an unmistakable look that was fortunately not caught on either the written nor the video records.

"My point is, excuse me—my QUESTION is—how do you feel about the fact that as far as the State and County of New York is concerned, you got away with murder and no other person or persons will be brought to justice?"

"How do I feel about it? I am not on your couch. I have no control over the New York District Attorney, nor do I have control of the police department. I have no control over whom they prosecute, or choose not to. It is quite out of my hands."

"You've been silent about it. If my husband was murdered and the police dropped the investigation, I would take action."

"Objection."

"Why haven't you gone to the press?"

"I've been vilified by the press. There was a gag order. My attorney asked for one on my behalf. You know this."

"Which didn't seem to stop them from plastering your face on television, newspapers, magazines .... On social media ...."

"Was that another improperly constructed question?"

"Why not play the game?"

"It was my game, wasn't it? I asked for the gag order, the Hunts simply couldn't control themselves. If I broke silence, I'd be violating my own gag order. The other media companies would follow suit."

"If it was me—"

"—It wasn't."

119

"Objection," Miranda interjected. "Linus, give me time to object."

"How about the Mayor then? You could have asked him to intervene."

"Not my ally."

"Your very influential Father-in-law then."

"Not predisposed to help me. Or Ellen apparently. Haven't you been listening? The Hunts were rather fixated on me. Hunt Media? Who do you suppose was leaking all of these so-called facts to their own media outlets?"

"Why is that?"

"Objection."

"You'll have to ask them."

"Why do you think, then? Because you got away with murder?"

"I've already answered that."

"Then why not put pressure on the Hunts to adhere to gag order?"

"To what end? One battle at a time."

"Then why not put pressure on the police to go after the supposed real killer?"

"I've been vocal about who that is as best I could, given the bloody gag order. I grow tired of repeating myself to the dim. Nobody able to do anything about it seems to care. Do you understand now?"

"And who is that?"

Another bit of eyeglass maintenance came before he said, "I've answered that as well."

"For the record."

"Again for the record?"

"Yes please."

"Doug Hart."

"Her lover?"

"The contractor. And yes, her paramour."

"Not yours?"

"Excuse me?"

"Your lover or paramour or whatever fancy word you'd like to use. You were also having an affair, were you not? Wouldn't that give you another motive to kill your wife?"

"Objection."

"Gone fishing again, hey?"

"Answer the question, Doctor Hampton. Wouldn't your lover have a pretty strong motive? You didn't think you could hide her forever did you? We have investigators as well."

Chapter 13
March 6, 2015
7:45 PM
Less Than Dirt

IN A NEARLY HIDDEN TABLE IN THE
homey back room of Jones Wood Foundry, an Upper East
Side eatery elevating United Kingdom canon, Linus
Hampton waited for his dining companion. On furlough
from house arrest, he enjoyed his pint of Boddington's and
a starter plate of Welsh rarebit toast while waiting for Chef
Jason Hicks to expertly prepare his main dish. And for his
tardy investigator to arrive. Amidst the dark wood, dim
lighting, tomes of Shakespeare, with the Angus & Julia
Stone folk-rock song *Draw Your Swords* softly playing in
the background, Hampton enjoyed his private table in New
York's snooty version of a proper British public house. In
the old days of two years ago, he was a weekly fixture.
Now, under house arrest, his visit was a rarity.

All of the veteran staff knew him. None seemed to
pass judgement. Without fuss, he was shown is usual
table, as if there hadn't been a lapse in visits. His usual
booth was hidden from view of other patrons and

whenever possible away from prying ears. Chef Jason came out to the table, asked if Hampton had anything special on his mind in the way of food, before retreating back into his kitchen to personally prepare Linus's selections. No small talk. Not a word about his legal troubles. Not so much as a hint about the length of time since Hampton's last visit or why. Just the way the professor liked it.

A server presented him his starter plate once it was prepared. After a time, Emmanuel Alvarez slid into the booth mid-bite without explanation as to why he was tardy or how he'd already had a craft cocktail called the Italian Diplomat in his left hand.

Manny, as he preferred to be called, was a large man. Latin men aren't usually over six feet and built like bulldozers. Manny knew how to handle himself despite his large potbelly. An intimidating sight to be sure and the man certainly stuck out in a crowd on his own. When he and his very effeminate, very petite, and very flamboyant husband were in a room, the couple did not go unnoticed.

Manny introduced himself and his husband, Carlos, to Ellen one night when they spotted her in a hot new club. Before being married he'd been hired by Linus on a number of occasions. Hampton often worked on cases outside his duties as a Columbia professor. In any of those times, Alvarez hadn't had the opportunity to meet Hampton's very beautiful and very famous wife—though not for a lack of trying. The next day, Ellen made mention of the interaction to Linus and asked how he thought the very large man and the tiny new boyfriend worked. "You know, sexually? It's like a grizzly bear and a chihuahua," she said. Linus sarcastically thanked his wife for the

123

imagery and said he would try very hard to burn that image out of his mind.

"More than a few ticks overdue, aren't we?" Hampton said by way of a greeting. "You know very well how I abhor tardiness."

Alvarez set a briefcase to his right in the booth as he slid in and immediately began to blurt out his investigative findings in broken spanglish, ignoring his client's quip. "This Hart guy is a real piece of work."

"Sssssssh." Hampton set down the rest of his final piece of toast, dabbed his mouth with the linen, and then took a sip of his heady beer before continuing. "Mightn't we keep the conversation we're about to have to a dull-roar? I'm not entirely sure I'd like the entirety of Manhattan to know that I'm having Handy-man Hart investigated. At least not yet."

"Yeah. Yeah. Sorry." His accent was part Latin, part Bronx. Sort of a male version of Rosie Perez. Though openly gay, Manny hadn't a hint of a lisp or overtly feminine mannerisms.

"I'm trying to enjoy my evening, so if you don't have anything truly enlightening to share, I don't want to hear it until the morrow."

"You called me here. You set up the meet."

"I set up the meeting in order to inveigle a judge to let me out of my home for a few hours. I can only leave my increasingly confining hotel room to see my lawyer or a finite number of other banal tasks. Since I'm not teaching, those tasks are few. For anything else I have to rattle my tin."

"You stay at the Mandarin. The Presidential Suite. I've seen it and it's gorgeous. What is it, three thousand square feet?"

"You try being forced to spend every waking hour there."

"I would love to. It's larger than my apartment and we don't have room service and spa treatments. When can Carlos and I move in?"

"I quite needed to stretch my legs. A change of atmosphere can be quite a cracking spur, wouldn't you agree?"

"Yeah. Sure. Whatever you say. But I do got news. We can do this now or I can just come to your suite tomorrow."

"You 'do got' news?" Hampton cleaned his glasses, pinched the bridge of his nose. "Out with it."

"He's a real lady's man. Always has been as far as I can tell," Alvarez said before taking a sip of his elaborate drink. "You have to tilt your hat. Except for the statutory rape charge when he was a minor. But that went away."

"What does that have to do with the fact that he was having a bit of the other with Ellen? We already knew that. Not exactly vanguard with current affairs, are we?"

"It shows a pattern with this guy."

"Leave the legal stuff to me. What else?"

"Bar room brawl went bad when he was in his twenties. Pled down to assault by mutual fray. Probation."

"Meaningless."

"He's violent. That's not meaningless. You asked me to dig into this guy and I did. I hit pay-dirt."

Hampton shook his head. "You have less than dirt. I need something that can be used against him in a court of

125

law. The mere fact that he was sleeping with my wife has done little to garner the interest of the authorities, so I need to ruin him in open court."

"He's a violent miso-gym-nist. You can use that in court."

Hampton almost cleaned his glasses again, but caught himself and took a sip of his beer instead. "Best leave the English language to me as well. It's misogynist, not —gymnist. A misogynist is a person who despises women, not one that loves them with the same enthusiasm as Handy-man Hart obviously does. You should know that, given your proclivities."

"Proclivities?"

"Preferences. Sexually. I'm not judging, I'm merely suggesting that you might empathize with someone who doesn't care for women."

"I don't have any problems with women. I love women. I just don't want to sleep with them."

"Your point is well-taken; however, I meant jealous. Gay men tend to be jealous of women."

"Whatever. I'll leave the legal stuff to you, and you leave your thoughts about how gay men think and feel to me. Okay?"

"Excellent. Then you *DO* understand my point."

Manny shook his head and went on. "He beat some guy's head in. Hart. He left the guy for dead in a bar after the fight. You can use that in court."

"Again with 'what I can use in court'. How is it that you are an investigator, *MY* investigator, and still know nothing about the law? Prior bad acts. Hart braining the other bloke has nothing to do with the case at hand, other than the fact that both of the injuries he caused are to the head? It can only prejudice a jury which is why no competent judge would allow it. We pulled Schriber for the trial. He is quite competent."

Alvarez looked confused. "But you see on tv all the time—"

"—You believe what you've seen on the tele before you believe a legal scholar? I've done wisely to hitch my wagon to your star."

This time the chef brought out a gorgeously presented plate of bangers and truffled mash personally, placing it in front of Linus. "Anything for your friend?"

"Not only is he not my friend, he clearly hasn't earned his daily bread. He won't be staying."

"Enjoy," Chef said before leaving. Alvarez looked hurt. "I should take my husband here. It's nice."

Hampton ignored his investigator. "The only way William Reid, Esquire, my lawyer, can bring up the bar room beating or his licentious behavior with regard to the opposite sex is if he says, under oath, that he isn't a violent person or has never hurt anyone or is a complete gentlemen. It can only be used to challenge the veracity of his statement and prove him a liar. Unless he is a complete idiot, which is entirely possible I'll admit, he's not likely to say any of those things. What else?" Hampton asked before putting a dainty bite of sausage, truffled mash, and a hint of British onion demi-glace into his mouth on an inverted fork.

"He went to school with your wife. A fancy school. A private school. They were an item back then."

"Hm. Interesting. Then he's not likely to be a complete wretch if he went to Chapin. I'll wager that was an influencing factor as to which contractor Ellen decided to hire. The first bit of news to pique my interest. Was Ellen the girl who accused him of statutory rape back then?"

The investigator looked pleased with himself and knew from past experience 'interesting' was as good a compliment as he could expect to receive from his client. "Minors records are sealed. I don't know."

"Disappointing that. See if you can't find out, yes? Anything else?"

"He hires illegal workers. Mexicans."

"Stop the bloody presses. A contractor in New York is hiring illegal Mexican workers to save money?"

Manny's pride was short-lived. "Yeah."

"Make yourself of some use, would you? Look into, at random, fifty construction enterprises in the tristate area and tell me if any of them *DON'T* use illegal workers."

"You really want me to do that?"

"Indeed. For no other reason than to give you an education. I am rather surprised that you would sell out your countrymen so easily. You thought that you were telling me something that I didn't know. What I would then do with that information, *YOU* didn't know. What If I had my legal team make a call to ICE, who then raided one of his job sites? How many of your cousins would have to go back to Mexico? Do you find yourself feeling a bit dirty for being such a cheap whore? I'm rather disappointed." Hampton rested his fork down on his plate before adding, "I do hope your papers are in order by the way. Or is that why you married your very pretty husband. For the green card?"

"My family is from Puerto Rico, asshole, and I've lived in New York my entire life," he said before draining his drink and all but slamming the empty glass down on the table. "That's on your tab." Emmanuel Alvarez squeezed himself out of the booth, retrieved his bag, and left the restaurant without a look back.

Hampton looked down at his plate and said to himself, "Finally. I can enjoy my dinner in peace."

Chapter 14
February 8, 2016
1:00 PM
Low Fidelity

THE CONFERENCE ROOM HAD TAKEN ON A very different tone since the fifteen-minute break. While Roya Dressner was still posing the questions, she was less inclined at courtesies. Instead, she was quite brusque. While her posture and facial expression hadn't changed, her tone told a different story. She reminded Professor Linus Hampton that he had to answer the question she'd posed to him.

"I remind you that you are still under oath. I'll ask the question again. You were also having an affair, correct?"

"An affair? No."

"You were sleeping with someone other than your wife. Ask yourself, 'Would she be asking me this question if she didn't have proof?'"

"Sleeping? No."

Roya removed a large envelope stamped 'PHOTOS DO NOT BEND' in red from a pile to her left. "Doctor Hampton, were you having sexual relations with a person other than your wife, Ellen Hunt?"

"Yes."

"There. See? Was that so hard?"

"Difficult."

"Excuse me?"

"Hard is an adjective referring to how solid or rigid the object of the sentence is. Or, in an alternate meaning; how potent, powerful, or forceful. You said hard when you meant difficult."

"People use hard to mean difficult all of the time."

"'People' say stupid things all the time. 'People' say things like 'lit' and 'woke' incorrectly. 'People' are not lawyers. Words have meaning. What you say will be public record. Be mindful of your words, counselor."

"I didn't realize you were also an expert on nomenclature, Doctor Hampton. Do you have a PHD in English as well?"

"Unfortunately correcting English comes with the territory when teaching young adults. As I said, language is important—especially in law."

"I'll keep that in mind. Can we get back to your affair? The legal version of a Jedi Mind Trick—getting me off my point by going on the attack—isn't going to work."

"We both know that there aren't any incriminating pictures in the envelope in front of you."

"We do?"

"We do. Else you'd have slipped them out into the light of day by now. Entered them into evidence as exhibits. Threatened to blow them up to five hundred percent at trial. We both know you're bluffing."

Roya flashed a disingenuous smile. "You were careful, I'll give you that."

"I wasn't hiding anything. Nor was I fooled by your feeble attempt at tricking me into an admission. I told you about the 'affair'—as you called it—to get on with it."

Roya upped the ante to a phony chuckle. "Let's not insult each other's intelligence, okay? If it had come out at your criminal trial that you were having an affair, it would have added another motive for killing your wife. Money was big, but an affair? That's the cherry. The police didn't exercise due diligence. We did."

"You think you've found something, have you? The police and the District Attorney might have known about the affair. Her affair. My affair. However, what is known and what can be proved are two very different things. "

"Maybe. But this is Civil Term. It's a different standard. You know I have you."

"Counselor, you are so intent on the grain of sand that you've lost sight of the beach."

"Is it time for clichés now? I'll bite. Enlighten me."

"I don't believe we have the time or strength."

"It's only natural to hate your wife for having an affair, is that why you had one? Revenge?"

"Don't be ridiculous. Hate is for children."

"So you're saying that you're above it?"

"Of course. I'm not a child."

"Then explain it to me."

"Neither of us wanted children."

"Surely the Hunts wanted future heirs. Ellen was their only opportunity to have grandchildren."

"Someone has to have the good-sense to refrain. And there are cousins with the Hunt name. The proud tradition will continue."

"And what does that have to do with you and Ellen having affairs?"

"We had an open marriage."

"Then why not bring that up in court? Without animus about an affair, we're back to one motive."

"The original motive. Money. That seems to have been enough. No need to give Hardison any more ideas."

"It's a lot of money."

"The open marriage wasn't relevant. Not as yet. Money was the supposed motive for my killing her. Which is why the subject of bringing up our arrangement was suggested and rejected. We focused on the real killer, and *HIS* motive for killing her."

"Doug Hart?"

"Yes."

"And while that gave him motive, it also gave you motive. Why not just be open about the open marriage? That is the point I'm driving at."

"Marital privilege. Surely you've heard of it. Any communication or agreement between married parties cannot be legally forced by third parties to divulge the substance of those communications or agreements."

Roya looked at Kettering and shrugged in bewilderment. "I don't get it. If what you're saying here and now, under oath, is true—which is up for debate to be sure—that would have been a big feather in your case."

"It would be throwing the baby out with the bathwater."

"I don't follow."

"I would be opening up my private life, the life that Ellen and I shared, to ridicule. Privacy is something I cherish. Something I would have to give up had I divulged our arrangement at trial. And for what? It wasn't even known, or at least able to be proved. Why shed light on a prickly thing that cannot and would not be used in open court anyway? And now that I have been forced to share it with you, you'll make a meal of it no doubt."

"We have to explore it. As you say, it can neither be proven nor disproven."

"Proved or disproved."

Roya ignored being corrected. "You're an intelligent man. You think you're smarter than everyone. So I have to ask, why throw a juicy steak out on the table if you don't want or have to? You didn't share it at trial for that reason. So why now? Because you *WANT* me to make a meal out of it. You know there aren't pictures in this envelope, because you know you were careful. So why not deny it? You know I can't prove it. I didn't force your hand, did I Doctor Hampton? You're forcing mine."

"Objection. I counted three questions with no time to respond," Miranda Wood offered.

"Noted. Answer this then. Why make me go down this road if privacy is so sacred to you? Why are we even speaking about an open arrangement between you and your late wife?"

"That's two questions," Miranda said.

"Miranda. I'll answer," Hampton said. "It is my experience that the most sexually talented partners are meretricious at best. Meaning they offer little else. While I enjoy the time spent love-making, I abhor any interaction before or after. The reciprocal was true of my wife."

"So you admit to having more than one extramarital affair?"

"I believe it was my wife who was found be unfaithful on more than one occasion."

"Yet you just said—"

"—That is not what I said, and you can replay the video or have the record read back to you if you wish. I enjoyed sex and my wife did not. At least not with me very often. I enjoyed her company and did not most other people. I have made quite an effort to form as few relationships as possible, then and now."

"That doesn't really answer the question does it?"

"If that is the case then you are absolutely as dense as I imagine."

"Why admit to it?"

"I've sworn to tell the truth."

"Yet you haven't."

"So you say. If I've been lying, you'll have the opportunity to reveal that at trial. If it comes to it."

"Did you have other affairs?"

"I tend to avoid commingling with the bridge and tunnel crowd."

"And again that doesn't answer the question. You like sex and your wife didn't give you any. Instead, she gave it up to other men. So naturally you looked elsewhere. You supposedly had an open arrangement, so why not?"

"There is a fidelity clause in our prenuptial agreement."

Roya looked confused again. She was about to ask another question but Linus preempted her.

"The arrangement was ours, not the Hunt's. Her father insisted on a prenup and further insisted that the fidelity clause be added. Clearly he didn't know his daughter very well. I was careful to ensure that my .... dalliances .... coincided with hers. We were free to see other people as long as precautions were taken, which they always were. So you see, if I wanted to leave my wife in a divorce, I would have been within my rights to do so."

"How do you know that precautions were taken? There was DNA from semen found in your bed. Doug Hart's semen."

"If it was in the bed, it wasn't inside my wife, was it?"

"You can't be serious."

"No?"

"I'm afraid I don't understand your position," Roya said.

"Ellen wasn't using birth control. Neither of us wanted children. Had she not used precautions, she ran the risk of pregnancy. We both used precautions."

"And in the event that you did leave her, how much money would you have been awarded?"

"Approximately twenty-million."

"A far cry from the entirety of the estate."

"A tenth. Are you terrible at maths as well?"

"Twenty isn't two hundred."

"You're like a puppy. I have to show you the stick before I throw it. Unless we dispense of this ridiculous charade, I'll get nothing. So why kill her? Twenty-million is better than nothing and going to prison."

"You didn't go to prison."

"But I wouldn't know that before I committed murder, would I? Honestly, watching your mind work is excruciating."

Roya looked at her partner who was less adept at a poker face than she. They were now on their heals, a one-eighty from where they were after the break just an hour ago. They needed to regroup. The look on Kettering's face made it plain not only to her but to the room.

"Now would be a good time to break for lunch. One hour?"

"We just had a break, didn't we?" Hampton asked.

"And yet now is a good stopping point," Roya replied.

"So you can lick your wounds?"

She gave him an exacerbated look. "So we can eat."

"You don't look to do that often, Miss Dressner. Far be it from me to interfere with nourishing your all-too frail body."

Roya shook her head. "We are off the record and will reconvene in one hour."

Chapter 15

July 4, 2013

9:00 PM

Sovereignty

THE HAMPTON-HUNT PARTIES WERE
always lavish affairs.   A who's-who of New York elites
inevitably in attendance. Linus and Ellen's penthouse held
Broadway celebrities, runway models, Wall Street moguls,
movie actors and directors, celebrity chefs, trending night
club owners, fashion designers, and sometimes a
Kardashian or two. A-listers only, or the people who could
buy and sell them. Friends of Ellen Hunt all.

Linus Hampton had no friends outside of Ellen's. He
spent a great deal of time and energy not to form
relationships outside those cultivated through his wife.
Another facet of his personal ethos. Friendly yet guarded,
he reluctantly worked the crowd of sophisticates gathered
in the spacious penthouse apartment.   He received
handshakes and kisses on the cheek from people he could
hardly say he knew, yet inexplicably called him friend.

It was the Fourth of July. Independence Day. The holiday shared Ellen and Linus's ten-year anniversary. The annual celebration was invitation only, and anybody who was anybody in Manhattan wanted to make the list. The events were Ellen's idea of how to spend their anniversary, certainly not his. Dozens of people loitering about his home was not his idea of fun. More like his idea of hell. One year Linus proffered the idea of spending their anniversary on their small estate on the island of Tortola. It had not gone over. His wife wanted an event where New York elites could come to her turf and be seen. How July Four was different from every other weekend was a topic best not brought up. His wife was always the socialite, always someplace where paparazzi eagerly captured the moment.

This year, like every year, fireworks could be seen from either their wraparound balcony or the private rooftop deck. Below their penthouse, millions of tourists gathered in Central Park or along the East River to watch the controlled explosions light up the sky.

While the ants below fought for a space to look toward the stars, NYK, a trending New York DJ, was spinning music to stars of a different sort. The noise was unintelligible to Linus and he wondered how anyone could enjoy it. Another of their DJ guests, TIESTO, was pressured by the dozens in attendance to step in for a set. Linus didn't find the sounds he made with the equipment he stood behind to be any better. Hampton's idea of music was *cello suite no. 1 in g major* with Erling Blöndal Bengtsson on cello, written by Johann Sebastian Bach in the 1700s. How techno or EDM/Pop or House or

139

whatever the mob was calling it had devolved from the genius of Bach was beyond him. These two knobs didn't even play instruments, they made obnoxious sounds with recordings from people who did. This was talent?

Some of the guests hung around the bar where his wife had a bartending staff making free drinks. Others were on the balcony. Still others mingled on the roof deck smoking marijuana, congratulating each other on achieving a station in life affording the ability to score the best weed in Manhattan. Once high, they would join others that were waiting for passed food to circle back on a tray by a catering service. The models taking small nibbles to be social only to then expel the food into one of their toilets, he reckoned. Small talk about what Linus felt was nonsense in virtually every circle. He had utter distain for all of it.

"As usual you seem in unalloyed pain."

Linus turned to the British voice. Brenna Lythe. A longtime friend and schoolmate of Ellen's. A former London model and failed actress. Linus wondered on the occasions in which he saw her if she'd changed her name to Lythe, or if her Cadogan parents had made sure to give her a different yet graceful name that would decrease her claim to old family money. Brenna was, after all, the product of a hushed extramarital affair.

Brenna wore a flattering yet revealing dress, undoubtedly by an elite designer. The small straps held the thin fabric which lightly draped over her non-existent curves. Brenna's moisturized, porcelain skin exposed no flaw or wrinkle.

"I loathe these gatherings in ways that even I cannot articulate," Linus replied.

"You could make it less obvious."

Her English accent was elegant, one of many traits he enjoyed about her. High praise from a man that found very few enjoyable traits in even fewer remotely tolerable people.

"I will have to work more diligently on my ability to posture."

"You can hide your true feelings from almost anybody. Almost. But not me."

"You forget, I've known you for quite a long time, Brenna."

"Poor Linus. So easily inconvenienced."

"When was the last time you had fifty-odd people in your home?"

"I think there is more like seventy here."

"My point."

"How is it that the two of you have been married for ten years and are about ten light years apart?"

"Opposites attract I suppose."

"That old cliché."

"There is something to be said for stability."

"What you call stability others call boring."

"Always a pleasure to speak with you, Brenna. Don't you have someone wealthy to rub up against?"

"Lighten up, Linus. I'm just having a bit of banter with you. No need for a fuss up," she said with a wry smile.

Ellen approached with a glass of Bollinger Les Vieilles Vignes Francaises for Brenna and a Stella Artois for Linus. "Finally someone to take Linus out of his misery." After handing Brenna the glass of bubbly they kissed cheeks.

"I don't think anyone can take him out of his misery," Brenna offered. "Fortunately I think we are the only two who know it."

"I don't need another beer," Linus said as his wife handed him the freshly opened green bottle.

"Of course you do. You look pathetic. And sober."

"I'm always sober, love. You know that."

"Yes, yes, can't lose control. I know all about it. Bren .... Save him."

"One more won't send you into a downward dervish, Linus," Brenna added in support.

"I ask you every year to invite some of your friends from the university, darling. I pains me to see you so unhappy. Have another beer. Unwind a little. Mingle."

Linus gave a fake smile. "I've already mingled. My presence is known."

"Strike up a conversation, don't just say hello in passing. You could make an effort. These are your friends."

"These people purport to be *YOUR* friends."

"And yours."

"I don't have friends. I have colleagues. These gatherings are my acquiescence to you, love. I know how important they are to you."

"This year particularly," Ellen said steering toward her friend.

"Ten years," Brenna raised her glass. "Cheers." After a small sip of her champagne, she added, "As always a lovely party in your lovely home."

"A last hurrah, if you will. This is all going to be completely redesigned," she said with a wave of her arm.

"After this, we demolish this space and make it livable again. This soirée is a final homage. Out with the old and in with the new."

"Quite the undertaking," Brenna said before taking another sip of her champagne.

"You have no idea. I've gone through design after design to come up with the final plan. Speaking of which, I need to find a contractor up to the task. I just can't settle on the right one."

"I do. I know just the one. And so do you," Brenna grinned.

"Really? Do tell."

"I'll text you a phone number. Blast from the past. Do give him a call. He'll sort you out."

"Bren, you are a godsend. Will you excuse me? I need to go see someone." Ellen stopped after moving two short steps and added as an afterthought, "And Bren? Please take care of him." She gave her husband a peck on the cheek.

"Will do."

"We just went through this three or four years ago," Linus offered as he watched his wife leave to recommence her circulation.

"I don't see anything wrong with it the way it is. Quite lovely actually. Lots of light. Open space. High ceiling. Balcony. Roof deck. What are you changing?"

"*SHE* is changing. Everything." He took a sip of his Stella. "I get to keep the bar, my study, and the tele room to watch my beloved Manchester United. The rest is gutted."

"Poor thing. What shall we do with you?"

143

"Beg Pardon?"

"Ellen said to take care of you."

"Yes, well, I believe what she was referring to and what you seem to be implying are two markedly different things."

"I'm not so sure. She tells me the two of you have .... An arrangement."

"After one too many martinis I'm sure."

"We are best friends. We share everything."

"Ah."

"Being around all of those young women about campus, surely you've wandered into other pools."

"Are you mad?"

"I'm practical, Linus. You are devilishly good-looking. A bit reserved, it's true, but I wonder if we made you improper what you might accomplish under the sheets?"

"A question that must go unanswered, I'm afraid."

"Oh come now. Those doe-eyed women with tight asses and firm tits in your classes must linger on your every word. Don't tell me you haven't taken advantage."

"That would be a rather stupid and reckless thing to do, wouldn't it Brenna?"

"It might be the thing to loosen you up a bit."

"It would be the thing that ruins me."

"Not if you had a pass. Hold on a tick. Do you like boys?"

"Are you listening to yourself?"

"There's nothing wrong with taking in a firm man now and again. God knows I enjoy it. Nobody would judge you."

"We all know you enjoy the time on your back, Bren. Always on the lookout for the next conquest, hey?"

"I just haven't found the right one yet. You could change me for the better. I'm not twenty but look at me. I am fit."

Linus revisited the tiny designer dress which left little to the imagination. Her ensemble was unencumbered by undergarments, else they'd be visible. The woman was every bit of what she claimed. At thirty-nine, she could pass for one of Hampton's students. Brenna Lythe could easily still be a model, if she had the yen for it.

"You're quite lovely, Bren, and I'm quite married," he said after looking her over without making it seem so. As he took another sip of his beer, he tapped his wedding band on the green glass bottle to audibly reinforce his point.

"Quite married with carte blanche to do as you wish. I know you've done it before. Ellen has told me all about them."

"The two of you carry on like school girls."

"We *WERE* schoolmates and we share everything. Save for you thus far."

"Yes, well …. I'm not a play-thing, am I?"

"You could be," she said cheekily.

"Are you quite finished?"

"Am I embarrassing you, Linus?"

"Don't be daft."

"How many have there been?"

"A bit indelicate, isn't it?"

"Since being married. In the last ten years. How many?"

"Always good to speak with you, Bren. Best I do as my wife asked," he said as he made to leave the area to circulate his own apartment.

"Don't leave," she placed her free hand on his arm. "This is getting interesting."

"For you. Do unhand me."

Brenna moved her hand up to his bicep and lightly rubbed. "I know she doesn't give you much affection, who can blame you for plunging into foreign waters?"

Linus appeared to be at a rare loss for words. Brenna leaned in and whispered, "I'm completely settled on being the kept woman, by the by."

Outside, the fireworks began to pop and twinkle in the sky.

Chapter 16
February 8, 2016
1:45 PM
Repose

A BLOCK DOWN FIFTH AND A RIGHT ONTO WEST
Fifty-sixth, Joe's Shanghai provided a relatively quiet place for Miranda Wood and her client Linus Hampton to eat dumplings, discuss the deposition thus far, and where things were likely to go when they returned. Dumplings were Miranda's comfort food of choice. When she'd had a rough day at the office, in court, or when her ex-husband decided to be an asshole about custody arrangements as leverage over the amount of his child support, she found some measure of solace in pork dumplings. The current situation had not yet risen to the level of utter despair, but it was on the horizon. She could feel it in her bones.

This particular Joe's Shanghai wasn't a regular haunt for her. Miranda preferred the one on Pell in the East Village which was very close to where she lived. As she and her client entered the restaurant, she gave the server a hundred dollars and name-dropped her friendly relationship with Joe Si, the owner, in order to secure the server's agreement to refrain from seating the booths on either side of them until it was absolutely necessary. The server took the money and bowed saying, "rú nǐ suǒ shuō."

Joe's is by no means five-star. The appointments are workaday. The dumpling shop is accessible to all and busy because the food and service are excellent as well as affordable by Manhattan standards. Patrons are made to feel that they are getting more than what they pay for. An enviable business model to be sure, which is why the small multi-location company is so successful.

It was nearing two o'clock in the afternoon, the main lunch rush was over, yet the restaurant was at nearly seventy-five percent capacity.

Miranda hoped that the money she'd given the server would provide the privacy she needed with her client, that the booths near them would remain unused for the duration of their lunch-meeting.

Once Miranda had ordered for the both of them—which seemed to irritate Linus as ever-so-slightly indicated by the curling of his upper lip—she got down to business. Two orders of pork dumplings and two green teas would refocus them for the conclusion of the depo. At least that was her hope.

"So let me ask, how do *you* think this is going so far?" she asked after giving the server their food order. "Because I have to level with you, Linus, it looks like you're trying to bareknuckle box with your face and hope it's hurting his hands."

"How vivid."

"I'm trying to illustrate a point."

"Well made."

"Was it? Because as usual I find it nearly impossible tell what you're thinking. I need to know that you realize what is happening, and that it's being recorded on paper and on film for them to dissect you in court."

"They don't use film anymore. It's not on film."

Miranda closed her eyes and exhaled in lieu of screaming at the top of her lungs and strangling the life out of the man sitting opposite her with her bare hands. "Are you taking this seriously?"

"Of course I'm taking this seriously. Do I seem the type to live the life of whimsy? I calculate which tie to where with my suit every day, let alone leave a bloody fortune—*MY BLOODY FORTUNE*—to chance."

"Well, you seem pretty fucking reckless to me."

"Aren't we feeling bold?"

"I'm simply trying to make my position plain."

"I believe you have."

"And you don't agree?"

"I do not."

"Then what am I missing, Linus?"

"Quite a lot, obviously."

"This is the rubicon. The point of no return."

"I know what a rubicon is. This is not it."

"You can't blow the depo."

"This is but a salvo. I have no intention of 'blowing' the depo, as you say."

"Then tell me what you're seeing that I'm not. Specifically."

"Those Capstone flunkies are trying to muddy the waters in the hope that we will take some sort of deal.

149

Throw excrement at me so I'll ponder the notion of taking a settlement for less money in forbearance of another exhausting trial."

"They haven't thrown a number out."

"They will."

"And what number would you entertain? Half? A hundred million, give or take?"

"Not on your life."

"Then what is the number?"

"All of it. Every bleeding penny."

"That's not very realistic."

"It's my money."

"And how much of it are you going to lose at the expense of a trial? My fees alone are—"

"—Are not the point. What can you buy with two hundred million that you cannot with one hundred? It's the point of the matter."

"You're willing to risk the entirety of the estate .... The money, the properties .... Every asset .... All of it .... To make a point?" Miranda shook her head in disbelieve. "I apologize, Linus, you're right. You're not reckless. You're *INSANE*."

"I'm innocent of the canard that has seemed to take root in even you. Why admit or settle when I've done nothing wrong."

"You were found to be innocent at trial. Criminal court. This is different."

"How so?"

"Really? You don't know? You've been on the television. Newspapers. Magazines. Social media has had a field day with you. You'd have to get a trial in civil term in another country to have jurors who haven't already passed judgement. You're the guy who killed his wife for a fortune. The guy who got away with it."

"It seems the rumor has become fact."

Miranda shook her head. "Perception. Perception is reality in civil term. And as far as I can tell, the two lawyers in that conference room are at the advantage. You *MIGHT* have rattled them for a moment, but they won't make the same mistakes in court. They will go over the transcript, they'll watch the video, and avoid the pitfalls they fell into today. That's why they invented depositions. I say settle. If they throw a reasonable number out there, my advice is to take it."

"If I settle, I will be stripped of reputation. Déclassé."

"You've already been stripped of your social status. Have you read your own press?"

"There was a gag order."

"A lot of good it did. Have you read it? You got away with murder and are now seeking the plunder. You can't go back to teaching. You're persona non grata at Columbia and in polite Manhattan society. The Hunt's have made you their family cause."

"I foment a coterie, don't I? Nothing brings a family together like an imaginary villain."

"Exactly.   In a time when nobody agrees on anything, you've broken through as the one person everybody can hate. Congratulations. That's quite a feat."

"Very well, Miranda. Let's do as you suggest. Let's throw in the bloody towel then. While we're at it, why not join a twelve-step program for underachievers? We can bravely run and hide from every prickly thing and call it day, shall we?"

"This is an enormous risk to take. Period. And why? To stick it to Capstone? If you lose—and in my opinion, that's where this is headed—that's that. You break it, you bought it, was ever thus. An appeal is not—"

"—I know a little something about the law."

"You're a legal scholar, not a litigator. And a trial is not your friend. You are not a likable guy, Linus. I don't know how to say it another way, or how many times I have to repeat the same thing."

"This is not going to trial. How many times must I repeat myself?" He removed his glasses to clean them.

"One more, I guess. Your position makes no sense."

"It will. Watch and learn."

The server arrived with their dumplings and tea. The Asian woman said nothing after placing the items in front of them, retreating to her other duties.

Miranda took a moment to compose herself.

After taking a sip of the hot tea, Hampton slid the chopsticks out of the wrapper, broke them apart and rolled them together in his hands as if trying make a fire.

Miranda shoved a dumpling into her mouth, very clearly enjoying the familiar flavor, savoring the bite. The food seemed to calm her. When the bite was fully consumed, she broke the silence.

"Do you have something up your sleeve?"

"Always."

"Care to share it with .... I don't know .... You're fucking lawyer?"

"You mightn't approve."

"It's not like you're leaving me much choice. I'm in the dark. Whatever you have planned is going to happen either way, approval be damned. So let me in on it. Tell me that there is a method to this madness before I have a heart attack. I don't think they have enough dumplings in this restaurant to calm me down if we blow this trial."

"Yes, yes. Your fees are what? Six million? More? Quite a lot of dumplings, isn't it?"

"It's not about the money."

"It's always about the money, Miranda."

"I'm your lawyer and I might just be able to help if you'll let me."

"You are—by being in the dark. Take comfort in knowing that I could not pull this off without you, Miranda. I promise, when this is all over, I will show you just how much with more than your astronomical fees."

"That's supposed to be comforting?"

"It's supposed to repose any distress you're feeling and let you know that you are off the hook. I have control of the situation. As I've said .... Watch and learn."

Before shoving another dumpling in her mouth she said, "Maybe I should get a pamphlet for that twelve-step program."

Chapter 17
February 8, 2016
2:30 PM
Alibi

THE DEPOSITION RECONVENED PRECISELY
on time, everyone back in their places exactly one hour
after the lunch break was called. Before going back on the
record, and while waiting for Dom the videographer to use
the restroom, Roya and Miranda were discussing what
each had eaten for lunch. Roya was fond of Joe's Shanghai
as well, she'd said, but had taken the seven-minute ride on
the E line to Shake Shack with Kettering because that is
where he wanted to go.

Kettering ignored the conversation happening in
front of him. If he cared to explain why he'd insisted on
Shake Shack and not acquiesce to wherever Roya wanted
to eat, he didn't show it. Instead, he buried his nose in a
file. He appeared to be preparing for the next segment of
the deposition.

Once Dominic was behind the camera at the exact
stroke of the sixtieth minute, Kettering announced that

they were back on the record, but acquiesced to Roya who recommenced the questioning.

"Let's see .... Where were we? Oh yes, you're claiming that you and your late wife had an open marriage."

Linus said nothing.

"Correct?" Roya added.

"Yes."

"You didn't mention this to the police. Why?"

"It was none of their concern. I believe I have answered that question."

"Your wife was murdered. You were accused of murdering her. Why not tell them everything and let *THEM* figure out what was and was not their concern? Because you had something to hide?"

"Proctor and Gamble—"

"—Brock and Gamble—"

"—Weren't interested in anything other than me."

"Did you know that at the time?"

"It was quite obvious," Hampton said. "While I was initially being questioned in my suite at the Mandarin, they reiterated how often murdered women were the victims of their husbands or boyfriends."

"Why didn't you point them in the direction of the boyfriend? Hart. If you're so sure he did it, why not tell the police?"

"By the time I was sure, I'd already been arraigned and placed on house arrest. I felt it best to sever communication with the police and focus on my own defense. They'd been less than honest with me, hadn't they? A Grand Jury was convened while I was sitting with the detectives in the precinct. If the police had conducted an actual investigation, I would have been more than happy to help. They didn't. So I communicated what I needed to through my legal team."

"Especially since you were having an affair of your own," Roya added.

"Yes."

"Make her ask a question, Linus," Miranda said.

Hampton put his left hand on his attorney's right forearm and continued. "Why muddy already soiled waters? They weren't interested in the truth."

"You hadn't given them the entire truth, how could you make that assertion?"

"I was arrested before my wife's body was even released from the medical examiner. Ellen was quite high-profile and an arrest had to be made. If they were interested in the truth, they would have conducted a proper investigation."

"Meaning questioned the woman you were having an affair with?"

"Brenna Lythe. Yes."

"Because you thought that it would make you look more guilty?"

"If one didn't want to know the truth, yes. My relationship with Brenna would have made me appear more .... Dodgy."

"Well, that's why we're here. To get to the truth," Roya said.

Hampton looked at Kettering. "Of course it is."

"Let's say for the sake of argument that we believe you. You were wrongfully accused and the system worked. A jury acquitted you because the facts didn't prove what

156

the prosecution was alleging. How can you fault the police or the District Attorney's Office for coming to the wrong conclusion when you hadn't given them all of the facts?"

"As I've said, they weren't interested in facts. Just as you aren't. You've been hired by Capstone to find a way to withhold my estate. My money. The fortune that I'm entitled to by law. To drag me through court to re-litigate this nightmare all over again."

"Do you think that if ADAs Hardison and Kemp had uncovered your affair that you would have been found guilty?"

"No."

"Really? Seems realistic to think that you wanted a new life but to keep the same lifestyle, don't you think? A jury would have questioned that."

"If Hardison had discovered it and subpoenaed Brenna, my lawyer would have cross-examined her and revealed that there is no way that I could have murdered my wife. The laws of physics preclude one from being in two places at one time."

Dressner and Kettering looked at one another suddenly and simultaneously. Both seemed shocked with the news. Had they been in the field of view of the camera, their consternation would have been captured for posterity. Had Miranda Wood been sitting slightly to her right, her amazement would have been recorded as well. Yet only Hampton's mug was in view. Only his rare smile, his first real sign of any emotion during the entirety of the proceeding thus far was visually recorded. The grin looked genuine.

"Uh .... Wait. I'm confused," Dressner said as she shuffled through files and paperwork. After nearly a minute, which seemed an eternity, Roya found the documents she was looking for and set them in front of her. "According to the police report, you claimed to have been held up at the university and walked home. That was your alibi, or lack thereof. You repeated it to ADA Kemp in the presence of your attorney when you were questioned at the police station. Are you now saying that those statements aren't true?"

"Yes."

"With such a weak if not non-existent alibi, why wouldn't you tell them where you actually were, if you did actually have an alibi?"

"For the—

"—Before you respond, I would like to remind you that you told us the same thing in this very room under oath."

Hampton's smile remained. "I did no such thing. Have the stenographer read it back to you if it will refresh your memory. For the record, I was not under oath when I was questioned by the police or the Assistant District Attorney. I didn't take the stand at my criminal trial, fortunately, so I didn't have to withhold where I was at the time of my wife's murder, nor did I perjure myself. Had Brenna been called to testify, she would have told the jury what I am now telling you. As I've said, the police never conducted an investigation, so Brenna was a non-issue. Fortunately the ADA's office is inept and didn't call her, so I didn't have to involve her in this muck and mire. I testified here, under oath, as to what *I TOLD THE POLICE*. I told the police that I walked home."

"Exactly. Which you're now telling us was a lie. Under oath."

"No. I told you, under oath, my lie to the police. I never said that I walked home from campus, not here. I'm telling you now under oath that I didn't. I said in my earlier testimony here today that, '*I told the police* I walked home from campus.' Which I did and was a true statement. Watch the video. Reread the transcript."

Roya shook her head. "You're walking a fine line here, Mister Hampton."

"Doctor Hampton."

"Whatever. You lied to the police, which is a felony. Or you're lying now. Also a felony. How can anything you say be believed at this point?"

"The former is hindering prosecution. MY prosecution. An 'E' felony at best. I'd like to see anyone make that stick, and in the remotest of possibilities that someone did? .... I'd be sentenced to probation at best. With what I've gone through? Time served. The latter is much more serious, yes. However, my testimony here today is not perjurious. Depose Brenna Lythe if you want to prolong this ridiculous exercise."

"You know we're going to go over the deposition transcript."

"I encourage you to."

"And we now have to depose Brenna Lythe."

"As I said, if you must. Threaten her all you like, she will corroborate my testimony here today."

"What were you doing with Miss Lythe on the night of your wife's murder, and why wait until now to tell us?"

"You can probably surmise what I was doing. I also wanted to show her my divorce papers."

Another stunned silence. Roya shuffled some papers and files before continuing. "I don't have any record of you filing for a divorce."

"I hadn't yet filed it. I drafted it that very day."

"Your lawyer had the obligation to disclose—"

"—*I* drafted it that very day."

Kettering interjected. "What? On a cocktail napkin?"

"You were leaving your wife for Brenna Lythe?" Roya asked incredulously. "Is that what you are testifying to? The very day that your wife was murdered, you're now saying that you were planning on serving her with divorce papers?"

"Yes."

Kettering was incensed. "Is this a joke? How do you expect us to believe this? There was no filing, no mention of it before now ...." He shook his head and looked at the ceiling in the room as if their was some answer above him.

"I very much wanted to keep Brenna out of the spotlight. Since Ellen was murdered, the divorce was moot."

"She's a supermodel. I would think she would be used to the spotlight," Dressner said in a tone but with less volume than her colleague.

"Not with respect to a murder."

"If you had an open relationship, why wait to come forward with your alibi? If you were going to file for divorce, why not disclose those documents? You were on trial for your life. Unless this entire story is a lie?"

160

"I'm sure there are witnesses that saw us going into her building. Or me leaving. There are security cameras in her building. I was in no danger of being convicted. Had I been, she would have come forward of her own volition. She's been in favor stepping into the light since I was arrested. I did the honorable thing by protecting her virtue."

"How chivalrous of you."

"As for the divorce, as I said, it was moot."

Kettering leaned in toward the center of the conference table. "That's some coincidence. 'Your Honor I was going to divorce my wife and leave with only the shirt on my back, but somebody killed her before I did it so it's all-good.' You would have been laughed out of the *FUCKING* courtroom. In handcuffs."

"MIKE," Roya nodded toward the camera. Kettering didn't seem to care.

"So you do understand why I didn't come forward with this information earlier," Hampton said without delay.

Roya shook her head at her co-counsel and then looked Hampton in the eye. "This is absolutely ridiculous. Is that your statement? Do you want to amend what you've just said on the record? Because you can clarify, or just say you were joking. You can go on record as saying you were just joking and that what you just stated did not actually take place. I'm not your lawyer, but I would recommend that you do that."

"Objection," his actual lawyer said.

"Brenna and Ellen were best of friends. People might get the wrong idea."

"You *ARE* joking. People already had the wrong idea, according to you. You were branded a murderer."

"A murderer who was unhappy in his marriage, if I had shared all. I am innocent. Nobody would have believed me."

"Nobody believed you anyway. Nobody believes you right now."

"Because of the Hunts. It seems the gag order was a mere suggestion. They couldn't help themselves."

"I don't have anything to do with the Hunts and I don't believe you," Dressner said.

Linus ever-so-slightly leaned toward Roya Dressner. "You work for them and don't even know it. The Hunts own a portion of Capstone. You work for Capstone."

"Be that as it may—"

"—You can believe me or not. What I've just testified to is the truth and can be corroborated. Do you think I would tell you such a wild tale if I couldn't prove it?"

"For two hundred million dollars?"

"Which I won't get one cent of if you can find one shred of evidence to the contrary of what I've said here today."

"Fine. For grins, let's say I believe you. You could have taken the Hunts to court for violating the gag order. You could have told the truth about Ellen and about Brenna, if it was in fact the truth. You could have ignored the order and gone public. You had remedies."

"I'm quite good at many things. Undoing what has been done so publicly is not one of them."

"I've had enough of this," Kettering blurted. "All of this is self-serving crap!"

162

"Mike," Roya said. Her eyes and head rolled toward the camera just behind them again. It was still recording. Kettering took a deep breath, as did Dressner.

"Your dog is biting off his leash," Hampton said. "I can produce divorce papers. They are now and have been safely stored in a safety deposit box. Notarized and time-stamped. I wouldn't have left with merely the shirt on my back as Mister Kettering here has suggested. Brenna Lythe is a former runway supermodel, not exactly poor. She will testify where I was at the time of my late wife's murder, and *HER* testimony can be corroborated by building security and a sworn statement from one of the tenants in her building if it comes to it. Everything I've testified to, under oath here today, is absolutely true and can be proved. I should think that will put an end to Capstone's position on this matter."

Dressner pretended to go through files and paperwork while her mind raced. It was obvious to everyone in the room. After a short time, her shoulders sunk. "I'd like to take a minute with my co-counsel. Fifteen minutes sound good?"

"I'm fine to continue," Hampton said. "We just had lunch."

Kettering stood and leaned in. "It's our deposition and we're taking fifteen minutes."

Linus was back to smiling. "Take your time."

Chapter 18

October 27, 2013

8:30 PM

Until It's Over

BRENNA RESTED HER HEAD ON THE SOFT spot between Linus's left breast and shoulder. They each looked at the faux plaster and moulding design of the ceiling in Brenna's flat as they lie naked in bed, enjoying the euphoria that post-sex provided.

"Penny for your thoughts," she said in a hush tone.

"I'm thinking about our earlier discussion."

"Really? I thought you'd be thinking of all those lewd things I've just done to you. On a bloody Sunday, of all days." She slid her hand down under the silk sheet and took hold of him. "And what I'd like to do again."

"There will be time for all of that," he said. "Were you serious? Before?"

She picked her head up of his shoulder and looked him in the eye, releasing his semi-erection from her hand. The sheet fell, exposing her small, firm breasts. The outline of her petite ribcage could be seen under skin that rivaled the silk sheets. "Of course I was."

"Because it will take some doing."

"It will take losing my best friend on earth. My closest friend since we were schoolmates. She'd fly anywhere on the planet to see me through. Runway or way station. If ever I needed to talk .... "

"I know, love. It's why I'm asking. We must be sure," Hampton said.

"I've never been so sure of anything in my life. I am willing to ruin a friendship for you."

He sat up, laying his back against the tufted headboard of Brenna's bed before taking a sip of Perrier from the glass on the nightstand. "How dedicated to this endeavor are you?"

"Are you questioning that I won't do what needs be done? I think I've shown you that I'm willing to let you put that thing wherever you like to make you happy."

"This is quite different, Bren."

"I'm not stupid."

"Nor am I suggesting that you are. But if we are to do this, we have to make a plan. A long yet intricate plan in which we cannot deviate. Meticulousness is essential. No matter how difficult or sideways things get, we stick to the plan. She is a Hunt, lest we forget."

"She's never let me forget it. I love her despite the fact that she's never let me forget it."

"I don't hate her," Linus said.

"Nor do I. I love her. I just love you more."

"I couldn't have said it better myself. Which is why after tonight, we cannot see each other again. Until it's over."

165

"It's a bit strong, that, isn't it?"

"Appearances, love. What will it look like?"

Brenna rolled and sat on his lap, facing him. "I couldn't give less of a shit what it looks like."

"Do you want to build a life together or not?"

"Of course I do."

"Do you want to scrape by or live the life that we deserve? Love is one thing. Threadbare is another."

"I've been modeling around the world for Guess, Vicki's, Vogue .... You name it .... For years. I have money. So do you."

"Forgive me but you didn't make Gisele money and you're not in as high demand as you once were."

"Fuck you," she said and slapped his pectoral area. "I haven't been out of it that long. I gave acting a go and it didn't take. But I could go back if I cared to. I still have calls to go back on the runway."

"Of course you could. By why when it's completely unnecessary?"

She hit him again but not hard enough to hurt.

"Please don't make my point for me. You can't get madcap if we're to do this. I'm simply trying to say that at your age, supermodel money will only last so long."

"I don't need as much as you do, clearly," she said.

"Nobody needs it. But why not have it if you can?"

"You're very wealthy."

"Ellen is very wealthy. She could burn my money and not feel a thing."

"And mine, but it's still quite a lot of money. You and I wouldn't have her kind of money, but we'd be quite wealthy."

"Not as wealthy as we could be, Bren. With a little bother, we can be."

"You're a lawyer. A highly respected professor at a prestigious university. To hear you tell it, you get a great many calls for your legal opinion."

"Academia, even Columbia, pays less than what I'm worth. As does the Defense League. Ellen spends more than my two hundred thousand dollar annual salary on yoga pants. I'm not talking about a quarter million, Bren. I'm talking about a quarter *BILLION*."

"She's not been faithful, Linus."

He kissed her on the mouth. "Nor have I and you've missed the point."

"You did it for love."

"I did it for the same reason she did."

"How much would you get in a divorce if she was proven to be unfaithful?"

"Proved. Twenty-million."

"That's a lot of money."

"Ellen's worth considerably more. We've both been unfaithful, so I would have a legal fight to get the twenty-million in all likelihood."

"Assuming she knows about us, yes?" Brenna asked, looking him in the eye.

"She does, doesn't she?"

"I would think so, yes. After the party .... Your tenth anniversary ...."

"I've come in and out of this building how many times, Bren? She could prove it without much of a bother."

"As you said, she did it first. What would anyone expect? She fucked her way across Manhattan and left my poor Linus home in the dark with his dogs. You were bound to wander."

"Yes, we both wandered. She has the money. And the prenup."

"What are you saying?"

"I'm saying we were both unfaithful and for the same reasons. For me, love came after. Legally, a divorce would render me all-but destitute."

Brenna smiled and kissed him on the mouth. "So you do love me?"

"That's what you've focused on? In all of what I just said, that is what you've fixated on?"

"I've never heard you say it before," she said with a wider smile.

"What are we talking about? Why would I risk—"

"—So you don't want to see me. After tonight. That's what you've come up with, is it? Just like that. Should I move back to London?"

"No. Don't be dim. We can see each other socially. Socially - not like this. Not in a way that can lead people to think. We all know how much people hate to do that. Anyway, as it happens you'll be needed here in New York."

"Then what? We just play like nothing happened? I see you from time to time and prattle on about the bloody weather?"

"Until it's over."

"When will that be?"

"Give it time. I have to craft a plan. *WE* have to craft a plan."

"It's only divorce, Linus. It happens every day."

"It's not just divorce, and it's the difference between nothing and hundreds of millions of dollars."

"We don't need her money. I have money."

"We've been through that. It's not nearly enough. The Hunt's will make sure I never work again. We'd be pariahs. For me that means far less than it does for you, but you get my meaning, don't you? We need to be certain that we never want for anything after this is all said and done."

"You're not going to leave her penniless, are you? She deserves better than nothing. She's treated you badly, but I don't think she'd survive being destitute. I don't wish that upon her, she's still my friend."

"A Hunt? Penniless? I rather think not."

"You know what I mean."

"I married her, Bren. Trust me. She'll get what she deserves."

Brenna shifted herself, grabbing ahold of the man she sat upon. As she stroked him, feeling him get hard in her hand. She leaned in and whispered into his ear, "Give me what I deserve."

Chapter 19

February 8, 2016

3:00 PM

The Petulant Child

KETTERING AND DRESSNER WALKED INTO the ad hoc conference room thirteen minutes after calling for the fifteen-minute break. The look of defeat ever-present in their expressions and body language, though each carried it differently. Roya's frustration manifested itself in fatigue. She looked tired. The tiny, frail woman had aged six months in the last six hours, making her appear to be weaker than ever in Hampton's view. Michael Kettering's expression was of anger. As he walked into the conference room, Kettering stared Hampton down. His eyes blazed into Hampton's as he walked around the table to find his seat. The muscles in his jaw pulsed. Nostrils flared.

Neither Miranda nor Linus had left the room for refreshment or a toilet, both sat in their seats waiting for the deposition to resume.

"When were you going to share all of this with me? I'm your lawyer for Christ's sake," Miranda whispered when they'd been left alone at the start of the break.

"I wanted it to be a surprise."

"And unnecessary. We could have avoided the deposition entirely. Maybe even your criminal trial."

"I doubt that. And your firm was well-paid, so I shouldn't think you'd complain."

"You can support all of this with actual evidence, correct? Please tell me you weren't bluffing."

"I wasn't bluffing."

"Where are these divorce papers?"

"In a safety deposit box, as I said. I had them notarized and date stamped. A copy of the CCTV footage at Brenna Lythe's apartment building was saved and deposited as well."

"Which bank? Specifically."

"Does it matter? The proof exists. Isn't that enough?"

She sat for a moment in silence before saying, "You know what this means?"

"I've always known."

Wood then went to her already opened laptop to send off an email while Hampton sat starched and expressionless save for the occasional hint of a smile. A corner of his mouth twitched upward now and again, then back to the default position as if Linus had caught himself exuding the rare emotion.

The attorney and her client remained silent and in their own small and separate worlds when the Capstone attorneys returned.

"Thank you for indulging us in a break," Roya said with obvious counterfeit sentiment as the two attorneys walked back into the conference room. "We needed to make some calls."

"Indeed," Hampton said.

"We are back on the record," she said to the two people recording the meeting, both of whom had also just returned to the room. "Before we broke you testified that you are now able to produce an alibi witness, a Brenna Lythe. A witness that you hadn't produced during your discussions with the police, nor during your criminal trial, but are conveniently sharing with us now. Is that still your statement or would you like to amend your earlier testimony?"

"As I mentioned in my earlier statement, I'd tried to avoid her involvement in this foolishness as best I could. Since it is now unavoidable, I am testifying, under oath, that I was with her on the night of my wife's murder and that I possess dated and notarized divorce documents, which I can produce in a civil trial if need be. I was going to serve my late wife with the papers the very night of her death."

"You realize that we are going to have to look into this. We are going to have to verify all of your new claims."

"I have been patient with you, counselor. I have been patient with Capstone. I have been patient with the police, the DA's office .... On and on. The legal system is slow and cumbersome and messy but it does work eventually. It is beyond time for justice to prevail and my patience has worn thin. I was acquitted of the ridiculous charge of murder, lest we forget."

"Your wife *WAS* murdered," Kettering interjected.

"Not by me. Twelve jurors saw through the subterfuge. I am innocent. Capstone has been the petulant child for quite long enough and it is past time to put an end to this tantrum."

"As you said, it's all part of our great legal system. It is my job to make sure that you don't get a single dime of your late wife's estate. We can tie this up in probate for another decade if we need to," Kettering said.

"Mike." Roya put her right hand on Kettering's left forearm.

Hampton filled the pause. "Taking the canon of 'zealously representing your client' to new heights, hey? Don't you get paid either way? Billable hours and all that?"

"You've made it personal."

"Mister Kettering, it is *YOU* who have made this personal. If you continue to—"

"—We have to investigate your new claim. This alibi witness," Kettering continued, "she is going to have to take the stand in open court. Are you sure she's gonna hold up?"

"As I was saying, if you continue to stall the money that is owed to me by taking this to civil term, I will take additional legal remedies of my own. I was acquitted. I have told you that I can provide additional proof beyond the reasonable doubt threshold of *CRIMINAL* law, much less *CIVIL*. Additionally, you've have just said—on the record—that you are making my situation your personal cause, Mister Kettering. Conclude your investigation all you like, I can produce my alibi witness and supporting evidence *TODAY* if need be. If you continue to prolong this charade, you will have left me no choice but to sue you for additional interest to the money you are holding in escrow for Capstone, as well as my attorney's considerable fees. Do you know what the interest on two hundred million comes to? Even at half of one percent? Beyond Capstone, I will then sue the both of you individually for liable in a defamation suit, as well as Abuse of Process."

"We are just doing our jobs," Roya said.

"Mister Kettering has said on the record that you are well beyond 'just doing your jobs'."

"Threatening us isn't the best way to get what you want, Doctor Hampton."

"I'm not making threats. I'm am divulging to you my next legal steps. You look tired, Miss Dressner. I assure you that I am just as tired of all of this nonsense. My patience has worn thin, and I'm quite finished with pleasantries."

"Ha." Kettering shook his head. "This is you being pleasant? That's rich."

"Mike," Roya said to her colleague before turning back to the respondent. "Doctor Hampton. We've been in contact with Capstone. During the break. Which is why I asked you again for the record if you would like to clarify your testimony when we returned. We will need a sworn statement from Brenna Lythe, along with any supporting documentation from the building CCTV or doorman or security. We will also need the notarized divorce papers you testified about from this alleged safety deposit box. If we receive those documents and if your witness is willing to state for the record that you were with her and nowhere near your apartment the night of your wife's murder, Capstone will forgo a trial and pay you the full sum of Ellen Hunt's estate."

"What choice do they have?"

Roya ignored his question. "We would insist upon having all of the mentioned documents before releasing the monies," she said instead.

Hampton looked at his watch. "I can call Brenna now. She's undoubtedly no more than an hour away. She could be here straight-away."

"That won't be—"

"—The banks close in less than two hours today. The documents can be couriered to your office by seven at the latest, I should think. I could meet you at the bank if that would help."

Kettering sat back in his seat, slumped with arms folded. "It's all about the money," he said under his breath but loud enough to be caught both digitally and by the stenographer.

"It's been two years. I've waited long enough, don't you think?"

Kettering leaned back forward to say something, then thought the better of it.

Roya offered, "Tomorrow morning would work best for us. We have some papers that need to be drafted."

"Very well. Tomorrow morning then. I'll call Brenna when we finish up here."

"Assuming we have everything tomorrow morning, we can either cut a check or wire the money into any account of your choosing by the end of business tomorrow."

"It's his girlfriend," Kettering said obviously unable to hold his tongue any longer. "They're in this together. Don't you see that? The contractor is a patsy, that's why the police didn't arrest him."

"Mike. This isn't helping." Roya turned to Dom and Nicole. "We're off the record." She then leaned toward Kettering and whispered to him, but both Hampton and Wood could hear her. "We talked about this outside. He was acquitted. If his girlfriend or co-conspirator or whatever you want to call her gets up on the stand at a trial, we have no shot at winning. Hampton will eat us alive and you just heard him say that he'll then go after us personally."

"Idle threat," Kettering said, not whispering.

"He'd be within his rights, and he'd probably win that litigation as well. Get it together Mike. You can't take this so personally. It's over."

Kettering shook his head but said nothing.

"We're back on the record."

"Did you get your dog back under control?" Hampton asked. "He's likely to get bit if he keeps on." Linus looked to his counsel who sat in silence. The look on her face was unreadable. He turned back to Roya Dressner. As he stood up, buttoning the top button of his suit jacket and pressing the non-wrinkles out with his hand, he said, "Tomorrow morning then. I'll be sure to get you my bank account information."

"We're not quite finished here, Hampton," Kettering said.

Hampton moved toward the conference room door and said, "Yes we are."

Chapter 20
April 14, 2016
6:15 PM
The Fix

THE CRYSTAL CLEAR WATER OF LOWER
Belmont Bay washed up in waves onto the white, powder-
soft sand of Smuggler's cove.   Though one of the two
largest beaches on the British Virgin Island of Tortola,
Smuggler's Cove was vacant on the North end. The North
end of the beach never has cruise-liners or couples on
holiday, because the northern end of the beach is not open
to the public.   The private beach is a half-mile of nearly
untouched oceanfront in front of a villa the size of small
hotel. Those driving past the gated driveway on Route 1
on the way to Gun Point or the yacht club know that
someone rich and glamorous stays beyond the gate and
behind the trees, but who was often unknown.

　　　　The tops of Linus Hampton's tanned bare feet were
covered in soft sand as he stared across the bay toward
Jost Van Dyke, a small island less than ten nautical miles
to the west. The sun would soon set behind the hills of Jost

Van Dyke, the warm colors in the cloudless sky beginning to radiate. His tanned skin matched the light brown checks on his Burberry swim trunks. The pure white fabric beneath glowed in comparison while the red checks would soon match the twilight sky.

Brenna sat on an outdoor chaise chair under a palm tree a few yards behind him, inland. Her Chanel sunglasses resting on her head, her eyes slowly moved back and forth as she read Rupi Kaur's digital version of *Milk and Honey* on her tablet. Brenna's skin was substantially lighter than Linus's as she took to the shade and religiously applied ultra-high SPF sunscreen. For her efforts, her light skin was as taut as her muscle tone. The Bermuda Double String bikini by Heidi Klein she was wearing did little to hide the bits that made her feminine.

As she finished a chapter, Brenna glanced at her left hand which now had a six carat cushion cut engagement ring with a platinum setting and matching wedding band on the ring finger. She hadn't become used to either ring yet, as the impromptu and low-key ceremony took place not quite a week ago. There had been no engagement, the two rings were purchased and put onto Brenna Lythe's finger on virtually the same day. The giant and accompanying diamonds reflected light in the setting sun. She then looked toward the water and took in the silhouette of Linus's lean back as he looked out across the bay. "Are you all right, Darling?" she called to him above the sound of softly crashing waves.

Hampton didn't move.

Brenna set her tablet down on the small table beside her chair and approached her new husband. When she came up behind him, she put her porcelain arms around his tanned, flat stomach. "What's wrong, darling?"

"Nothing. Just thinking."

"About what?"

"Doug Hart."

She pulled away and came round to face him. "Look at me. I'm half naked on our own beach in the middle of the Caribbean and you're thinking about Douglas fucking Hart? Take a sip of your beer and forget him."

He looked in his right hand at the bottle of Stella Artois then back to her. He'd forgotten it was in his hand. The sun had warmed it to the point where it was now undrinkable.

She moved closer to him and slid her hand inside his swim trunks. "Better yet, get inside me and put him out of your mind."

"It's the anniversary, Bren. She was murdered two years ago today."

Brenna withdrew her hand from his shorts. "Yes I know. Is that what has you melancholy? You're not second-guessing our elopement are you?"

"I'm neither melancholy nor second-guessing. I'm just thinking. What do you think he's doing right now?"

"I hadn't given it much thought. But now that you mention, maybe he's spending the money you sent him."

"Where?"

"Who knows? If he's smart, not in New York. Forget about him."

Linus lifted his Maui Jim's onto the top of his head and pinched the bridge of his nose. "Doug Hart is many things, but smart is not one of them."

"I never understood why you gave him so much money to begin with."

"He did us a rather large favor by killing Ellen, wouldn't you agree?"

"I suppose. But if anyone was tracking the money—"

"—Our money is in the Caymans. Untraceable and just a few islands away."

"What about his accounts?"

"What about them?"

"If the DA's office were to look into his accounts, they would see a rather large payment. From you."

"For services rendered on the apartment, love. He was renovating it, wasn't he?"

"I've put him out of my mind. I didn't think much of him when we were schoolmates, I certainly don't think much of him now. We don't have anything to worry about do we?"

"No. Of course not."

"Then why let him ruin the day? This is our home now or until we tire of it anyway. We can go anywhere we like, do anything we like. If they catch him, what can he say? That you put him up to it?"

"But I didn't, Bren. I certainly benefitted from it—WE certainly benefitted from it—but I didn't hire him to kill Ellen."

"Bollocks that." She tilted her long neck and looked at Linus in disbelief. "Come now. Don't be coy. You can tell me the truth."

"I am telling you the truth."

"Then why pay him? Why torture yourself about where he is and what he's up to?"

"I paid him to finish the bloody apartment so I can sell it. He finished it inside of a month. Can you believe it? If he'd spent more time working and less time inside Ellen, it would have been finished a long time ago."

"Has it sold?"

"The asking price is nineteen-point-five million. It'll take some time. A murder having taken place there doesn't help matters."

"So you're trying to make me believe that all that money you gave him was for the renovations? A bit cheeky, even for you."

"With a handsome tip, I'll admit. He did put quite a lot of additional money into my pocket without the headache of having to divorce Ellen. Whatever you may think of me, I did love her once."

"I know you did. But you didn't shed a tear when she was murdered."

"I'm not a sympathetic man, you know that. I'd fallen out of love with her and she was worth more dead than alive. But I didn't want her dead. Not really."

"Of course you did, darling. That was your plan all along."

"Don't be daft. My plan was to divorce her and evoke the fidelity clause, which I couldn't do if we were seen together. I needed to expose her as the wanderer. I needed to be innocent. Ever the devoted and doting husband. Her death was a coincidence."

"Mm-hm. A happy one." Brenna turned around to watch the sun set, entwining her arm with his.

"Ellen was your best friend."

181

"Ellen's best friend was Ellen, you know that." She rested her head on his arm for a bit before adding, "So why are you thinking about him?"

"He's a loose end. I don't like loose ends."

"Oh yes, of course. Everything has to have a proper place, yes? Not to worry. He can't hurt us. Not anymore."

"Everything does have a proper place, Bren. An order to it. I'm thinking about calling Manny."

"Who?"

"Manny Alvarez. The investigator. I want to hire him. I need to know what Doug is up to. I need finality."

"Let it go. Stop thinking about it and be happy."

"I'll never be completely happy until I know. You must know that about me. I'm incapable of not knowing."

"Oh darling .... Have it your way then. But there's no need to hire anybody. In fact, it's best you don't. Doug Hart is quite final."

Linus pulled away from Brenna and looked into her eyes. She was grinning. "I don't follow," he said.

"Douglas Hart is dead and gone. Once he was finished with that gaudy apartment, he'd outlived his usefulness."

"How?"

"A rather unfortunate accident on the Hudson River," she said sheepishly. "I'm not entirely sure if it was on the New York or the New Jersey side. I suppose we'll only know if he's ever found."

"What did you do?"

"You're always on about how clever you are. Sort it out. I'm quite surprised you haven't already."

He continued to look into her eyes to find the answer. The sound of the waves and the faint sound of the

182

dogs barking up in the villa were all that could be heard while he worked through the problem. He cleaned his sunglasses and pinched the bridge of his nose before replacing them on top of his head.

"You killed him. He killed Ellen and then you killed him. It was all you. You cornered me at the anniversary party. You set them up, Doug and Ellen. You knew them from school. You knew they were together back in school and it would be easy to reconnect them. The renovations were just a means to get him in the door. You made me think of leaving. This was just the latest in a list of her dalliances, but you knew this one would eat at me. That Ellen revisiting an old love would secretly gnaw at me and so you swooped in, didn't you? You set this entire plan in motion. This was your doing all along."

"And now we're married," she said wiggling her fingers showing him her engagement and wedding rings.

"Which means you are now entitled to half of everything." The shock of the news visible on his usually stoic face.

"Plus or minus a hundred million."

"You played me. I see the game and eschew the pitfalls. But not you. I didn't ...."

"I gave you a nudge. You did the rest. You are nothing if not predictable, darling. A hint here. A naive question there. You thought you had the entire thing sorted. Getting Doug to do his part was a bit more challenging."

"You had to get him to kill her."

"I had to make it *HIS* idea."

"How?"

"Men and their egos," she said shaking her head. "He always felt inferior, even in school. He still held her ridiculous Statutory Rape claim against him to heart."

"—And you stoked the fire."

"Doug Hart was as dense between the ears as the hammer he used to kill Ellen. While I crushed the man's ego, I also filled Ellen's head when we would go out to dinner or a club. At first it was 'Aren't you do for a renovation?' I knew it was about time. Then I pushed her to hire Doug. 'You owe him something for trumping up that rape charge,' I said. Then it became 'What do you see in that neanderthal? I never understood your attraction to Doug-*FUCKING*-Hart even when we were kids.' And 'He's so beneath you.' I'd fill her head with things like that. I'd tell her over and over and over again knowing she'd eventually say them to him. Once she realized the only use she had for Doug was the meat between his legs, and that she could get that anywhere, she grew tired of him. Nature took its course."

"And he bashed her head in with the hammer," Linus said. "When she decided to leave him, she repeated all of the things you filled her head with and he beat her to death. I knew it was him."

"You just didn't know why. Not exactly.

"Nobody believed me."

"I believed you."

"Of course you did. It was all you."

"He did what he was programmed to do. Naturally he called me directly after."

His eyes widened in immediate understanding. All pretense at hiding his emotions lost. "The phone call on

184

your cell. That night. I brought the divorce documents over to your flat. After we made love to celebrate. That's why you sent me home that night, after the call. He'd murdered her, so you sent me home."

"Very good, my darling. You had to find your wife."

"I underestimated you."

"Most men do."

"I'm not most men," Linus said.

"I would normally agree. Though it seems you do have an equal. And now you've married her. I don't have to remind you that this conversation is protected, do I?"

"I'm a legal scholar. Of course you don't have to remind me that spousal communications are privileged. That's why the rush to get married. You wanted to make sure we eloped before I put it all together."

"You're very clever. You would have sorted it out on your own at some point. I worried that you would sort it before we were wed."

The sun was now extinguished. The timer turned on the lights, illuminating the path up to the now fully lit villa. The beach was as quiet as it was dark. His dogs were now quiet, one of the staff was probably feeding them their dinner.

After a long bit of silence she took his hand in hers and moved toward the villa. "Now let's end this silliness. Take me to bed."

"I don't know that I'm in the mood just now."

"Oh darling. I'll fix that too."

AUTHOR'S NOTES AND ACKNOWLEDGEMENTS

The previous work is one of fiction, any resemblance to specific and true incidents is purely coincidental. The names of real places, people, music, et cetera are either coincidental or simply to give the story an authentic feel. None of the events that took place in this novel are real to my knowledge.

New York is a massive city. I return often, usually for business, though I will often try to mix in some pleasure. With each visit I try to explore a bit more of the Big Apple. I could easily spend a decade tasting my way around the menus of the restaurants of every possible culinary genre and not have begun to touch the surface. The restaurants I used in this novel are real and just a few of my many favorites. The Mandarin Oriental is by far my favorite hotel in New York and several other cities.

Because of New York's enormity, many of the communities therein stick to their neighborhoods. For one, there is little reason to venture more than ten blocks in any direction as everything one would need is—in all probability—just around the corner. Manhattanites stick to Manhattan just as most of Brooklyn remain there. The line I used about the 'bridge and tunnel crowd' was not meant to demean any borough, it was to highlight the very real sense of territorial segregation that exists in my view. And not just in New York. Many of us live in our own bubbles, never venturing out of our comfort zones.

For those readers who have read other novels or scripts I've written, I delve into the legal system quite often. None more so than this novel. This novel was an undertaking because I had to research both criminal and civil law. It is amazing to me how different the two really are—and how little one faction relates to the other. I went through a vast number of public documents researching civil case after case and have come to conclusion that anybody can sue anyone for just about anything, whether a criminal law has been broken or not. Tort reform is not only necessary, it is imperative.

As always, thank you for your time and I sincerely hope that you enjoyed the story. I hope to share another one with you soon.

-sw-

ABOUT THE AUTHOR

Scott Wellinger is a well-traveled writer and novelist. He has written many novels, articles, scripts, musical lyrics, and essays under pseudo-names. His more popular novels feature, among others, the fictitious private investigations of Warren Dennihan. A native of New England, he was born in Vermont and was educated in Boston, Massachusetts. He holds a Master's Degree in Applied Economics and when he is not traveling, writing, playing music, cooking or painting, he is on a golf course.

For more author information: www.scottwellinger.com

Also by scott wellinger:

Use It Up (2015)

The Season for Moths (2016)

Novels in the Warren Dennihan crime-fiction series:

CRASH

A Warren Dennihan Novel (first of series)

Venom

A Warren Dennihan Novel (book 2)

Sinn

A Warren Dennihan Prequel (book 3)

Ebb

A Warren Dennihan Novel (book 4)

Juror

A Warren Dennihan Novel (book 5)

Flight

A Warren Dennihan Novel (book 6)

These novels can be purchased in Ebook and print wherever books are sold.

Thank You for Reading!

If you enjoyed reading this novel, please help others appreciate it as well.

Recommend it. Please help other readers find it by recommending it to friends, reader groups, discussion boards, or wherever you purchased the book.

Review it. You can add your thoughts to Amazon, GooglePlay, iBooks, kobo, Barnes & Noble, at the publisher website for me at www.scottwellinger.com, reader clubs like goodreads or LibraryThing, Shelfari, etc., etc. If you do write a review, please share it with me through my publisher at www.scottwellinger.com, or to me directly through social media.

Follow me on twitter, Instagram, and SnapChat for updates and special offers. @wellinger_scott , @SCOTT_WELLINGER , and @scott_wellinger respectively.

Best Wishes,

~SW~

The following is an unedited sample of CRASH, book one in the Warren Dennihan series. The novel is available in ebook and print wherever books are sold.

Scott Wellinger

CRASH

a Warren Dennihan novel

PROLOGUE

THE NIGHT HAD DRAWN DOWN LIKE A THICK BLANKET over the small New England town, tucked in the mountains of southern New Hampshire. A cloudless, late summer sky made the bright stars the only form of illumination, which were little more than pinholes of light off in a distant universe. The pine forest which shot up from the fertile ground gave off a rich perfume reminiscent of Christmas, which was less than half a year to come. Above the tree-line, the natural rock formation known as *The Old Man on the Mountain* was a slight, silhouetted backdrop bidding the tourists a final goodnight whilst he slept. The narrow, windy roads meandering through the hills below that watchful cliff north of Boston, Massachusetts, were fortified with guardrails and graveled pulloffs to accommodate the looky-loo tourist vehicles. The fall foliage leaf-peepers were still a month or so away, but the hiking and camping season was still in full swing. The heavy traffic from the visitors trying to get a last trip in before the arrival of colder nights, was nonexistent in the hours after dusk. The hikers, campers, and naturalists had long since ventured home for the night or abandoned their parked vehicles on one of the pulloffs on the side of the road, as they made camp somewhere in the darkened forest.

The *Old Man* was the sentry for several communities below his perch on the White Mountains; the county and township of Wayland, New Hampshire was by far the most affluent. The old and new money was drawn from the financial hub of Boston in the form of large salaries. The town flourished as the commuters preferred to spend their ample earnings in the sanctity and "tax-free" state of New Hampshire over the Metropolis of Boston which fed them to the South. Another form of income for Wayland is the tourism, though the affluent of the community continue to be torn in that while the outsiders boosted the economy, they trampled over their turf. The visitors should be felt yet not seen. The people of money from Wayland did appreciate the financial relief from the tourism, which was their dilemma in refraining from ousting their numerous intruders. While there is no sales tax on goods in New Hampshire, there is a nine percent tax on the prepared food served. Tourists eat out, contributing to the town's revenue. Restaurants are aplenty in Wayland, filled with a wait by those who don't live in the area permanently.

The winters were the most difficult for the citizens of Wayland in avoiding the onslaught of outsiders. The skiers would come from the flatlands by the SUV load and deface their great State. No matter the season, invaders inevitably made way toward the Old Man and the natural wonders he stood sentry over. The affluent of the community spent their time and income away from the flatlanders at the Wayland Country Club. Golf was just one activity taken in there, and in truth many claimed to play more often than they had a tee-time for. The sanctuary was more for camaraderie and companionship than the activities the club promoted. A place for the wealthy to rub elbows with others of their kind in the same area.

This particular night, those with money were keen to show off just how much they had and were willing to part with. The Gala and Charity event that was taking place in the pavilion was under way, all of the who's-who in place and opening wallets for the silent auction, though whom or what charity would be receiving these sums was anybody's guess. While the sprinklers were misting water over the lush back-nine of the manicured golf course, which could be seen out of the large windows, elegant gowns and tuxedos flattered the bodies of the occupants in the club. Live, light jazz music and the mumbled conversations of the local power couples mingling under the giant chandelier could be heard faintly in the distance, while the rest of the community went about their Saturday night. The well-to-do's had the evening festivities, freeing their assistants and staffers to have theirs.

Arelia Diaz had made her plans weeks prior, when she learned that she would have a rare night off. She was a live-in maid for one of the rich and beautiful, though she called herself a caretaker, and was looking forward to blowing off some built-up steam with a night of dancing with her girlfriends. The initial response from her friends at her invitation for a night out on the town was a jealous decline, until they too were informed that they would have the night off. Her friends in the area were also in the employ of other event attendees and would also have the night free from; babysitting, nannying, serving, cleaning, maintaining, cooking, or the myriad other tasks their employers were too important to perform. A night of dinner; gossiping over the comings and goings of their respective power families, and certainly dancing would be just the cure for the tedium that ailed them. Only one friend, Marina could not make it. She was told that she would have to take care of a child, though her employer didn't have any children.

Arelia Diaz, a mid-thirties Brazilian woman, left her own family back in Recife to make a better life for herself and said family. A large portion of her income was sent back to Brazil to lift the station of her once poor family in Recife, keeping just what she needed to live on for herself. Other than her gaggle of female friends, she was alone in the United States. She had no spouse or children, which was the mainspring for many nights of tear-soaked cheeks and a saturated pillow. The oldest of four daughters, she saw limited opportunities in her native village and networked into an immigrant sub-community tucked into the American northeast almost ten years prior. Alone but not alone, she was content in managing a dream household, though it was not her own.

Miss Diaz did not consider herself to be what the Americans called a *cougar*, she was too young to be considered for the part, though she was going to be on the prowl this night. All women had needs, this was a rare opportunity, and she was going to make the most of it. She painted on a pair of the most expensive jeans she could afford, her ample bosom bursted out of the front of her new, sparkling, black-yet-shear blouse, exposing her black push-up bra, and donned a pair of high heels which lifted her four inches higher than her usual five-foot-three inch frame. With her raven hair done (in what was coincidentally called a Brazilian Blowout), and her makeup applied to accentuate her big, beautiful brown eyes, she would be turning some heads. She still had what it took to bag any man she wanted, despite her lack of practice.

She would not be bringing anyone back to her suite at her employer's palatial home, this was not allowed, nor did she have any intention of staying with an interested gentleman. Her duties would resume bright and early in the morning. Her employers would likely be as moody as usual, as demanding as usual. Maybe they would even be a little hungover, though they would never in a million years admit that to the help. The agenda for the night would be dinner, *Forró* dancing, and a copious amount of flirting. Unfortunately the line would have to be drawn at flirting.

She was given an older, red, Honda *Civic* to use for her daily errands, which she was using while on her way downtown to meet her girlfriends. It was a small yet able car, in spite of the age, much like Arelia believed herself to be. She had plenty of life left, this was just a means to an end. A way to go back to Brazil with enough money saved to provide for a family back home and the new one she would make, and for their families after she was gone.

Diaz was used to the car and all of the idiosyncrasies that came along with it. She loved the limited freedom that the car provided her, but she loved the stereo system the most. In the ten years of being the caretaker, she was never allowed to listen to her music loud enough to be heard by anyone in any part of the house. Nor was she allowed to use headphones as she was always on call. Always. Failure to hear, much less respond to a call from the main house would mean an immediate end to the life she had built here and the inability to send money back to Brazil. Relegated to vehicular sonic therapy, she would blast her beats as loud as the car stereo and tiny speakers could muster.

She had the windows down, feeling the night air through her already blown raven locks of hair. The outside sounds were competing between the crickets, the sounds of the Country Club in the distance, and Arelia belting out the Portuguese lyrics over the loud music of her favorite band *Falamansa,* at the top of her lungs.

"Se um dia alguém mandou
Ser o que sou e o que gostar
Não sei quem sou e vou mudar
Pra ser aquilo que eu sempre quis
E se acaso você diz
Que sonha um dia em ser feliz
Vê se fala sério"

She was blissfully unaware that this would be her final concert.

As she rounded a sweeping blind turn on Wayland Country Club Road, the singing and car-dancing was immediately interrupted by the harsh LED, high-beam headlamps glaring into her eyes from seemingly nowhere, yet everywhere. She knew nothing of candlepower light measurements, but the retina-burning headlamps blinding her surely could have illuminated Fenway Park. Diaz could not see anything, much less navigate the rolling left turn. She could not see the lever protruding off of the steering column to flash her own high-beams at the offensive driver coming towards her. Nor could she get her bearings on the road. Arelia was desperate to see a yellow line. A white line. Anything to pinpoint if she was in a lane. There were no vibrations from the warning grating on the side of the road, because there wasn't any grating on the side of the road. No reflectors, not that she would have been able to see anything being reflected in the already blinding light. She would have welcomed the grazing of a guardrail, just so she could sort out where she was in both time and space. Everything was happening so fast. Brakes were unused. The stereo remained at full, deafening decibels. There was no time to turn it down. No time to think. No time to sweat. Was there somewhere she could pull off? But that question did not register in the time it took her to sail off the road.

The little-Civic-that-could missed the end of a guardrail, grabbed the bit of gravel just off of the pavement, bulleted her through the small graveled pulloff area. The car continued, severing a maple tree that was contemplating the changing leaf colors, continuing on to impact the base of a large rock formation. The car came to an immediate halt from the forty-plus miles per hour it was traveling just seconds prior. The rear of the

197

car was the last to learn of the immediate stop being insisted upon by the fixed and rooted boulder. The rear-end of the Honda had no choice but to follow the rest of the cars' lead after jetting into the air, the rear tire spinning as it tried to continue beyond the mess. It failed.

The sound of the dance music halted, replaced by the sound of the mangling of metal and the pulverizing of bone. The jagged metal sliced through flesh which added to the cacophony of horrific sounds. The macabre series of sounds lasted but a beat, but the devastation would be permanent.

Nothing would be continuing beyond the crash. Not the maple tree, not poor Arelia Diaz formerly of Recife, Brazil and more recently of Wayland, New Hampshire. Where her body existed in the cab, where she was car-dancing to her favorite band, singing as loud as her beautiful lungs could project, was a sick sculpture of metal, plastic, glass, rubber and human organs. The front of the car no longer existed. It was impossible to discern car from body, where the red paint from the Honda started, through all the blood, and the end of the former occupant. Her lifeless face rested, burning on the steaming engine that now occupied space in the back seat; searing what was left of her beautiful features, her head and neck was being pressed toward the truck of the Civic.

The offending headlights stared onto the wreckage for a time, determining what was already known. The lights crept slowly toward the destruction, attached to the black vehicle that was camouflaged by the dark of night. They would abandon the devastation they had caused. The upbeat, accordion-based dance music and singing, followed by the horrifying reverberations of the crash were no more. The sounds were replaced by the ticking of the cooling and destroyed engine; the sizzling of flesh against it; the acceleration of the fleeing murderous vehicle; and crickets.

1

UGLY. THE IMAGE APPEARING BACK AT HIM IN THE makeshift mirror was ugly. No other word could summarize the reflection and the atmosphere surrounding it; his every thought and emotion. The stainless steel metal above the all-in-one, Willoughby sink-toilet reflected pure ugliness. The image itself superimposed upon the backdrop of the institutional beige walls, the florescent lighting, the grey concrete floor.

Jacob Grantes had never been considered a hunk, nor an Adonis by any account. He was not a physical specimen for which to lust. He had never been compared to the likes of George Clooney but he had been somewhat attractive, smart, confident. His six foot one inch frame, his square jaw, his sea-green eyes were some of the features that admirers had named when defending him as 'a catch'. The image that had once stared back at him, however, had disappeared, morphing into the figure that was reflected back at him in the polished steel. He splashed water on his face, one push button on the faucet at a time, yet no matter how much water he applied, how much he washed, and how much he scrubbed his face, he could not cleanse the ugliness inside or out.

Grantes, inmate #437261, had been a guest at the Wayland County House of Corrections for the past six months, having been denied bail. He had not been in trouble with the law prior to the events leading him to this very moment, which made the denial pending trial quite unusual. Jacob was accustomed to living in a large home with his family and the picket fence, which made the current accommodations all the more intolerable. His cell was an eight by twelve foot concrete room with a double bunk, a small desk and a sink-toilet which he had to share with his celly. The space was tight and the nerves were stretched even tighter. Twenty hours per day were spent in this tiny space. Best friends could be put together in such a way and it would not take long to become mortal enemies. To make matters worse, the door to the cells lacked bars; a solid door, which allowed little air flow, with a narrow, horizontal slot at waist-high for food trays to be passed through, or to be handcuffed prior to exiting. The small, vertical window was convenient only for the Correctional Officers who had to execute head counts. This solid metal door was manufactured to make the most loud, god-awful clanks and noises when opened and closed. Studies had been done on this; millions spent, to craft an audible assault on inmates in an effort to make them uncomfortable, on edge, and contemplating the actions that had led them to their current place of residence.

The CO had awoken Grantes with a loud, mechanical unlatching, the grinding of metal as his cell door was sliding open at 5:30 AM.

"Grantes. You got 15 minutes to shit, shower 'n shave. Court. You'll get chow on the ride over."

"Yeah," he said between splashes of water on his face.

His grumbled reply indicated his malcontent, as this was to be a real shit day. It was to be a different kind of shit day, but a shit day all the same. All other days had the exact same schedule; filled with misery, meetings with so-called counselors, and a myriad of conversations with fellow inmates all of whom proclaim to be innocent or screwed by their lawyer. This day would be a shit day of a different color but a shade he knew quite well. Jacob Grantes had previously spent most of his adult life immersed in the muck and mire of the legal system, only on the other side of it. As a defense attorney, he knew exactly what this day would entail. The splashing of water on his face would make none of it go away.

"Jesus Christ, can you shut the fuck up? What time is it, bro?"

The shout came from a lump in the sheets, covering the body laying on the top bunk in his cell. Grantes' celly had a very low tolerance for anything beyond sleeping away his bid. This is known in prison as a bed-bid, and he is not the only one trying desperately to dream away the time.

"It's early. Sorry. I have court today. But it looks like you'll have the cell to yourself for the day," Jacob said to his cellmate in an effort spin a positive light on the early morning disruption to his much-needed beauty sleep.

"Goody." He said this without removing the covers which made him appear as though he was levitating five feet above a filthy concrete floor.

"You'll be able to shit in peace at least. I wish you'd spent a little time out of the cell so I could crap without an audience."

"You really gonna shower?"

"Yeah, I'm getting my shower bag ready now." Each inmate fashioned together a bag of toiletries to cart to the open shower area. Everything in the area was wet, as were the products after using them, requiring the cosmetics to be taken out of the bag to dry and then refilled before each visit to the showers.

"That means that the door is gonna open and close a couple more times. Why you gonna shower anyways? Gonna be front and center with a jumpsuit and shackles anyway, clean ain't gonna matter."

"They'll let me change into a suit."

"Ha - you're funny. You're an idiot, but you're funny. Where are you gonna get a suit asshole?"

"I came here in a suit. My lawyer will have another one if they won't let me have that one out of property."

"You're gonna be in a holding tank, good luck getting one of the courthouse COs to let you change. Lazy assholes might have to do extra work," he said. "Whats today anyway?"

"February fif—"

"— the case moron. What part of the case is it?"

"Oh. Discovery and motions. It's when — "

" — I know what it is. Fifteen minutes tops bro. They're not lettin' you change into a fuckin' suit. Two bus rides and a day in the tank for fifteen minutes. Have fun."

"Shithouse lawyers," Grantes mumbled aloud. It amazed him how much legal knowledge inmates had. Especially those with high recidivism. Grantes's cellmate had a very vast and intimate knowledge of the law from a certain prospective. He was, therefore, known throughout the prison as a good shithouse lawyer. During the short rec-times, inmates would leave there cells and seek out the shithouse lawyer for legal advise about their specific case. His services were never free yet many would line up to pay for his legal knowledge.

His celly was of course aware that Jacob was a real lawyer, which only caused that many more passionate discussions. One incident a few weeks prior, Grantes was accused of stealing his business because an inmate on the first tier chose to seek his actual legal expertise rather than his cellmate's. Jacob was no fighter and gave him the ramen he was paid for his legal services in order to keep the peace.

Jacob was determined to be in a suit for his appearance in court today. He was forced to wear a jumpsuit every day, all day, and he was tired of it. The entire ugly situation. As he left to go to the showers, he tried to convince not only his celly that he would be afforded the change of clothes, but also himself.

"We'll see."

2

JACOB GRANTES AND HIS BEST FRIEND RYAN WELLS
had started a law practice together fifteen years prior. They had,
over time, cornered the bustling criminal and legal market of
nowheresville. The small southern New Hampshire town of
Barstone, in Wayland County, was considered to be the other
side of the tracks by the more affluent locals. Those elevated
locals being the residents of the affluent town of Wayland, which
was literally just across the train tracks of the commuter rail
which took commuters into Boston, Massachusetts. The clichéd
delineation was real. The constituents of Wayland Township
made it quite clear to all of the inhabitants of Barstone, and really
anywhere else for that matter but less vocally, that they were not
welcome. The elected Sheriff of Wayland County, his office
located in the town of Wayland by design, was well aware of
what would happen if the petty crimes and riffraff of Barstone
were to bleed into the backyards of the wealthy community only
a nine-iron away. And so the two towns within the same county
coexisted; the town with the same name of the county reaped all
the rewards, while the slums went about being the outcasts.

The law office of Grantes, Wells & Associates was
strategically located in Barstone, on the border of the two towns.
They needed the criminal element to pay their salaries, and
therefore the business from the Barstonians, and the partners
wanted the much more civilized legal filings of Wayland. The

two townships utilized the same courthouse as they were in the same county. Life was never boring for the two attorneys. Defending the proprietors of a Meth Lab in Barstone one day; defending a restraining order filed by scorned trophy-wife against an unfaithful husband in a messy fourth divorce on the next.

The *Associates* in the name of the firm was a mistruth. An embellishment to look bigger and more established. JG, as he was called, and Ryan were the only partners, the only lawyers, and there were no others seeking partnership. None would be sought out either as they were not seeking any new blood for such an arrangement. The associates consisted of their part-time private investigator, Warren Dennihan; and their full-time secretary in Ryan's wife, Angie. Warren had his own thriving business in Boston, with his own partner, and was subcontracted by the New Hampshire law firm whenever an investigator was needed. He was rarely, if ever, in the Barstone office. Angie was in the office every business day, much to Ryan's chagrin, and she had almost no legal knowledge. What she lacked in legal prowess, she made up for in organization and efficiency. She was invaluable and JG had said in the past, in plain language to Ryan, that whatever problem he had with the arrangement, to get over it.

The arrangement had been Ryan's doing in the first place. He had hired Angie Grummond, as was her name at the time, without consulting JG on the spot at the first interview. Rather than ask the prospective employee out on a date upon their first meeting, which was ultimately what Ryan wanted to do, he decided to hire her instead. The would-be sexual harassment suit in waiting didn't last long, as they were officially an item by the time she was finished her training. JG didn't mind as much as he had initially let on, not even annoyed if truth be told. The headache of starting a firm was a larger migraine than that of an office romance. Besides, Ryan had been JG's best friend since law school, almost for as long as he could remember, and he had never seen his friend so happy.

The startup capital for the small firm came from the money bestowed to Jacob via his surrogate family. His in-laws had been more than good to him, they had filled a hole left in him by the passing of his natural parents. His wife, Anna, had come from money and while she had married for love, her parents could think of no reason for them to struggle financially. Anna's parents had made the idle threats to rescind the money once they learned that Ryan was to be made full partner from the outset, but all concerned knew the threats were empty. Their apprehension came from genuine concern as they saw their son-in-law, Jacob, as the much more talented of the two-lawyer partnership. With Jacob viewed as having a much higher potential than his friend, especially since he had no money invested in the venture, they felt Ryan was there for the ride instead of the build.

Ryan was not a bad lawyer. He was no Alan Dershowitz either. He was talented but he was also a free-spirit. Wells would get caught up in the spirit of the law rather than the black letter. He took flyers. Rather than take on more legitimate claims, he often went to the hoop with little on evidence and heavy on the liberal sentiment. He would often take on the lost cause that was rejected by JG; acknowledging that he might win some, but he would lose more. Ryan was an idealist. His interest and passion for the law was in the good it could do. He actually thought the lady with the scales was indeed blind. He still does to this day.

JG had depended on Ryan to bring in fees not necessarily wins. Billable hours were billable hours, each generating income. Winning of course would draw the big cases, but with a location in Barstone, New Hampshire, who was he kidding? The business would come from the petty drug cases, larcenies, B&Es, DUIs, assaults, and the ilk from people who couldn't afford to be choosy when it came to a criminal defense. They knew they were going to prison with a public defender, at least with the hippie they had a chance.

JG had the wins, Ryan had the passion. But that was all in the past. What JG needed from his friend and partner now was a win. A big win. Ryan was going to defend him when and if this case went to the hoop. Today was discovery motions. The *I'll show you mine and you show me yours* part of the case. Today they would see what the State of New Hampshire had, and if this case was going to trial. If so, Grantes needed Ryan to win the case of his life. For Jacob's life.

3

"All RISE. PLEASE COME TO ORDER, COURT IS NOW IN session. The honorable Judge McCaglia presiding." The bailiff shouted with much too much in the way of volume. There were few people in the fourth session of the Wayland County Superior courtroom. It was entirely unnecessary to shout at that level, but Grantes decided that the loud volume coordinated nicely with the loud color of the neon, hazard-orange prison jumpsuit he was wearing.

He had asked the Correctional Officer, politely mind you, if he could change into a suit that his lawyer had brought for him to wear to court. The CO guarding the prison property room hadn't even entertained the idea of fetching inmate #437261's suit from the cage. "No fuckin' way," were his exact thoughts on the subject. Jacob had reckoned that this would be a possibility when he called his attorney from prison, which is why he'd asked Ryan to pick one out and bring an extra one he had on the rack in his office at the firm. If truth be told, he preferred the one from the office, the suit he'd been hauled off to prison in was probably quite wrinkly at this point. Now in the tank below the courthouse, he repeatedly asked the jailhouse CO about seeing his lawyer and changing into a suit. He even bargained to leave on the shackles, but the request didn't warrant any response. He repeated the question in case the officer didn't hear him. The CO had heard the request because he gave the sternest of looks upon hearing it a second, third, fourth, and fifth time. In each instance the guard gave no response. Ryan then got involved but the plea to the Deputy Sheriff was in vain. The officer said he didn't like the hippie lawyer in the linen suit, and never liked any inmate ever. He was appointed to rid the county of these unwanteds, and this nonconformist was working to free them. Chalk one up for the political right, getting one over on the liberal left.

"You may be seated," said the judge. She was the moderately attractive Judge Grace McCaglia. Wearing the usual black robe, matching black hair that may have been colored specifically to do so, and mystic blue eyes that could virtually see through a person. She confidently presided with a no-nonsense efficiency that would make Ryan's wife Angie proud.

In her late forties, she had accomplished more than most attorneys had in the course of their entire career, in a fraction of the time. In the *Live Free or Die* State of New Hampshire; there were rumors of political favoritism, affirmative action, and sleeping her way into a judgeship. Any explanation was more plausible than that she'd earned her position. These whispers did not go unnoticed which is why she once prosecuted as an Assistant District Attorney and now presided as a judge strictly but fairly. There would not be any second-guessing her rulings. She would not allow anyone to be justified in criticizing her for not being the right person for the bench.

"Where are we in the matter of the State of New Hampshire v Grantes?"

"Where are Anna and Brady is the better question." JG whispered into Ryan's ear as they sat in their seats at the defendant's table. He looked around the room but with few

210

people in it, it was quite clear that his wife and son were not present.

"No idea. Three messages without a response this morning. Maybe they gave her a hard time about a four year old in the courtroom?"

Ryan finished whispering the response as he stood to address the judge to answer her question.

"We would like to request a continuance, your honor."

"On what grounds? This has been ongoing for six months, time is ticking here sir."

"We are still in discovery, judge."

"I must be confused. This *IS* the discovery hearing, is it not?"

"We've not received any of the ADA's documents, Judge. How can I file a motion or motions to exclude evidence or dismiss all charges without notice of said evidence?"

"Dismiss? Mister Wells, a Grand Jury was convened and subsequent to Rule 8, they found probable cause to sustain an indictment. The 90-day threshold was met. Do you want to weigh in here counselor?"

She swiveled her chair to her right so she could face the prosecuting Assistant District Attorney. 'Weigh in' was a poor choice of words and she immediately realized it.

Pierce La Fontagne was an enormous man. Fat. He was an unhealthy glutton that could blame whatever or whomever he wanted with regard to his obesity, but it was a fact that he tipped the scales at over four hundred-fifty pounds. He was always disheveled and just as disorganized. How he'd lasted as an ADA was a mystery, but his nickname was not so mysterious. They called him Jabba, after the enormous creature in *Star Wars*, behind his back. And he knew it. He spoke with as slow a purpose as his metabolism.

"We have … Ah … Given the defense … Ah … And have enough to provide the people to move … Ah … Forward with the case, Judge. We … Ah … Don't need much, but we do need a little more time." The fat on his neck jiggled when he spoke. He never looked up to face the judge when he spoke to her, as he shuffled his papers in the disorganized mess he had created at the prosecutor's table. Besides his disorganization, not making eye contact when speaking infuriated her. She felt it was a sign of disrespect.

"Does that mean you are ready or not? Kind of late in the game aren't we, counselor? You had enough to sustain the charges, do you have what you need to move forward or don't you?"

"Ah … We feel confident that the current evidence will prove our case beyond the threshold of reasonable doubt."

"I can tell." She had to pause to control her anger. She was a professional to her very core. She swiveled back toward the defendant.

"Mister Wells?"

"I'm happy for ADA La Fontagne that he feels so strongly about his case. If there is so much overwhelming evidence in moving forward against my client, why haven't I received it?"

"Again I'm confused," she said turning back to the ADA. "How about it? Did you send the material to the defense or didn't you?"

"I … Ah … Believe—"

"—Do you have the discovery documents with you now?"

"Ah … Yes."

"Excellent. Problem solved. Hand them across the aisle to the defense. Now. Speedy trial gentlemen. The defendant has the right to one, he is remanded and sitting in prison awaiting the disposition of this trial. Continueance? I would think his lawyer would be more adamant about moving this forward. He pleaded not guilty. ADA La Fontagne and the state requires a speedy trial, and frankly I demand it so I don't get backlogged. Six months gentlemen. This has been going long enough, wouldn't you both agree? We move ahead forthwith." Efficiency experts could learn a thing or two from Judge McCaglia.

"I agree that six months is a long time, your honor. Especially for my client, who was only remanded due to an imminent threat justification, which we will get to in a minute with the motion you have before you."

Ryan had filed to have the issue of bail revisited. Jabba had used a justification arguement that Jacob Grantes was an immediate danger to society and should be remanded as to allay any danger to the community. Additionally, she was clearly disgruntled with the prosecutor today, which he hoped to use to his and therefore his client's advantage.

"But with all due respect, judge, I do not agree with the a forthwith," Ryan continued. "In order to provide a proper defense against the charges, I need to ensure that the burden of proof and all pertaining evidence is met and provided to me by the prosecution. The ADA has just told you and I, after some equivocating I might add, that they now have all the evidence they plan to use when and if this goes to trial. I need time to assemble all the counter-evidence and exclusion motions supporting our claim against the charges, and that proving that my client is innocent."

JG nodded his approval. His friend and partner was doing well. Unlike television and movies in Hollywood, the State cannot come out of nowhere in the last minute of a trial with a damning piece of evidence. It was now time for the prosecution to put up or shut up and Ryan had just spoken legalese saying so.

"Whether you agree with my ruling or not, Mister Wells, is not my concern. You heard the ADA, he's moving forward, and unless you're going to change a plea to GUILTY, we're moving forward."

"With or without my continuance, Your Honor?" Ryan pressed.

The judge shook her head. "Just out of curiosity, how long would you need?"

"We request ninety days."

"Three months for discovery that was just given to you and prep for trial? You are joking right? Nice try." She turned back to the ADA. "I don't have a green sheet in front of me. Is there a deal being offered?"

"We … Ah … Haven't—"

"Get it together, Mister La Fontagne." She again shook her head in apparent disgust. "Is there anything else you would like to state before I rule on this?"

"Ah … No Your Honor. I would just like to … Ah … Reiterate that — "

"—No need to reiterate anything, I heard you the first time. As much as it pains me, you've got thirty days." She turned toward the clerk to dictate. "Let's set a date for pretrial and jury selection at or about one month from today."

"Your Honor with that being settled, I would like to revisit the issue of bail. The motion should be before you," Ryan said.

He was hoping that since things had not exactly gone his way thus far, Judge McCaglia would throw him, and more importantly JG, a bone on the motion to revisit the issue of bail. Her disapproval about the performance of the presiding ADA could only help the cause.

"That has already been denied. I denied it six months ago. Is there anything new to bring forth where I would reconsider?"

"He is a prominent attorney in the area, Judge. He has a family, is a husband and father. He is the sole breadwinner. This has created an enormous hardship. His driver's license has been reinstated at this point, but we would surrender it again in lieu of incarceration if the State is still concerned that he is an imminent threat. But if we are now talking another thirty days before jury selection for a trial, I see no reason to continue to remand him. He has been a model inmate, never been in trouble with the law prior to this case, and he has — "

"Save it Mister Wells. You have nothing new here. A woman is dead. The allegation is that she is dead because of your client. Drinking and Driving is serious and a blight on our society. When a child is in the car on top of this, allegedly, the crime is reprehensible. I continue to believe that he may be an imminent threat. The fact that he is a prominent figure in this community; and that he is an attorney; that has been before me and this court in the past; is not a reason for him to benefit. He cannot garner favor from a court that is supposed to judge his alleged crimes. Any defendant before me with these same allegations would get remanded, remain alcohol-free, surrender their license to drive a motor vehicle, and pending the outcome of the trial, matriculate a Substance Abuse Program. I'm sorry Mister Grantes, but you are to stay at the Wayland County House of Corrections pending trial. Stay in the Substance Abuse Program or there will be consequences, sir. As your attorney just stated it is only thirty more days."

She paused only for a moment while she briefly looked over the rest of the documents regarding this case in front of her.

"So unless there are any other motions, we will resume these proceedings in thirty days. No more delays gentlemen, either one of you. Court is adjourned."

215

The gavel was only tapped onto the sound block but it sounded as though it was slammed through to the other side by a sledgehammer.

4

THE TRUTH IS THAT THE HARDSHIP THE GRANTES FAMILY
was facing was not at all financial. It was Jacob who was
suffering the most, to be sure, but they were all unaccustomed to
this torment. Spending six months in that horrible place was a
battle of its own, however not being with his wife and four year
old child was all but killing him. Brady was not supposed to be
without his father. He hadn't been in his life up to that point and
'away on business' was the story that his wife had sold him.
Anna was good about sparing the boy the truth, that his father
was accused of manslaughter with special circumstances, and at
least played the role of understanding wife until now. Anna had
been distant in most recently.   They had dealt with serious
difficulty in the past, but this was a big ask. He promised himself
to make it up to her. They would get through it. Their college
romance had started blissfully and had some serious downs
despite their intense love for one another. Their eventual vows to
take each other through good times and bad had taken significant
meaning both past and present.

Norman and Olivia Craig had done whatever they could to
encourage the college romance of their only daughter, Anna.

Jacob, not Jake or JG as others called him (his natural parents had taken the time and effort to pick a name for him, and it was rude to bastardize that effort, they'd said repeatedly), was decidedly the perfect match for their Anna. Especially with the boys she had brought home in previous courtships. True, Jacob's family didn't come from wealth, nor had they built any. The Granteses weren't new money, they were no money. The Craigs had faith that this legacy would change with Jacob. He had work ethic, was smart, and pre-law. Yes, this is what they had in mind for their girl and they would do whatever they could, financially or otherwise, to support Jacob's goals. As long as Anna was included in the equation.

Jacob was always humbly appreciative, respectful in declining the offers of money or the "just because" expensive gifts, but relented over time. Anna joined in on the pressure to accept these material tokens of affection for they were deemed as simple manifestations of parental approval. She viewed the entire subject as "only money". Of course it was only money to her, she had been privied to these same gestures and more over the course of her entire life. These gifts were just an extension of her expectations from her wealthy parents.

"You should just get used to it honey, they won't let up. They love you and they just want to show you how much. Besides, you deserve to live a certain lifestyle even if you don't know it yet," she said in one of their more memorable spats on the subject. There had been more discussions regarding this very subject, all of which she'd won with some version of the same statement.

Jacob's fight for financial independence with her was a broken alliance, however. He would say things like, "I'm used to doing things for myself, babe. It's not that I am unappreciative of it, but there's something honorable in building a life for ourselves, by ourselves. I feel like I'm forever indebted to them."

These declarations would fall on deaf ears and would either reluctantly fade or would be the impetus for a battle royale, depending on the value of the gesture and how much Jacob really wanted to press the issue. Eventually Jacob acquiesced, as he did each and every time. As the relationship developed, the lifestyle became de rigueur. He had lost every battle and the war as well. In truth, he had built up enormous debt and was very thankful for the financial help. Boston University was not cheap, Boston University School of Law even less so. The money, cars, apartments, the ability to go to Law School (only 11% of those applying to BU School of Law get accepted. The competition is stiff, but Mr. Craig was friends with someone on the Board of Trustees, or so he said).

"It's not bribery," Norman Craig explained. "I love Anna," he also said. It was to ensure that they had a strong foundation on which to build their life together. Of that, Jacob was sure.

Jacob's biological parents loved him with all of their hearts, albeit with fewer trinkets to show for it. Actually, there weren't any trinkets. Reginald and Elizabeth Grantes had to work and toil for every nickel of property or possession they owned, and even then the nickels didn't add up to anything of worth. They doled out hugs and kisses the way Norman Craig doled out money. Before the Craigs, Jacob had been a wealthy man. His parents attended or coached every athletic endeavor their only son struggled to perform. Neither parent had attended college but made it a priority for their son to get the education they did't have. They would not, could not, contribute financially. But they were motivating and supportive as best they could.

Young Grantes left upstate Vermont to attend Boston University and achieve his and his parent's goals for him. His parents remained there, driving south for visits or sending care packages of sweets to their starving student. They were pleased to learn that as of his sophomore year, their son would no longer struggle financially. The ends would more than meet. Unfortunately, in the end, they would never meet Anna.

✳✳✳✳✳✳

It was the start of Jacob's second semester, of his second year at BU. Reggie and Liz decided to drive down to Boston to visit their son, as they had done two other times in his tenor there. He had been home for Christmas break and every other sentence was, "Anna this" or "Anna that".

Jacob had been a social mingler in high school, never the most popular kid but was a welcome addition to any clique. He was better than averagely attractive. He was polite, and was familiar with many a female as well, in large part because of his standing in a plethora of social circles. He had many dates, with a few sporadically retained as official girlfriends over the years. He certainly didn't have any that he had prattled on about for days on end.

His freshman year had been new and exciting, but also the most difficult endeavor he had undertaken in his life up to then. There were precious few stories regarding the fairer sex as he said there wasn't any time. That was only half true. The other half was that going to University was not about settling down but about exploring, both academically and socially. It was novel that this Anna would commandeer so much of a conversation, which made necessary the trip to Boston.

Interstate 89 is a long, windy, treacherous highway running north-south over and around the Green Mountains, crisscrossing Vermont and into New Hampshire. This is one of two major highways in Vermont, and is the quickest way south to Boston, Massachusetts. The two lanes of patchy, frost-heaved road are tricky to negotiate any time of year; soft shoulders, ice, elevation changes, with notorious fog make it more so during bad weather.

January brings major snow storms almost every year, often dropping several feet of snow in a relatively few number of hours. This particular *Noreaster* should have postponed the trek south to Boston, the storm well-tracked and advised in advance. But in the Northeast, weather personnel and meteorologists, were wrong as often as correct. Though every attractive weather girl, on every channel, was forecasting the same snow advisory. The days had been requested off, however, cashing in vacation and/or personal time, so the show must go on. The trip was planned, and the senior Grantses would stick with that plan. And so on that January afternoon, Reg and Liz Grantes of Burlington, Vermont embarked on their journey south.

Jacob found it odd that his parents had not called him once they'd arrived in Boston. They'd had a reservation with a late check-in scheduled at the Buckingham Hotel on Commonwealth Avenue, as was customary when they visited. When he had not heard from them, the thought of the big storm resonated in the back of his mind. He almost immediately disregarded it, however; his father had driven in the snow his entire life, had taught him how to drive in the stuff. He called the prepaid cellphone they used only when traveling, as cell phones were not the rage with his parents. Neither contended to be that important where they needed to be available for a phone call at every hour of every day. He could not get through to the cell when he called. Their voicemail was not set up, of course. It was not until he called the hotel and informed that they had not checked in that he began to worry. More phone calls to their friends and to their places of work without a definitive answer to their whereabouts led to panic.

By 10:00 AM the following morning, panic became horrified shock. The Vermont State Police informed him by telephone that neither had survived a severe car crash. Neither had been alive when authorities had arrived at the scene.

"We hate to inform you over the phone," they said. "How very sorry we are," they also said. "Please come to Montpelier, Vermont to identify the bodies of your parents."

They had not made it out of their own state. The reports showed that the snowy weather conditions inhibited sight; mixed with the unplowed snow on top of black ice, with an unfamiliar rental vehicle that was not equipped with all-wheel drive, were some of the variables contributing to the disastrous formula. The guard rail was ill-placed, meaning that there wasn't one in place. A guard rail would have at a minimum kept the vehicle on the road. The lack of this safety measure did the opposite and did not keep them on said road. The rental vehicle launched off the elevated section of highway on Interstate 89, into the icy ravine below. The final element in their premature demise.

The aftershock of the catastrophe had left Jacob scarred both emotionally and financially. Anna and her parents were there to reassemble the pieces as best they could. The financial piece was easy. Norman took care of the massive debt in one phone call. Anna was there for the emotional part. This was not as easy. But they dealt with it.

Reginald and Elizabeth Grantes, formerly of Burlington, Vermont, had loved life. They cared not for money but for the happiness it could provide from joyous memories. They loved each other and they loved their son, and in that they were rich.

Realistically, they were not. They lived paycheck to paycheck and didn't manage those very well at all. There were always events deemed too important to pass up, spending money earmarked for bills; spending in lieu of life insurance, savings, or a 401k. They were upside down on their mortgage in part because of the market, but primarily because of the repeated refinancing and remortgaging.

Without life insurance, in their terrible financial condition, and most recently with the cost of their final expenses, they had left their only son with an enormous financial burden. He was already in debt because of his educational loans and the catastrophe would make him more so without a house or substantial property to sell. And so at the ages of 58 and 56, Reggie and Liz respectively, had left their son broken and broke. Had it not been for the Craigs, he would have been broke for the rest of his life.

5

JG WAS ANXIOUSLY AWAITING THE ARRIVAL OF HIS
lawyer at the table in one of the courthouse conference rooms
after the hearing. He was immediately escorted there after his
brief legal fray in the fourth session upstairs. Ryan had scheduled
a meeting in advance with his client before being bussed back to
the prison, should he not make bail. Which to his misfortune is
exactly what happened. Ryan seemed to be taking a long time
doing whatever he was doing in the eyes of JG; leaving him alone
in the dark, windowless conference room with a court officer
standing watch in the corner. It was an awkward silence which
made Ryan's absence seem even longer. He was not in any hurry
to get back to his cell, nor to his cellmate, but he was
overwrought with how his case was progressing thus far. Or not
progressing, which consumed his thoughts every minute of every
day in prison.

The large wooden door opened with a start, ending the
tension that had been building in the small room, adding a
different sort of unease. Ryan moved quickly to a chair opposite
his client, setting his leather briefcase down on the oversized
table between them.

"I'd like to be alone with my client please," he said over his left shoulder to the officer.

"Sure thing. I'll be outside the door when you're finished."

Once the babysitter had left, the lawyer-client pretense was abandoned. "Well, that didn't go very well." The hearing had not gone well, they both knew it, and neither one would needed to sugarcoat it to pretend that it had.

"Ya think?"

"Look pal, we have them on the ropes, right where we want them," Ryan said.

"Rope a dope, huh? Who's the dope? They're kicking our asses, Ry."

"Well, I don't know what I could have done differently in retrospect. Thoughts? I mean what would the Great Jacob Grantes have done?"

JG's elbows were on the table, head in hands. He needed a lifeline. The sarcasm and mucking it up with his friend needed to cease. He was on the verge of breaking down.

"You did what you did, Ry. I mean you did what I would have done. That woman is a ball-buster."

"McCaglia has always been brutal, you knew that going in. You've been in front of her before. Hell, she kicked asses and took names as an ADA, she's doing the same now that she's on the bench. She has something to prove, always has, and she doesn't cut breaks unless she absolutely has to. And she doesn't have to here. We don't have anything going for us, and Jabba isn't chomping at the bit to cut a deal either."

"Exactly. So what *DO* we have we going for us?"

"I was just speaking with tons-of-fun upstairs after our hearing. That's what took so long. I've got the 'one and only green sheet' right here. This is the only deal he is offering, or is ever going to offer, he says. It's not a good one, I'll warn you."

He reached into his briefcase that he'd set on the table, removed the green court document that La Fontagne had given Ryan a few moments prior. It was conveniently on top and quickly slid directly in front of his jumpsuit-clad friend. A green sheet is a bargaining document with legalese and three vertical columns in the middle horizontal third. The form is on No Carbon Required (NCR) paper with three sheets; one for the ADA, one for the defense, and one for the judge. The first column is for the prosecutor, which offers a sentencing recommendation if the defense forgoes the expense of a trial. The middle column is the defense counter offer, which typically chips away at what the State wants. The final column on the right, is the deal formed between the two and goes to the judge. He or she reads the statutory minimums to ensure nobody is ponying up the courthouse, then usually rubber-stamps the deal. When all is said and done, all the judge wants is to clear their docket, keep justice moving just like everyone else. This is called a green sheet for the complicated reason in that the color of the document is a light green. Though it must be signed by all parties, it is only legally binding when and if a formal hearing takes place and agreed to on the record in front of a judge.

"He likes where he is," Ryan continued. "As you can see, the offer is Vehicular Manslaughter with special circumstances, OUI 1 with injury, leaving the scene. He drops the child endangerment, and puts a recommend of eight to ten on the VM, concurrent. Loss of licenses, two years after release on the drivers, law for life because we're talking felonies."

JG shook his head. "Not much of a deal."

"You'd get fifteen years on the VM alone at trial. Add in the OUI-with, leaving the scene, and depraved indifference would get you another ten-plus separately. Tack on the child endangerment charge if we go to the hoop, and you would not be able to see your kid without someone watching over your shoulder until he's legally an adult.   Eight to ten, to run concurrent means with good time, two years off the minimum. You've been in for six months already, so you would be out in five and half. No child supervision, no probation. It's not good but it's the best we're gonna get I'm afraid."

The drivers license didn't make that much difference to JG. The loss of his ability to practice law could also be dealt with, he had money, thanks to his wife and in-laws, and he could always find something to occupy his days. Maybe he could teach. The five and a half years away from his family was intolerable. He could not lose his family for any longer than he already had. Supervised visits with Brady was unacceptable also but at least he would be able to see him other than through glass. These thoughts were going through his mind but he wasn't vocal about them, which caused a long pause. He continued to stare at the offer, lost in the ramifications if he agreed to what was written.

"What's going through your mind?   Talk to me.   There's nothing saying that you can't be behind the scenes at the firm, you just wouldn't be able to take cases when you get out."

"You think that is what's bothering me, Ry? How long have you known me? You really think that is what's hanging me up?"

"No, I don't. I'm just trying to help. But Jabba isn't going to budge. It's this or we go to the hoop. But you have given me nothing to work with on defense. We go to trial? I think unless we come up with something really damned compelling, you're going to go away for a long, long time."

"Have you been in touch with Anna yet? I'd like to discuss this with her."

"She isn't, nor was she, here today.   No answer either. Voicemail is full. I'm really not sure where she is, but I'll keep trying." He pulled out some other documents from the briefcase, spreading out the pile on his side of the table. "What I would like to discuss is all of this circumstantial evidence and see if anything jogs your memory. Anything we can hammer away at. If we weaken anything he has, maybe the deal gets better. I doubt it, but maybe."

"We've been through this, I don't remember anything about that night. Well, other than Sully's anyway."

"Yeah well, we're going to go through it again anyway. You admitted to quote, 'being hammered' when the cops picked you up at your house. You were passed out by the way. Again, Brady was upstairs asleep and legally unsupervised because you were out of it."

"I can't believe I drove in that condition, much less with Brady in the car. Then left him on his own like that in the house? I just can't believe it."

"Thats what they're going with. I have a sworn statement from the bartender, Jenna, that you left Sully's between 8:00 and 8:15 PM. You also admitted to being at the bar in the back of the cruiser, which means you had to be really banged up. You, of all people, know better than to say anything to the police after you've been arrested. But anyway, you left and picked up Brady at the Destriers at 8:20 PM; the servant that was watching him told Chamille Destrier that she put him in his carseat in the back of the running car, that you never spoke or left the driver's seat. She said she found it odd behavior, but this is all third hand through Chamille because the servant doesn't speak English, apparently. Double hearsay. We can attack that at trial if need be. The police never spoke to this housekeeper lady directly to confirm or deny anything. Chamille was at the charity event next to your wife, so we strike the kid being in the car as hearsay. I think that is why the big-boy is dropping child endangerment to begin with, the kind soul. I don't think he can prove it."

"Yeah, what a sweetheart."

"Right. So you drove away and must have bounced off a tree, veering into the opposite lane where this poor woman happened to be coming right at you. She goes off the road and plays chicken with a big tree and an even bigger rock. She lost and you went home to sleep it off."

"It's not funny, Ry. Please don't make light of the fact that this woman was nearly decapitated by a smoking-hot engine. I feel awful."

"Sorry, just trying to add some levity. You're right. It's not funny. Anyway, they have matching paint from the tree, black sapphire pearl, and the scrape on your Volvo has wood and bark all through it. Exact. No real credible argument there, I'm afraid. Furthermore the rubber zig-zagging on Wayland Country Club Road matches the Michelin 235/60R18s on your ride. Cops investigated your tires, they've got you dead to rights there too."

"Match? *Cops* are matching this all up? Can we get experts to refute them? Volvos are a dime a dozen in New England, hell I have two of them."

"Lab techs. This isn't *CSI*, they didn't stop everything they were doing and get top experts from all over the country to fly in on the state's dime, no. But you don't have to be an expert to see that all of this doesn't look good. Picking apart their lab technicians with our expensive ones is not going to win over a jury, if that's what you're thinking."

"That's exactly what I am thinking. The techs are overworked, underpaid, they make mistakes — "

" —This is New Hampshire, JG. They are neither overworked, nor are they underpaid. These aren't MIT grads by any stretch but they don't have a whole lot to investigate, trust me. Just between you and me, I looked at your car, the road, the tree. You killed this poor woman. If you were anybody else — "

229

"—So what are we doing here then? I should take the deal and kiss my family goodbye. My life is over?"

"You're my best friend. I'm trying to mitigate your responsibility here. I'm trying to help. I don't know? Find a technicality. What we're doing here is trying to get the best deal we can."

"Great. Just great. You think five and half is the best I can do?"

"We haven't discussed the 911 call yet. Anonymous, but that's how they nailed you. How they knew to go to your house to grab you."

"What is there to discuss? You've already told me to take the deal, right?

Ryan paused. He shuffled the stack of papers containing all the condemning evidence. He really wasn't sure why he was against taking the deal but he was. He knew his friend, knew him better than any other male on the planet, and something was not right. Endangering the life of his only son, the one they had so much trouble conceiving, was not scanning. True, he had been drinking more in the months before the accident, but to get that blackout drunk was not something he would expect from his friend. He was mister safety. People disappointed. But not JG. Not Jacob Grantes. He had never disappointed. Not until now. "Look, I'm not telling you to take the deal. At least not yet. We finally have all the evidence that fat-body has compiled; so we put Deni on it and see what he comes up with. I mean, the cops didn't pick you up at your house until 9:45 PM, which gives you a huge window to get shattered in the comfort of your own home. If everything comes back the way it looks here, which admittedly is really fucking bad, then we pick away at the bartender and the illegal lady."

"Please leave the vic alone. Arelia, right? Jenna too."

"Look. Jenna is a sweet girl, we go there and knock a few back, have a few laughs, and she's always good to us. But she over-served you. She claims not, but obviously she screwed up and is covering her ass. As far as the victim ... She's dead. Which is unfortunate. But she shouldn't have been in this country to be dead. She was illegal. I feel for her just like you do, but when it comes to my friend or someone who may or may not even pay taxes? I might be a 'hippie' but I look out for my own. We've kinda got a role reversal here, huh? You're usually the cutthroat."

"Prison changes people I guess. Usually for the worse, not more sympathetic. But it is what it is."

"Maybe. But if shit goes south, all the cards lead to what we have before us? We go after the ladies. The bartender has some responsibility here, and so does the vic. This *is* New Hampshire. We don't like drunk drivers but we don't like illegal aliens more."

"Not very politically correct of us, is it?"

"Unfortunately, like you said, it is what it is. Peace, love, and get a green card."

"Well lets hope it doesn't come to that. Just get Deni going because we don't have much time."

"I'm on it. I'm not going anywhere. You need anything?"

"Actually, yes."

"Name it."

"Find Anna."

6

RYAN WELLS WAS JG'S LONGEST AND CLOSEST
personal friend.   They had both grown up poor but not
impoverished, had been instilled with a strong work ethic, and
were the first in their respective families to go to college. They'd
met at BU during freshman orientation and were all but
inseparable since.   Grantes had been a loyal friend in pulling
Wells into the fold of the partnership and Ryan had been loyal in
many other ways, including during the death of Jacob's parents.
They were each the brother they'd never had.

The two were so alike in so many ways that they could have
been biological brothers.   Ryan was good looking, tall and had
what was once an athletic build.   They would both be forty this
year and had previously made plans for both families to go on
vacation together to celebrate.   Until the incarceration, all had
looked forward to the time away.   The only major difference
between them was professionally.   They were both strong
advocates, but the hippie would live in the shadow of his more
talented, leaning to the right, brother.

As Ryan left the courthouse, he pulled his iPhone out of his long winter overcoat to call Warren Dennihan, the firm's ad hoc investigator.

"Deni, how are you?" He immediately regretted not using his bluetooth ear device to make the call as he juggled his briefcase, the phone, and his car keys to open his parked car.

"Same shit, different pile. What's up?" Warren Dennihan was a *Southie*, or from the district of South Boston and had the severe accent to prove it. Bad. Or 'wicked bad, guy'. It was almost like he spoke a different language, as *pahk tha cah in hahvid yahd*, just doesn't quite describe how broken his English really is. He didn't pronounce *r's*, unless of course they were not in the word like *drawr* instead of draw. It was work to hold a conversation with him unless you were familiar with him or those from his neighborhood.

"I just finished up with JG's hearing. It didn't go well."

"I figured. I got my partner workin' my other shit, so how much time do I gotta clear up?"

"Ah shit," Ryan said. He dropped his phone while opening his car to get it started and warmed up. He had to retrieve it out of the snow but fortunately it still worked. With the new synthetic oils and the fact that he drove an Audi A6, he didn't need to get the car warmed up for performance reasons, but he couldn't get the winter-fighter to work on his cold body until the engine was pumping warm air at him.

"You ok?"

"Yeah, Yeah. I'm here. Just dropped something. So everything we talked about? That's what they've got. The whole shah-bang. We've gotta work on it."

"By we, ya mean me."

"It's been a tough morning, are you really gonna give me a hard time right now?"

233

"Always. Hey listen. I've been callin' WHOC, I know a few guys over there. Not much I can do to look after him in there. Its all political. He's a lawyer, so nobody trusts him, and he can't gang up. At least he knew not to PC, just take a beat'n like a man if thats what they wanna do."

"If it was going to happen, it would have happened by now."

"Not necessarily, but we can hope. How much longer?"

"That depends on you, Deni. Thirty days if this goes to the hoop. Trial will probably take about two weeks or so, after that depends on what we get. I was hoping we could get enough to kill a trial, maybe enough to get a deal. They are offering eight to ten, which means five and half when all is said and done."

"All depends on me? No pressure. Who's breakin' balls now?"

Ryan was still sitting in his car, which was starting to kick out the warm seventy-four degree air that was set on his digital thermostat on the in-dash computer. He still couldn't drive, however; the car had not yet picked up the signal for the phone and you cannot drive and talk on the phone in New Hampshire unless handsfree. "Hey where are you?"

"Around the corner from you, I'll be there in thirty secs or less."

"Good. This might be easier face to face. I have a ton of documents you should look at."

"Do you still drive the silver Audi?"

"Yes, of course. I love this — "

" — I'm behind ya."

"Holy crap. That was fast."

Deni parked his blacked-out Escalade and relocated to the passenger seat of Ryan's vehicle. This was the part that took the thirty-seconds. "Let's see it all," he said without explanation of how or why he was in the immediate area.

"So this is everything." He handed Warren the stack of evidential material from his briefcase, then continued. "I know we discussed it when this thing happened, and since, but something just isn't sitting right about this case. You think I'm nuts though don't you?"

"I don't think you're nuts, per se, but would you really go through all this bullsh for anybody but JG? I agree that somethin' ain't stirrin' the kool-aid, but you and I both know he did it. He was drinkin' like a fish for months before this all happened. I was thinkin' family trouble at the time, but who knows? That kid is his life, so I can't see him throwin' that away. But we all fuck up, doesn't have to be on purpose for it to do damage."

"So does that mean that you're on board? I gotta know that you're on this."

"Loyal as lab, huh? Yeah, me too. I'm in, and you know it. I just need somethin' to work with here, guy."

"Look I never ask how you do what you do, because I'm not sure I want to know, but we're going to need all you've got on this. We need to dig into; Jenna, the bartender we know from Sully's Tavern, the Destrier servant or au pair or whatever the hell she is, the 911 call is a bit wonky, and if all else fails — we make the vic the most despicable person who has ever illegally entered the borders of this country," Ryan said before pausing. "I was kind of hoping for a sliding scale on this one. I know you have to clear your calendar and this is going to take some time, but with me taking this case, I have all of his cases I have to work, and mine, and of course he isn't in the office taking cases so the firm is really financially tight right now and — "

" — Hey relax, kid. I can't dig up what ain't there, but I'm on it. As legit as possible anyway. As for the fee, don't worry about it. I owe him. He's been good to me over the years."

"So what are you thinking?"

"I've got a couple of ideas. Mostly hunches, but I know people."

"I know you know people, that's why you are so good at what you do. Anyone I know?"

"Stop kissin' my ass Ry. I wanna check out the bar first. Jenna."

"Business or pleasure?"

"Both."

"I've got another project that's just as important."

"I'm listenin'."

"Find Anna and Brady. They didn't show up at court today and she's not answering phones. It's weirding me out, and JG is really freaked out."

"Huh. That ain't like her."

"Tell me about it."

"Lets go over to the house. You drive."

"Right now? Deni, I've got — "

" —You said it's important. Was that fact or bullsh?"

"Fact."

"Then start drivin'."

I wish to dedicate this book to my father, George Gamow, and my dear friend, Stan Brakhage, who both helped me to bridge the schism between Art & Science.

- R. Igor Gamow

"What we remember lacks the hard edge of fact. To help us along we create little fictions, highly subtle and individual scenarios which clarify and shape our experience. The remembered event becomes a fiction; a structure made to accommodate certain feelings. This is obvious to me. If it weren't for these structures, art would be too personal for the artist to create, much less for the audience to grasp. Even film, the most literal of all the arts, is edited".

- Jerzy Kosinski

Contents

Illustrations

PREFACE: THE REALITY OF REALITY

Of all the great disappointments that I had suffered over these many years my first and greatest disappointment was when I learned that my childhood heroes were fictional. This included a bevy of individuals almost too many to name and would include The Lone Ranger, Robin Hood, King Arthur, The Hardy Boys and even "Nancy Drew". Upon this realization, I assumed that since I was a child, these fictional characters were created for children. But if I read stories written for, let us say, my parents, these stories would depict real people and real events. In the evenings, almost every evening of my childhood, my parents, Rho and Geo would, after I was put to bed, read to each other. This was a time before the ubiquitous television set. At the time of my revelation about reality they were reading the collected stories of Somerset Maugham. I randomly read a story from their book entitled, *The Colonel's Lady*. I was tremendously moved. But of course, I was then only eight or nine, and now, I am 75. The entire story was only ten pages, so I read it in one sitting. The highlight of the story is when the colonel discovered that his wife, with whom he had basically a loveless marriage, had written a book of poems entitled *When Pyramids Decay* that had suddenly become a best seller. The poems describe a middle-aged married woman who had a love affair with a much younger man. The young man suddenly dies, leaving the women devastated. Theses poems appear to represent a love affair that the colonel's wife had. She had published the book using her maiden name, never dreaming that the book would ever to see the light of day, much less be a bestseller. The colonel had two problems. First, he could not imagine that anyone would have an affair with his mousy wife. Second, if in fact she had had such an affair, he wanted revenge. I'm sure that I only vaguely understood the male problem back then. When I asked my mother about some of the details, it turned out that I had randomly chosen a story that both my parents knew and loved, and that the whole story was made up, as was the book of poems published by the colonel's wife. I actually asked my mother to get the book of poems the colonel's wife had written only to be told that it never existed. It was from that time on that I decided that not only what I was reading was not real, but nothing was real. What we now call reality was just an illusion of reality.

Many years later in college, I learned that Plato had made a similar assumption. This preface would not be complete if I did not have at least one quote from Einstein: "There are only two ways to live your life. One is as though nothing is a miracle. The other is as though everything is a miracle." I know it is presumptuous to modify anyone's quote, especially Einstein, but I would change the word miracle to "real" in order to

6

convey my present belief. Another reason for me to quote Einstein is the fact, that Einstein had joined the three of us, at our home, for dinner. I was four years old! Now after more than 65 years, I am quite comfortable knowing that my literary heroes were made up, because I am completely comfortable believing that everything is made up, thus nothing is real. In my mind, the one exception is mathematics. Even if humans never existed or even if our universe was completely lifeless, mathematics would still exist. Perhaps I'm wrong, but it would not be the first time. So, if nothing really exists, then the natural extension of this statement is that all nonfiction books, such as history books, biographies and memoirs, are in fact fiction. It is only our illusion that there is a difference between fact and nonfiction literature. In other words, fact and fiction may be different in degree but not in kind. So my book, *The Professor's Daughter*, is clearly fiction and for me to call it a fictional memoir is redundant. One of my all-time favorite storytellers always finished her stories saying "some of what you just heard is real and some is not—it is up for you to decide." I had decided a long time ago to accept everything and believe nothing. Happy reading.

R. Igor Gamow
Summer 2010

ATHENA

LOST

How could I hear my cell phone ringing at a moment like this? Music was blaring and a male stripper named James was gyrating in front of me, giving the come-hither sign to jump out of my chair and join him. It was my 30th birthday and my friends were throwing me a private little party in a back room of O'Grady's Bar, an upscale watering hole in Chicago. As everyone downed their third shot of Patron, I noticed three guys peaking through the half opened door to admire my friends. Why not? Ten pretty young ladies in sexy summer outfits all throwing down a shot of tequila. Priceless.

I couldn't be coaxed out of my chair to dance with James. So, Ava, our group's resident exhibitionist, heeded the call and slithered into action. Ava was more fun to watch and much sexier than the hired talent. Our stripper was cute and buffed, but he couldn't dance. Time to send him packing, no pun intended, and get on with our evening. The guys at the door watching Ava dance were mesmerized, hoping they might join us for the rest of the night. Ava grabbed the stripper by the necktie that hung over his bare chest and tangoed him around the room. At this point, "Dancing with the Stars" would have had to cut to a commercial break while Bruno fanned Carrie Ann with a towel. The guys watching at the door couldn't resist any longer and crashed the

9

party. No one seemed to care, least of all me. I never liked being the center of attention. My male strip-o-gram had come with a card that said "Time to forget the ex and start looking for the "n-ex-t." Since my divorce, almost a year ago, I'd had one uneventful date and my friends were on a mission to find me a new guy.

As Ava began a faux strip tease act, teasingly unbuttoning the front of her blouse, one of the guys began to video the performance with his iPhone. Here we go, I thought, she'll be on YouTube in ten minutes. It used to be that one in a million got lucky and found their ten minutes of fame; now everyone has a shot at it. My cell phone rang again. I wasn't going to answer, but some calls just feel important and I pulled the cell out of my purse to see who it was. I knew the area code, but I didn't recognize the number.

"Hello."

"Athena, oh thank heavens you answered." It took me moment to place the voice.

"Arthur?" I said.

"Yes, dear, it's me," he answered.

Arthur Doyle was my father's attorney and confidant. Doyle and Associates was one of the most prominent law firms in the West.

"There's no good way to say this, Athena," he said. "I have bad news - your mother has died."

Everything seemed to freeze. I wasn't aware of the party, the music, the people. It was like a tidal wave had washed over me and stopped time.

"Athena, are you there?"

"Yes," I said, and then began to sob uncontrollably. My friend, Ann, put her arm around me and asked if I was alright. I let out a loud wail that stopped the party dead. Everyone stared at me. I got to my feet and stumbled out of the room. The bar was noisy and chaotic and I walked out the front door to the street. I still had my cell phone in my hand and put it back to up to my ear.

"Arthur?"

"Yes, I'm still here," he said. "Your mother had a heart attack."

"Where's Father? Why hasn't he called me? "

"Because we can't find him," Arthur said.

"What do you mean?"

"I found out that your mother had died yesterday when a courier delivered a letter to my office this afternoon. Your father left instructions for me to contact you and have you arrange your mother's funeral." Arthur told me he'd spent the afternoon trying to locate my father with no luck. "He's vanished and we can't find him anywhere," Arthur said. I was too stunned to be rational. My mind was reeling. I tried to say something to Arthur, but I started sobbing convulsively and couldn't speak. "Go home and try to get some rest," Arthur said. "I'll keep looking for your father and call you soon." I thanked Arthur and stuck my cell phone in my purse.

Ann found me out in front of the bar, leaning against the wall, crying. She took me in her arms.

"What's wrong?" she asked, "Was the stripper that bad?" When I responded with more tears, Ann realized it was serious. "Athena, I'm sorry," she said. "What's the matter?"

I told her about my mother and asked her to thank my friends and tell them I had to leave because of an emergency.

Back at my apartment, I tried calling my father on his home phone, office phone and cell phone, but nothing. I left urgent messages for him to call me. At ten o'clock, Arthur called to say he still hadn't been able to locate Father. He'd arranged a flight for me at ten o'clock the next morning and we agreed to meet for lunch once I arrived. I drank a glass of wine and sat on the couch staring blankly at the wall. I'd already been depressed and lonely, although you wouldn't know that by looking me up online. Such an upbeat profile! The exciting life of a pretty young woman in the big city. With pictures to prove it. But let's not analyze that in detail. Let's just say that as an advertisement for myself, it was a very misleading description of the product.

Since my divorce, my life had seemed a bit pointless. I was in the midst of a mini existential crisis. I'd moved back to the city, met a few friends whom I barely knew, and found a job that didn't suit me. I'd only seen my mother twice over the last five years, and we rarely talked by phone. In that whole time, I can't remember feeling much about her at all, because I didn't really think about her at all. Now I was suddenly overwhelmed by the emotional loss. It was like sitting on a chair and having one of the legs cut off. Until it was gone, you didn't notice the chair leg at all. Then you hit the floor and realized how much you counted on it. I had two more glasses of wine and fell asleep on the couch.

The next morning I flew to San Francisco, picked up a rental car at the airport and drove into the city to have lunch with Arthur. I'd been calling Father repeatedly, but no answer. From the car, I tried the house yet again and someone picked up. It was Britta, our longtime housekeeper.

"Britta, hello, how are you?" I said.

"Athena?"

"Yes, Britta, it's me. Do you have any idea where my father is?"

"No, dear, I'm sorry. The house has been flooded with calls and I stopped answering the phone."

"When was the last time you saw him?"

"The morning after your mother died, he came home from the hospital in shock. He didn't say a word to me and went to his room. The next morning I couldn't find him anywhere."

I told Britta that I planned to come to the house later and she said she would see that my room was ready. Britta was from a small town in Scotland. Her father had raised sheep, and as a girl, Britta often tended the flock along with the family's three border collies. She herded the flock on horseback, and by the time she was a teenager, she looked like she'd been born in the saddle. Britta's brother was an avid climber and took her on treks climbing the Munros, Scotland's highest mountain range. Britta became an accomplished climber and went on to climb two of the world's tallest peaks. In high school Britta was an exceptional student, but never got the chance to go to college. She moved to Dublin and for years made a living as a street musician. She came to New York with her musician boyfriend and lived in the Village where she met my father. The two loved talking about mountain climbing, horses and dogs.

After Father moved to California and became a professor, the two kept in touch. Many years later, Britta wrote Father to tell him that she had gotten a degree in biology at night school, but it didn't help her find a job - she was still waiting tables. Out of the blue, Father invited her to California to be his teaching assistant. To help make ends meet, he paid her to do chores around the house. Britta was a natural at caring for the animals, and she also helped father to test his various climbing inventions. Over time, she evolved into our all-around Gal Friday. Besides training and caring for the animals, she would schedule Father's trips abroad, line up his speaking engagements, and help Mother with social events. Britta became a member of the family. She lived in a small one-bedroom cottage that was in the woods in back of the house. She always seemed perfectly content and was unflappable under any circumstance. Britta also looked after me when I was growing up. Although we weren't particularly close, we got along fine. Her true loyalties were to Father. I often felt that she knew more about my parents than I did.

My cell phone rang and I anxiously pulled it from my purse. Caller ID revealed it wasn't Father calling, but Hank, my husband, actually my ex-husband, but I still hadn't gotten use to that designation.

"Hello," I said

"Hey, I'm sorry to hear about your mother. How are you doing?"

"Not great … Just dealing with the funeral, it's all kind of a blur."

"When's the funeral?"

"Friday."

"Is there anything I can do?"

"Ah, no, I don't think so, but thanks." There was an awkward pause and I wondered if I should invite him to the funeral. What's the protocol? He hadn't said he planned to be there. Suddenly my cell phone beeped with another incoming call.

"Hank, sorry, but I have to take another call," I said. "I'll call you back." The incoming call was from Arthur's secretary, informing me that Arthur was running twenty minutes late for our lunch meeting.

I thought of calling Hank back, but didn't. At the moment, the last thing I wanted to do was awaken the emotional cold war that simmered in the wake of our divorce. Dealing with my mother's death totally consumed me. I felt physically numb, in a kind of altered state of consciousness where normal daily realities were suspended as I searched for some final spiritual bond with my mother. As people called me to pass along their condolences and inquire about the funeral, I realized that for most of them it was something they had to fit into their schedules.

I met Arthur at a seafood place called The Outrigger. He greeted me with a warm hug. Arthur had known Father for over thirty years. They'd met when father hired Arthur's big city law firm to do patent work on father's inventions. Over time, Arthur put together some very profitable deals for him, licensing a number of his inventions to big companies. Arthur was also a restrauteur, a gourmet chef and an extremely talented landscape painter. He was friends with the renowned western artist Russell Furman and had a big collection of his artwork. The only person with a larger collection was Jack Nicholson. Furman once took Arthur and Father to a party at Nicholson's house and I was green with envy.

"Still no word from father?" I asked.

"Nothing," he said. "I'm sorry." Then he showed me the detailed instructions father had left for mother's funeral. Elaborate floral arrangements, a eulogy from Father Edwards, a list of pallbearers and a list of speakers. As I read over the letter, handwritten in his meticulous longhand, conflicting emotions welled up. I vacillated between dread that he might have gone off in his grief to kill himself, and at the same time, I was furious that he'd vanished and left me to arrange Mother's funeral. There was a huge guest list, a who's who of their friends. The waiter delivered vodka martinis and Arthur raised his glass.

"To your mother," he said. I choked back the tears and took a sip of the martini.

"What are we going to tell everyone about Father and why he isn't here?", I asked.

"Good question," Arthur said. "There's the truth, and then there's our version of the truth." Spoken like a true lawyer, I thought. We debated various cover stories like that Father had fallen gravely ill, or that he was out of the country in a remote place like Tibet and his flight back had been cancelled. Finally, we decided to stonewall for another day and hope he'd show up. To close friends and colleagues we'd say that father was in mourning and talking with no one. Arthur had alerted the police and the coast guard. He'd even hired a private investigator.

"It won't be too long before your father's disappearance becomes public knowledge," Arthur said.

"And then what?" I asked.

"One thing at a time, my dear," he said. "First let's deal with the funeral. I'm here to help you." I took Arthur's hand and held it tight.

17

"I can't thank you enough, Arthur," I said. "I couldn't get through this without you." Arthur agreed to meet me the next day at St. Paul's Cathedral and help make arrangements for the service.

I left the restaurant and on my way out of town took a drive through the U.C. Santa Cruz campus, which is nestled in the redwood forests overlooking Monterey Bay. My father had taught here for the past thirty years. I found a classical music channel on the radio and turned up the volume on Beethoven's Fifth. It was so loud inside the car, I barely heard my phone ringing. The caller ID showed that it was my father's best friend, Stan. I flipped open the phone.

"Hello Stan," I said

"Athena, I'm so sorry about your loss. It's a loss to all of us," Stan said. Then he lost it and began to cry. "I'm sorry, Athena," he said. "Here I am calling to give you support and I fall apart. What will we ever do without your mother?" Then I began to cry.

"It won't be easy Stan," I said, fighting back the tears.

"And where's your father?" he asked. "I can't reach him."

"He's in mourning, he hasn't talked to anyone since mother died."

"Tell him to please call me. I'm coming to the funeral, when is it?"

"Friday afternoon," I said.

"I'm in Hungary, doing a film, but if I can arrange a flight, I'll be there," he said.

"But Stan, won't you have to stop filming?" I asked.

"It doesn't matter, it's only a movie. I'll call you tomorrow," he said. "Should we be worried about your father?"

"No, I think he'll be alright," I said. It was a lie, but what else was there to say at the moment?

"Okay my little angel," he said. "I'll call you tomorrow." Stan had called me his "little angel" since I was nine years old. He'd first met my father over forty years ago in New York City when they were both struggling artists. Back then, father's passion was dance. When he was fifteen, he saw Jose Greco perform at the Joyce Theater in New York, and it changed his life. When Greco leapt up onto a coffee table and performed a thundering flamenco solo, Father was spellbound. He dropped out of boarding school and moved to New York to pursue ballet. His first three years in New York, he lived in a cold water flat in the West Village. There he met Stan, a struggling young poet. Stan was an inspired, passionate force of nature. He was ruggedly handsome with a head full of jet-black hair and dancing eyes that were always alive with curiosity. He always dressed in black and had the aura of a 50's movie star.

Stan was born in New York City at St. Vincent's Hospital, often called the "Poet's Hospital" because Dylan Thomas died there.

Stan never knew his father, who supposedly had been "exiled" to Italy because he was wanted as a minor Mafioso. Stan's mother was an unstable alcoholic who couldn't hold down a job and put Stan in a foster home at the age of twelve. Stan proved to be a gifted student with a talent for music. At fifteen, he left the foster home and lived on the streets of Little Italy, often sleeping in the subway at night. Stan spent most of his days at the library consuming the Greek and Roman classics and reading history and literature. He sometimes panhandled in Times Square playing guitar and singing songs he'd composed. Writing songs led to writing poetry, and he began to audit a class on Keats at Columbia University, where he met Allen Ginsburg, a Columbia student. Through Ginsburg, he met Jack Kerouac and their literary mentor, William Burroughs, who had graduated from Harvard years before. Before long, Stan was part of their literary circle, reading his poems in coffee houses in the Village and soon after publishing his first book of verse.

At a poetry gathering with Ginsberg, Burroughs and Gregory Corso, Stan helped a young filmmaker film the reading with a 16-millimeter Éclair film camera. Stan enjoyed the filmmaking process so much that he shot and edited a documentary on the group that Kerouac had dubbed "the Beats." Stan fell in love with the art of film and began making experimental films and dramatic shorts. He knew the musician John Cage and teamed up with him to make an experimental film called "Vibration," a visual interpretation of Cage's original music.

One day, Stan was sitting in a coffee shop in the West Village reading the *New York Times*. On the front page of the *Times Arts* section, he saw a picture of a tall Russian in tights, a leather jacket and a long ponytail, sitting on a classic Indian Chief motorcycle. Sitting behind him on the motorcycle was a beautiful ballerina in costume. The man in the picture was my father, and the article was about his upcoming performance in the National Ballet Company's production of "Swan Lake". The *Time's* deliciously romantic story profiled Father's life as a struggling artist and how he supported himself as a daredevil motorcycle courier for CBS News.

As he was reading the article, Stan heard a motorcycle pull up outside and was surprised to see the ballet dancer in the picture getting off his bike. A big believer in fate, Stan dashed outside and followed Father down the street into the Eighth Street Bookstore. He found Father looking through poetry books.

"Aren't you the ballet dancer whose picture is in the *Times* today? " he asked.

"I hope so," father said, "but I haven't seen today's paper."
Stan held up his copy of the *Times* and showed father the picture.

"That's me," father said.

"I've yet to be in the *New York Times*," Stan said, "but once I win the Pulitzer they'll be knocking down my door. Looking for anything in particular?"

"I'm after a translation of Eugene Onegin," Father replied.

"Forget it!" Stan said, "There are no good translations of Eugene Onegin. Pushkin only works in Russian."

"How well I know," Father said, "I'm reading it in Russian, but my Russian is a little rusty and I want an English version to help me along."

Stan and Father headed off for lunch together and talked about Vladimir Nabakov for the rest of the afternoon. By ten o'clock that night, they were drinking vodka at Stan's favorite bar, the White Horse Tavern, where legend had it that Dylan Thomas poured down eighteen straight shots of whiskey before expiring at the nearby Chelsea Hotel. By midnight, Stan and my father were best friends.

MOVIES

As I drove past the biology building where Father's office had been, I saw happy looking students strolling across campus. And why wouldn't they be happy in such a setting, studying with the world's elite scholars? The university had a stellar academic reputation in medical research, atomic physics and marine biology. It was an artsy college community, its own little fiefdom of intellectual endeavor isolated from the working world that surrounded it.

My grandfather, George, had been a world-renowned theoretical cosmologist, and spent the last five years of his life here in Santa Cruz as a visiting professor. He taught a class for graduate students, developed his theories on black holes and wrote a series of very popular books about modern physics. In the world of science, George's career was the stuff of legend. He risked his life trying to flee the oppression of Stalinist Russia, seeking the freedom to pursue his scientific research. His first attempt to defect with his wife involved trying to kayak across the Black Sea to Turkey, but was foiled by poor weather. Finally, with help from Niels Bohr and Madame Curie, he managed to get permission to attend the historic Solvay Congress on Physics in Brussels.

Niels Bohr, Danish physicist

g. Gamow

George and his wife then went into exile and never returned to their native Russia. Over the next three decades, George became part of the inner circle of physicists, including Albert Einstein, Niels Bohr and Ernest Rutherford, who developed modern physics.

Lord Rutherford (*left*) and Sir J. J. Thomson.

G. Gamou

Father loves to tell the story about Einstein coming to his house for dinner. At the time, Father was only four years old. His idol was Roy Rogers and he dreamed about getting his own horse. While Father was out in the back yard busy being a cowboy, George would sit around the house with Einstein, or Robert Oppenheimer or Edward Teller, busy figuring out the future of nuclear physics.

$$R_{\mu\nu} - \tfrac{1}{2} R g_{\mu\nu} = -\kappa T_{\mu\nu}$$

Albert Einstein.

G. Gamow

26

As a college student back in St. Petersburg, George had loved the ballet. And when my father dropped out of high school to pursue a ballet career, George supported his decision. By the age of twenty-five, though, father decided to give up ballet. He loved the art of dance, but he disliked the rich patron culture that surrounded ballet. George told father that he'd pay his college tuition if he came to Santa Cruz. First father had to pass a high school equivalency exam since he'd dropped out of high school. Then Grandpa pulled some strings and got Father admitted. Unlike most college freshman, father had already lived the life of a bohemian artist in New York. College life seemed dull by comparison. He found his academic courses boring and began teaching ballet on the side. He once told me that by his junior year he'd decided to quit school.

"I was having dinner with your grandfather," he said, "trying to get up the courage to tell him that I was going to drop out of the university. We were talking about genetic biology and he pointed out to me that all life, from bacteria to whales, could be described by the ordering of the four letters of the genetic code. I found that concept just unbelievable. The revelation so inspired me that I decided molecular genetics was going to be my life's work."

With his newfound passion for biology, father returned to his studies with the same dedication he'd applied to becoming a dancer. He once calculated that he'd studied over 10,000 hours to master the art of ballet. He believed that if he now applied himself for another 10,000 hours, he could master the academic challenge ahead of him. Three years later, father earned his PhD. By then, Stan had directed his third movie, a satirical comedy called "Utopia." The film became a cult hit and won Stan an Oscar nomination for best director. He was becoming well known in the filmmaking world as a maverick, an independent who spurned the Hollywood studios to make his own personal movies. But Stan was always struggling to find money for his films and was often broke himself. Whenever Stan came to Los Angeles to cast a movie, he would always come up to Santa Cruz and visit Father. Father was now a full professor and had his own research lab. Somehow, he persuaded the college's liberal arts department to hire Stan as a visiting professor to teach a film studies course. It was a hard sell. Now almost every college has a film department, but back then it was rare. Stan's courses on screenwriting turned out to be hugely popular, even with directors, producers and actors from L.A., who would come to Santa Cruz just to take Stan's class.

I drove out of town on the two-lane highway that snaked up the coast toward home. I'd driven this road countless times over the years. It had become like a meditation. I knew the road so well that I just floated along, hardly conscious of driving the car as the ocean swirled below. Fourteen miles later, I turned off onto the gravel road that led up to the house. It had been two years since I'd been home, and whenever I came back, I always marveled that I'd grown up in this storybook house. A white, two-story Victorian structure sitting perched on a bluff overlooking the ocean.

The Professor's Victorian home that
overlooks the Santa Cruz Bay.

You could sit on the front porch and watch the sun set over the ocean and it would send shimmering golden needles of light dancing through your spine. I thought of it as nature's acupuncture. It was a ritual that I'd enjoyed countless times over the years.

I knocked on the front door. "Britta," I said. No answer. I called out her name louder and still no response. Before going in the house, I decided to go see if Britta might be in the barn. Subconsciously, I was probably screwing up my courage before going into the house, because I knew that the empty house with mother's presence everywhere would overwhelm me. I wanted to ease into the pain. I walked around to the back of the house. Next to the white clapboard barn was the clay tennis court that Father had built. The net was a bit tattered and the surface a bit cracked, but I could tell that he was still playing. When I was a girl, Father and I would often play Mother and Stan in doubles. Stan wasn't much of an athlete. Whenever a ball sailed out of the court into the woods, Stan would call a "nature break" and go retrieve it. Stan's "nature breaks" usually lead to a ten-minute tennis delay as he lit up his cigar and enjoyed the scenery.

I pushed open the large sliding door to the barn and went inside. When people first stepped into the barn, they were always surprised at how enormous it was. Father had the interior of the barn divided into three sections: the lab, the horses and the toys. What caught your eye at first was a gigantic transparent bubble that created an enclosed atmospheric chamber. This was the lab were father worked on his inventions. Inside the bubble were scattered all sorts of devices: cylindrical compressions chambers, fancy treadmills, stationary bikes and rowing machines all equipped with scientific monitoring devices. Scores of top-notch athletes had come here to buy hypobaric chambers that father would design specially for them to improve their conditioning and performance. Father used to call it "legal blood doping". Over the years, I'd met Olympic medal winners in cross country skiing and swimming, a Tour de France winner, NFL football players, and a host of famous marathoners and mountain climbers.

There were three horses, Pegasus, Zeus and Helen, all Arabians. They had three comfortable stalls in a corner to themselves. Helen had been my horse as a girl, and I suppose it still was my horse, even though I hadn't ridden her for over ten years. Pegasus was Father's horse and Zeus had been Mother's. Another section of the barn was set aside for father's toys, essentially motorcycles and cars. There were two Harleys, a BSA and a replica of the chopper from Easy Rider, one of father's favorite movies starring Peter Fonda. In the movie, Fonda rode a chromed and chopped LAPD motorcycle that he called "The Captain America." There were four of these "chopped motorcycles" in Easy Rider and before the movie was finished, the Hell's Angels broke into the movie lot and stole all of them. They were upset that some sissy Hollywood types were depicting their cult motorcycles. The stolen motorcycles were never found, although bits and pieces of them occasionally showed

31

up. The public was so impressed with the chromed chopper that Peter Fonda started a motorcycle company, California Motorcycles, which made replicas of his Captain America motorcycle. Father bought the first one produced.

Father had a collection of sports cars, including a Porsche Roadster, and Aston Martin. His favorite was a Bugatti sedan that was a gift to him from one of his Middle East clients. When Jay Leno heard that Father had this particular car, he visited him and wanted to buy it for his own collection. Father said no, but told Jay that he could have visitation rights. Father also had a custom-designed, off-road, four-wheel-drive camper that he called "Arnold." It was kind of a Hummer before there were Hummers. Arnold could take you just about anywhere, to the most remote mountaintop, through the dense backcountry and across desert wasteland. And once you got to your destination, you could camp there for days in Arnold, which Father often did, researching and testing his latest inventions. Although he was a professor of biology, which he taught at the university, Father's academic background was the biology of extreme environments. And his research about life at the extremes often required spending time in extreme conditions, from very hot to very cold environments, and from very dry environments to very wet environments. This research took him to the highest mountains, the deepest seas, the driest deserts and the wettest rain- forests. He was fond of saying that he studied life from "pole to pole."

The barn also had one other important function; it served as our own private movie theatre. Father's cars and motorcycles would be moved outside, replaced by chairs, benches, pillows and cushions. A large movie screen was mounted on the wall and huge speakers were in place on the rafters above. Stan had given my father an old reel-to-reel 35-millimeter projector as a gift and he'd taught me how to use it. I became the official projectionist on most "movie nights." There was no set schedule for movie nights; they would occur randomly. Through his connections, Stan would get a print of a movie, and we'd have a screening. I became a very efficient projectionist and hence, indispensable. Stan taught me how to thread the film through the gates in the projector and make a loop so that the sound was in sync with the picture. He also taught me how to splice the film back together when it broke using a special glue and a film cutting block. The 35-millimeter movies were always in three reels with about 3,000 feet of film on each reel. On warm summer nights, as many as forty people would gather in the barn. After they got a drink and found a seat, I'd turn off the lights and it was movie time. When the first reel would run out, there would be a quick "intermission" while everyone refilled their drinks and I got the next reel threaded up on the projector.

As the projectionist, I felt like a magician casting a spell. It was the alchemy of film, as Stan used to say. The film images flickering away at twenty-four frames a second put the audience in a trance, and our movie screenings were often like group séances. Everyone would fall into a dream- like state and watch the movie for two hours and then awaken and excitedly talk about it late into the night. My parents would send me to bed after the movie ended, however, since my projectionist duties were complete. But rather than go to my room, I would sneak up into the loft in the barn and listen to everyone talk about art, science and politics into the wee hours of the night. One of father's favorite topics of debate with Stan was the issue of art versus science. Stan often brought friends to movie night, usually artists of some sort, painters, poets or musicians. Invariably, when father met a new artist friend of Stan's, he would greet them with his "art vs. science" gambit; and even though I'd heard it numerous times, it never lost it's charm.

I remember the night we screened Felini's "8 1/2"". Stan brought his friend, the painter, James Chatam. Stan introduced James to Father and before they were done shaking hands, Father launched into the "art vs. science" debate.

"So you're an artist?" Father asked.

"Yes, I am, sir," answered James.

"James, tell me this, why is science progressive and art is not?" James seemed a bit puzzled.

"I'm not sure what you mean," he said.

"I'll give you an example," Father said. "If you take the greatest scientists of the past, like Aristotle or Newton and you brought them to the present, they'd be complete idiots. They wouldn't know anything. They'd have to go to school to learn how much they didn't know. But on the other hand if you took artists, like Michelangelo, Mozart or James Joyce and brought them to the present, they'd be right at home."

"What's your point?" James asked.

"Well," Father said, "it shows that science is progressive and art is not, it doesn't change." James became a bit agitated.

"Now wait a damned minute here," he said. "As an artist, I'm not sure if I feel insulted or honored." After father's opening salvo, Stan would always jump into the fray.

"Whatever artists are doing," Stan said, "at least they're not threatening the extinction of the human race like science."

"So science is evil, eh?" Father said. "But science has the power to improve the quality of life, alleviate poverty, cure illness. What can art do?"

"Art," replied Stan, " has the power to make people investigate the mystery of their own lives." There was never any clear winner to the "art vs. science" debates. They invariably ended with everyone agreeing that neither art nor science had yet to figure out the meaning of life. So why not relax and watch the evening's movie?

Father loved movies. He could talk endlessly with Stan about cinema. Father took Stan's screenwriting class where they deconstructed great movies to see how the screenplays served as the artistic blueprints for production. Father became fascinated with the mechanics of moviemaking and told Stan that he had a great idea for a screenplay. Stan told him to write it and he'd show it to his Hollywood agent. So, father wrote a Michael Crichton-like science thriller. It was so good that Stan's agent optioned it to a major studio. Father ended up writing more screenplays; to him, it was just an entertaining hobby. He would think up a story idea and pace around his office at night and dictate the whole thing into a cassette tape recorder. He would imagine the whole movie as if he was watching it in his head. As he told the story he would play all the characters, speaking the dialogue in each of their voices. In five nights, he would record eight hours of cassette tapes and then have a typist transcribe them. Then, with a little editing, he'd polish up the script and be done. Over the years, these spec scripts that father wrote made him quite a bit of money. Father had always loved the process of invention. He used to joke that he found writing screenplays to be his favorite form of inventing, because you could create value out of thin air. You just thought up a clever story, wrote it down and someone bought it. You didn't have to really make anything, whereas his inventions in bio-engineering required him to make real working devices.

Some nights I had my own private movie screenings. I'd re-watch an old classic like "Love in The Afternoon," because the print was still in the barn and Stan hadn't returned it yet. One Friday night, my parents were out for the evening and I invited my quasi-boyfriend friend, Gordon, over to watch a movie. We weren't really girlfriend and boyfriend yet, but we were getting there. This would be the night we'd make it official. We pretended that it was our own private drive-in theatre and left father's cars parked in front of the screen. I loaded "Shampoo" starring Warren Beatty on the projector, started the film, and then jumped in the front seat of the Buggati with Gordon. He put his arm around me and I snuggled right in.

As the first act ended, Warren Beatty was kissing Julie Christie and Gordon was very aroused. Of course, I was fantasizing about Warren Beatty and had become quite flushed myself. Gordon had managed to kiss me twice and was inching his hand inside my blouse. I had taken a personal oath that I would not have sex until I was sixteen, as an odd form of reverse rebellion against my father. At the moment, my personal oath was in serious jeopardy. As I kissed Gordon while watching Warren Beatty kiss Julie Christie, fantasy and reality blended together. I let Gordon unbutton my blouse and bury his head in my breasts. Beatty and Christie started making passionate love on the bathroom floor. Suddenly the movie stopped and the screen went dark. There was dead silence, punctured only by the sound of Gordon's amorous moaning and the metallic clanking of the film reel slapping the loose end of the film against the projector. Gordon didn't seem to notice.

"Hold on, Gordon," I said.

"What?"

"I have to change the reels."

"You can do that later; let's make our own movie."

Good try, Gordon, I thought, but I was no longer in the mood. My fantasy lover had abandoned me. Up on that big screen, Warren Beatty was so confident, so charming and oh-so-handsome. In the movie, he's a hairdresser and the women all swoon over him. He would make them look beautiful and then devour them in bed. I even imagined how delicious he smelled as he cut Julie Christie's hair and then hugged her in that steam filled bathroom. Gordon smelled like a musty t-shirt. What was I up to anyway? It wasn't like I was embarrassed by my virginity like so many of my girlfriends, who thought being sexually experienced was cool. My friend, Maggie, had sex with a number of college boys and bragged about it. I guess I was looking for some moral code to base my sexual relations on. My father was a borderline atheist, which, given his passion for evolution and science fit the bill. Mother found her deeper meaning through her art, not formal religion. She'd go off for days hiking in the wilderness and return with a radiant Buddha-like calm. That left me to concoct my own philosophy about life, including my own attitudes about sex. It's still a work in progress.

I pushed Gordon away and jumped out of the Bugatti. I put up the second reel, started the projector and got back into the car. I put on my denim coat and zipped it up. Five minutes into the next reel, Gordon was hot and bothered again.

"C'mon, Athena, I thought this was our own private night at the drive-in."

Gordon was still at half-mast, but I'd become distracted. I found myself thinking about Hal Ashby, who'd directed "Shampoo," and Robert Towne, who'd written it. I'd learned about them through Stan, who knew them both. Towne had co-written "Shampoo" with Warren Beatty.

"Gordon," I said, "did you know that the screenplay for this movie was nominated for an Oscar?" I don't think that Gordon even heard the question. Just as he began to force himself on me, we were interrupted by a loud booming noise from the back of the barn.

"Athena, are you in the Bugatti?" It was my father, home early. I was busted, caught in his prized car. With a boy, no less! Father had a temper and I braced for a nasty outburst. But as he walked up to the car, I saw a broad smile on his face.

"Just like at the drive in, eh?" he said. "Watching a movie in the car. Great idea, Athena. Why didn't I ever think of this?" Without waiting for me to answer, Father hopped into the back seat.

"And who's this young man?" he asked.

"Um, Gordon, Gordon Sykes, sir," Gordon said. Gordon's studly demeanor had crumbled and his amorous passion had vanished. He looked like a deer caught in the headlights.

Meanwhile, up on the screen, Warren Beatty was riding his motorcycle. "A Triumph. I had that bike once," Father said. "Do you ride a motorcycle, Gordon?"

"No, never have, sir."

My father was quite an imposing figure, six-foot-four, broad shoulders, long hair braided in a ponytail, penetrating green eyes and a crushing handshake. He could charm you or intimidate you, depending on the occasion. I caught myself imagining Gordon as a younger version of my father. Charming and witty and smart, which, of course, all added up to sexy. The real Gordon was an un-romantic dullard in comparison. But then, father out-charmed and outwitted most mortals, so poor Gordon didn't stand much of a chance.

Up on the screen, in the film's dramatic climax, Jack Warden finds Warren Beatty and Julie Christie in the throes of passion on the kitchen floor and delivers one of those memorable movie lines: "Now that's what I call fucking!" he says. Father laughed while Gordon watched stoically.

"Well, I better get going," Gordon said. He got out of the car.

"Goodnight, Athena," he said, "and good meeting you, Professor." He reached out and shook hands with my father and then walked out to his car. Poor Gordon. First he was matched against Warren Beatty and then against my father. He never stood a chance.

After Gordon left, Father suggested that he and I plan a drive-in movie night of our own. We made a date to watch "Shane," one of his favorite films. Since he owned his own print of the film, we scheduled the screening for the following Monday. Mother would be out of town at an art dealer show, so it would be just the two of us.

When Monday night arrived, I went out to the barn and put up the first reel of "Shane" on the projector. Father walked in ten minutes later with a bowl of popcorn, a bottle of coke for me and a tumbler of vodka for him. I started the film and hopped into the Porsche with him. Even though he'd seen "Shane" dozens of times, he always went into a dream-like trance the moment it started. "Shane" was the epitome of the outlaw hero story. And Father had always fashioned himself as an outlaw, a maverick. For me, the film was almost like a Freudian analysis of our family. The film is set in the Wyoming Territory in 1889. Shane, played by Alan Ladd, has no first name. He arrives out of nowhere and we know nothing of his past. He's hired as a ranch hand by the Starret family and we soon learn that in his mysterious past he was a gunfighter. An evil cattle baron named Ryker, played by Emile Meyer, is trying to run the Starrets out of their homestead.

As the film unfolds, Starret's wife becomes infatuated with Shane. And their son, Joey, is enthralled by Shane's prowess as a gunfighter. Meanwhile, Starret becomes frustrated with Shane's detachment and refusal to take up arms against Ryker. When

41

Ryker brings in a hired gunman to kill Starret, Shane reluctantly takes action. Shane knocks Starret unconscious in order to save him from being killed by a professional gunfighter. Then he straps on his gun and rides into town alone for the showdown. In the shootout, Shane kills both the hired gunman and Ryker. It's the perfect reluctant hero story.

I always identified with Joey. For Joey, the combination of his father and Shane add up to the ideal father. But Starret and Shane have conflicting values. Shane's reluctant hero represents the life of solitude, self-determination and freedom. While Starret represents family values and responsibility to society. As Starret's wife wavers between which man she prefers, the audience wavers between which set of values is better. Shane's distrust of civilization is represented by women and marriage. Women represented the very entanglements that the outlaw hero sought to escape. Women involved the responsibilities of settling down and accepting the conventions of society. So the outlaw hero had relations with "bad" women, whose decadent morals were not fit for family life and settling down. No need to worry about marrying them. Yet, as Joey sees it, society depends on the self-determined, un-entangled outlaw heroes like Shane to preserve it. Shane has his own code of what's right and wrong. He doesn't feel bound by the conventional laws of society. In the movie's big moment, when Shane says goodbye, Joey breaks down in tears. As Shane rides off, Joey calls after him, "Come back, Shane, come back."

For me, Father was a composite of Shane and Starret. A family man who provided for his wife and daughter, and an outlaw hero who often rode off and left us on our own. The family man who loved the women in his life and lived by society's rules at home. The outlaw hero lived the life of freedom away from home and lived by his own code of right and wrong. And as a girl, I'd often felt like Joey, fascinated by my hero outlaw father when he came home and preferring him over my family man father. And then crying, "come back, Father, come back" when he left. This made me think that I didn't want an outlaw hero for a husband. Being the daughter of one was enough – or so I thought.

After the film was over, Father started up the Porsche, drove it out of the barn and parked under the stars. We sat looking at the stars until two in the morning, talking about movies, evolution, the galaxies above, and mother's mysterious recipe for rum cake. It was one of the few times I'd ever had my father's undivided attention. Just us, talking. I always felt that Father loved me, but that he just never had the time to tell me. His life burned so bright and fast with creative energy that it consumed all his time.

"Athena," he said, "this was a wonderful evening. We have to do this again."

But we never did.

STARTING OVER

The next morning, I had some of Britta's homemade coffee cake along with her extremely potent French press coffee. It provided just the instant jump- start I need to face the day. Now sixty-two, Britta was stocky and very fit. She had red hair and a large round face with lively green eyes. She showed me a list of people who had already called about the funeral. We spent the morning calling and emailing people with details about the funeral arrangements. After passing along condolences, many people asked how Father was doing and we told them that he was taking it extremely hard. A few good friends asked to speak with him and we said he was in seclusion, not taking any calls.

I called Father's colleague, Max Schneider, a renowned physics professor at the university, and asked him if he'd give a eulogy for Mother at the memorial service. Like Mother, Max was German. They both came to America in their teens and both still had family in Germany. They shared similar childhood experiences growing up in World War II Germany and living through the crushing Russian invasion that culminated in the fall of Berlin. Whenever Max came to our house, I always loved to listen to Mother and him talk. They seemed so worldly and sophisticated. Switching back and forth from German to English, they would talk about their trips back to Germany, and about physics and art. Over the years they became the best of friends.

I left the house at noon and drove into town. I stopped at Mother's art gallery to meet with Renee, her best friend. She was a fellow artist, who often helped out at the gallery. Renee was the shy introvert to Mother's outgoing extrovert. I asked her if she'd speak at the memorial service and she was non-committal at first. She told me she was not a public speaker and was terrified to be in front of a large audience. We talked about Mother for the next hour. Renee told me that her sculptures were now in art galleries around the world and some were selling for six figures. When she said that Mother's spirit would live on in her art, I found myself crying and smiling at the same time. Renee said she'd think about giving a eulogy at the service and I hugged her goodbye. Ten minutes after I left, she called me in the car and said that she wanted to speak at the funeral, and that she wanted to show slides of my mother's art.

From the gallery, I went to Paulson's Funeral Home and met with the funeral director, George Paulson, a tall, balding man in his mid forties, dressed in a black suit. We talked briefly in his office and then he took me back to see Mother. When I reached down and touched her arm it was hard and stiff like wood. I shuddered and then began to cry. How could her life force just disappear? I felt faint and my knees buckled. The funeral director put a steadying arm around my shoulder.

"It's alright my dear," he said. "She's in peace". His blank expression turned slightly sympathetic and without another word he guided me out of the room. It was his job to move things along. He led me into a sitting room.

"Take a minute," he said, "and then we can discuss arrangements."

He left the room and my cell phone rang, startling me. I felt like a fool for leaving it on.

"Hello," I said.

"Athena, it's Arthur. How are things going?"

"Alright, I'm a bit numb, but carrying on."

"There's still no word on your father," he said. "Can you meet me at my office by four?" I told Arthur I'd be there as the funeral director slid back into the room and sat down beside me. He had a large three ring binder with laminated pages that showed various styles of caskets. *Where in the hell is Father*, I thought to myself.

Stan called as I was driving over to the cathedral. He told me that he had arranged to digitize some old film footage he shot of Mother and Father and was going to edit a special film tribute to show along with his eulogy.

"Sounds good," I said

"Look," he said, "could you arrange for a video projector with at least 4,000 lumens to be at the church?"

"Stan," I said, " I have no idea what you're talking about. But I'll try my best." He gave me the type of gizmo he needed and I called Britta to see if she could find one to rent somewhere.

At the cathedral, I met with Father Andrews. We agreed that he'd give a brief memorial sermon and then introduce those who would be giving eulogies. I left the church and drove to the Outrigger to meet Arthur. He ordered us each an Absolut martini.

"Well, there's still no word about your father," Arthur said. "I've hired a private investigator and he's come up with nothing."

"So we have do decide what we're going to tell people," I said.

"Exactly."

"I've already mislead some people by telling them that father was in seclusion," I said. " So the word's probably gotten around that he's at the house."

"Maybe we should leave it at that," Arthur said.

"What, and tell people he's not at the funeral because he's grieving at the house?" I said. Arthur shrugged and took a sip of his martini.

"It just seems so ..."

"So what?" Arthur asked.

"So preposterous, I guess."

"A most accurate definition of the situation," Arthur said. And then he ordered us another martini.

It was dark by the time I got back to the house, past eight o'clock. On the dining room table, Britta had left a detailed list of everyone who would be attending the funeral. As I paged through the list, I realized there were over 700 names. The church could only hold 500, so I'd have to make arrangements for the rest to sit outside. Britta had meticously noted those people who were the closest to Mother and should be seated inside.

There was no sign of Britta, so I assumed she'd retired for the night. I made yet another futile attempt to call Father on his cell phone. I selected a bottle of single malt scotch from the extensive liquor cabinet, and poured myself a generous amount. Then I went into his study, sat down at his desk and logged on to his computer to check my email. I read through a number of emails from my friends passing along condolences and hoping I was alright. Then I found an email from Hank and read it.

> *Hey darling, I don't know if you're checking your email, but we didn't get to finish our call yesterday and I've been unable to get you back on the phone. Again, sorry about the loss of your mother. I could come for the funeral if you like. Or would that be awkward? I suppose you're staying with your father. Even though he and I only met a few times, I think we have a good relationship. Anyway, if not now, hopefully soon, you'll give me a chance to meet with you and talk about us.*
>
> *Love, Hank*

I found it hard to believe that Hank wanted to try a new "us." How did he think the new "us" would be different from the old "us"? And I had no idea why he thought that he had such a good relationship my father. The truth was that father couldn't really

48

see what I saw in Hank, other than his horses. Father thought that Hank was a bit of a dullard. In hindsight, I must say that I agreed. I guess I had taken for granted the environment I'd grown up in – a place where artists, scientists and various near-geniuses drank vodka in the kitchen and after dinner talked passionately about their fascination with evolution, Turgenev, Niels Bohr, black holes and the films of Billy Wilder. I thought I'd create a home like that with Hank. We'd work hard, have children and create our own world of creative, stimulating friends. But the reality was nothing like the fantasy. Hank was a macho, self-centered, provincial rancher. I was so smitten with the cover that I forgot to look inside the book until I bought it. And then by page five, I found an ultra-conservative Baptist who hadn't read more than five books his entire life. He had no interest in art or science and his music collection was limited to Merle Haggard and Waylon Jennings.

Father had imbued me with a love of art. He'd also given me an understanding of the language of physics and biology. Once you knew this language you could sit on the porch under the stars and discuss the evening sky like a trained musician discussing Beethoven's Fifth. Hank's friends were good ol' boy farmers and ranchers. Interesting characters, but not the least interested in, say, the big bang theory of the universe, quantum mechanics or the films of Woody Allen. For them, the point of science was to provide a good weather forecast and improved seed crops. Not a bad thing, but not the kind of stimulating environment that I was after.

I replied to Hank's email and told him that I had my hands full dealing with arrangements for a large crowd and that it was probably best that he didn't come. I told him that I appreciated his offer and I'd call him in a few days. Of course, I didn't mention that Father was missing. I finished my scotch and went up the stairs to my bedroom. My old room was exactly the same. My old hand-made wooden desk and my ornate wrought-iron bed frame with a gorgeous quilted bedspread were still there. Everything was neat, tidy and clean, no doubt thanks to Mother. On the wall were pictures of me with friends, with mother, and riding horses with Father.

I opened the window and looked out at the shimmering ocean under a full moon. I'd enjoyed this view thousands of times growing up. Then one night, just days after my sixteenth birthday, I witnessed a scene from this window that changed my life. That particular night I was in bed sound asleep when I was awaken by a commotion outside. I sat up in bed and heard a woman screaming. I went to the window and out on the front lawn I saw a woman sitting in a wheelchair throwing rocks at my father. Father dodged the rocks and attempted to approach her without getting hit. I eased open my window to hear what was going on. The young woman in the wheelchair kept screaming and cursing at Father with the most vulgar language.

"Now, Artemis, please calm down," Father said.

"Why? Because you don't love me anymore?" the woman screamed. "Because you abandoned me for your wife?" She was screaming loud enough to rattle the windows. Then she reared back and threw a large rock at my father's head. He ducked and the rock sailed across the porch and smashed through a picture window. For a woman in a wheelchair, this girl had one hell of an arm.

"For the love of god, enough," Father pleaded. But Artemis just launched another rock, which hit father in the arm. With that, Father charged her before she could reload. He struggled to subdue her arms and then started to lift her out the wheelchair into his arms.

'You goddamned bastard!" she screamed. She managed to get one arm loose and slapped Father in the face. I was glued to the window in shock. As Father carried Artemis toward the house, I got a better look at her. A very pretty woman who couldn't have been older than twenty-five. Indeed, she looked almost as young as me. Then I heard my mother at the door

"For god's sake, get in the house, you're disturbing the animals," Mother said. Father, who had the strength of an ox, carried the woman to the front porch and started up the stairs. I heard them enter the house and close the front door. My heart was pounding with excitement. I slipped out of my bedroom and ever so quietly padded down the hallway to the head of the stairs. I heard our late night guest bellowing like a captive animal. I peaked down the stairs, but saw nothing.

"Goddamit, put me down," she said.

"Here, here, calm down," father said.

"I'm going to make her some soup," mother said. Mother had a large arsenal of dispute mediation techniques. Making soup was one of her mothering strategies, which she'd used many times on me. There was something about warm soup that had a calming effect, plus one had to shut up to sip it. As mother went into the kitchen, she caught me peeking down from the top of the stairway. She gave me a firm look and waved her hand, signaling that I was not invited. "Get back to bed," she said in a hushed voice.

I retreated back into my room. I realized that the woman in the wheelchair, who could have been my older sister, was my father's lover.

The next morning, I found Mother sweeping up broken glass from the shattered window. Father was in the kitchen drinking coffee and reading the paper. I walked into the kitchen without saying a word, grabbed an orange and a piece of bread and walked back up the stairs. The events of the previous night were never mentioned again by my parents, but that night changed my life forever. I realized that the many times my father was away on one adventure or another, he was probably not alone. I began to hate him. How could he dare sleep with someone other than my mother? I also began to have issues with my mother. Not only was she aware of my father's secret life, but she seemed to condone it.

All morning I stayed in my room, brooding and feeling sorry for myself. I was angry at my parents, angry at the world. The girl in the wheelchair had shattered my fairytale image of my family as the "perfect family." I made up my mind that I was going to go live life by my own standards. I was full of youthful idealism and high-minded morals. I knew what "love" was, or so I thought. If I had to exclude my parents from my life, so be it.

That afternoon, I went out to the barn, fed the horses a few carrots and then took the jeep into town. As I drove down the coast, I saw a lone sailboat, out in the bay. It was Father. A wave of conflicting emotions welled up inside me. I thrilled at the sight of him tacking through the wind, admiring his skill.

At the same time, I felt rage, almost hatred at him for his marital indiscretion. How did I know that there weren't other women, other affairs? And if there were, was my mother aware of them also? The two of them seemed to have a secret life that I was never aware of, a life that excluded me.

The Professor sailing hard into
the wind in his beloved sailboat.

In town, I picked up my best friend Ellen at her house and we hung out for the day. As a national merit scholar who'd graduated first in my class, I had scholarship offers to numerous schools across the country. After endless hours of soul searching, I had decided to join Ellen and go to college the next year right here in Santa Cruz, even though it was the provincial choice and didn't offer the adventure of exploring a new place. But all things considered, Santa Cruz was a great school set in a spectacular location. Academically, it was top notch. I took Ellen out for coffee and told her that I had some bad news.

"I don't mean to ruin our plans," I said, "but I've reconsidered going to school in Santa Cruz." The news upset Ellen more than I would have guessed. We had planned to share a dorm room our first year and then find an apartment to share.

"How can you change your mind at the last minute and abandon me? " she said. "What have I done ?"

"It's not you at all," I said. I told her that I had come to the conclusion that I had to get away from my parents. Much further away than Santa Cruz. My father was a professor here and my mother had her business in town. My rationale didn't sit with well with Ellen. She stormed out of the Starbucks and walked home.

I picked Brown University in Providence, Rhode Island. It had a good architecture program and was geographically about as far away from home as possible. After getting an undergrad degree at Brown, I stayed another two years in Providence and got a graduate degree in Interior Architecture from the Rhode Island School of Design. Over those six years of schooling, I saw my parents a total of four times. Three Christmases back home and one visit from my mother to Providence for my graduation from Brown, which Father couldn't attend because he was doing research in the Himalayas. I never went back home for summer breaks, but instead busied myself with intern projects, a study abroad program and summer school. In hindsight, I regret the pain my "rebellion" might have caused my mother. We still got along fine, but I knew she was hurt by how scarce I made myself. My emotional boycott was really directed at my father, and I often wondered if he ever really noticed or even cared.

After finishing college, I got a job at HOK Group in Chicago, one of the world's biggest architectural firms. I loved Chicago, the home of Frank Lloyd Wright. I spent much of my spare time visiting Wright's simple, hand-crafted Prairie School houses designed with indigenous materials. I became a Frank Lloyd Wright expert and was always spouting off about "organic architecture."

After three years as a glorified assistant on other people's projects, I finally got a chance to be lead interior designer on a project to build a new house on a ranch in Montana.

Athena prepares herself for a day's
work at her architectural firm.

My first big project led to something I never would have expected,
a husband. We made our first presentation for the project at our
offices in Chicago. We were among three firms in town making
presentations to design a new 5,000 square-foot house for the
Circle K Ranch. The client was Hank Conroy, and when he
showed up at our offices in Chicago, I was smitten. As I stood at a

large screen in the conference room reviewing a set of artist's sketches for the project, Hank watched me so intently that I was a bit unnerved. After the presentation, he told me that he loved the design and the job was ours. I was thrilled. Hank thanked me for the inspiring presentation and said that he couldn't wait to get started on building his dream house. As we shook hands, he clasped my hand firmly.

"A beautiful house and a beautiful designer, it was meant to be," he said,

"I can't wait to get started," I said.

"Well, why wait, I'm flying back to the ranch tomorrow," Hank said. "Why don't you come with me?"

"I'd love to," I said, "but I have to make company arrangements first." In reality, I wasn't sure what came next, since this was my first real project. Our company's vice president, Frank Pearson, who had sat in on the presentation, suddenly piped up from the end of the conference table.

"Why don't you go, Athena." he said, "We'd just send you up later in the week anyway to survey Hank's property."

"I guess I could," I said. "But I'll have to check on travel arrangements."

"That's all taken care of darlin'," Hank said. "We'll fly up in my plane." Frank called for a bottle of champagne to celebrate the deal and we toasted the new project. Little did I know that it was about to change my life entirely.

Hank took five of us to dinner at his favorite Chicago restaurant, Morton's. We talked a lot about horses. Hank was impressed that I was an experienced rider and had my own horse as a girl. "I've got just the horse for you, Athena," he said. "And we'll take a ride at the ranch that will make you one happy cowgirl." After dinner, it was late and I scurried home to pack and prepare for the trip. The next morning, I took a cab over to Hank's hotel and found him waiting in the lobby. Hank was tall, and wearing his Stetson hat, he stood out like the Marlboro man. As usual, he was dressed in a rodeo shirt with the Circle K logo embroidered on the pocket, tight fitted jeans, a custom belt with a silver-faced buckle and beautiful hand-tooled cowboy boots. Instead of luggage, he had a large a pair of saddlebags draped over his shoulder. Hank was charming the pants off two attractive, well coiffed forty- something women. When he saw me, he tipped his hat to the ladies and strolled over to greet me. I watched the two women whispering to each other, seemingly giddy about their encounter the mysterious cowboy.

"Mornin' darlin', " Hank said. "Let's hit the trail." *This is going to be fun, I thought.*

We took a cab to O'Hare. I was expecting a private Learjet with a pilot, but Hank had a single engine Cessna, which he flew himself.

"Been doing it for twenty years," he said, "comes in very handy in Montana. It's kinda like having your own private highway in the sky." We walked out to Hank's plane and threw our bags in the back seat. Hank did a quick exterior inspection of the plane, hopped in, started up the engine and radioed the tower for permission to take off. It was a very foggy morning and I couldn't see much beyond the propeller. And as we taxied out to the runway, I suddenly realized that I was trusting my life to a stranger. At least he was a confident stranger. Two minutes later, my confidence was shaken as we lifted off the runway and Hank headed straight up into the fog. I felt like I might fall out of my seat.

"Relax, darlin'," he said over the propeller noise. "I'm just gonna get us above this cloud cover."

Relax! Ha! It was like being launched in a tiny spaceship. I was sitting on my back, pointed straight up in flimsy, shaking tin can. I tired to remain calm, but my heart was in my stomach and all I could think was: is this how John Kennedy Jr. died? Then suddenly we popped out of the fog into a brilliant blue sky. Hank leveled off the plane and we glided along over the clouds below like sailing over the ocean. It was just us in our own private glowing world. Hank reached over and gave my hand a squeeze.

Athena and Hank flying in his plane from
San Francisco to his Montana ranch.

"Y'all right?" he asked.

"Just fine," I said. "It's so peaceful up here." Father always told me to throw my sense of security out the window every chance I got. Nothing like a raw dose of reality to jolt your senses alive, he always said. And I felt totally alive.

We landed at a little airport in Johnston, population: 3,200. Hank's ranch was fifteen miles out of town and the drive was splendid. I could see the magnificent peaks of the Rockies shimmering in the distance. Ten miles out of town, we turned off the paved two-lane black-top and headed through the sage brush on a gravel road. Hank's 8,000 acres rolled gently into the hills. I saw a herd of horses in one pasture and cattle in another. Hank's old ranch house had been built over seventy years ago, a quaint little wood-beam cabin with a modern kitchen, a small living room and a few bedrooms. The new house would be built up on a nearby bluff. We saddled up two horses and rode up to take a look. I rolled out the blueprints and we walked off the layout of the house. Then we stood in the spot that would be the master bedroom and looked out the imaginary window at the view. It was spectacular. Hank walked up behind me and put his arms around my waist.

"Athena," he said, "I must tell you that I was attracted to you from the moment we met. I hope I'm not being too pushy, but I'm sure glad you're the one designing my house. A beautiful, horse-riding architect."

There was a long pregnant pause. Whose move was it? My heart took over and I scripted Hank's next move in my mind: he would take me in arms, kiss me passionately and say he was smitten the moment we'd met. One touch and I would melt.

"You want to ride up the hill," he said, "and see if we can spot some elk?"

"Um, sure," I said, and for the moment the spell was broken. We rode through beautiful wooded terrain up to an old abandoned bunk house. Hank handed me his binoculars and pointed out a lone elk in a meadow below. Then we dismounted and sat on the porch of the bunk house. Suddenly we were kissing passionately and the next moment we were making love on the floor of the bunkhouse. I remember the sun streaming through the porous barn wood walls as we lay blissfully entwined.

Two months later, Hank and I were married. It was like a fairytale and reminded me of my childhood in the country. I was surrounded by the beauty of nature and, again, had my own horse. More importantly, I had a new man in my life and I was in love. Hank shared my vision of what love meant, that marriage was an exclusive bond. Or so I thought. It all changed in the blink of an eye when I came home unexpectedly from a trip to Chicago and found him in our bed with another woman. I was devastated. My illusions about the perfect loving family were severely shaken. Hank told me it wouldn't happen again, but for me that was it. I divorced him and moved back to Chicago. Suddenly I was single, a working girl again, living in the big city with the opportunity to start over. Still, I couldn't get over my disillusionment. I had a series of "casual relationships," but they were all emotionless. A sense of inner rage had returned. I found myself blaming my parents again, as if by shattering my youthful image of the loving family, they had somehow ruined my ability to trust men altogether. My relationships with men seemed doomed before they began. And I didn't seem to enjoy the sex because I felt guilty that

I was betraying my so-called ideals. How could I sleep with men I didn't love and who didn't love me? I finally stopped going out with men altogether.

GONE

The next morning, I ate a bowl of Britta's Irish oatmeal and drank two cups of her French press coffee. It was a lovely morning, about to dissolve into a somber afternoon. I called Arthur and he told me that there was still no word about my father. Then Britta drove with me into town.

At the cathedral, abundant floral arrangements scented the air, and with Arthur at my side, I greeted the guests at the door. Once the cathedral was full, the remaining guests were seated outside under a canopy. Stan arrived at the last minute. He gave me a long hug and quickly introduced me to his companion, Paulina. Paulina was exotically pretty with dark olive skin and slate grey eyes.

Father Edwards gave a short eulogy. After that, Max, talked about his long friendship with Mother and the bond between them that grew out of their shared heritage. Renee gave an emotional remembrance of working with mother and showed slides of her sculptures. It was a lovely presentation. Stan came to the podium and said that he had put together a short tribute to her. The lights were dimmed, a screen came down from the ceiling and it began. Over the black and white home movie images, Stan spoke into a microphone at the podium, narrating the film. Stan's fluid montage of images was cut to Mozart's Requiem, one of Mother's favorites. There were shots from Mother and Father's wedding cutting the cake and dancing together and then driving away from the church in Father's MG Roadster with the top down and Mother waving and smiling blissfully. Then came shots of her sculpting in her studio and riding her horse. The last image faded out and the audience sat for a moment emotionally overwhelmed. Then the lights came up.

"May she be in our hearts forever," Stan said.

I came up to the podium, hugged Stan, and then thanked everyone for coming to celebrate mother's life.

"I wish I could have the last five years of my life to live over," I said, "so that I could spend that time with my mother. I guess I took it for granted that she'd be there on my terms. All of you who had the good fortune to live life with my mother know just what I mean."

At the reception afterwards, I told everyone that Father had gone into seclusion when Mother died and then became so delirious that the doctors wouldn't let him out of bed. Stan told me that he had to leave in two days and that he was going to come to the house and see Father even if he had to just whisper to him through the door. For a moment, I thought about telling Stan the truth about father's absence, but I decided to deal with that particular situation the next day. Stan said he would call me in the morning.

When I got back to the house late that night, I should have been exhausted, but I was wired. I had a glass of wine with Britta. We reminisced about Mother and talked about the people we'd seen at the funeral. I felt numb and giddy at the same time. Talking to Britta helped to keep my mind off all the chaos swirling at my feet. I thanked Britta for all her help and she said goodnight. I realized that I didn't know what my immediate plans were. I had to deal with a missing father, the house and Britta. Arthur was going to meet with me the next afternoon to help sort it all out.

I pulled a bottle of Glenlivet from the liquor cabinet and poured myself a healthy drink. Then I went into father's study to see if there were any phone messages or emails. Nothing on either front. Sitting at his desk, I scanned over the books on his bookshelf and a VHS tape caught my eye. On the box cover was a picture of Father performing in Swan Lake. He's in ballet tights and holding a young ballerina aloft above his head. I used to watch this tape often as a girl, amazed at how father gracefully pirouetted across the stage. I took the video tape out of the box and slid it into the VHS machine. I turned on the TV, pushed play, then sat back and drank my scotch.

Father had great strength and agility as a dancer. As always, I marveled at his pas de deux with his partner. He did a perfect tour en l'air, spinning around 360 degrees in the air and landing arabesque on one foot. It had taken him years of hard work to make it look so effortless.

THE PROFESSOR

HOME AGAIN

I stood in the door to my study watching myself on the screen performing in Swan Lake. Athena was sitting in my stuffed leather chair watching the television, oblivious to my presence. On the screen, a beautiful ballerina jumped in the air and as she flew through the air and twisted, I caught her and held her aloft.

"I got that part because I was the tallest male dancer," I said, "and the only one with the strength to hold up our leading lady."

I hadn't meant to startle Athena, but she jumped out of the chair.

"Father!" she said. "You scared me to death!"

"I'm sorry, dear," I replied, trying to calm her down. But my daughter was not about to be calmed down one bit.

"Where have you been?" she screamed at me. "Everyone is worried to death!"

"Do I sense concern or anger?" I asked.

"My concern is over because you're here and alive." she said. "But angry? You better believe it. I just held Mother's funeral without you, wondering all along if you were alive. You disappeared! Why?"

"I'm sorry Athena," I said. "I couldn't face it. I may never be able to face it. Leaving was unfair to you, I know that. But I was suicidal." Athena just glared at me. I guess I didn't deserve any

69

sympathy and there was none offered.

"I don't know what to say right now," she said. "I need to leave and think all this through. I'll call you tomorrow." Athena started to walk out, but I blocked the door.

"Please, don't go," I said. "Stay the night, at least. I know you're furious with me. I know you're very hurt. But we're both grieving. So please, don't go. I want you to stay." I gave her a hug but she didn't respond. As I held her in my arms, she looked up at me, sighed and then sat back down. I sat down beside her.

"You and your mother never resolved things," I said. "I know at this moment, you might not really care, but I don't want the same thing to happen with us. Maybe we can try to work things out."

"This may not be the time," she said.

"There may never be another time," I said. "Couldn't you stay a few days?"

"I'm not sure where we'd even start," she said.

"We can start wherever you like," I said.

"I'm not sure that either of us wants to go there," she said.

"Go where?" I asked. Athena took a sip of scotch. Then she looked at me for a long moment, as if deciding whether to proceed or not. When she finally spoke, her voice was subdued, almost a whisper.

"Well, for me it all started that rainy night when I was sixteen," she said. "I guess I've just never understood …" She paused, searching for the right words to continue.

"Never understood what?" I asked. She looked up at me and blurted it out.

"Dammit … I've never understood how you could have fucked that women in the wheelchair!" she said. I was momentarily speechless. That's some starting point, I thought.

"Well, we were never exactly in the wheelchair," I said.

"I'm sorry," Athena said. "I didn't mean to be vulgar."

"Don't worry, no offense taken," I said. "That's as good a starting point as any. I sense for you that it's right at the heart of the matter."

"It is," she said. "Maybe it's something you don't want to talk about. But for me, that's what I'd want you to hear about. It's like you had a secret life with other women and Mother went right along with it. When I realized what was happening I became unglued. I felt rudderless. Your lifestyle was so unconventional that I rebelled and became conventional. I was looking for a normal family life. I blamed you for being unfaithful to Mother, but then when I realized that she condoned it, I was confused. I hated you and couldn't understand Mother for putting up with you." Athena slumped back in the chair and closed her eyes. She was exhausted, physically and emotionally.

"Look, Athena," I said, "if that's the discussion you want to have, I'm willing. But let's call it a night, we're both tired. Will you stay and continue our talk tomorrow?" She opened her eyes and nodded a weary "yes".

"Alright," she said. "Let's talk in the morning."

"Thank you, dear," I said.

After Athena went to her room, I picked up the bottle of scotch from my desk and poured some into my glass. I sat down and stared up at the large oil painting of my father that hung on the wall over my desk. The portrait, painted in 1932, captures an intense, serious young man. At the time, he was the most celebrated scientist in Russia. But under the Stalin regime, he was rarely allowed to travel outside of Russia to share his theories with the world's leading scientists. The communist regime thought his theories would be stolen by the West. I stared at Father, as if looking for him to give me some fatherly advice on how to deal with Athena. But what advice could he really give? He, too, had fathered an only child, me. But, of course, I was a boy and ours was a father / son relationship. A relationship he relished, but had little time for. I was sent to a military academy and learned about the birds and the bees from my fellow cadets and the local town girls.

"You're not going to help me on this one, are you?" I said aloud to him. Then I picked up my scotch and toasted him goodnight.

I poured myself a bit more scotch and walked out to the barn to consult with Pegasus, who was always glad to see me. He rubbed my neck with his nose, snorted, stomped around and then ate an apple out of my hand. It was a ritual I'd performed with him for the last twenty-one years. Whenever I made late nocturnal visits, he knew that I was coming to unburden myself. I would ask him a rhetorical question and he would calm down and stare solemnly at me, acting like he understood the importance of my ruminations. I sat down on a hay bale to drink my scotch, and Pegasus assumed the role of psychologist.

"So Athena wants to discuss my secret life," I said. "That could turn out to be an awkward journey, don't you think?"

It wasn't something parents talked about with their children. Neither side wanted to hear about the private sex lives of the other. But this was different. Athena wanted to know about my values, my code of ethics and what my moral standards were. How did my philosophy of life justify having lovers other than her mother. And I suspected, since she could no longer ask her mother, she wanted to know from me just what kind of relationship that we'd had.

How to tell Athena that I considered love a religion? It was a high-risk quest between two people that involved vulnerability and suffering. An adventure that opened one's senses and emotions to the ultimate levels. Of course, it would seem on the surface that I was just chasing sex. But nothing could be further from the truth.

And in this day and age of instant sexual gratification, sex has become almost a mere sport. Today, the idea of love seems considered quaint, almost foolish – something that just gets in the way of having sex. Romantic love, the real attraction between two people, is lost. But how to explain this to one's daughter? My marriage was certainly unconventional. And I never wanted to teach Athena that she should live her life with the same values that her mother and I did. In her rebellion against us, she had tried to establish a view of life that saw love as a romantic ideal with Mr. Right. Unfortunately, she married the concept, not the man.

Tomorrow would be an interesting talk. One that might end quickly without any resolution. I certainly had no regrets, no confessions about elicit sexual affairs to tell my daughter about. On the contrary, just like her mother, the other women I'd loved had been the most important and life affirming experiences in my life. I only hoped that I could make Athena understand how I loved them and they loved me. I finished my scotch and looked up at Pegasus, who had been keenly watching my deliberations. I stood up and scratched his neck.

"So, what do you think, love," I said. "Will Athena really want to hear what I have to say? "

As I left the barn, I walked past my BSA motorcycle, one of many that I owned over the years. The BSA was a custom replica of the same motorcycle my father rode as a young man when he spent a summer working at the famed Cavendish Lab in Oxford with Ernest Rutherford. When he arrived in England, Father bought himself a second-hand BSA (Birmingham Small Arms) motorcycle to get back and forth from the Cavendish Laboratory and to drive around the countryside. He used to tour the English countryside with Niels Bohr or Edward Teller riding in tandem behind him. Rutherford once warned father to be careful not to kill Bohr and derail the development of quantum physics.

MAKING MOVIES

The next morning, we had a quick cup of coffee and then went horseback riding. When we returned, we ate breakfast in the kitchen and I asked Athena about the funeral. For a long moment she stared at me as if she didn't want to talk about it. Certainly not with me. I told her again that I was sorry for not being there. She sighed and in a flat monotone said, "Max's eulogy was very moving, and Stan actually showed a video. It was film he'd shot of your wedding. Stan brought Paulina Lusk with him, the actress in his new film. Apparently they're engaged."

I almost fell out of my chair.

"Engaged!"

Then right on cue, Britta walked in with the news that while we were out riding, Stan had called to say that he was on the way over.

"Did he say if he was bringing anyone with him?" I asked her.

"A lady friend," Britta answered.

"Do you know anything about Paulina?" I asked Athena.

"Who doesn't," she said. "Her story has become a tabloid headline."

How true, I thought. Three months ago Stan had called from Prague and asked me if I'd heard of Paulina Lusk. She was becoming a movie star in Europe and he'd just cast her as the lead in his new film. Stan told me he wasn't too impressed with her acting skills, but that he needed her in the movie because her name value would secure the financing. A month later, Stan called to tell me that after the first week of rehearsals, he was pleasantly surprised with Paulina's acting. Although, when he told me that they had become romantically involved, I questioned his objectivity.

Athena seemed to perk up a bit at the news that Paulina was coming over with Stan. It momentarily took her mind off her mother's funeral and our father-daughter summit. I heard the dogs barking and looked outside to see Stan's car coming up the drive. Athena and I walked out to the front porch to greet him. It was a crisp sunny day, but it did little to improve our depressive moods. Stan got out of the car and marched up the stairs to the porch and gave me a long silent embrace.

"I'm so sorry," he said.

Then he hugged Athena and stood looking at us both with tears welling up. Stan was a bit overcome with the moment and hadn't introduced Paulina. She walked up the stairs and introduced herself. Paulina was an exotically gorgeous young woman and knew it. She was wearing a short skirt, a sheer silk blouse and enough bracelets on her right arm to start a jewelry store. "Hi, I'm Paulina," she said to me. "Stan has told me so much about you. He talks about you more than he does about himself."

We sat out on the porch and Britta brought out a plate of cheese grapes and almonds. Stan, who knew the house well, walked inside and returned with a bottle of vodka and four glasses. He poured everyone a healthy shot, raised his glass and offered a toast. "May she always be with us."

Stan told a few stories, including the epic tale of my wife appearing in one of his films as an extra, and the time that she had rescued Stan and me when we crashed my jeep in the river. I found myself daydreaming, staring blankly off into space. Stan was such a vivid storyteller that I expected my wife to walk out the front door any second.

Stan told us about the movie that he was shooting with Paulina. It was the first movie he'd shot in hi-definition video.

"I swore I'd never abandon film," he said. "But hi-def is so much cheaper and so much quicker. And I've found I can make it look just as good as film."

"We'll see," said Paulina. "Stan promised me that I would look beautiful in this hi-defy stuff, but is he right?"

"You have to trust him," I said. "Stan's an auteur."

"Yes, but a very fussbudgety one," she said. "He slaves over every detail from the props to the wardrobe."

Paulina's favorite topic was Paulina. For the next half hour she told us about her plans to become a major star in American movies. She was hoping this little "indie" with Stan would get her noticed at Sundance and open up the right doors. I wondered to myself if Athena had the same impression of Paulina as I did: a self-absorbed actress using Stan to advance her career. This was the first time I'd known Stan to get romantically involved with such a shallow women. His first two wives and subsequent longtime lover had all been fascinating women. Smart and worldly - a concert pianist, a doctor and a film editor. By comparison, Paulina was a child who needed constant attention.

After lunch, we all walked out to the barn. Paulina trudged along with us as if she'd been ordered to do chores. Most people usually found something of interest in the barn between the horses, vintage cars, the compression chamber bubble, and the mini-movie theater. But not Paulina. Once inside, she plopped down on a hay bale and talked on her cell phone, ranting about something or other in Czechoslovakian. When she finally got off her cell phone, she wanted to go for a walk and headed out with Athena, leaving me alone with Stan.

"Paulina seems like a lovely gal," I said.

"Yes, my friend, but I know what you're thinking, that I'm just being an old hound dog, right?" Stan knew me too well, that's just what I was thinking.

"Of course not," I said.

"And don't make any references to *Lolita*, he said. "In an odd way she was forced upon me since I had to have her in the movie to get the financing. Then after we'd made the deal and cast her, it almost all fell apart."

"Why?" I asked.

"Well, unbeknownst to me, it turned out that Paulina had a bit of a drug problem."

"Oh my," I said.

"Yep, so the insurance company that was bonding the movie threatened to shut it down unless we paid a bigger premium. They had Paulina submit to urine tests every day during filming. If she tested positive, they'd pull her off the film. When Athena called me about the funeral, I decided to bring Paulina with me so I could keep an eye on her."

"Chaperone by day, lover by night, eh?" I said. "Athena told me it's serious; is this true?"

"You mean could Paulina be my future ex-wife?" Stan said. "I don't think she's interested in marriage. Speaking of relationships, how are things between you and Athena? "

"I'm trying to make peace with her," I said, "but I don't know if she's interested in my attempts at rapprochement."

"Ah yes, rapprochement," Stan said, "a very apt description, like two countries that have been at war trying to re-establish relationships. Of course, the outbreak of this particular war was mostly your fault."

"My fault?"

"You were much too absent during Athena's childhood, and now you've only grown farther apart. You have to make amends or lose her forever."

"How do you suggest I start?"

"You might begin with a simple apology and let her know how much you love her."

"Message received," I said. "But, she also wants to hear about the other women in my life. Or I should say she wants a justification. How do you make anyone, let alone your daughter, understand that?"

"You're the expert on that, not me," Stan said. "My relationships with women have brought me only pain and sorrow. You, on the other hand, have somehow found joy and happiness with women, including a divine wife who really loved you."

"Yes, but I'm not sure how to explain our version of marriage to my daughter. Most people think that if they give up their outside lives and bind themselves together in marriage that they'll find happiness, but they don't."

"You had a true marriage," Stan said.

"I know," I said, "but it's very risky to tell people what I think a true marriage really is– it offends their sensibilities. Our love wasn't exclusive. It wasn't based on strict fidelity, but it was based on honesty."

"As Balzac said, 'Grand passions are as rare as masterpieces' ", Stan said, "and your marriage *was* a masterpiece."

"I thank you for that my friend," I said and gave Stan a hug.

"I'm counting on you to make it right with Athena," Stan said. " You need her in your life."

Stan and Paulina left at nine o'clock and headed to the airport to catch a red eye flight to Honolulu, en route back to Prague.

"The travails of making a movie on a shoestring budget," Stan said.

Right, I thought, a paltry eight million dollar film budget. Maybe a shoe-string budget by Hollywood standards, but a boatload of money to most people. After directing six movies, Stan had yet to have a box office hit. Which meant he'd yet to have a big payday and was by no means a rich, big time film director. In Hollywood, you were only as good as your last picture and "good" was defined by how much money it made. It was not like other professions, where you were rewarded financially as you got better at it with age. Most film directors found it harder to raise money for their films the older they got. I'd always felt Stan was a little envious of my financial success. Even though I never had multi-million dollar budgets like him, I'd managed to parlay hundred-thousand-dollar research grants into inventions, which I'd patented and sold for substantial sums of money. From a return on investment perspective, you could say I'd done much better than Stan. However, many of Stan's movies were artistically brilliant. Works that would stand the test of time.

Athena had perked up a bit with Stan, but once he left, her sullen mood returned. I'm sure much of it had to do with her mother's death. Then there was our situation, we obviously weren't providing each other with much support. Maybe this wasn't the best time to try a heartfelt reconciliation, but I thought if we didn't try now, we might never try.

"So, you want to know about the woman in the wheelchair," I said.

"That and the rest of your life that you kept secret," she said.

"At first, your mother and I had a very conventional marriage," I said. "But after five years, I realized that I could no longer deal with monogamy. I loved my present life but I missed my life as a Bohemian dancer with all its freedoms. Deep down, I wanted the joy of a married man with his family and, also, the freedom of a bachelor. I wondered if this was even possible? Is that possible? Jimmy Carter famously said that he often lusted in his heart, but he implied he never acted out these desires. I think most people would accept that he and his wife, Rosalynn, truly loved each other, even in the presence of his lusting heart. But I cannot accept that if he had indeed carried out a lustful act, he and his wife would immediately stop loving each other. This concept just does not play out for me, and thankfully, it didn't play out for you mother, either. There has never been a day, not even a second, that I ever stopped loving your mother and I am sure her love for me was the same. So over time, my marriage with your mother became somewhat unconventional. We often discussed whether we should try to impose our set of values on you. Ultimately, we decided that we shouldn't; that you should have the freedom to discover your own moral compass without us tipping the scales. We thought our lifestyle might have been unacceptable to your peers and their parents. We worried you might get ostracized. A backlash would be directed at you because your parents were so unconventional. So the irony is that the one of the most important things I've always wanted to share with you, I didn't. In fact the only person I shared that part of my life with, other than your mother, was Stan. I now feel it was the biggest mistake of my life that I didn't share it with you. I am so very sorry."

"And just what is it that you wanted to share with me?" she asked.

"The idea of romantic love," I replied, "about finding real love between a man and a woman that is not necessarily based on fidelity."

"Are you trying to tell me," Athena said, "that a man could love two women simultaneously, or perhaps even more?"

"That is exactly what I am trying to tell you," I said.

"Well, good luck mister, that's a tall order." Athena wasn't making it easy to talk about matters of the heart. I took a drink of scotch and let it warm it's way down. It had a way of diffusing the urge to trade sarcastic retorts with her. "Father, I realize that most men are not strictly monogamous," she said. "But I can't conceive that any wife, my mother included, would happily accept a marriage in which the husband maintains a mistress. I don't see how that could really work."

"There's many examples of it working," I said, "some of them in the public's eye."

"For instance?" she Athena asked.

"President Franklin Delano Roosevelt had a long time mistress," I said, "and there is no evidence that Eleanor loved him any less. Or take Jacqueline Kennedy, it's inconceivable to me that she did not know about JFK's girlfriends while he was in the White House. And Eisenhower's inner circle knew about his mistress, a fact that Mamie Eisenhower also must have known about."

"I don't see how these are examples of wedded bliss."

"Why not?" I asked. "Their marriages lasted."

"Yes, but you're missing the point," she said. "Eleanor Roosevelt was furious when Franklin took a mistress and told him to get rid of her or she'd divorce him. Jacqueline Kennedy was heartbroken by JFK's constant skirt chasing; and by the way, these women certainly weren't loving mistresses, they were mostly one night stands. I don't know much about Eisenhower, his one affair happened while he was overseas, so it was out of sight from Mamie, anyway. The rumor was that Ike had become a bit impotent, so it was more of a platonic than a sexual affair."

"I'm impressed with you knowledge of history," I said.

"I have you to thank for that," Athena replied.

"How so?"

"I was a history minor in college and you paid the tuition," she said. I laughed aloud and it cut the tension a bit.

"You should have tried biology," I said. "Then you'd have a better idea of what I'm talking about."

"Very funny."

"Athena, do you really believe that if the average happily married man could keep a mistress who truly loves him, with the consent of his wife, that he would the turn the offer down? I think the average man, given this offer, would think he had died and gone to heaven."

"I believe that, also," Athena said. "The problem is getting the consent of one's wife. And if a man wants to have a number of mistresses, why get married at all?"

"Well now, that is a very good question," I replied. "I believe that the average, middle-aged bachelor, playing the field, is as miserable a creature as the average, monogamous married man, who must maintain monogamy, or lose everything."

"I not sure about that," Athena said. "But you broke the conventional rules and it certainly seemed to work for you."

"That's because your mother and I had an understanding that our marriage would not be monogamous," I said. "We may not have disclosed every aspect of our lives to each other, but we never kept secrets from each other. Perhaps, part of our secret of success is to always treat each other with respect and discretion. Your mother had only one rule for me: if I must be with other women, then I should really be in love with them and not just use them for pleasure or ego. It may have been a problem in disguise that I've never been able to have sex with a woman without being in love with her."

"So it's not just sex you're after?" Athena asked.

"Of course not," I said "to be in love is an experience way beyond just sex. And when you're in love you're more alive, it gives you more creative energy. It makes you curious and expands your knowledge. For me it's always been my muse."

"And you felt that you could find this romantic love with more than one woman?" she asked.

"Why not?"

"Because isn't it living a lie, a deception?" Athena said.

"But you see there was no deception," I said, "Your mother and I told each other everything. The other women I was with knew that I was married. Some of them even knew your mother and became best friends with her."

"What about all your students," Athena said, "I imagine that they often pursued you."

"I could have had love affairs with students, but didn't," I said. "They say that over 10% of the students at most colleges have affairs with their professors."

Athena said, "Both of my roommates did just that."

"And let me ask you," I said, "did you think they were victims?"

"Victims?"

"Yes, you know, taken advantage of by a professor in a position of power who used his power to make the poor girls submit."

"Are you kidding?" Athena said, "Amber, who was my roommate for two years, could have seduced a fire hydrant. She was a theatre major, and I think she liked to practice her acting techniques on unsuspecting professors. She went through five professors in two years. One in Physics, one in Economics and three in English. She told me she liked the English professors best because they all read her poetry. My other roommate, Vivian, was a different story. She was an intellectual. Her method of seduction was to admire various professors for their minds. These professors were always impressed that such a good looking young woman had such a good grasp of their intellectual theories and Vivian would beg them to teach her more."

"I'll bet it didn't take much begging," I said.

"Practically none," Athena said. "It would start out as intellectual flirtation that quickly lead to romance. Vivian told the professors that making love with them was her way of thanking them for sharing their knowledge with her."

"A win-win situation," I said.

"One professor wanted to leave his wife and marry Vivian. Vivian wasn't at all in love with him. The professor threatened to give her an F if she broke up with him. She went to Greece right after graduation and I got a letter from her telling me that the professor kept emailing that he wanted to come live with her in Greece."

"What did she do?" I asked.

"Changed her email." We both laughed and I realized it was the first time I had heard Athena laugh since she'd been here.

"These days," Athena said, "with all the new sexual harassment rules it would be very risky for a professor to have an affair with a student."

"Actually the new rules make it much safer," I said.

"They do?"

"The new rules require that a professor request permission from a school administrator to have an affair with a student. The school then arranges a third party to grade the student so that if their relationship eventually sours, neither the school nor the professor can be held libel."

"What a dreadful rule," Athena said. "I can't imagine being the father of an eighteen-year-old freshman who finds out that his daughter has received permission to sleep with a fifty-year old professor."

I took the last sip of my vodka and settled back in my chair. "For some reason," I said, "the story about your roommate reminds me of the time I was threatened by a teacher, although the circumstances were quite different." Childhood memories came vividly alive. "As you know, when I was a boy, just twelve years old, my parents enrolled me in a college preparatory school,

Staunton Military Academy. I started in the junior school, sixth and seventh grade, and then I graduated to the Staunton High School, eighth through twelfth grades. My parents persuaded me to go to Staunton by emphasizing that the academy had horses, a shooting range and a swimming pool. My parents were hoping that I would take my academic studies at Staunton more seriously than I had in public school. In the end, I think we both achieved our expectations. All our teachers at Staunton wore military uniforms and they all had a rank. A few of the teachers that had not served in the armed services held a fake rank and wore a fake uniform. The students all wore gray wool uniforms, similar to West Point cadets, with a tie and hat whenever they were out of the dormitory, except when they were doing athletics. I really liked the faculty, especially the tennis coach, the swimming coach and our history teacher. The one teacher who was a real turn-off for me was one of school's fake officers, "Colonel" Taylor, who was our English teacher. For the most part, the academy's faculty were snappy dressers as they tried to set a good example for us cadets. Colonel Taylor was a notable exception. He was sloppy, plump and insufferable. He looked down at us cadets as people he could barely tolerate. Rumors circulated through the school that he had been denied a university teaching position and settled for this present post. I considered him a pompous ass and for the most part just ignored him. During one memorable class while Colonel Taylor was writing on the chalkboard, someone loudly passed gas, eliciting muffled laughter from the cadets. Colonel Taylor demanded to know who was the culprit and threatened to dock the entire class ten demerits unless someone fessed up. We all, of course, knew who the culprit was, but we all held fast. One for all—all for one! In mid-semester, we had our midterm essay to complete. He handed out a sheet on which he documented how many points would be subtracted for any and all infractions in spelling, punctuation and so forth. We had to turn in our essays and he would return them to us the following week. I uncharacteristically worked very hard to obtain a perfect score, since he had bragged to us that he had never given a perfect score to any student and never would. Well, a week after turning in our essays, he walked around the room and returned, as promised, each essay to us students. He made a few general comments and then dismissed the entire class but pointedly asked me to remain behind. I had not received my essay back. He then closed the classroom door and straight away accused me of cheating, saying that no student of my age could write such essay, and he gave me two options. The first, admit that I had cheated and then write a new essay for which he would give me a grade of C. The second option was that if I refused to confess he would give me an F! I chose the second option. He also refused to return my essay. Farting in class is one thing, but accusing me of cheating is quite another. I've never hated anyone else in my life with such intensity. I daydreamed how I could kill him. I thought that rat poison would be a real possibility or pushing him in front of a moving car."

"Isn't killing your instructor because he falsely accused you of cheating a bit extreme?" Athena asked.

"Yes, perhaps, but I was enraged."

"I hope you are not going to tell me that you actually killed this man and you're now confessing this to your daughter?"

"No, no. I didn't kill him, but something almost as bizarre occurred. Our class met three times a week and during our Friday evening mess, our dinner, the commandant came to our table to inform us that Colonel Taylor needed to be out of town for a personal matter for a week. Stories circulated around the academy that the colonel was being disciplined because a number of us cadets had filed complaints about him. His wife, who was also an English teacher, would teach his class. Athena, you cannot imagine in your wildest dreams how excited we all were that a female would be in our dormitory. Our testosterone levels were all at red-alert. Although, given what a slob Colonel Taylor was, we didn't expect his wife to be a beauty. Monday morning we were all in our seats and when the commandant came in with Mrs. Taylor, we all, as protocol demanded stood up at attention next to our desks. She was the most beautiful female we had ever seen. She was absolutely perfect, wearing a lovely flowery summer dress and medium height heels with a smile to kill for. The commandant said 'at ease' and we all sat down. Then as he left, he said, "They're all yours." How we all wished that to be true. She gave us a radiant smile and asked each one of us our name and where we came from. Her husband never knew any of our names and made it clear that he did not care to know any of our names. After doing her roll call, she said that if she could do anything for us, to just ask. Someone in the back of the class in a stage whisper said, "How about your phone number?" We all glared at the cadet. It was the first time I'd seen a woman that I'd longed to touch. We were all in agony. The surprising upshot was the realization that if a slob like her husband could have a woman like her, then that meant that someday we could all have such a wife. She taught our class that Monday, Wednesday and Friday. That Friday, I had an appointment in Charlottesville, so I needed to miss her class as well as parade practice that afternoon.

When I returned that afternoon, the dormitory was empty because the cadets were at parade practice, so I had the dorm to myself. Since the dorm had no women's facilities, and all the cadets were gone, Mrs. Taylor must have decided to take a shower in our facility. As I walked into the bathroom, she was just stepping out of the shower and rubbing her hair dry. She was standing right in front of me. She smiled at me, continued to dry herself off and just ignored me. Other than a few art pictures of nudes my parents had at home I had never seen a nude woman. Never! I backed out of the bathroom and ran down the hallway whooping and hollering like a Banshee. It was the most wonderful experience of my life—how in the world was I so lucky to receive this gift? Well, neither Colonel Taylor nor his wife were ever seen again. The rumor was that the school had fired him. The fact that I was possibly one of the reasons he was fired gave me great pleasure."

"Not to mention the thrill of seeing a woman naked for the first time," Athena said,

"Somehow," I said, "at that moment in the shower, the great hatred that I had for her husband just simply disappeared—just like that. My reasoning was something like—Okay, you have unjustly accused me of cheating, but I have seen your wife in the nude, we are now even. But it was much more than that. Since that time, I have been annoyed with people from time to time, but my ability to hate another human being just disappeared that day in the shower room with my teacher's nude wife. Many years later in college I became fascinated with the biblical story of David and Bathsheba when he first saw her making her bath."

"Mother told me that you named me Athena because Athena was Odysseus's favorite goddess and you admired Odysseus beyond all others. I should be thankful that you did not name me Bathsheba."

"No, my darling, you were and you will always be my warrior Athena, not my Bathsheba.

TIBET

As we sat in the living room nursing our scotch, Athena's cell phone rang, startling both of us.

"Excuse me," she said, and pulled her cell phone out from a sweater pocket to take the call. "Hi. I'm talking with my father," Athena said, "but I'll call you back after we finish up." Athena flipped her cell phone shut. "It was Hank," she said.

"How is Hank?"

"He wants to get back together."

"And you? "

"Not at all." Athena finished off her scotch and set the glass down. She looked worn out from a long day.

"It's late, my dear," I said. "Why don't we continue in the morning?"

"Good idea." As she started up the stairs to her room, I said goodnight.

"Goodnight Father," she replied. Her tone was flat and formal, as if we were two ambassadors from different countries taking a break from negotiating a nuclear arms deal. Maybe we were. What a depressing analogy, I thought. The house was dead quiet, not even a whisper of a breeze from the ocean. I could hear Athena's footsteps in her room above me, pacing, probably talking to Hank, my distant ex-son-in-law. I say "distant" because I only met the man a handful of times. Not model father-in-law behavior on my part. After her divorce, my daughter had branded Hank with her version of the *Scarlet Letter*, a "C" for cheating husband. It was a club for lying philanderers of which Athena included me as a member. Unlike her husband, however, I'd never been a cheater. To be a cheater you actually had to cheat on someone, then usually lie about it to cover it up. Many of our most prominent politicians were quite adept at it. I was trying to get Athena to understand that I hadn't cheated on her mother. Maybe it just wasn't a lifestyle or philosophy that Athena could embrace. And it was easier for her to put me in the same boat as her cheating husband, Hank.

I poured myself another scotch and headed out to the barn to confer with Pegasus. I was something of an insomniac, rarely falling asleep before four in the morning. It was great for creative contemplation, late nights pondering a new invention, writing or just reading. However, in the morning it made me a bit slow on the uptake, which is why all my classes at the university were in the afternoon. Inside the barn, I said hello to Pegasus, but he wasn't in the mood to hear me ruminate. He didn't even want to share an apple. Absent-mindedly I began toying around with a hyperbaric chamber known as a Gamow Bag. I was working on a design to adapt the bag's altitude-lowering principles for use aboard space shuttle flights. The nearby wall was covered with photos from various expeditions I'd taken to the Himalayas. I fixed on one

8x10 photo of me with eight of my students who had gone on a research trip to Everest base camp three many years ago.

Looking at that picture, I thought maybe I'd told Athena a white lie earlier that evening when I said I'd never had a romantic relationship with a student. Although frankly, I'd never thought of the incident in that way. To this day, I still sometimes wonder if it ever really happened. Maybe it had all been a hallucination caused by the altitude in the Himalayas. In the picture, I was standing with seven students next to a very large yak upon which another student is sitting. Beth, the gal sitting on the yak, was strikingly pretty with piercing green eyes and was an engineering major. She loved adventure and was an accomplished kayaker and climber. Standing next to me in the picture was Angela; she had a round angelic face and was an avowed Buddhist. To the right of Angela stood five male engineering majors, the tallest among them my teaching assistant, Ralph. He was a skinny, energetic fellow with a keen intellect. At the end of the line was Nike, who stood out among the rest because she seemed to be in the wrong picture.

The other students were all equipped with slick brand name gear – North Face jackets, top shelf REI backpacks, Oakley sunglasses and hi-tech Gortex hiking boots. Nike, on the other hand, looked like she might be walking down the street in Haight-Ashbury. She had on a plaid flannel shirt, a denim jacket, blue jeans, high-top sneakers and an old canvas backpack that looked like a remnant from World War One. Topping it off, she wore a

Nike,
the champion
high school
basketball player,
experiencing life
in the high
Himalayas.

baseball cap with a ponytail gathered together by a colorful red scrunchy. When she arrived at the airport to embark on the trip I asked her if she'd packed the right gear for the trip. She just nodded yes, without saying a word.

We were on our way to Everest base camp to study the effects of high- altitude physiology. I'd brought along two of the portable Gamow Bags that I'd invented two years earlier. They were now being marketed by Dupont and over the last year had become so popular with climbers that they were now standard equipment on most Everest expeditions. I'd always felt a bit self-conscious that they had named the bag after me. Although, it hadn't hurt my reputation; I was now a brand name in the world of mountaineering.

Until recently, the country of Nepal had been a monarchy. It's perched on the southern flanks of the great Himalayan Mountains. We flew into Kathmandu's Tribhuvan International, the only international airport in Nepal. It's a brick and glass building six kilometers from the city. The moment you walk out of the airport, you're engulfed by an intoxicating mix of energy and color. We had a day to spend in Kathmandu before leaving for the mountains, so I played tour guide and showed everybody around the city. We wound through the streets dotted with Buddhist and Hindu temples: multi-story pagoda-like buildings and stupas adorned with the all-seeing eyes of the Buddha, which seem to gaze in all directions. Angela, our resident Buddhist, wanted to go see Bodhnath, one of the most important Buddhist temples in Nepal. According to legend, the Kathmandu Valley was once a holy lake inhabited by giant serpents, and when the first Buddha threw a lotus seed into the lake, it burst into a thousand-pedaled lotus flower.

"When the Buddha saw the beauty of the flower, he caused the hills to part, draining the lake and forming a valley," Angela said, "so that the lotus would always be protected by a rim of mountains." Strings of prayer flags in five bright colors, each of symbolic significance in Tibetan Buddhism were strung everywhere. "As the flags flutter in the breeze," Angela said, "Buddhists believe that prayers are dispersed across the land and into the cosmos." Ralph closed his eyes as if to meditate and rubbed his stomach. He said that he was trying to disperse his hunger into the cosmos, but it wasn't working. Now there was a universal truth, I thought. Young males are always hungry.

For lunch we had Dal Baht, a traditional Nepalese dish of vegetables with a mild curry, rice and dal, which is like a soup made of mashed lentils and spices mixed with vegetables and rice. The food was delicious. There was hot lemon tea and milk tea and plain boiled water, which tasted rather smoky from sitting on top of a wood stove. The water was taken right from the river and either had to be filtered or boiled or both. After lunch, we drove out to Pashupatinath, a famous Hindu temple located on the banks of the holy Bagmati River. The temple complex was bustling with activity. Worshippers giving their offerings and tending cremation fires, souvenir-sellers hawking their wares and wandering Hindu mystics called Sadhus posing for photographs. The Sadhus wore ochre- colored robes and many had their faces elaborately painted. They had renounced all material and sexual attachments and lived in caves and temples throughout Nepal. Many of them were smoking charas, a handmade hashish. Ralph called it the elixir of the mystical magic tour. "They smoke it to suppress their sexual urges and concentrate only on meditation," Angela said.

That night we stayed at the Vaishali Hotel, a popular spot for climbers on their way to Everest. At the lobby bar we drank bottles of Thongba, a Tibetan beer made from millet. Nicole sat next to me at the bar and we talked about using the technology of my compression bag for endurance training. Being a competitive tri-athlete, she was interested in peak performance. Over the last few years, a number of high-profile athletes had shown up at my lab to test out the chamber. They thought of it as legal blood doping. One Olympic cross-country skier bought one of my compression chambers and squeezed it into the back of his VW camper van. When he was training on location, he would get into the van at night and sleep in the chamber. After her second beer, Nicole told me that she planned to get up early and take a run in the morning before we left. She said that she was going to jog over to the Monkey Temple and run up the steps.

"Want to come with me?" she asked. It was an invitation delivered with a flirtatious undertone.

"No thanks," I said. "We've got a long day tomorrow. Remember, after we get to Lukla we start trekking in the afternoon."

"No worries," Nicole said. "A quick run just gets me warmed up, keeps me in shape." Looking at Nicole's fit, athletically tuned body, it was hard to argue with her about conditioning. I told her that it was fine with me if she went for a run in the morning, but only if she took someone with her. We agreed that the only two who might consider it were Phil or Max, and Nicole slid down the bar and began pitching the idea to Phil. A few minutes later she gave me a big smile and the thumbs-up sign. I walked over and told her and Phil that breakfast was at seven and we left the hotel for the airport at eight. Then I told everyone to listen up and repeated the same information. With that I said goodnight and headed up to my room.

The next morning, everyone sat around the breakfast table eating fried potatoes, porridge with hot milk and Tibetan bread with honey. Nicole and Phil were conspicuously absent. Angela had shared a room with Nicole and said she heard her slip out early. Thirty minutes later, the two appeared in the restaurant, packed and ready to go. Nicole showed us pictures on her digital camera while she woofed down a few chapattis. They had gone to the Buddhist stupa of Swayambhunath, and run up the steep steps to the Monkey Temple.

At the airport, we boarded a Twin Otter 18 seater. The pilots fired up the propellers and off we flew to the small village of Lukla, nestled in the foothills. From Lukla we would begin the 8-day trek to Everest base camp. The flight to Lukla took less than an hour. From the plane we could see the breathtaking Himalaya foothills below. The terrain was so steep that the villagers had to build narrow terraces to farm on. Lukla's tiny landing strip is carved into the rugged foothills. At an elevation of 9,000 feet, it's one of the scariest airstrips in the world and landing there is a white-knuckle experience. At first you have the sensation that you're flying smack into the side of the mountain. At the last minute, you see the landing strip, which looks like it's painted on the steep sloping side of the mountain. Your immediate reaction is "We're going to land there!" I looked at my group of intrepid travelers who now appeared much less intrepid. Angela and Nicole were holding hands tightly. They had their eyes closed and Angela was leading Nicole in a Buddhist chant. Phil was looking out the window wide-eyed, breathing rapidly, trying not to hyperventilate. The rest of the guys were sitting with their heads down staring at their knees, curled up in fetal positions as if to cushion the impact of the landing. Nike was sitting alone in the back, looking calmly out the window, smiling. We hit the airstrip, which ran uphill to help stop the plane on the short runway. After we bounced a few times and came to a stop, some Nepalis came running out and blocked the plane from rolling backwards down the hill. Then they turned the plane around so it faced downhill and was ready to take off after we deplaned.

We went to a local teahouse and everyone went inside except for Angela, who stayed outside to do tai chi. Everybody drank sweet milky tea, while I hired a sherpa named Pemba to be our lead guide. Sherpas are often named after the day they were born.

Pemba means Saturday. He spoke good English, and like most Nepalis, was very friendly. At our next destination, Phadding, Pemba would hire porters. The porters would carry extra luggage and supplies, and each day during the trek go on ahead to set up camp for us. An hour later we were off into the fresh mountain air, trekking downhill across the mountainside to the banks of the Dudh Kosi River. Four hours later we crossed a long swing bridge decorated with prayer flags and arrived at our destination, the village of Phakding. It was an easy first day and gave everybody the chance to get acclimated to the altitude.

We stayed overnight in a guesthouse and were off early the next morning for a long day's trek. Our goal was to reach the village of Namche, a long trek up to 11,300 feet. The students got along well. They were an energetic bunch and no one seemed too affected by the altitude. Angela kept up a running commentary on Tibetan culture. The guys took turns flirting with Nicole, who continually teased them that she could out climb, our run and out trek any of them. The "odd man" out was Nike, who always lagged a bit behind, never socializing with the others. I'd often look back and see her trudging along under her bright red cap, which she wore pulled down so low that her eyes were barley visible, her ponytail rhythmically swinging to and fro. I usually got to know the students well on these trips. I'd learn their goals and aspirations and find ways to excite them about the mysteries of science. Nike, however, remained an enigma.

Each day when we stopped for lunch, someone would give a short presentation on some aspect of high-altitude physiology and then we'd discuss it. There's no better place to study high-altitude sickness than the world's highest peaks. So many climbers make the trek up to Everest that there's a steady supply of victims suffering various degrees of mountain sickness. A virtual mountaintop lab for doctors and scientists like myself.

Climbers call the area above 26,0000 feet "the death zone," and with good reason. Oxygen deprivation can bring on Acute Mountain Sickness (AMS).

As we sat in a circle eating dal baht and chapattis, Phil gave a presentation on high-altitude pulmonary edema (HAPE). He unfolded an anatomy chart on the ground that showed the respiratory system and explained how oxygen deprivation and increased pressure on the pulmonary arteries caused the lungs to fill with fluid. The victim began to drown in their own body fluids.

The only treatment was rapid descent to a lower elevation to raise the victim's atmospheric pressure. But often, the victim was too sick to move. In emergencies like this, putting the victim in a Gamow Bag could artificially raise the atmospheric pressure around him. Phil laid picked Angela as our volunteer victim and slipped her into the bag. We were at an elevation of about 10,000 feet and Nicole pumped the foot pump vigorously to get the pressure inside the bag down to 5,000 feet. The sherpas all found this experiment quite amusing. Phil tried to explain how it worked to Pemba, but he didn't grasp the science involved. I told Pemba to think of it this way – getting in the bag was like going to Lhosha. Pemba smiled broadly, now he got it. Lhosha was a sherpa village down in the valley with an elevation of only 1,500 feet. Pemba told the other sherpas the "joke" and they all laughed.

After lunch we trekked through pine forests until we came to the long rickety suspension bridge that crosses high over the river below and leads into Namache. It was a clear day and from the bridge we got our first look at the snow-covered peaks of Mt. Everest, glistening in the distance. "Chomolungma," Angela said. "That's what the Tibetans call Everest. It means the "mother goddess of the world."

Namache was bustling with activity. It's the main trading center in the Khumbu region and has shops, restaurants, hotels with hot showers, a police checkpoint, a moneychanger and even internet service. It's the last chance to stock up before heading toward Everest. Pemba hired two more sherpas and eight porters. We stayed in a guesthouse, our last night sleeping inside for the rest of the trek. In the morning we enjoyed the luxury of a solar shower, ate breakfast and headed out. The next three, days our routine was pretty much the same. We'd trek till noon, eat lunch and give presentations. The porters would go up ahead and set up camp for the night. By the time we arrived, they had the tents up and were preparing food for dinner. For the most, part the students were exhausted after a day of climbing and trekking. They slept in two-person tents and were often fast asleep by sunset. I slept in an oversized single tent that was some distance from the others. While we slept, a few of the porters stood guard against possible robbers. Outside my tent, I could hear them singing and playing cards throughout the night.

In the morning, a sherpa would bring tea and biscuits along with hot water to your tent. After you washed up, you'd join everyone in the big mess tent for breakfast. On our fifth night, we camped near the village of Pheriche, at an altitude of nearly 14,000 feet. Phil and Angela were having headaches due to the altitude. When I asked Nike how she felt, all I got was "fine." The next morning after breakfast, our plan was to go into Pheriche and visit the small medical clinic. I knew one of the doctors there who specialized in treating high-altitude sickness and he was going to spend time with the students.

We'd just finished breakfast and were about to break camp when a tall Frenchman came scurrying up to our camp. He introduced himself as Henri and told us in halting English that a member of their climbing party had been stricken with severe mountain sickness. He was immobile, vomiting and they feared it was pulmonary edema. By any chance did we have a Gamow Bag.

"This is your lucky day, Henri," Phil said. "Not only do we have a bag, but we have the man who invented it."

Phil nodded toward me. Henri ran over to me and laid a big kiss on my cheek and engulfed me in a bear hug. Their party of six was four miles up the trail. Henri's brother Pierre had grown weak and dizzy and then suddenly collapsed. Henri had hustled ahead hoping to find help. I decided to take a Gamow Bag and follow Henri back to his group. I told the students to wait at our camp and put Ralph in charge. I picked Nicole to come along in case I needed help. She was the strongest trekker in our group and knew how to use the bag. The rest of the students expressed their disappointment that they weren't coming on the rescue mission, but it would be more efficient without them.

Pemba, Nicole and I followed Henri at a brisk pace up the trail. It was steep and we were breathing hard in the thin air. After three grueling, hours we came upon Henri's group. Pierre was in a sleeping bag inside a tent. His skin was blue and he was wheezing and coughing as he gasped for air. Nicole laid out the Gamow Bag and we pulled Pierre out of his sleeping bag. He was a big guy and it was tricky stuffing his limp body inside the compression bag. After we got him zipped inside, I watched through the small plastic window as Nicole worked the pump. We got a reading equivalent to 10,000 feet, but Pierre didn't respond. We kept up the pressure for another 45 minutes with Nicole pumping away steadily. Finally I saw Pierre open his eyes. He looked around dazed and confused at being inside the bag. I got Henri to look in and wave at him. Pierre responded with a slight smile.

It was dark by the time Pemba, Nicole and I arrived back at our camp. The weather had taken a turn for the worse and a dense fog engulfed us. For dinner, we all huddled shoulder-to-shoulder sipping on an endless supply of sweet Nepali tea. I gave a brief account of our rescue mission and then we all retreated to our tents to snuggle up in our warm sleeping bags. There had been rumors of robbers in the vicinity, so the sherpas kept a bright fire burning throughout the night. I had just fallen asleep when I heard my name called just outside my tent. It was a female voice and something told me that Nicole had come for a visit. I unzipped my tent door and was shocked. From the light of the campfire, I could see it was Nike. She was shivering and looked distressed. She ducked inside my tent and told me that she was frightfully cold and asked if she could stay with me. I just stared at her dumbfounded. Suddenly she was unzipping my bag and a moment later she was inside with her arms about me. It took me a moment to realize that she was completely naked. Was I really awake or was this all a dream? Every part of her body was in contact with mine. Her lips were just next to my ear and she kept repeating, "Hold me tight because I am so cold." I tried to tell her that she felt warm as toast but the moment I tried to speak she put her fingers on my lips and said, "Shhhhhhh."

Then her lips were everywhere and she kept saying how she loved me and that we would always be together. Her crotch was on my hipbone and she was gently humping me. My resolve to remain calm had vanished. I'd become wildly aroused and grabbed her bottom with both hands, but she quickly removed them.

"Please don't," she said. When I felt her firm round breasts I got the same response.

"Please don't."

I could feel her full weight lying on top of me. She was light as a feather. I breathed in deeply and she smelled delicious, like sweet incense. Then she slid down my chest, gently kissing my stomach as she went. It made me quiver with warm spasms. She disappeared inside the sleeping bag and slid off my polypro pant legs. Her mouth and hands were just amazing and when I was just ready to climax she gently stopped her caresses only to start up again a moment later. It was tremendous. I had to stifle myself from moaning loudly. And then I exploded. A current of intense pleasure surged through my body from head to toe. A moment later, I heard Nike giggle.

She slid up and whispered in my ear how good I tasted and how much she loved me. Then she started rubbing herself against my hip and came repeatedly in a wave of violent contractions. She collapsed on my chest with her arms around me.

"We should sleep," she whispered.

My mind floated through the pure atmosphere of the Himalayas. Somehow having sex so unexpectedly in such a wild isolated place didn't seem so much a sexual experience, but rather a mystical experience. With our bodies entwined inside my sleeping bag and our nervous systems seemingly meshed together, I fell into a heavy sleep.

The next thing I knew, I was awakened by Pemba outside my tent.

"Chiya and biscuits," he called out to me. I sat up in a panic. How was I going to explain that one of my students was naked in my sleeping bag? But she was gone. Absolutely gone! Was it all just an old man's dream of a beautiful wood nymph? I then noticed that my polypro pants were half off. Pemba returned with a bowl of hot water and soap. I unzipped the tent door and stepped out. I set the bowl of water and soap inside his tent without bothering to use it. I wanted to see Nike and walked briskly across the campsite to the mess tent. Inside, the students were sitting around in a circle eating. I saw an empty spot next to Nike and walked over to her. But as I went to sit down by her, she gave me the slightest nod that told to me once again, "Please don't." Message received. I sat down at the other end of the circle.

The last week of our trek was so abnormal because it was so normal, absolutely normal. We went to Everest Base Camp and then trekked back down. I gave lectures to the students. Nike called me "Professor," but avoided talking to me. And I never once caught her looking at me. It was all bewildering.

When we returned home, I had the students all submit a paper describing their experiences on the trip. I wondered what Nike might have to say. All the students turned in a paper except for Nike, who I never heard from. One afternoon, I saw a girl in a red cap outside the library. Excitedly I hurried over, only to discover that it wasn't her. I never heard from her or saw her again. It was as if she'd vanished. I began to think that maybe Nike was just a hallucination I'd had trekking through the Himalayas.   At high altitudes, climbers often suffer wild hallucinations.   Then a month later, while I was organizing my gear for another expedition, Nike's red elastic hair band fell out of my sleeping bag.

In 1911, one of the world's most famous dancers, Vaslav Nijinsky, performed a ballet entitled Le Spectre de la Rose, in which a young school girl returns from a dance and is full of joy. She sits down on a chair in the center of the stage; the stage is empty except for the chair and a large open picture window. Sitting in the chair, she falls asleep. Suddenly Nijinsky, covered with roses, flies through the window and lands in front of her and asks her to dance. They dance together as if in a dream and then as the music rises in a crescendo, Nijinsky jumps magnificently into the air and again flies out the window. The girl returns to her chair and again falls asleep. She awakens and is puzzled by her vivid "dream." Then she sees a lone rose on the floor and picks it up. It is, of course, a real rose. Just like Nike's red elastic hair band that I found in my sleeping bag so long ago was real.

I suspect Nike was once terribly abused by someone—perhaps her father who had complete control over her as the ultimate authority figure. Or perhaps she had a really abusive boyfriend? Maybe I represented an authority figure and by seducing me she felt the power, if only for that moment, over me and all the other men in her life. But who really knows?

RAGE

Athena asked me if I'd ever broken my rule about love being a prerequisite for sex.

"No," I answered. "However, there were a few times when what I thought was love turned into something else entirely. It made me realize how the heart can be fooled. I once had an experience where sex turned into an act of aggression. Until it happened, I didn't know it was even possible for me to act in such a way."

"What happened?" Athena asked.

"It's something so out of character for me, I really don't like to talk about it. And besides, it doesn't really have anything to do with our discussion about love and relationships."

"Tell me anyway," she said. How did I open this can of worms, I wondered. One reference to a story I never planned on telling Athena, and she was now pestering me like a police detective to divulge the details.

"Look," I said, "this isn't a story about love, it's a story about betrayal and revenge. You won't find it at all enlightening."

"Try me," she said. My daughter the police detective was not giving up. It was beginning to feel like an interrogation.

"You sound like a detective," I said. "You're acting like Peter Falk in Colombo, the sly interrogator."

"But let me assure you," she replied, "whatever you say will NOT be used against you by your daughter."

"Remember 'Love in The Afternoon' with Audrey Hepburn?" I said.

"Sure," Athena said, "I think it's on your top ten list, isn't it? I snuck into the barn one night when you screened it at one of your film parties with Stan. I only saw a little of it, though, because mom spotted me and sent me to bed. It's about a rich, middle-aged playboy, played by Gary Cooper, right?"

"Right," I said, "and he has a romance with a teenage girl, played by Audrey Hepburn. Audrey Hepburn's father is a famous Parisian detective, played by Maurice Chevalier. The detective is investigating the scandalous romantic goings on of our rich playboy. Audrey Hepburn is fascinated with the playboy and reads all about him by sneaking into her father's office and reading his files. She cleverly arranges to meet him on her terms, the playboy that is, and they start a romance. The film really is a comedy with a happy ending, if you consider a teenage girl marrying a middle-aged playboy a happy ending. My story somehow reminds me of 'Love in The Afternoon' because it's also about a young woman who pursues an older man, me. Unlike 'Love in The Afternoon' however, this version, has a decidedly unhappy ending."

"One fall morning a science student named Circe came to my office and asked me if I remembered meeting her. I told her I was sorry, but she didn't look at all familiar. She took a seat and said that it wasn't surprising that I didn't remember her, because she was only ten years old when we first met.

'My father, George Rach is a scientist,' she said, 'and you came to our house to discuss a project with him.'

'George, oh sure,' I said, 'Now I remember. That was a number of years ago.'

'Ten years ago,' she said, 'I was only eleven. We all went out to the horse barn to look at our horses. I was wearing my 4H outfit and you asked me about my 4H project.' Now I remembered her. A little girl with braces and thick glasses. She was still small, barely five foot, with tightly curled brown hair. And she still wears thick glasses, which she constantly took on and off.

We talked about her parents and their horses. She seemed to know a lot about me. Not only my science career, but my study abroad programs. After that first meeting in my office, we met often over the next few weeks and had long conversations about her science studies and about our shared love of horses. There was never any hint of romantic interest between us.

One weekend, Circe invited me to go horseback riding with her family up in the high country. I trailered Pegasus up to the arranged meeting place and Circe was there waiting for me alone. She told me that her mother had gotten sick and her father stayed home with her.

Circe and The Professor on one of
their early morning horseback rides.

Riding our horses, we got caught in a frightful electric thunderstorm, and were both soaked to the bone when we got back to the horse trailers. Circe's clothes were soaked through and she was shivering. She had almost turned blue, she was so cold. I helped her out of her wet clothes and wrapped her in the only dry thing I had, a horse blanket. I closed my eyes to undress her so she didn't think that I was trying to take advantage of her.

'Professor,' she said, 'Why do you have your eyes closed?'

'There is, a lovely Greek myth,' I said, 'about a mortal,

117

Tiresias, who accidentally comes upon Athena bathing in the forest and she immediately renders him blind. And for the rest of his life the last image he ever saw was the beautiful bathing Athena in the nude.'

'Ah,' she said, 'and you wouldn't want the last image you ever saw be little old naked me.'

'No it's a perfectly wonderful image,' I said, 'I'm just not ready to be blind yet.'

Not long after that, Circe dropped into my office and invited me to go horseback riding again. Her parents wouldn't be coming, she told me. It would just be the two of us. We rode our horses through heavily wooded terrain and unlike last time, the weather was beautiful. We stopped at a clearing by a stream and dismounted to eat lunch. I asked Circe if she had a boyfriend.

'No, I've never had one,' she said, 'in fact I'm still a virgin.'

After we got back down the trail and loaded our horses into their trailers, we said good-bye and I walked back to my truck to leave. Suddenly Circe came running after me. She seemed emotionally keyed up about something.

'Can I talk to you?' she asked.

'Sure,' I said. "What's on your mind?" We walked back up the trail a short distance and sat on a wooden bench. She told me that she was getting her own place and was worried about moving out of her parent's house.

'You'll do fine,' I said.

'My real worry is about meeting men,' she said.

'You're a lovely gal,' I said, 'you'll have no trouble finding all the guys you want.' Then she divulged her real fear. Being a virgin, she was terrified about having sex. I was caught off guard by her rather candid admission,

'Sex is the spice of life,' I said. "You just need to get out and experiment.' She gave me an overly dramatic serious look.

'I want to save my virginity for someone special,' she said, 'and not just give it away.'

'That's certainly your choice,' I said. As we walked back down the trail, Circe reached out and held hands with me.

'I'd still like to experiment though, would you help me?'

'Help you?' I said.

'Help me experiment and have an orgasm,' she said.

'And still be a virgin?'

'Yes,' she said.

She pulled me off the trail into the trees and spun around into my arms with her back against my chest. She took my hand and slipped it inside the front of her jeans. She was very aroused. I pulled my hand away and spun her around to face me.

'Circe,' I told her , 'we can't do this, it's not appropriate.'

'So you want me to be a virgin all my life? ' she said, and then gave me kiss on the cheek.

I stopped and took a sip of scotch and looked at Athena.

119

"Surely that's not the end of the story, is it?" Athena said. "What made Circe think that you would do this for her?"

"I don't really know, perhaps since I'd seen her in the nude she thought I was her boyfriend. In any case she came onto me pretty strong," I said. "Maybe I shouldn't continue, I'm not sure this story will help us any. Why don't we call it a night?"

"No, no," Athena said, "now you've got me curious; continue."

I took another drink and tried to figure out just how to continue.

"I think the real reason I enjoyed Circe's company was that we shared a passion for horses. Circe knew everything about horses. She somehow spoke their language and could intuitively tell what a horse was feeling. She showed me things about training our horses that were just amazing. I'll admit, though, it was a bit strange that she wanted me to coach her about her sexuality. But my rationale was that since we weren't really involved sexually, there was no problem."

"It reminds me of Bill Clinton's defense," Athena said.

"Right. And just like it backfired on him, it backfired on me," I said. "Do you remember the faculty Christmas parties that your mother and I had at the house every year?"

"Of course. Mom was always throwing parties at the house. I used to hide at the top of the stairs and listen all night."

"Well, I'd invited Circe and her parents to the Christmas party and your mother wasn't happy about it. She thought I was seeing too much of Circe. I was drinking eggnog and brandy and mingling

120

with the guests when I noticed that Circe was greeting new arrivals at the front door and then leading them over to say hello to me. I thought she was just trying to be helpful. Then I saw your mother wave Circe into the kitchen with one of those "get-the-hell-in-here" gestures. Through the kitchen door, I could see them having a heated argument. Later that night, after the guests had left, your mother was furious. She not only told me that she deeply resented Circe acting as the hostess in our house, but that Circe had confronted her and said that I would leave her because she was too old. I realized that my riding pal was a real witch, the devil incarnate. I apologized to your mother and then sat up all night brooding. I was furious with Circe."

"This story is beginning to sound more like 'Fatal Attraction' than 'Love in The Afternoon,' Athena said.

"Exactly," I said. "The next day I received a voicemail from Circe saying that I should call her as soon as possible. I called the number she left and she told me excitedly that she was house-sitting for one of her parents' friends and I should come over and visit on my way home. She said to come through the ally and go to the back door so the neighbors wouldn't notice. When I left the office that afternoon, I drove past the address she'd given me and then drove the alley in back and parked. As I approached the back door, I could see Circe talking on the phone in the kitchen. She waved at me to come in. When I walked in the door, she held her hand over phone and whispered in my ear that she was talking to her mother. Circe had gotten a job at a real estate company and her new work outfit was an ill fitting pin-stripped paintsuit that clearly looked out of place."

Now that I'd started to tell Athena the story about Circe, all the lurid details were playing in my head. I told Athena I'd get us another scotch and walked out to the kitchen. I'd become agitated by my memory of this experience with Circe. The x-rated version was best kept censored. Especially from one's daughter. I was having a vivid memory of walking up behind Circe as she talked on the phone and putting my arms around her waist. As she talked to her mother, I started to fondle her and she smiled. I started to slowly undress her while she tried to keep up a normal conversation going with her mother. I stripped off her pin-striped gray pantsuit and her silk blouse. Circe was standing naked in her high heels and I rubbed the inside of her thigh and then gently brushed my fingers across her vagina. She was very aroused and told her mother that someone was at the door and she abruptly hung up. She threw her arms around my neck and wrapped her naked legs around my waist. I threw her down on the kitchen floor and in one violent motion entered her. Never in my life had I ever made love to a woman that I so despised. Her head was banging on the hard kitchen floor but she was squealing in pure delight. She climaxed quickly and I told her to get some butter out of the refrigerator. Then I told her to get on her hands and knees and I

122

covered her with butter and penetrated her anus. Every time I thrust myself into her she cried out with a mixture of pleasure and pain. Then I carried her into the bedroom and laid her spread eagle on the bed. I went and found a bottle of Jack Daniels and poured a glass full. Back in the bedroom, I told her to take a big drink, no arguments. She choked down two big gulps, then handed me back the glass. She fell back on the bed and I left.

Before I went back into the study to continue my chat with Athena, I took a deep breath to calm down. Then I pulled the bottle of scotch from the liquor cabinet and filled our glasses. I walked back into my study and handed Athena her glass.

"Where were we?" I said.

"You had just found Circe in the kitchen. She was on the phone talking to her mother and you began to get amorous with her."

"Right," I said. "Except that I was more enraged than amorous, and I forced her down on the kitchen floor. I was being rough and aggressive with her, but she loved it. My rage slowly subsided after I left. I drove over to the university and worked out in the gym. Then I showered changed clothes and went home. A few hours after I got home I received an email from Circe saying it had been the most wonderful experience of her life and she loved me as no other women could ever love me. I emailed her back that I was so disgraced by my behavior, I could never see her again. I said I was so deeply ashamed that I was considering taking my own life."

"Seriously!" Athena said. "You were actually thinking of suicide?"

"Absolutely not." I said. "I was lying through my teeth. And I was secretly pleased that she never knew that I'd acted in a fit of rage, not love. Still, my last encounter with Circe was unacceptable under any circumstances. I realized how rage against a women could lead to an uncontrolled passionate sexual encounter. It was a dark, dangerous impulse."

"You've left me rather speechless," Athena said.

"Believe me," I said. "I understand. Let's call it a night."

LOVE IN THE AFTERNOON

The next morning, I found Athena out on the porch drinking coffee and reading the newspaper. I told her that I had to run into town and grab some paperwork at the university.

"Nice morning for a motorcycle ride," I said.

"Bit chilly isn't it?" she said.

"No, c'mon, a couple of leather jackets and some sunshine and we'll be fine," I said.

"Alright, let's go," she said. We rounded up the necessary jackets, gloves and goggles, then I rolled the Captain America out of the barn and fired it up. Athena hopped on back and off we went. Riding a motorcycle puts you right in the moment, and gliding through the woods and down the coast enveloped in the ocean air is a 3D experience. I'd taken that ride hundreds of times and it never ceased to thrill me.

In town, we rode across the campus to the physics building. I maneuvered the bike down a narrow alleyway in the back of the building to my secret parking spot under a lamp pole. I kept a chain and lock around the pole, which I always used to secure the bike. We walked in the back door to my old lab and went upstairs. Since I'd only recently retired, my office and mailbox were still there. I ran into a few colleagues who gave me sincere hugs and passed on their condolences about my wife. I picked up my mail and grabbed some paperwork from my office. To get back downstairs we took a shortcut through my old lecture hall. I stopped to look around the place that for so many years had been my own private performance space.

It's a wonderful room, a 400-seat theater with a huge stage down in front. There was a full-size retractable movie screen, portable lab sinks, an enormous smart white board and various other state-of-the-art presentation tools. But all I ever really needed was that stage. When I lectured, it was always show time. My hair stood on end before I took the stage. I tried to infuse my students with a passion for discovery. Every one of them had a switch, and if you found a way to turn on that switch you would ignite the boundless creative energies of youth.

"Have a seat," I said to Athena.

She gave me a 'whatever' look and sat down beside me.

"All those years you were growing up you never once came see me teach," I said.

"You never invited me," Athena said.

"Did I need to invite you?"

"Touché," she said. "Actually, I did sneak in once when I was in high school and watched you lecture."

"Really!" I said. "You never said anything. What did you think?"

"You were fantastic. I wanted to tell everyone 'that's my father.'"

"I loved this lecture hall. It was a theater where I presented the ideas of the world's greatest thinkers. For many years I taught a large class on 'Creativity' which gave me a platform to discuss both my past and present inventions and speculate on future inventions. One spring semester, I had a particularly intelligent group of students. They had the highest grade point average of any class I'd ever had. They were a challenging bunch and it was very inspiring. Among them was a girl named Alpha, the smartest student I'd ever taught. Alpha had been a child prodigy. A concert pianist by the age of twelve with a brain hard-wired for math and science. At fifteen, she'd won a national science competition by designing a computerized motion-control program for robots. Elite universities across the country offered her scholarships, but she'd chosen to come here. Alpha told our admissions board that the main reason she chose Santa Cruz was because she was inspired by my research and wanted a chance to study with me."

"That must have scored you some points with the university," Athena said.

"Indeed," I said. "Even the Chancellor with whom I had a running feud over research grants called to give me a proverbial pat on the back, the same back he'd been trying to stab me in for years."

"So, did Alpha live up to her genius billing?"

"At first I wasn't sure about her. The first lecture of the semester, I surveyed the audience, wondering where she was, trying to pick her out." I pointed to the middle of the first row of seats in the auditorium. "It turns out that she always sat right there. But even though I'd seen a picture of her on her application, the first time that I looked at her, I had no idea it was her."

"Why not?" Athena said.

"Well, the girl sitting right in front of me in the front row was totally punked out in full Goth attire. Her hair was three colors: black, pink and some other color not found in nature. She had as much ink as an NBA superstar. Tattoos everywhere, including one ornate dragon that started on her shoulder and ran all the way down her left arm. And piercings with lots of hardware, a nose ring, a lip ring, and earrings too numerous to count. She also had a black motorcycle jacket that I really admired. Alpha had striking good looks with piercingly blue eyes. During my lectures she would listen and occasionally raise her hand. When I called on her she wouldn't actually ask me a question.

Alpha in full Gothic garb on her big
black Harley, ready for any adventure.

She'd always say 'am I to understand correctly that' and then
repeat back to me what I just said in her own words, sometimes
adding her own additional thoughts which were always quite
enlightening. Never in my entire university career had I been so

challenged by a student, let alone a freshman!"

"Of all the students in that class, Alpha was the one student who did not need to come to my office-hour help sessions. But she never missed one. We rarely talked about course material. She probably could have taught the class herself. She'd sit in my office and talk so much that I nicknamed her "chatter box." She liked to pick my brain about the research that went into my various inventions and ask detailed questions about my compression bags. Other times, we'd launch into discussions about whatever was on her mind, from black holes to string theory and even Bobby Fischer's queen sacrifice in what she considered the greatest chess game ever played."

"One day we got into a discussion about her tattoos, which she pointed out had all been designed with layers of symbolism. On her arm she had a tattoo with the traditional Chinese yin / yang symbol of Confucius.

'Are you into Zen?' I asked her.

'Personally, I'm an atheist,' she said, 'But I do find Taoist philosophy quite interesting. For me, this tattoo has two meanings. One is the dual nature of men and women.'

'What's the other?' I asked.

'It's a special relationship I have with someone in my family,' Alpha said, holding up her tattoo again for me to see.

'Let me guess,' I said. 'You have a twin?'

'Believe or it not, you're right. I have a twin sister,' she said.

'An identical twin?'

'Yes, monozygotic twins as we're called. From the same egg.'

'And with the same identical DNA,' I said.

'Yes, but once we came out of the womb, we split into two separate archetypes, symbolized by the yin and yang of my tattoo.'

'And what might those be?' I asked.

'That, you'll have to find out for yourself,' she said. Alpha told me that her twin sister's name was Beta and that she was coming out from LA for a visit the next week. 'May I bring her to class so you can meet her?' she asked.

'By all means,' I said.

"My next lecture was four days later on a rainy Tuesday afternoon. As I took the stage and said hello to everyone, I noticed Alpha front and center, as usual. She was wrapped in a motorcycle poncho and wearing a leather thug cap. Sitting next to her was a girl I assumed was her twin sister. But it was hard to tell because she was wearing a full-length plastic raincoat, pink aviator sunglasses and a big floppy hat with a brim so large that her face was barely visible. After class, I was surrounded by students on stage. I looked around for Alpha, but she and her sister had vanished. Two hours later, they both appeared at my office. They sat down and Alpha introduced me to Beta, who was still wearing her raincoat, sunglasses and big floppy hat. I asked Beta if she was going to school in L.A. and before she had a chance to open her mouth, Alpha answered for her.

'No, my beautiful twin sister is a model. She's on the verge of supermodel fame. Which can only mean that I'm next, right? After all, I'm a carbon copy.' Beta sat calmly in here chair, listening. She looked either bemused or bored, it was hard to tell behind those huge sunglasses. We talked for another fifteen minutes and each time I asked Beta a question, Alpha answered. Alpha rattled on non-stop for twenty minutes about fashion as an art form and then my next appointment showed up. On their way out, Alpha stopped at the door and told me that she was having a luncheon the next day for her friends to meet Beta.

'Could you come by? We'd love to have you,' Alpha said. 'You could just drop by for desert and coffee if you're short on time.' She wrote down her address and handed it to me.

'I'll try to make it,' I said.

'One o'clock,' she said. Almost imperceptivity, Beta wiggled her fingers, waving me a small goodbye. Was she as shy and reserved as she seemed?

'Good day, ladies,' I said, and as they left, I realized that Beta had never said a word the whole time.

"The next day, on my way in to the campus, I decided to drop by Alpha's little soiree for her sister. I'd become captivated by Alpha's brilliance and always enjoyed her company. And I was curious to see if her sister was indeed a carbon copy, having always been interested in the biology of twins. The address of

132

Alpha's house was in Spanish Hills, an affluent, upscale part of town. Arthur lived nearby and I'd been in the neighborhood before. Alpha's place was a beautiful two-story brick house surrounded by elaborately landscaped gardens. As I parked my bike on the street and walked to the front door, I wondered how she managed such lavish accommodations as a college student. Maybe the chancellor had bribed her with extra incentives to sweeten her scholarship offer. I knocked on the huge oak door and a moment later it cracked open to reveal Beta peeking out at me. What a transformation from the girl I'd seen the day before! She looked stunning. She was in full make-up, her soft lips scarlet red, and her sparkling eyes rimmed with eye shadow.

'Good, you're here!' she said. She swung open the door and ushered me inside. For a moment, I was speechless. Beta was wearing a spectacular white wedding dress. It all seemed a bit surreal.

'Is that a wedding dress?' I asked.

'Indeed,' she said. And then spun around gracefully to show it off. 'Do you like it?'

'It's gorgeous,' I said. 'What's the occasion?'

'I design clothing and I made this for my friend who's getting married. We're the same size and I'm trying it on to see how it looks. You're my first critic.'

'It's perfect!' I said. 'You're the next Vera Wang.'

'Thank you,' she said. 'I know Vera, and she'd charge twice

133

what I'm charging for this dress.'

'And what did you charge?' I asked.

'Oh, let's not talk money,' she said. 'It ruins the moment.' Gone was the shy reserved girl, replaced by a poised, gorgeous young woman. She was exquisite, a young Grace Kelly! It felt like an almost mystical experience. As many times as I'd looked at her identical twin sister, Alpha, I'd never found her to be this beautiful. Inside, the house seemed oddly quite, no evidence of a lunch party whatsoever. I wondered if I'd come at the wrong time.

'Where's Alpha ?' I asked.

'She's at her boyfriends house celebrating her 18th birthday,' Beta said.

'That means it's your 18th birthday too,' I said. She gave me a playful smile with a hint of mischief.

'Very good,' she said. 'Alpha told me you were smart.'

'Well happy birthday,' I said.

'Thank you.'

'I take it the lunch gathering was cancelled,' I said. 'I didn't get the memo. But Say hello to Alpha for me and tell her let's all try to get together before you leave.' I handed her the bouquet of flowers that I'd stuffed in my black leather jacket and then started to leave.

Beta opens the door in her wedding dress
and finds an astonished Professor.

'No, please stay,' she said. 'I'm having my own birthday party
and I want you to be my guest. I've made a special desert for the
occasion. My own birthday cake.' I was both surprised and a bit
unnerved! I told her that perhaps it was not a good idea for me to

stay. Beta looked quite hurt by my rejection. She told me that she'd dreamed about making me this dessert ever since her sister told her of me. Then she begged me to stay. How could I refuse? We walked into the dining room and she offered me a seat. On the table was very large slice of chocolate mud pie.

'Chocolate mud pie!' I said. 'How could you possibly know this is my favorite desert in the world?'

'I've done my research quite diligently,' she said.

'Perhaps, but you'd have to be a mind reader to know that I love mud pie.'

'Not really, Alpha and I talk every day and she mentioned that you once said in a lecture about biological cravings that your favorite desert was mud pie.'

'I thought you were a model,' I said, 'not an FBI agent.'

'The pie is very rich,' she said, 'would you like a glass of milk to go with it?'

'Now you ARE reading my mind, I'd love one.' As Beta waltzed gracefully into the kitchen, I noticed the contours of her perfectly shaped body evident under her tight fitting dress. A moment later she returned with a tall cold glass of milk and sat down beside me. I asked her why she didn't have a piece of pie and said she wanted to watch me eat. As I savored each bite, Beta watched me intently. Then suddenly she took the fork from my hand.

'Let me feed you,' she said, and feed me the next bite. I took a hold of her wrist before she picked up another bite.

'That might be enough,' I said.

'Please let me continue,' she said, 'I've fantasized about this moment with you for a long time.' Slowly she feed me two more bites and then I took the fork and feed her. Oddly, I felt very comfortable with her even though she was a complete stranger. And to have a beautiful young woman feed me was quite arousing. We ate the last bite of mud pie and I finished the milk. Beta pushed the plate away and looked me directly in the eyes. Her charm was hypnotic.

'That wasn't so bad was it,' she said, 'Letting me feed you.'

'No it was delicious.'

'I have one more special birthday request,' she said.

'And what is that?' I asked.

'I like you to indulge me in one more fantasy and give me a spanking.' Well, being feed desert by a stranger was one thing, but this was quiet another. I hadn't come here to have sex with her. Over the years a few women had told me their fantasies of being spanked. Supposedly many women shared this particular fantasy which some say is a desire to be tamed by a lover. A young Russian ballerina I'd known told me that when her lover spanked her it made her fell like a naughty girl who was being punished and she found it very arousing. Maybe the person being spanked has all the power because they're giving the orders and their wishes are being fulfilled. But where did one draw the line between consensual love play and sadistic behavior? Some say men are more aroused than women by fantasies of being restrained or spanked. They like giving up their power and being dominated.

'Just indulge me,' Beta said, 'and then you can leave.' I told her I'd give her a spanking but only if I could do it my way.

'It's a deal,' she said. I told her to bend over my lap and hike up her dress. She had a perfectly round, pink hard bottom. I slipped off her panties and gently caressed her silky smooth skin. Then I started spanking her, each time just a bit harder. Beta began to writhe and moan and hug my legs. As I slapped her rosy behind the sixth time she cried out "Oh god, I'm coming," and then she shuddered as I spanked her softly a few more times. She lay blissfully in my lap for a moment. Then she sat up, leaned against my chest and whispered in my ear. 'That was my first sexual experience,' she said.

Then Beta stood up, straightened her dress and brushed her hair back. She told me that her sister had started having sex when she was twelve. 'I was revolted by her addiction to sex,' she said 'and I made a childish vow to die a virgin. Alpha told me that you were the first man she had adored, but didn't want to sleep with. The more Alpha told me how much she adored you the more I wanted to have you. I want you to be my first and only lover.' It was most flattering to hear this from a beautiful young woman. But at the same time I felt that Beta was being overly dramatic.

'I'm flattered,' I said, 'but I must way this is all a little sudden.'

'You don't believe in love at first sight?' she said. Then she gently kissed me and stood up. 'I'm going to have to say goodbye, I have to leave soon to get back to L.A. for a modeling job,' she said.

And with that she gave me a little farewell wave and started up the stairs. It occurred to me that I might never see her again and suddenly I was in no hurry to leave. I heard her running the water for a bath. I walked up the stairs and looked in the bathroom door. It was a lavish marble tiled room with a semi inlayed bathtub in the shape of oyster shell. Beta was filling the tub with bubble bath.

'Can I bathe you?' I asked her. She smiled at me, and then gave me an embrace. Slowly I began to undress her. I unzipped the back of her dress and slid the thin straps off her shoulders. I peeled the dress down to her waist and then she wiggled her hips and it fell to the floor. She unhooked her lacey black bra and dropped it at my feet. Her breasts were superb, round and firm. I reached out and gently traced a curve around her nipple. Beta closed her eyes and opened her mouth and I leaned in and kissed her and she abandoned herself passionately to the kiss. When I put my hands on her naked back her porcelain skin was smoother than silk. She quivered in my arms with small warm spasms. I lifted her up into my arms and then set her down softly into the bubbling bath water. Playfully I dunked her head and she popped back up spitting water at me. Then she splashed at me and I grabbed her arms and we kissed. I washed her feet and soaped her back. Then I took a washcloth and scrubbed her face. She kicked and giggled and it reminded me of bathing a squirming puppy dog.

Screaming, kicking and laughing, Beta receives the scrubbing of her life.

We wrestled playfully and I almost slipped and fell into the water. With her wet hair and freshly scrubbed face, Beta was transformed from glitzy fashion model to the girl next door, freckles and all.

I threw a bundle of towels and a terry cloth robe on the floor. Then I lifted Beta out of the tub and laid her down. After I peeled off my wet clothes I kneeled down beside her and ran my fingers through her wet hair. Our bodies found each other and just seemed to blend together naturally. We didn't say a word, it was like we already knew everything about each other and could feel each other's personalities through our lovemaking. We both seemed to be hearing the same music in our heads and our bodies rocked together to the rhythm. There was no dramatic climax, just a peaceful warm glow that seemed to roll along for eternity. It was like communicating to each other our hearts secrets. Afterward I wrapped her in a robe and she watched me put my clothes back on. She gave me a little kiss on the cheek.

'It felt like we were playing a song together,' she said, 'like we had the same melody in or heads and were moving together with it.'

'Like dancing,' I said.

'Exactly,' she said. 'Right up to the last note.' I dried her hair with a towel and then gave her a hug.

'Now, I'm running late,' she said, 'and it's all your fault.' She gave me that playful smile of hers and I wanted to carry her right into the bedroom. She put her finger on my nose. "Goodbye my love," she said. I started to ask when I'd see her again, but she put her finger on my lips and cut me off.

'Let's just remember this moment for now.' She gave me a soft light kiss and I floated out the door and danced down the stairs doing my best Fred Astaire impression.

As I rode my motorcycle up the coast back to the house, I was out of my mind with happiness. But by the time I got home, my euphoria was replaced by a sense of dread, because I knew the gods would not let me ever see her ever again. I could hardly fathom what had happened, the experience was too magical. All that night and into the early morning I recreated every second I had with Beta and then it struck me. What had I done with her silk panties that I so gently removed? I raced to the hall closet and pulled out my suit jacket. In the pocket I found Beta's silk panties! They were real and thus she must have also been real!

The next day, Alpha was in class sitting in her usual seat, front and center. Later that day she came by my office.

'I thought you were having a lunch party yesterday,' I said, 'where was everyone?' Alpha apologized and told me that the party had been moved to her boyfriend's house.

'Beta told me that you came by the house,' she said, 'did you two enjoy your visit?'

'Yes,' I said, 'most enjoyable.' And left it that, wondering if Beta had told her all the details about our amorous afternoon. Of course, I was dying to ask her about Beta. How long would she be in L.A., where did she live? But I didn't. It was strange. Yesterday, I seemed so familiar with Alpha and Beta was the stranger, and now, it was the other way around. Or maybe it was all just a game between Alpha and Beta; and Beta had seduced me just to show up her sister. So, what should I do? That weekend I couldn't concentrate on a thing. I went sailing with Arthur, but hardly said a word because I was too absorbed thinking about Beta. The weekend came and went and by Monday I was convinced that I would never hear from Beta again. Perhaps our moment in time was only a moment and there would be no more. But the next day, I found a thick hand addressed envelope sent from L. A. sitting in my department mailbox. My heart raced as I opened the letter."

"What did she say?" Athena asked.

"The letter was long and detailed," I said. "And it moved me more than I can express. Beta said that her letter was inspired by "Eugene Onegin," the famous Russian novel written entirely in verse by Pushkin in 1836. I knew Pushkin by heart, since I was brought up on him as a boy. Pushkin was my father's favorite poet and he could recite all two hundred pages of "Eugene Onegin" by memory. The story is about a seventeen year old, bookish country girl, named Tatiana, who writes a love letter to a Russian aristocrat. For the past 150 years, every Russian schoolgirl has been required to memorize Tatiana's letter, whose circumstances were not unlike Beta's today. Although Tatiana was a simple

143

country girl, she devoured French romance novels in which the heroines openly expressed their erotic desires. Beta's is also addicted to modern romance novels and read one or two a day. For Beta, what started out as a simple erotic fantasy resulted in me becoming the love of her life; not unlike Tatiana, who never ceased loving Onegin from that first day she saw him."

"It must be quite a letter," Athena said.

"I left in on the desk in my study," I said. "I'd like you to read it."

"I will," she said. And we said goodnight.

BETA'S LETTER

My Dearest Igor,

  I do hope you do not mind that I call you Igor? I love that name and Alpha thought that it would be OK for me to call you by it. You are and always will, be my "Prince Igor."

  Firstly, I would like to tell you that I am completely and irreversibly in love with you and I will love you for the rest of my life completely and unconditionally. I am committing myself and my love to you not because of the various events that occurred between you and me when we last met, although that is certainly part of it, but it is because I have searched for you since I was a little girl and had only the vaguest idea of what being in love really was. I now know. You are and will always be my

"Knight in Shining Armor" that I dreamed of all my life.

Secondly, I promise you, with all my heart, and on my mother's grave, that I would never ever deceive you. I will love you forever unselfishly and unconditionally. I am fully aware that you must certainly think that Alpha and I had, in fact, deceived you and that you might never be able to forgive us, well, at least to forgive me for this deception? There was, of course, some deception, for which I apologize for, but I promise you it will never happen again. Let me try to explain why I use the phrase "some deception" and I can only hope, and pray, that you will understand and will forgive me. Nothing in my past life, present life and certainly my future life makes sense except in the light that Alpha and I are identical twins and we cannot be understood individually but only as a pair.

We have been called, by scientists who study identical twins, "Yin/Yang" or even "Abel/Cain." Neither metaphor really is very accurate, even as metaphors go. Another group of scientists who studied us when we were little girls considered Alpha to be a dominant left-brained person, rational, masculine, aggressive, whereas I was considered dominant right-brained, intuitive, feminine, passive and yielding. Alpha, geek and nerd that she is, uses the metaphor that we are analogous to the North and South Pole of a bar magnet. A uni-pole bar magnet cannot exist, although Alpha will argue that there are some theoretical exceptions! Because of Alpha's outstanding ability to create and solve very complex mathematical equations in her head and her ability to dominant the game of chess at the highest levels while doing these calculations in her head, we were both thrown into the spotlight—she as a mathematical savant and I as a language savant. When we were ten years old, our mother was suddenly and tragically killed in an auto accident and our father prohibited us from being used as scientific guinea pigs.

My dearest beloved Igor, I am sure you are still puzzled about what any of the above stories have to do with you spanking me on your knee, or of us taking a bath and then me giving my virginity to you on the bathroom floor? Let me further summarize the findings of scientists before their studies on us were discontinued. We both, Alpha and I, have photographic memories, a really terrible term, and we both have total recall. I am a diarist and a reader and I am painfully shy. I have read all the great books from the Great Book series and I write and speak, when I do speak, the three romance languages fluently, French, Spanish and Italian. I am told that my penmanship and grammar are practically flawless. In order to deepen my love for you, as if that was possible, I will learn Russian, since I believe it will bring me closer to you. I am basically modest and I almost never use the word, "I" in a conversation. I was, obviously, neither shy nor modest when you and I were together, as I am not shy or modest when I write in my diaries, really my journals, or in this letter to you and any possible future letters to you. I started writing in my journals at the age of about three and I have filled some dozen notebooks. I have not, generally, recorded specific events, but I have recorded almost every thought I have had since I was three years old until the present time. No one, and I mean no one, has ever read a single word from these diaries. Since I have seen you, I have instructed my attorney, yes I have an attorney, that upon your request to him he would turn over all these diaries to you, along with some pieces of my mother's jewelry. You are free to do with these items as you wish. Alpha, in contrast to myself, virtually never writes and has read only one novel—'Moby Dick'. Her tutor told her, in his frustration about her lack of interest in literature, if she would read 'Moby Dick 'and if she passes an examination prepared by him on 'Moby Dick ' that he would give her a hundred dollars. Since Beta will do almost anything, well anything, for money she sat down and at one sitting read the entire book and made a perfect score on her examination and collected her hundred dollars. She later told me that reading that book was the worst experience of her life! She then challenged her tutor, if he would give her a thousand dollars she would read and pass an examination on 'War and Peace'. The tutor refused the offer. Alpha, on the other hand, devours any and all chess books and mathematical books almost daily. We also differ in handedness. Alpha is a left-handed hooker and I am a right -handed hooker. It implies that the handedness center and the speech center are on the same brain hemisphere, ipsilateral, in contrast to most people where they are located on the opposite hemispheres, contra lateral. In handwriting jargon the hooker's wrist is bent towards the centerline when she writes giving the wrist a hook like appearance. The researchers think that we are completely unique in this aspect?

Ok, here we go. You are not only my first lover, you are the first man I have ever kissed or have been kissed by. Do you remember that it was only after we made love that we kissed and kissed and then kissed even more? I have never had a date with boy or man. Since my one claim to fame is in my modeling career, it is really rather easy to pass myself off as an object with no more of a personality other than a pretty vase. Alpha, on the other hand is a pure ally cat, no disrespect to ally cats. She first attempted to seduce her tutors, sometimes successfully, including one lady tutor. Later, she seduced her motorcycle friends, and the list goes on. Her seductions, as best as I could tell were mostly "one-night stands." She would do anything to get her way and then just lost interest. People who turned down her advances became her life-long enemies. I was never interested in attending any university. In fact, I dropped out of home schooling in the tenth grade! Alpha, on the other hand, had offers and scholarships from all the world's leading universities. She scoured dozens of university's catalogs for interesting professors she could study with and possibly seduce. Your name caught her fancy, so she researched you and she decided to attend your university although it was not a world-class university. Then a miracle occurred. She had only been at your university a few weeks when she started writing me, well emailing me, how much she enjoyed your classes and your office hours and she went on and on. She went so far to use the word love, love his class, love his stories, love his office hours, but not a word about having, or even thinking of having sex with you. Not a single word. I must admit that this one simple fact simply fascinated me and puzzled me and I was sexually excited by this fact. It was about mid-semester when she suggested I visit her at the university to celebrate our 18th birthdays together and she would introduce me to this fabulous professor. I was on my way to L.A. for a modeling gig, so I said I could visit her for a couple of days. As I was flying to our visit I noticed that your name kept coming up in my daily journals—could you be "My Knight in Shining Armor"? My love, I really do not have any obvious vices except one—I am addicted to, if that's the correct term, to reading junk romance novels—sometimes, several a day. You may know, or maybe not, the heroes and the heroines in these novels have a lot of physical contact but they never have any sex, never. So in my fantasies, I would be dressed up to my teeth, and then I would meet this handsome older man who I could cook for, perhaps hand feed him, and after he has rejected all my sexual advances, he would then spank me over his knee as a naughty child, punishing me for my

154

indiscretions. As I grew older I fantasized that I would climax while I was being spanked. I should add that I had started to masturbate quite young, before menses, and I masturbated daily and sometimes several times a day. I loved the feeling it gave me but I was a singularity. My masturbating was just my way of loving myself, plain and simple. My two orgasms with you, well multiple orgasms, were completely off the chart. Now I only think of you while masturbating although I think of you even when I am not masturbating, i.e. I think of you all the time! I cannot sit on a toilet without imagining that you and I are in the throws of love on the bathroom floor just ahead of my toilet. Never in my wildest dreams did I think that this would ever happen to me, ever. As you know, Alpha invited you to our birthday party lunch. I was to prepare lunch because Alpha with all

155

her brains cannot even boil water not to speak of cooking. You did mention apparently in one of your classes that you loved mud pie and so she asked me to make this for you. She also asked me to dress up, "doll yourself up" in contrast to my sister who lives and breaths in motorcycle garb. The only elegant dress I had with me was the wedding dress I'd made, so I wore that. I was pleased that Alpha, apparently, wanted to show me off to you as if to say— this is what I can look like if I wanted to. Somehow, being used as bait excited me. I assumed you would come to us, congratulate us, eat your dessert and then leave. Since she invited her other friends, I just assumed it would just be normal congenial gathering. And then she changed her story, telling me that her other friends were meeting at her boyfriend's house so she abruptly left me alone with you to serve you your dessert. You were obviously uncomfortable being alone with me and attempted to leave. It was then, and only then, that I decided to play out my childhood fantasy—it was now or never. So my love, I really did not deceive you and I was not Alpha's accomplice. Perhaps she had a birthday party planned and at the last minute but decided to have it at her boyfriends house, who knows? It is suspicious that she never told me she even had a boyfriend? I could ask her what really happened but I will not because, firstly, I do not really care, and secondly I would not believe anything she told me. She returned to her home some few minutes before I had to catch my L.A. flight and told me that her party had ended early. She casually asked me if I enjoyed meeting her professor and I answered, 'of course' and I then I left. No matter what, those few hours with you were the most wonderful hours of my life and on top of all of that I also found my lifetime true love. Let me finish with a quote I found in a magazine. "One senses, after finishing 'Byron in Love' that for all his ugly mischief, her hotel now has a room for the consummate romantic as well." My dear love, I have many rooms in my brain, my hotel, and you are now part of each room. I will love you, forever and forever and forever more. I could not, should not, will not ever ask you to love me but, please believe me that my love for you is eternal! I would end my life if you asked me and I would die happy. Please do not let these words scare you—just realize that I am a young girl, a happy girl, a girl on cloud nine, who has just fallen in love. I love you!!!!!

Beta

PS. In my literary studies I did read
Yevgeny Onegin by Alexander Pushkin, and
I was so moved, as I am sure that every
Russian girl student has been moved, for the
past 150 years, by a love letter written by a
simple country girl, Tatyana, to a Russian
aristocrat, Yevgeny Onegin. Her letter
finishes with this final stanza, quoted
below. My love, I wish to learn Russian in
order to be able to recite this letter to you in
Russian, if only in my dreams. Oh my God,
how I love you.

I finish - I tremble to read it through,
With shame and terror my heart sinks low,
But your honour is my guarantee
And to that I entrust my destiny

"On the last page of the letter there was a notecard paper-clipped to the bottom. Beta had made one side of the card up to look like a faux invitation. It read:

'From: Beta

To: Igor

Event: Private Lunch

Where: The Cliff Hotel, Poolside in Room 214

When: Saturday, the 24th at 1PM'

On the other side of the card, she wrote, 'You are the only invited guest, so I'll have to eat alone if you don't show up, You can reach my room through the pool area and PS, please don't tell my sister that I'll be in town.

Your Private Chef, Beta'

MODEL

"That Saturday I rode out to the Cliff Hotel, a beautiful hotel that overlooked the ocean. I wandered through the hotel lobby and found my way out to the pool. A dozen or so hotel guests were lounging by the pool sunning. I found Room 214 and saw that the door was slightly ajar. On the door handle hung a "Do Not Disturb" sign, but someone had crossed out the "Not." I pushed the door open a bit further and saw Beta standing in front of a mirror brushing her hair. The moment I saw her, I became instantly relaxed. She was wearing a simple peasant blouse, Capri pants and had bare feet. No make up. She looked radiant. Beta saw me in the mirror and smiled. She came over to me and we embraced.

'You look hungry,' she said. 'I hope you brought your appetite.'

'I brought all my appetites,' I said.

'Hhhmmm,' she said, and playfully pushed me back onto the bed. Then she stretched out beside me and for the longest time we just stared at each other without saying a word. She asked me if I was ready for lunch and without waiting for an answer jumped up from the bed and darted out of the room. She returned pushing a cart with an array of food and two glasses of white wine. I joined her at a small table by the window table and we ate.

'Are you ready for desert,' she asked.

'I'm still recovering from the mud pie,' I said.

'Fewer calories this time,' she said, and leaned over and kissed me. Then she took my hand and led me back to the bed. We made love gently and then lay together in each other's arms.

"Beta told me that she was born in Madison, Wisconsin. Her father was a lab technician at a local hospital and her mother was a high school teacher. When she and Alpha were three years old, their parents realized that their daughters were extremely gifted. Alpha was fascinated by numbers and could perform calculations in her head for which her parents needed a calculator. Beta meanwhile was reading the classics and had a knack for composing poetry. Alpha completed all her high school courses by the age of fourteen and won a national merit scholarship award. She had scholarship offers from one side of the country to the other, from Stanford to Harvard and back again. Beta, on the other hand, didn't get as much attention for her literary pursuits as Alpha got for her math genius.

"By the time they were fifteen, the two sisters had grown into beautiful young women. Alpha was a brilliant chess player and when she won the state championship, the local newspaper printed a picture of Alpha and Beta celebrating the victory. The picture, captioned "Beauty and Brains Times Two," was seen in newspapers around the country and a talent agent from the Elite modeling agency in New York came calling and told Beta's parents that their daughter had true beauty.

'My father told the agent that I was a smart, cute kid,' Beta said, 'not a model. I never thought that I was beautiful, either. Just a gangly, skinny kid with an ugly front tooth that I'd broken playing football with the boys. Nevertheless, the agent persuaded my parents to let a photographer take some pictures of me and put together a modeling portfolio. The agency loved the pictures and entered me in Elite's Look of Year contest and I won second place. And then things started to happen really fast.'

'I was sent to New York for the summer to live in the agency's townhouse, a chaperoned dormitory for the models. Two girls to each room and we slept in bunk beds. Until the models were eighteen, they weren't supposed to go out alone at night. But I'd sneak out all the time and go to the theatre and art galleries and fell in love with New York.

'During the day, the agency would send me around to fashion magazines and to meetings with top fashion photographers. One day, my agent asked me to run an errand and drop off a contract at the studio of the famous photographer, Randy Mize. When I arrived, he was finishing a photo session with Kate Moss. Everyone was drinking champagne and a Verdi opera was blasting through huge speakers on the floor. I stuck around and watched them finish, then I noticed Kate do a few lines of cocaine and prance off to her limo. I told Randy that I liked the Julian Schnabel painting he had hanging in the studio, and he was surprised I knew of Schnabel. I told him that I also liked Schnabel's films and Randy took a sudden liking to me. We went out for an espresso and he loved the fact that I could carry on an in- depth conversation about modern expressionism. Randy got so excited he said that he wanted to go back up to his studio take some pictures of me. How could I refuse an offer from Randy Mize! So we went back to his studio, I touched up my make-up and he took a series of photos of me posing with his collection of nude sculptures. He loved the pictures and within a week he was using me in high-end fashion shoots for *Vogue* and *Mademoiselle*. Bingo! Against all odds, I made it. I was the new "it" girl, and I decided to drop out of high school and pursue modeling.'

'What did your parents think?' I asked.

'Oh, my father was very disappointed,' Beta said, 'He thought I was wasting my life, unlike my genius twin sister who was using her brains to pursue a worthwhile, honorable career. Little did he know about Alpha's secret life as a sex addicted, wild party girl. Ironically, as a hot model, I was supposed to be the drugged out party girl bedding rock stars and having orgies. Such role reversal! But I'll be the first to admit that modeling is not a very stimulating business.'

'Orgies and rock stars,' I said, 'sounds stimulating.'

'I mean the actual job of modeling,' she said. 'I was never into orgies and rock stars. You spend the day putting on make-up and changing clothes. And you spend all your time with photographers and other models, neither group known for its superior intellect. The other girls were always kidding me because I'd sit around the studio reading Tolstoy and Dostoevsky while they paged through

mindless fashion magazines. We went to the Sahara to shoot
photos for the *Sports Illustrated Swim Suit* issue. I dragged along a
big trunk that was a bit inconvenient to haul around the desert and
Randy asked why I had to bring half my wardrobe, when we were
just shooting bikinis. It wasn't clothes in the trunk, I told him, but
books. That really pissed him off. I realized that for me, modeling
meant freedom.'

'Freedom,' I said.

'Yes, once I was successful and started to make insane amounts
of money and invest it smartly, no one could tell me what to do. I
could pursue my passions, literature and art. And I could travel the
world whenever I pleased. I loved comic books and I found that
being a model was a bit like being a superhero.'

'How so?'

'Well, my job as a model is to fill up the frame, which is just
what a comic book superhero does. Comic books are about a
person who at first is just average, but they're smart and have a
rich fantasy life.'

'And then,' I said, 'they're put into an unbelievable situation
and discover that they have superpowers.'

'Exactly,' Beta said. 'And as models, we use our beauty, our
superpower, which we manipulate in pictures to get the look that
people fantasize about.' Beta told me she needed to catch a plane.
At the door as we kissed good-bye, I could feel her breasts against
my chest and I was almost embarrassed. The women I had so fully

165

known a week ago, I was treating like a virginal daughter. Her last words to me that evening were, 'I will keep in touch.' "

I looked over at Athena, who was listening intently. "I'm sorry dear," I said, "perhaps this is too awkward for you."

"No, please continue" she said, "I want to hear everything."

"After that second meeting," I said, " I received a letter from her every day, without exception, throughout the fall and winter and into the beginning of spring. On Mondays I received three separate envelopes, one letter for each day of the week. Her handwriting was a sculptured script that could have been written by a school mom who taught penmanship to her young students. Her letters were extraordinary. She once wrote a full letter telling how much she loved me while she was sitting on a toilet. When she peed she said she imagined that it was my urine splashing in the toilet! I pictured her sitting on the commode writing on a tablet. She often described in excruciating detail her fantasy of me as she was masturbating-it was beautiful for me to read. She marveled how different the sensation was whether she masturbated right after going to bed or in the middle of the night or just before rising. I bring this up because I vividly remember my freshman English teacher, Professor Ratner, telling our class that when he was in WW II, the soldiers would amuse themselves by imagining pinup girls like Betty Grable and Marilyn Monroe peeing and we all laughed because these pinup girls were beyond having bodily functions, at least in the soldier's imaginations. Beta was my ultimate pinup girl and the fact that she peed and even pooped just made her more magical. She wrote about everything in her childhood, her hopes and her dreams, her first puppy and the first time a school bully made her cry. She wrote one long and full letter about her experience at a butterfly pavilion and the miracle of their bodily transformations. She wrote a poem about walking in slow motion through the Butterfly Pavilion as a shroud of psychedelic colored butterflies fluttered around her. The one thing she never, absolutely never wrote about, or ever talked about, was what would eventually happen to us. She lived only in the present. She never wrote about our future plans, other than what was absolutely necessary in order for us to meet, somewhere throughout the whole world. In three and half months she wrote me over 100 letters and I never wrote her one. I didn't have her mailing address because I never really knew where she was. I'm sure she would have told me, but I guess, I really did not want to know."

"She wrote you 100 letters in a few months?" Athena said.

"Amazing, isn't it?" I said. "There is a mental condition known as hypergraphia in which a person writes and writes and then writes more. Vincent van Gogh was afflicted by it. Doctors call it temporal lobe epilepsy. Perhaps Beta had a touch of that."

"Or perhaps she was just a born diarist," Athena said.

"In any case, there was never any doubt in my mind that I was the love of her life," I said, "and I never dreamed of questioning any of her motives."

"Writing letters is one thing," Athena said. "but traveling the world for secret rendezvous, staying at fancy hotels and eating in exclusive restaurants is another. How did she afford it?"

"I wondered about that myself at first," I said. "You know my boyhood hero had always been the Lone Ranger, but it always bothered me how could he afford his fancy silver saddle and those pearl handled matching silver six guns. Supposedly Tonto had a silver mine that supplied money for their needs."

"No, Father, it was actually the Lone Ranger's uncle, Dan Reid, who had the silver mine."

"The Lone Ranger had an uncle?" I said.

"You don't remember," Athena said. " You're the one who told me all this."

"You're welcome," I said. "Anyway, from all her modeling Beta had become wealthy."

"Beauty has its benefits," Athena said.

"Indeed. Wherever we met in the world I was on my own getting there, but once we were together I was her guest. I felt like Cary Grant!"

"Even Cary Grant would envy that arrangement," Athena said.

"Beta told me that her fantasy was to keep me as a lover. For an old man to keep a young women was pretty common, but for a young women to keep an old man, well, that was really different. It was also a turn-on for me because it is not much of a trick to sleep with a woman if you pay her enough, fur coats or dinners and so on, but for a woman to pay a man, well, that is a rush! As you know, I did a fair amount of traveling when you were young, and nine times out of ten she would find me wherever I was. Several times I had a two-hour layover in Chicago and boom, there she was, to walk me to my next plane. I never had a clue when or where she would appear. She was a master of disguise, some of them quite elaborate, and I often did not recognize her at first glance. In public she never made eye contact with me and in the theater she sat apart. Most people just assumed we were father and his rather plain daughter. It was very handy."

"Did you ever think about sleeping with your real daughter?" Athena asked. I was a bit taken back by the question.

"No, never my dear," I said. "Even as beautiful as you are."

"I think that many a young teenage girl fantasizes about sleeping with their father," she said.

"Did you?" I asked. Athena ignored the question and held up her empty glass.

"Shall we have another?" she said.

"Allow me," I said. I took her glass and got us each another scotch. I returned to find Athena lost in contemplation. I sipped my scotch and wondered if we making any progress.

"Should I continue?" I asked.

"By all means," she said, "I want to hear how it ends. Or maybe it never has."

"A few weeks after Beta had left town," I said, "I emailed her my itinerary, as I promised I would, for my upcoming Christmas trip to Nepal. I had done this particular Christmas trip many times. We would fly to LAX, then stay "overnight" in Bangkok and take a short flight the next day to Katmandu. A few days later I received a surprising letter from Beta that included every possible detail of where I was staying in Katmandu and a detailed description of my teaching schedule as well as the exact route of our trek. In her next letter, she rhetorically asked me if I was wondering how she got all the information on my trip to Nepal. She revealed that she simply called the institute for which I teach and she said she was a potential student and would like to have all the details of the present winter course and they faxed them to her. Then she bought the Nepali trekking guide and memorized our route."

"One smart gal," Athena said.

"Yes, very," I said. "Anyway, the time arrived for me to give my winter course and off I went with my students. When we arrived in Bangkok from LAX, the students went from the airport to downtown Bangkok to stay at a cheaper hotel and to sample the exotic nightlife. As always I stayed at the airport hotel. When I checked in I was hoping to find Beta waiting for me in the lobby. But no such luck. There was only an email from her wishing me a good trek. We spent 10 days in Katmandu where the students were paired up with Nepali families. I spent my time visiting a rinpoche each day. I was interviewing him for material on a documentary I hoped to do with Stan. You know how much I always loved *The Tao of Pooh*?

"Only too well. When I was in grade school you always read it to me and forced me to listen."

"Well, I'm sure it's paid off in the long run," I said. "Here's one that I never shared with you," I said, and picked up my dog-eared copy of *The Tao of Pooh* from a nearby shelf. I opened it and read a passage aloud:

"But sometimes the Knowledge of the scholar is a bit hard to understand because it doesn't seem to match up with our own experience of things. In other words, Knowledge and Experience do not necessarily speak the same language. But isn't the Knowledge that comes from Experience more valuable than the Knowledge that doesn't? It seems fairly obvious that a lot of scholars need to go outside and sniff around, walk through the grass, talk to the animals. That sort of thing." I closed the book, set it down and looked at Athena.

"And I'm sure there's a point to that," she said.

"Oh, profoundly so," I said, " 'Getting outside and sniffing around' was the best advice I'd ever gotten. It became my personal credo. As a professor, you can spend all your time locked up in your ivory tower, thinking you know all about a world you've never even experienced. My trips to Nepal became a transforming experience. Sure, the field tests on my hyperbaric chamber were a great success and I had been embraced by the mountain climbing culture of Nepal. But the real discovery was Nepal itself. I fell in love with the Nepali people and I was captivated by my first hand encounter with Buddhism."

"So, did you ever find Beta in Nepal?" Athena asked.

"After a 10-day trek though the Himalayas along with a 4-day field trip around the Katmandu area, we arrive back in Bangkok. Our flight back to the U.S. was the next morning. The students went off to their hotel with plans to spend one more night on the town. When I checked in at the airport hotel, the receptionist handed me a large bundle of letters tied together with a red ribbon. The letters were obviously not sent by mail, so they must have been hand-delivered. I looked across the lobby area, and next to the inside water fountain, sitting in a huge chair was Beta, grinning from ear to ear. She held up her room key and wiggled it in the air. We both had rooms on the same floor, so I deposited my backpack in my room, washed off two weeks of Nepali road dust and I went to Beta's room. We bundled ourselves in the hotel's white terry cloth bathrobes and went for a swim in their outdoor pool. Back in her, room we ordered food and drinks from room service and ate by candlelight. Under any circumstances this would have been spectacular, but since I'd been camping for the last 10 days and eating only dalbat, a hot shower, swimming with a beautiful women and an elegant dinner was out of this world. That night was everything one could ask for. Beta kissed me gently and we

172

promised to always be there for each other. It was a splendid night.

"The next morning I arose before dawn. I went in the bathroom to dress so as not to disturb Beta. But as I was leaving, she awoke and said she had a parting gift. It was a gorgeous silk shirt and she asked me if I would wear it home. Of course, I said. I went back to my room, packed and then met my students at the airport to fly back home. As we scurried through the airport to board their plane, I noticed the cover of an international fashion magazine on the newsstand. Beta was on the cover and she was wearing a silk shirt that matched the one I was wearing, the very one she gave me that morning!"

Athena finished off her scotch and sets the glass on the desk. "Well, I must say, she's a most interesting women," Athena said. I nodded agreement and finished off my scotch. "Shall we continue tomorrow?" Athena said.

"By all means," I answered.

Athena headed up to her room. I sat back to ponder our ongoing dialogue, our own personal chautauqua. All stories are edited and I decided there was no need to give Athena a detailed account of my amorous encounters with Beta. It was strange enough talking to one's daughter about relations I'd had with various women. And I was being totally candid with her about what I'd felt for these other women. The whole point after all was to try and explain the how it all related to the relationship I had with one particular woman, namely, her mother. But telling these stories brought back vivid memories of that night in Bangkok with Beta. For me, lovemaking always created a new form of communication with one woman. It was like learning a new language and getting to play with a whole new vocabulary.

I thought again about that night in Bangkok with Beta. After we'd finished eating in Beta's room, I poured more champagne. Even though it was December in Thailand, the temperature in Bangkok was in the seventies. Beta looked vibrant and sexy in a sheer wraparound leopard print blouse and purple Thai silk pants. Her hair spilled over her shoulders and gave off an intoxicating lavender scent. When she gently stroked the top of my hand with her fingers, a ripple ran through me. Then she got up from her chair and stood in front of me. She unbuttoned my shirt and peeled it back off my shoulders and gently massaged my neck until all the tension in my body dissolved away. I untied the string that fastened her blouse and it fell open, revealing her naked breasts. She smiled at me, spun around and sat on my lap with her back facing me. She stripped off her blouse and took my hand and put it on her breast. We could see each other in the large mirror on the wall and I watched as my hand caressed her breast. Her naked back brushed lightly against my chest and I could feel her shiver in my arms. Then Beta, my beautiful poet, began to softly recite a verse from Pushkin.

"A magic moment I remember:
I raised my eyes and you were there,
A fleeting vision, the quintessence
Of all that's beautiful and rare."

Beta knew hundreds of poems by heart and often recited them to me. She knew that I was found of Pushkin. I looked through the mirror into her eyes. She smiled at me and continued.

"I pray to mute despair and anguish,
To vain pursuits the world esteems,
Long did I near your soothing accents,
Long did your features haunt my dreams."

Agile like a cat, she twisted around and kissed me. It was like a shot of adrenaline. She turned back and I kissed her neck and her back and ran my fingers through her hair. She looked at me again in the mirror, then recited the next verse:

"Time passed. A rebel storm-blast scattered
The reveries that once were mine
And I forgot your soothing accents,
Your features gracefully divine."

I watched as my hands glide across her breasts with the lightest touch. As my fingers slid over her nipples, they became hard. I ran my hands down her stomach and back up her sides. Beta leaned back against my chest and bent her head back on my shoulder and I buried my face in her neck. She took my hand and rubbed it along her smooth silk pants and then pressed my palm over her groin. She rubbed my fingers firmly against her and in the mirror I saw her close her eyes and moan softly. Moments passed as we swayed back and forth rhythmically, Beta opened her eyes and pulled both my hands around her waist and whispered another verse.

"In dark days of enforced retirement
I gazed upon grey skies above
With no ideals to inspire me,
No one to cry for, live for, love."

With her back against my chest and our faces side by side, I was overwhelmed with desire. "Your feel so warm," she whispered in my ear. She slipped out of her silk pants and now sat totally naked on my lap. She smiled at me into the mirror and she could feel that I was dying to please her. She looked at me in the mirror and I could see she was also yearning to please me. Beta reached back and untied the drawstring on my pants and she almost giggled as we wiggled and pulled to slide off my pants with her sitting on my lap. Then, blissfully, we were both naked. From the open balcony door, a warm sweet breeze drifted across us. I put my hands on her thighs and slid into her from underneath. Beta rose up and down on my lap and in the mirror we could see each other begin to tremble feverishly.

With my hand on her chest I could feel her heart beating strongly and then she let loose with orgasm after orgasm that seemed to pound in unison with her heartbeat. Engulfed in Beta's passion, a wave of intense pleasure coursed through my body. I could feel my nerves tingling and I felt like I was radiating an electric force field. My body seemed like it had no physical borders, I felt momentarily infinite. I wanted this delicious sensation to last forever.

After our climax, we sat shuddering in each other's arms. Then I picked her up and we both spilled onto the bed. I lay on my side, leaned on one elbow and looked into her face. Her eyes were shining as if she was in a trance. She smiled at me and recited the last verse of Pushkin's poem:

"Then came a moment of renaissance,
I looked up - you again are there,
A fleeting vision, the quintessence."

I poured myself a nightcap and went out to the barn. It was almost a full moon and Pegasus was in the mood for company. We shared an apple and then I sat down in front of his stall and looked into those enormous eyes of his.

"You agree that all stories must be edited, don't you?" I said to him. "Otherwise they'd go on forever, wouldn't they?"

Pegasus just looked at me as if to say "Take your time, I'll listen forever."

SNOW CAVES

The next morning, I was sitting at the kitchen table reading the newspaper and chewing a celery stalk when Athena appeared. She grabbed a cup from the cupboard and poured herself some coffee.

"Good morning," I said. "Care for a Bloody Mary?"

"Father! It's nine o'clock in the morning!"

"More accurately, it's exactly five days since your mother passed," I said.

"I'll take one." I poured her a tall Bloody Mary as she sat down at the table. We clinked glasses and somberly sipped the drinks. "Well, what happened after Nepal?" Athena asked.

"Oh my, I don't know that I'm in the mood to continue," I said. Athena took the pitcher of Bloody Mary and filled up my glass.

"C'mon, you can't stop in the middle of the story," she said.

"Rather than repairing our relationship, maybe we're just straining it further," I said. "I'm beginning to wonder if these stories are just making you angrier with me."

"I was angrier at first, but now I feel more confused than angry."

"Confused?"

"About my own notions of love and relationships," Athena said. "Certainly, my love life has been a mess, but my rationale is that

I've never found the right guy. Maybe I don't understand how to be the right woman."

"It always takes two to tango," I said.

"Maybe I'm learning something from how well you tango," she said. "So tell me some more about Beta. What ever happened with you two?"

"Well, a month after returning from Nepal, I was scheduled to give a lecture at the Wilderness Society Convention at Lake Louise in Canada, which is considered the birthplace of Canadian mountaineering. Although I'd sent Beta my itinerary, I didn't expect her to show up since Lake Louise was so remote. Ironically, every step of my trip, there she was. That month's issue of *Conde Nast Magazine* had Beta on the cover. It was an ad for the ski resort in Banff and Beta was the model. She was in a form-fitting one-piece ski outfit that showed off her perfectly shaped body. She had on skis and was perched atop a magnificent mountain peak in the Canadian Rockies. She was wearing a confident expression that seems to say "I'm a daredevil, how about you?" You were ready for James Bond to show up any second and chase her down the mountain. The magazine was everywhere, from the airport newsstand to the hotel gift shop to and lying around coffee tables in the lobby. It was like Beta was watching my every move."

"The convention was at the Chateau Lake Louise, where as a boy I'd stayed many times on summer vacations with my parents. We'd tour the Canadian Rockies on horseback and canoe on Lake

Louise. It was always a delight for me to return. The Lodge is truly spectacular. It was built in 1890 and sits right on the shore of Lake Louise surrounded by majestic mountain peaks. The water in the lake is so brilliantly blue, it seems to glow. My mother told me that the water was so blue because it was distilled from peacock feathers. Father, ever the scientist, however, disputed that theory. He told me that the nearby glaciers grind up limestone into fine glacial silt called rockflour, which flows in the lake and makes for a bright blue glacier lake. By the 1930s Lake Louise became known as the "Hollywood of the North" and over the years all sorts of stars came there to film or vacation, from Douglas Fairbanks to Marylin Monroe.

I arrived a day before my lecture to meet with an old friend, the famous mountaineer, Lars Anderson, who bore a striking resemblance to the actor, Steve McQueen. Lars had guided climbing expeditions all over the world. He'd dragged Hollywood studio chiefs to the summit of Everest and Wall Street executives up the Eiger. Lars had also helped field-test early versions of my compression bag and had since used it many times on his expeditions.

After lunch with Lars, I went to my room and worked on the lecture that I would be giving the following evening. That night there was a benefit party at the Chateau's ballroom hosted by the Wilderness Society. It was a hundred bucks a ticket and featured live music with a fabulous jazz quartet. I dressed up in an outfit I call my western formal wear: a leather sports coat, a bolero tie, my finest cowboy boots , my prize ten gallon cowboy hat and a handmade Concho belt. The ballroom was surprisingly crowded with lots of couples out on the dance floor. I found Lars at the bar and ordered us each a Stoli martini and we talked about his upcoming expedition to Everest. As Lars sipped his martini, I caught him staring at someone on the dance floor.

"Oh my," he said, "my fantasy woman. Isn't that the girl on the cover of this month's *Conde Nast Magazine*? She was so beautiful in that picture, I didn't think she could actually be real."

I looked out on the dance floor and was stunned to see Beta dancing cheek-to-cheek with a dashing young man in a tuxedo. Beta looked fabulous in a backless dress, high heels and a pearl necklace. Was this really happening, I wondered, or had I fallen asleep in my room and caught in the middle of a nightmare? The song ended and as the couples on the dance floor applauded, Beta looked right at us and winked.

"Jesus God," Lars said, " I think she just winked at me. Do you think she knows who I am?" Then Beta walked right toward us. "Let's hope she loves mountain climbers," Lars said to me.

Beta had gone out of her way to keep our relationship secret, in part to protect me from being hounded by the press. I had told no one about our relationship, except for your mother and Stan. As Beta reached the bar, Lars introduced both of us to her.

"Professor," she said, "I've heard so much about you, I had to say hello, it's an honor to meet you." As she shook my hand she pressed a small note into the palm of my hand. "I hope I'm not interrupting," she said.

Lars was crestfallen, he was certain that Beta had come over to say hello to him. "Aren't you the beautiful skier on the cover of Conde Nast this month?" he asked.

"Guilty," Beta said, "but it's all an illusion. I've never skied a day in my life."

"Can we buy you a drink?" Lars asked.

"Sorry," Beta said, "I have to run off to another event, but have a great evening, gentlemen." With that, Beta sashayed out of the ballroom with her tuxedoed escort.

"Wow, she's even more beautiful in person," Lars said.

"Isn't she," I said. I finished off my martini and then peeked at the note that Beta had left me. Was this her bizarre way of saying farewell ?

"Dearest, I've left a package for you at the front desk. Please take a look ASAP – Beta". I said good night to Lars and went to the front desk to retrieve Beta's package. I took it back to my room and opened it. It was a small bundle of letters wrapped in a red ribbon with a small note. I felt a rush of excitement as I opened the note. It read: "Beta requests your presence for a late dinner. Meet her at the sun dial at ten o'clock and come very warmly dressed."

I tried to read over my lecture notes, but couldn't concentrate on a thing. All I could think about was Beta and the guy I saw her with earlier. At 9:30, I dressed as warmly as I could and headed for our rendezvous. I asked the bellman where the sundial was.

"It doesn't work very well at night, sir," he said jokingly.

"Most of them don't," I said. He told me that the sundial was on the path that led down to the lake and I tipped him ten dollars.

"Bundle up, sir," he said. "It's cold out there tonight, barely above zero."

I walked out the front door of the lodge and was greeted by a bitingly frigid wind blowing off the frozen lake. I zipped up my leather coat and headed down a small path that lead to the lake. It was a clear starry night with a good bit of moonlight. After I'd walked about fifty yards, I saw Beta standing by the large sundial. She was wearing a fur-trimmed white ski suit with a fur-lined hood. Illuminated by the moonlight, she looked like an angelic apparition. She greeted me with a hug and gave me a quick kiss. Then without saying a word, she took my hand and led me into the woods. When I asked her where we were going she put her finger over her lips. "Shhh," she whispered, "it's a surprise." For the life of me, I couldn't figure out where she was taking me. The bellman had been right, it was indeed, very cold out, but I was so excited, I didn't notice. We walk through the woods following a snow-covered path. The woods shimmered in the moonlight. After we'd walked about a mile, Beta stopped and pointed to something. At first I saw nothing but snow and then realized that I was looking at a snow cave!

"Our accommodations for the night," Beta said. At first I was speechless and then I thought she must be kidding. "C'mon," she said. "Dinner's waiting." And she started to crawl into the cave. I wedged my way in behind her and found her sitting snuggly inside. She'd turned on a small battery-powered lantern. Blankets and down sleeping bags lay on top of a tarp. It was quite cozy and much warmer. Knowing Beta, I assumed that she'd single handedly built our little wilderness bungalow.

"You built this?" I said.

"No," she said. "I read that there was a workshop at the Wilderness Conference on how to build a snow cave, so I went as an observer and they told me that the cave would remain until the end of the conference. So I just moved in."

"Squatters rights, eh?" I said.

"Exactly," she said, "squat yourself right down." We wiggled out of our clothes and slid into a two-man sleeping bag. Beta opened her backpack and pulled out a bottle of wine along with bread, cheese, grapes and smoked salmon.

"So," I said, "who were you dancing with earlier tonight?"

"You mean Brad?" she said. "He's the male model who was in the skiing photo spread we did for the magazine. He's a ski instructor at Banff. We were all just down the road this week for a launch party. I talked him into dropping in on your party so I could surprise you."

"Brad certainly seemed to be enjoying your company," I said.

185

"Sweetheart, don't worry, he's gay and as you well know, there's only one man that I allow into my sleeping bag." She leaned over and kissed me. I put down my tin cup of wine and kissed her back. She smiled looking into my eyes. We made love, then snuggled up and slept like love birds in our nest. In the morning, Beta managed to slide down inside the bag and I was awaken most pleasantly. Then we hiked back to the lodge, where Beta kissed me goodbye and scampered off to catch a plane.

I met Lars for breakfast back at the lodge.

"Sleep well?" he asked.

"Splendidly," I said.

"That was wild meeting the supermodel last night," Lars said.

"Gorgeous gal," I replied.

"She certainly seemed to admire your work," he said.

"I was surprised she even knew who I was," I said.

"If I see her today," Lars said, "I'm going to talk to her about climbing, see if she wants to go on an expedition someday." I finished my eggs benedict and ordered another cup of coffee. "I looked her up online last night," Lars said. "You know that she's one of the highest paid models in the world? And guess how old she is?"

"Ah," I said, "twenty-three?"

"No," he said, "eighteen! And she's got a twin sister. Supposedly they're both near geniuses."

"Really?" I said, "I've always been fascinated by twins." That night after my lecture, I thanked the Wilderness Society and said that I had a wonderful time. Little did they know how wonderful it had really been."

THE DEEP BLUE SEA

We ate lunch out on the porch and then Athena went up to her room to make a phone call. I wandered into my study and looked through some paperwork. I started to page through some pictures of fan worms that were part of an article I was writing for *Scientific American*. I had to pick out which photos would accompany the article. Athena walked in and looked at the photos, which I'd spread out over my desk.

"They're fan worms," I said.

"Kinda pretty for worms," she said.

"I used them for a study in what I loosely call the 'structure and function' problem. So many colossal mistakes have been made by researchers trying to deduce a biological function based only on knowing its structure." I picked up a book and opened it to the picture of a stegosaurus and showed it to Athena. "For instance," I said, "these large vertical plates on the back of stegosaurs appear to be a fighting weapon to some researchers, but to others they appeared to function as sex magnets to attract females and still others have proposed that they are really just cooling fins. Who knows, really?" I opened a file on my computer that displayed an animated graphic of how fan worms work. "When I first started SCUBA diving I became enchanted with a beautiful creature that is commonly called a fan worm. They belong to the same family as earthworms, but they have long feeding tentacles resembling pedaled flowers."

I picked up one of the pictures from my desk and handed it to Athena.

"They look enormous," she said.

"As big as the palm of your hand," I said. "They live in a cocoon-like tube that functions much like a turtle's shell. When the turtle is undisturbed, the head sticks out of the shell, but is quickly withdrawn into the shell at the slightest threat." The video animation on my computer screen demonstrated what I meant. "What makes the appearance of the fan worm so spectacular," I said, "is that at the head end there are many long beautiful feeding tentacles waving in the water's currents, capturing all kinds of micro sea organisms. As soon a fan worm senses any danger it quickly draws all its tentacles into the protective tube."

"Father, this is all fascinating," Athena said, "but does it have anything to do with the story about Beta?"

"Please dear," I said, "indulge me a moment. I'm getting there. You see, all worms, as well as sea stars, have an uncanny ability to regenerate an entire new organism from a small amputated piece. In one famous case, sea stars were so abundant and such a nuisance that in one harbor the fisherman dredged up tens of thousands of sea stars and chopped them up into little pieces and threw the pieces back into the harbor. Well, the next season the sea star problem was worse then ever because every piece they threw back grew into another sea star. So, this gave me an idea for my experiment with fan worms. On the Hawaiian Island of Kauai, I collected a number of fan worms, chopped them up into little pieces and then observed how the intricacies of the withdrawal response behavior reappeared as they regenerated into a new mature fan worm so that I could connect structure with function."

"But even if you could document the return of a behavior during regeneration," Athena said, "how would you document the structure that was responsible for this behavior?" I gave Athena a big smile.

"Ah, my dear, that's a wonderful question!" I said. I gave her a little hug, not sure how she'd react, hoping she wouldn't recoil. She smiled up at me and it felt wonderful. "I had arranged with a microscopist back home at the university," I said, "that each piece of the fan worm that had exhibited a certain behavior would be placed in a bottle of formaldehyde to trace out the new neural pathways that were apparently responsible for this behavior. Then we could associate a particular behavior with a particular structure. And voila!"

I pointed to a framed picture on the wall. In the picture, a group of grad students and I are standing on the deck of a dive boat. The ocean water is pure blue and white sand beaches carpet the coastline.

"That's off the shore of Kauai with my research team," I said.

"During the mornings we collected our various samples at sea and in the afternoons we worked with them in the laboratory. The marine lab was housed in a funky quonset hut on the beach. It was actually quite a spectacular location if you didn't mind roughing it a bit. I had been at lab for almost a week and hadn't heard from anyone, including Beta, which was a bit unusual. We were working in the lab late one afternoon when a dilapidated taxi drove up and parked out front. I looked out the window and saw the taxi driver walking toward the door carrying a large manila envelope. He knocked and gave the envelope to one of the grad students, who walked over and laid it on my desk. I noticed that the driver got back in his cab and just sat there. A few of the students were curious when I opened the envelope and pulled out a bundle of letters neatly tied together with a red ribbon. I could feel them watching as I opened a note from Beta. It read: 'Go to Kona Beach an hour before sunset and walk north along the beach. The cab driver will take you to the beach.'

"I told the students that I had some visitors in Waimea and would return the next day to the laboratory. I put my lead research assistant in charge until I got back, grabbed my jacket and jumped in the cab. The driver was a native Hawaiian who drove at a maddeningly slow speed. Maybe he thought I wanted to see the sights. After about forty-five minutes, he finally pulled off the road into a small parking lot. Jeeps, vans, trucks and two large motor-homes were packed into the tiny lot. I got out, paid the driver and found a large wood sign that said 'Kona Beach' with an arrow pointing toward the ocean. I scrambled down the path and walked along an empty beach. It was a spectacular day. The sunlight sparkled like diamonds on the breaking waves. A big ripe orange ball of sun was about two hours from setting over the ocean.

"I'd walked for about ten minutes when I saw a big group of people up ahead on the beach. It was a film crew the size of a small army. A fellow with a fancy walkie-talkie approached me. He had an air of authority, as if he was policing the beach.

'Sir', he said, 'this section of the beach is closed for filming. I'm going to have to ask you to go around that way please.' He pointed to a path that was marked off with orange cones laid out in the sand. Then someone hollered up to us from down by the water where they were filming.

'It's Okay, Jimmy, he's with me.'

"I recognized Beta's voice immediately and spotted her standing on the beach wrapped in a robe surrounded by make-up artists and hairstylists. Jimmy suddenly became very hospitable and ushered me over to a canvas chair on the beach.

'Anything I can get you sir?' he asked, 'Water, soda, lemonade, something to eat?'

'Don't worry about me, son,' I said, 'I'm fine.'

"Jimmy shuffled off to guard the perimeter like a good foot soldier and I sat back to watch the magic of filmmaking. I'd been on many film sets before with Stan and discovered that the magic of filmmaking is really more like a tedious construction project. However, in this case, there was a beautiful woman to watch.

"Beta took off her robe and handed it to a wardrobe assistant. She was wearing a skimpy two-piece bikini and she looked very sexy. The director huddled with her, pointing here and there, obviously giving her instructions for the next shot. I figured they must be shooting a TV commercial. A beautiful girl on the beach in a bikini could sell us almost anything. Guaranteed to get our attention. The film crew for this mere thirty-second commercial looked bigger than one's I'd seen on Stan's movie sets. I took a quick head count: besides the director and producer and all their assistants, there were two cinematographers, eight assistant cameramen, a six-man sound crew, a twelve-man lighting crew, two make-up gals, two hairstylists, four wardrobe people, over a dozen grips and electricians, caterers and slews of gophers. There were at least sixty-five people strewn out on the beach to get a shot of a girl in a bikini. Even though the sun was shining, they still had large film lights set up powered by mobile generators. One of the cinematographers had his camera on a big camera crane, ready to swoop down from the sky. After about twenty minutes of prepping, they were finally ready to try a shot. The director called out action and Beta ran through the water. The cameraman rode on a dolly, filming Beta as two guys pushed him across fifty feet of dolly track on the beach. The director sat under a make shift awning, out of the sun, watching the shot on a monitor. He called 'cut' and said, "Perfect, let's do it again". I guess 'perfect' wasn't good enough. Beta looked gorgeous bathed in the setting sun's golden light. Again the director called 'action', and she effortlessly pranced down the beach like a ballerina. On the next shot, the camera swooped in on the camera crane as Beta frolicked in waist-deep water. The camera glided down across the water and came to a stop ten feet in front of her. Beta looked provocatively at the camera and said, 'Hurry, I'll be waiting'. After repeating four takes of the shot, the director hollered out, 'That's a wrap' and the crew all applauded. The wardrobe lady wrapped Beta in a kimono. She waved at me, then ran over and gave me a hug.

'Fancy meeting you here,' she whispered in my ear. After Beta said goodbye to the director and the ad agency people, we took a stroll on the beach.

'That was quite the production,' I said.

Beta said, 'I heard they spent two million dollars on that silly commercial.'

'Two million,' I said, 'and you shot for one day!'

'Two days,' Beta said.

'So only a million a day,' I said.

'Don't be so sarcastic,' she said. 'And anyway, think how much I made.'

'How much?' I asked.

'None of your business,' she said, and put her arm around my waist.

'Two million is more than the entire budget of Stan's last movie,' I said.

'Sweetheart,' she said, 'that's art. We're selling shampoo, which is much more important.'

"We both laughed and then Beta ran up the beach ahead of me. The sun sat perched like a gigantic golden beach ball on the edge of the ocean. It looked like it was about to sink in the water. Beta was twirling through the surf and the mist from the water created prisms of colored light around her. I took off my shoes and ran into the surf after her. She shrieked as I picked her up in my arms and ran with her through the waves. A big wave slapped us from behind and we tumbled onto the beach lying together in each other arms.

'Just like Deborah Kerr and Burt Lancaster in 'Here to Eternity', she said, and gave me a kiss. I was wildly aroused and pulled her tightly to me.

'I wish right here, right now could be eternity,' I said.

'Now, now,' she said, 'this is just an appetizer, the night is young.' She gave me another kiss, jumped up and ran back onto the beach. Amazing, I thought, lying in the surf like Burt Lancaster with a beautiful woman. Beta had a way of making my fantasies all realities. And with her, the realities had a way of turning out better than my fantasies.

"As the sun set, we walked up the beach and took the path back to the road. Then we jumped into Beta's rental jeep and took off.

Beta told me that she'd agreed to shoot this commercial in Hawaii on one condition, that they shoot it on Kauai. As always, her way of arranging a date. We drove to Beta's villa and went up to her suite. 'I'm going to take a shower,' she told me.

'Need company?' I asked.

'No,' she said, 'but look in the closet; I did a little shopping for you.' In the closet I found a Hawaiian shirt, sandals and a Panama hat. Beta emerged from the bedroom wrapped in a Hawaiian-print sarong. We sat on the porch outside the suite and drank tall iced cocktails.

'I've found a place for dinner that you're going to love,' she said.

'I can't wait,' I said. "I'm starving."

'Follow me,' she said, 'our captain awaits.'

'Captain?' I said, following her out the door. We walked down to the Villa's pier and there waiting for us was the Villa's dive boat.

'I've reserved it for the night,' Beta said. The boat's captain ushered us aboard.

'Good evening folks,' he said, 'Captain Orta at your service.' He drove us out to the outer harbor, moored the boat and handed Beta the keys. 'Have a good evening, Miss Beta,' he said. 'I'll see you in the morning.'

Then he jumped into a Zodiac and zoomed off into the night. We were suddenly alone on a forty-foot dive boat, that swayed gently in the evening breeze. Beta brought out a large cooler with two bottles of wine and an exotic spread of lobster, scallops, shrimp and clams. Starved, we sat on the deck in the open air and inhaled the food. Then Beta opened the big equipment locker on the deck.

'Let's go for a dive,' she said. We pulled out facemasks, snorkels and fins, suited up and jumped into the water. The underwater lights from the dive boat illuminated the water below and we could we see fish of every size and color attracted by the bright lights. It was spectacular, like the ocean was our own private aquarium. A huge silvery barracuda approached us and then in an instant darted off into the darkness. Our light attracted some half dozen spectacular manta rays. They weigh up to three thousand pounds and have enormous wing-like fins that stretch twenty-five feet across. The manta rays, always curious about humans, swam right up to us. Illuminated by the underwater lights, they looked like alien spaceships. We spent almost an hour exploring and then swam back to the boat.

Beta and The Professor frolic together with
manta rays and the occasional barracuda.

We scrambled onto the dive deck and stripped down in the
cabin below. Then we wrapped each other in large towels and Beta
tossed seat cushions on the cabin floor. The cabin was tiny, but
compared to the snow cave, it was a palace. We lay down on the

cabin floor. Our love making was again very gentle and we were awake almost to dawn.

The next morning I awoke to the smell of bacon and eggs. I could feel the dive boat rocking gently in the water and outside the sunlight was sparkling on the water. As we sat on the deck finishing breakfast, the Captain pulled up in his Zodiac. He came aboard and then piloted the dive boat back across the bay. Beta flew off to Japan for another job and I went back to my fan worms.

"And what did you find out?" Athena asked.

"About Beta?" I said.

"No, about the fan worms?"

"Well, I made the connection between 'structure and function'. But what I really discovered was that I always needed a muse to stir my imagination".

"I'm beginning to see that," Athena said.

"I'm tired of talking about myself," I said. "Let's get some air and go for a ride."

Athena and her father, The Professor, share a quiet
moment with each other and their horses.

NEW YORK

It was a glorious afternoon with sunshine peeking in on us as we rode up the wooded trail. Athena led us through her favorite stand of giant sequoias. Riding through the towering three-hundred-foot-tall trees was awe-inspiring. At this point, I really didn't know what I was feeling about my talks with Athena. It was such a strange cathartic process grieving for my wife and at the same time telling my daughter about my past life with other women. But of course, Athena was the one who wanted to hear about it. And by now she seemed to have become quite interested. By the time we got back to the house, it was almost dusk. We sat out on the front porch and drank vodka while Britta made us dinner.

"So, when did you see Beta again?" Athena said.

"That next spring. I was invited to give some lectures on Long Island," I said. "Beta contacted me and said she had a surprise for me. She asked if I could come a day early to New York. I said 'yes' and she instructed me to meet her at the conference center at JFK airport." When I arrived at JFK, I found Beta standing at the Sky Bar, sipping a glass of white wine. She looked stunning, like she just steeped off the runway at a fashion show, dressed in haute couture, heels and all. She gave me a kiss and I was the envy of every man in the room. At first I was a bit flustered, because previously in public we had always behaved as total strangers. But

Beta certainly wasn't hiding our relationship this time. There were no disguises, or no father / daughter subterfuge. It was obvious we were lovers.

'We're in New York,' Beta said, 'it's my favorite city in the world and I'm going to take my favorite man in the world out on the town and show off a bit.' Outside, we hopped into Beta's chauffeured stretch limousine. A bottle of Dom Perignon was on ice and Beta poured us each a glass.

'Where to, miss,' the chauffeur asked.

'Sardis, please,' Beta said. I'd heard of Sardis, it was the restaurant where all the theatre people in New York hung out. Beta told me she often went there after seeing Broadway plays and that she had discovered something she'd thought I'd find quite interesting.

'What,' I said, 'that they have real Russian vodka?'

'No darling,' she said, 'but you're close, it is about something Russian.' I had no idea what she was talking about. Henri, the maitre'd of Sardi's, greeted Beta at the door. She introduced me to Henri and he showed us to a reserved table. Sardi's is known for the caricatures of famous actors and artists who adorn the walls of the restaurant. As we walked to our table we passed by sketches of Frank Sinatra, Judy Garland and Arthur Miller. As we were seated, Beta asked the maitre'd if he might tell me the history of the caricatures at Sardi's.

'Certainly, miss,' he said. 'Mr. Sardi had always admired the jazz club Zellis in Paris because the walls were decorated with the caricatures of famous movie stars. In the twenties, Mr. Sardi hired a Russian refugee named Alex Gard to do drawings of Broadway celebrities for this restaurant. He drew the caricatures in exchange for one meal a day.'

'And I reserved this particular booth today,' Beta said, 'because of the caricature on the wall behind us.' I turned to look at the picture and was shocked.

'That's my father!' I said in disbelief.

'That's your father!' the maitre'd said. 'My, my, your father's picture and Einstein's are the only two scientists in the restaurant. It's an honor to meet you.'

'Well, this calls for a toast,' I said. 'Henri, you wouldn't happen to have real Russian vodka in this establishment, would you?'

'But of course we do, and for you Professor, it's on the house.' Henri ordered a bottle of Moskovskaya vodka with a plate of pickles to the table and joined us in a toast. We held our glasses up to the portrait of Father.

'Za vas!' I said. We downed our vodka and Henri refilled our glasses. Then we ordered caviar for lunch and Henri bought us a bottle of champagne.

'What a surprise,' I said.

'Sweetheart,' she said, 'that was just a little treat. I'm saving my real surprise for later.'

"The word must have gotten out that Beta was at Sardi's, because when we walked out the door after lunch, the paparazzi had the place staked out and snapped Beta's picture as we jumped back into the limo. Beta told me that we were just blocks away from the Empire State Building.

'Believe it or not,' she said, 'I've never been to the top.' The limo cruised through Times Square and let us off in front. We took the express elevator to the observation deck on the 86th floor. It was a sunny, clear day and the panoramic view of New York City was breathtaking. Beta scanned the skyline through the observation deck's high-powered binoculars. 'Look, she said, there's where we're headed next, home sweet home.' I looked through the binoculars and could make out Central Park and various buildings on its periphery.

'What am I looking at?' I said.

'The Plaza Hotel,' she said. 'Do you see that French looking palace?'

'I'm not sure,' I said.

'C'mon, let's get a closer look,' she said. 'You'll love the Plaza. But first I have to make an appearance at Bloomingdales.'

'An appearance?' I said.

'Yes, it's for the debut of my couture line of evening wear,' Beta said. 'I have to drop by for a press conference and sign a few autographs.'

The limo pulled up in front of Bloomingdales and a flock of paparazzi snapped pictures and hollered questions as we got out. Bloomingdale's fashion director ushered us inside where a large crowd was waiting for Beta. Huge framed pictures of Beta modeling her new clothing line were on display in the aisles. The fashion director led Beta up onto a small stage and introduced her to the audience who applauded enthusiastically. Beta told the crowd that she had been designing and sewing her own creations since she was twelve; and that it had always been her dream to one day have her own clothing line. Then a model appeared wearing one of Beta's creations, a stunning dress made from layers and layers of sea foam organza. I was quite impressed. Unlike most fashion models and famous actresses who put their names on a label, Beta had actually created everything. After the presentation, Beta mingled with the crowd and signed autographs.

Back on the street we jumped into the limo and drove a few blocks over to New York's famed Plaza Hotel on Fifth Ave. The Plaza Hotel is a place of legend in New York. The twenty-story French Renaissance style chateau looks over The Pond in Central Park. When Donald Trump purchased the Plaza in 1988 for $408 million, he said, 'I haven't purchased a building, I have purchased a masterpiece — the Mona Lisa.' Over the years, everyone from the Winston Churchill to the Beatles stayed there. Truman Capote held his legendary "Black and White Ball" in the Plaza's Grand Ballroom. Dubbed the 'party of the century,' the masquerade ball was considered the social event of the year in New York City and the guest list was a who's who of movie stars, writers and politicians. Rooms started at $700 a night. 'I've booked us a suite that overlooks Central Park,' Beta said. A doorman at the Plaza helped us out of the limo and ushered us into the lobby The concierge waved at Beta as she led me across the lobby straight to elevator. Inside our suite, fresh flowers were everywhere and chilled champagne was already opened. Beta poured me a glass and said it was time to change into our evening wear. When I gave her a quizzical look, she pointed to the couch. A tuxedo was draped over the armrest.

'I had it tailor-made exactly to your size,' she said. I poured us each some more champagne and went into the bathroom to slip into my new tux. Beta emerged from the bedroom wearing a strapless evening gown.

'We have just enough time for an early evening ride through the park,' she said. 'Our carriage awaits.'

'Carriage?' I said, as I followed her out the door. Outside the front lobby, a horse-drawn carriage was waiting at the curb. We rode around the pond behind the Plaza and through Central Park, stopping to ride the carousel and to watch people race model sailboats in the lake. Then Beta had a sidewalk artist paint a portrait of us sitting in the carriage. After the carriage dropped us back at the Plaza, we walked two blocks down to the Russian Tea Room.

'I thought the Tea Room might be the right place to stop before the ballet,' Beta said.

'Excellent choice,' I said. I told Beta that during my days as a ballet dancer in New York, I'd been to the Russian Tea Room a number of times with my dance mentor, Leon Fokine. The Tea Room had been built in the mid-twenties by former members of the Russian Imperial Ballet and Fokine knew many of them personally. Fokine's uncle had choreographed Nijinsky's legendary first ballet performed in St. Petersburg at the Maryisnky Theatre in 1907. Leon was the son of the world famous ballerina, Alexandra Fedorova, who had been a mistress to a relative of

Nicholas II, the last Czar of Russia, and had lived a privileged life amidst the nobility of Russian high society. Leon was raised in the court of the Czar, where he inherited an aristocratic elegance and sophistication that was conveyed by his every move and gesture. In the 1940s, he came to New York and started a small dance company. It was as if destiny had brought the Jedi master of Russian ballet to the United States and plunked him right down in front of me at the exact moment when I wanted to become a dancer. He was a master at teaching the technical skills of ballet. I found in Fokine a Russian soul mate, and he became a mentor to whom I could devote myself. I took a part- time job as a grease monkey to support myself and spent every other waking hour studying ballet. By nineteen, I had been studying dance seriously for three years. I funneled the wild adrenaline of youth into the rigorous discipline of ballet. And Fokine was a strict disciplinarian. There was an elegant, old world formality to his teaching style. For each class, Fokine would arrive in a tuxedo. Then halfway through the lesson he'd remove his tie and jacket with a flourish and continue teaching. He was an exacting taskmaster and expected perfection from us.

Leon Fokine,
founder and director of the
National Ballet Company.

Beta and I left the Russian Tea room and walked over to Lincoln Center to see Swan Lake. I'd seen the great Russian ballet dancer, Igor Youskevitch, perform Swan Lake here over forty years ago. The night before that performance, I'd met Youskevitch at a party at Fokine's apartment. I was impressed by his warmth and artistic passion. When I watched him perform Swan Lake, I marveled at his artistry. When the curtain went up at Lincoln Center, I got goose bumps. I wanted to be out on that stage once again and feel my body respond fluidly and effortlessly to the music. The ballet dancers performed magnificently. Perhaps the lead could not quite execute a perfect pas de deux like the great Yousekvitch, but very few ever could. Igor was so strong and athletic, that when he leapt into the air, one thought that he might never return to the stage. Using her cache as a celebrity, Beta got us backstage after the performance. The dancers greeted me warmly and had me tell them stories of working with the legendary Fokine, and about seeing Youskevitch perform Swan Lake on this very stage. It was a magical night.

"We caught a cab back to the Plaza. I couldn't stop talking about ballet and what an amazing night that Beta had arranged. I wanted to stop at the Oak Room Bar for a nightcap, but Beta said we had to go to up to our suite.

'Remember, love,' she said, 'I have a surprise for you.'

'I thought the surprise was our evening at the ballet,' I said.

'Come along,' she said. 'We'll dance in our room.' Inside the suite, Beta led me to the couch. Two gift-wrapped boxes sat on the coffee table and she handed one of them to me. 'Open it,' she said.

"Inside the box, I found a pair of royal blue silk pajamas and a matching silk robe. Beta opened her box and pulled out a matching set of silk nightwear. She threw my robe and pajamas over her shoulder, took me by the hand and led into enormous spa-like bathroom. We undressed and washed each other's naked bodies in the shower, then slipped into our silk pajamas and robes. Beta lit the candles on the dining table in the living room and as if on cue, a bellman arrived and served us dinner and champagne. I was dying to know what Beta's surprise for me was … being treated royally like a king was already more than I'd imagined. But why rush things, I thought. I was loving every second. Why should I be in a hurry for this to end? After dinner, we went into the bedroom and lay on the bed drinking champagne.

'Do you remember the night we spent in the snow cave?' Beta asked me.

'Of course,' I said, 'how could I ever forget that! Especially the way you said goodbye.' Beta unbuttoned her pajama top and lightly tapped a finger on her naked stomach.

'Kiss me here,' she said. I gladly obliged and she took my head in her hands held it against stomach. 'Do you hear anything?' she asked. For a moment I didn't understand. 'Perhaps the sound of OUR baby?' she said. I sat up and looked at her. She took me in her arms and kissed me.

'I can't believe it,' I said. 'It's beyond my wildest dreams!'

'I'm going to quit modeling to have the baby,' she said. It was all rushing at me so fast, I was barely thinking about the future. 'You don't have to worry about a thing,' she said. 'I'll take care of everything.'

"So, this was her surprise and what a surprise it was! The next morning as I headed off to my appointment on Long Island, I opened a note she'd tucked into my briefcase. She said she would write and tell me her every thought on bearing our child, being a mother and sharing it all together. And those were the last words that I ever heard from her."

"She never wrote you another word, " Athena said, " But why?"

"A few days later I received a late-night phone call from my dean informing me that one of my former students, Alpha, had been killed in a car accident in L.A. by a drunk driver. He wanted me to tell her fellow students the news. I asked the dean if she was alone, and he said no." I put my head in my hands, trying to suppress my tears, but I was overcome and sobbed.

"Beta was in the car with her?" Athena said.

"Yes. Thank heavens they both died instantly. 'Thank heavens' hah! What kind of god could ever allow such a horrendous thing to happen?"

Athena reached over and put a comforting hand on my shoulder.

"The pain was overwhelming and I was alone in my grief.

212

Every memory of her was too painful. The next day, I burned Beta's letters and the silk shirt she'd given me. The only thing I saved was the very first letter she sent me."

"But the memory obviously remains," Athena said. "How else could you have spent the last week recounting it?" For a moment, I stared intently into my daughter's eyes.

"Until now," I said, "I've never spoken to anyone about this."

THE LADY IN THE WHEELCHAIR

I went out sailing early the next morning. On the way in, I saw Athena walking across our large lawn that leads to the cliff overlooking the ocean. I waved at her and she saw me and waved back. I realized that I hadn't even told her about the 'girl in the wheelchair' yet. When I got back up the house, Britta told me that Athena had gone horseback riding. I spent the afternoon sitting on the porch reading a new biography of Darwin. By the time Athena returned, it was early evening. I grilled some game hens and made wild rice and we sat out on the porch and ate.

Beautiful Santa Cruz Bay, as seen at sunset
from The Professor's front porch.

"Now," I said, "do you still wish to know about the lady in the wheel- chair?" Athena nodded.

"It had been almost two years since Beta's fatal accident," I said. "I never allowed myself to think about it. I fell back into my routine at the university, teaching my class, writing and bickering with the administration. In an odd way, I felt content. All the important things in my life had happened - your mother, you, Beta and my inventions. I could now retire to a life of reflection. But it turned out to be the calm before the storm."

"One afternoon, I received a call from a young woman named Artemis who told me she had read about my inventions in the field of bioengineering. She was an amputee and a spinal cord patient. She wanted to meet me to discuss a design she had for a possible new prosthetic device. It sounded intriguing, so I invited her to sit in on my class the next day and said we could meet afterwards. The next day, she didn't show up at my class and I didn't give it another thought. I was back in my office working on the computer when I heard a tapping noise on the door."

'Come in,' I said. The door swung open and an exotic woman in a wheel chair rolled into the office. It was love at first sight. She had a dazzling smile that radiated like a hypnotic force field. I was lost in an instant.

'I'm sorry for missing your class,' she said, 'but I got lost in the engineering building.' She pulled out a large binder from a

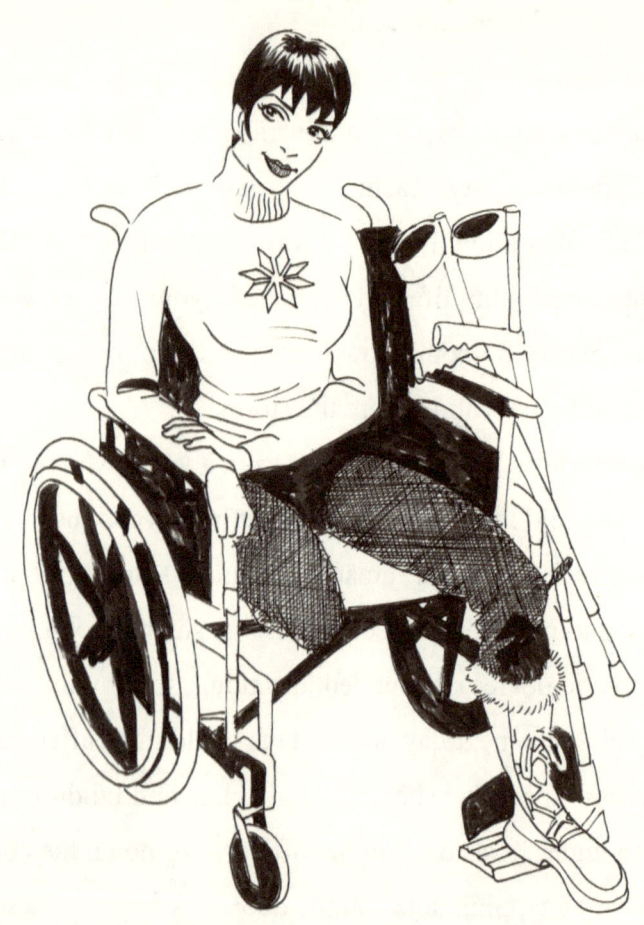

Artemis demonstrates her drop-dead and enchanting smile.

saddlebag on her wheelchair and opened it up on my desk. Inside were sketches of an energy return crutch.

She wasted no time on small talk and got right to the point. 'I want you to help me design the prototype for this device,' she said. I paged through the diagrams and read over the descriptions of how the device functioned.

'Your design is quite ingenious,' I said.

'Thank you,' she said. 'I hoped you'd like it.'

'I do,' I said, 'but it would take considerable research and engineering to make a prototype and get a patent.' She gave me that dazzling smile again.

'I know,' she said. 'So when do we start?'

'Have you thought of the expense,' I said. 'To do all this will cost a good bit of money.'

'I'll pay for everything,' she said. 'So do we have a deal?'

And without giving it another thought, I said, 'It's a deal.'

'Fabulous,' she said. "Let's go to lunch and celebrate our new business partnership.'

"Sounds like you were enchanted from the start," Athena said.

"Oh, I was. She was so vivacious it was overwhelming. She had the charm of a movie star and it reminded of me how as a boy I use to fall instantly in love with my favorite screen goddesses. And even though she was sitting right in front of me, she seemed as unattainable as a Hollywood starlet. We went to lunch and she ordered champagne and we toasted our new business partnership. She had rented a house near the university and was going to form a company for our new venture."

'Here's to success, partner,' she said. As we shook hands, she looked at me with the most penetrating eyes I'd ever seen."

I told Athena that Artemis wanted to build a spring into the crutch that would help propel a person forward. "Like flubber in the movies," Athena said.

"In a way, yes."

"This reminds me of the amputee mountain climber you worked with," Athena said.

"Hugh Herr," I said. " Hugh was a double below-the-knee amputee. When he was seventeen, he lost both feet in a mountaineering accident. While he was still in rehab, he designed rock climbing feet for himself so that he could continue climbing. He built different kinds of feet for specific rock types."

"Amazing," Athena said. I told Athena that in my bioengineering class, I used to demonstrate that the human foot is not naturally made for running, but rather for walking.

"Humans can eventually out-walk almost any animal," I said. "But a human's feet and legs are short and heavy which makes them less suitable for running. With their heavy legs and big flat feet, humans are "plantigrade" like a bear, instead of "digigrade," like a horse or a dog.

Hugh and I worked together designing a prosthetic foot for running. In the machine shop, I crafted steel leaf springs that could be inserted into the prosthetic foot, which would allow it to function like the energy return system of a horse. A horse has what is called springing ligaments. When a horse is running its hoof impacts the ground and compresses its spring-like ligaments that store energy. As the horse's center of gravity goes over the leg, the spring un-compresses and releases its energy propelling the horse forward."

The wind began blowing things around the porch. I grabbed the bottle of wine and Athena followed me inside to my office. I showed Athena a picture of Artemis balancing herself on her one foot while holding her crutches in the air.

"Such a pretty girl," Athena said. "How sad she lost her leg."

"Artemis hated it when people made that comment," I said.

"What do you mean?" Athena asked.

"She didn't want people to pity her because of her handicap," I said. "When people told her it was a pity she'd lost her leg because she was so pretty, she would fire back, 'Should only ugly people be handicapped? Would it have been better for me if I wasn't pretty?' But she was used to people being turned off by her handicap."

"Obviously you weren't," Athena said.

"You're right," I said. "After all, my first girlfriend was confined to a wheelchair with polio. But for me, a person's handicap never diminished their beauty. I was attracted by their inner quest, how they overcame their handicap. After all, body parts always get broken and dinged up. They can be fixed, even improved upon. I always saw a physical handicap as an engineering problem."

I spread out a batch of pictures on the desk. They showed Artemis snow skiing in a competitive downhill ski race.

"She skied?" Athena said.

"Oh, did she ski!" I said, " She was a world champion. She climbed mountains, too. But this was all before the airplane accident that made her an invalid for the rest of her life. When you first meet her, you'd never guess that she was anything else but a bubbly carefree athlete, but it was only a front. In reality she lived in deep pain. Part of the magic she projected came directly from her incredible smile and her wild laughter. I often saw her laughing, even giggling, entertaining an admiring crowd, then she would excuse herself to go to the restroom and swallow a handful of painkillers. This is not to say that she did not have good days for she had many, but her bad days would just be heartbreaking."

"So what happened after you agreed to help Artemis design her prototype?" Athena said.

"Well, that same day we first met and had lunch, I got back to my office and there was already a message from Artemis giving me her address and asking that I come by the next day at noon. She ended her message with 'regrets only.' As I cancelled meetings and rearranged my schedule so I could meet with her, I thought to myself, this is madness, it's as if I've fallen under a spell."

Athena took a drink and gave me a skeptical look.

"What?" I said, "I know that look of yours."

" I thought Beta had cast the ultimate spell over you," Athena said.

"Ah yes, but that was divine madness," I said. "This was

something else entirely. And so it began. The next day I rode my motorcycle over to her house and parked on the street. I was about to knock on the front door when I saw a note taped to the door. The note said: 'Please come in.' So I let myself in and found Artemis sitting on the sofa with her leg tucked underneath her and a broad smile on her face. There was absolutely no hint of her handicap. She told me to go into the kitchen and bring out two glasses and the pitcher from the refrigerator. I grabbed the pitcher, found the glasses and returned to the living room and poured our drinks.

'This is my favorite drink,' she said, 'cranberry, grapefruit and vodka.'

'Delicious,' I said. Then without saying another word, she handed me an old yellowed newspaper. On the front page of the newspaper, the headline read: 'Only One Survivor from Plane Crash in Mountains.' There's was a gruesome picture of the downed plane, pieces scattered in the snow. The date on the newspaper was ten years earlier. The article detailed how a plane carrying group of young skiers crashed in a remote mountain range. All but one were killed. The lone survivor was Artemis. When the rescuers reached the plane the next day, she was barely alive. She had multiple injuries, including a broken back and her legs and feet were severely frost bitten. She was in intensive care for six weeks and they had to amputate her right leg. I looked at Artemis and tried to imagine the pain and trauma she must have endured. I was in awe. I noticed a copy of *Business Week*

Magazine on the coffee table with a picture of Artemis on the cover. The caption read: 'Olympian Motivates Corporate America.' She'd made a miraculous recovery and became an internationally famous motivational speaker. Along with the settlement from the airlines after the crash and the money from speaking engagements, she was evidently quite wealthy.

She showed me around the house. The whole main floor had been turned into a large office like workroom. There were partitioned-off cubbyholes with desks and computers and a large open area with big worktables covered with prosthetic devices. Artemis showed me some of her old prosthetic devices and pointed out their limitations. We talked about how the new design would be a revolutionary step forward. Then she gave me a draft of the new business plan for our venture to take home and look over. As I was about to leave, I offered her a handshake to officially seal our deal and then leaned forward to give her a parting kiss on the cheek. She put her arms around my neck and kissed me passionately. Then she abruptly let me go.

'Goodbye,' she said, 'I'll call to arrange our next meeting.'

Driving home, I was really angry with myself. I'd let myself get involved in something that I new was trouble. I was sure that by the time I arrived home she would have already left a message. I began thinking of the reasons that I could give her why we needed to break things off before they went any further. I was too old for her, I couldn't take having my heart broken again. I even thought

222

of telling her that I was gay. When I got home, I was relieved to find that there was no new message from Artemis. In fact, the rest of the week I didn't hear a word from her and it was driving me wild. I found myself thinking about her all the time. I told myself that I'd wait another week and if I hadn't heard from her, then I'd call her. Then I realized that I couldn't possibly wait another week and called her. She answered the phone immediately and I tried to sound as casual as I could.

'Are you making any progress?' I said.

'Of course,' she said. 'Working around the clock.'

'Well, let me know when you have something to show me,' I said.

'It might be another week or so,' she said. Maybe I had it all wrong, I thought. Maybe Artemis had no romantic feelings toward me and it was all just business. 'But why don't you come by for lunch tomorrow,' she said, 'I'd love to see you.'

'Great!' I said, almost shouting into the phone. I sounded like an excited schoolboy. 'I'll bring a pizza,' I said.

'I hate pizza,' she said, 'just bring a red rose and I'll make lunch.' I could hardly wait. The next day I showed up with a dozen red roses. Again, there was a note taped on the front door, but I ripped it off without bothering to read it and let myself in. I found Artemis sitting in the dinning room with an elegant lunch already on the table. She gave me a kiss on the cheek as I handed her the roses.

'Lovely,' she said. She asked me to put the roses in a vase and make us a few drinks. 'I've been thinking a lot about you this last week,' she said.

'Really,' I said.

'Yes, I think you're wasting your god-given talent lecturing a bunch of spoiled rich kids at the university.' It was the last thing in the world I expected her to say and it made me feel a bit defensive.

'How could you know,' I said. 'You've never seen me lecture.'

'Au contraire,' she said. 'I attended every one of your lectures last week. I watched through the door to the balcony. You were fabulous.'

'So why should I quit?' I said.

'How many of those students have the ability to absorb what you're telling them?' she said. 'You should be spending your time in the lab, on your inventions, why waste it in the classroom?' She had a point. I'd often had the same thought. But the truth was I loved trying to turn on these young minds and hook them on the wonders of science. Even if just a few in each class became motivated, it was worthwhile. I often formed ongoing scientific collaborations with students that lasted a lifetime.

'Maybe I'm just being selfish,' Artemis said. 'I just want to be sure that I have enough of your time to work on my..., or I should say our project.'

'Not to worry,' I said. 'I'll give it all the attention it needs.'

"Artemis pushed herself up from her chair and on her one leg she gracefully maneuvered around to where I was sitting. She plopped down on my lap and gave me a coy look.

'And what about me?' she said, 'I also need attention.'

"I gave her a kiss and she wrapped her arms around my neck and kissed me back. At that point I knew that I was in big trouble and there was no turning back. I had fallen in love with this truly dangerous creature. My luck had run out and the gods were going to get even with me. I lifted Artemis up out of the chair and carried her up the stairs into the bedroom."

I took a sip of scotch, got up from my chair, and went to the window to look out at the ocean. Athena tried to stifle a yawn.

"That ride I took tired me out," she said. "Should we continue tomorrow?'

"I'm taking a sailing trip tomorrow," I said.

"Then please, finish your story," Athena said. "I'm all ears."

"Well, my relationship with Artemis was a romantic nightmare," I said. "I'd never been with such a domineering woman. I'd always been the domineering one. But Artemis rarely listened to a word I said."

"A little role reversal, hmmm?"

"You could call it that," I said. "We had almost finished work on our new prosthetic device. In fact, we had companies interested in buying it. And then everything just fell apart."

225

"What happened?"

"Her spinal injury had taken a turn for the worse and the doctors had prescribed a new cocktail of painkilling drugs. She was confined to her wheelchair and the doctors were pessimistic she'd ever get out of it. I took a leave of absence from the university to help take care of her increasing medical needs. To my own amazement, I was a good caregiver. In the past, I'd always been rather stoical about my own health and equally stoic about the health of others."

" How well I remember," Athena said. "You only sent me to the doctor once, for a broken arm."

"And here's to your everlasting good health," I said and raised my glass. "Anyway," I continued, "between my work at the university and taking care of Artemis, I was working around the clock. The situation created a severe strain at home with your mother. She was always the homemaker, the one who took care of my every need. Now, here I was nursing another woman in ways that I'd never done for her. The situation couldn't last. Artemis was having a hard time recovering from her latest setback. She became depressed and quit giving motivational speeches.

'I can't stand up there anymore and tell people why things were great,' she said.

"She wanted me to quit the university altogether and be her full time companion. She told me that I could live with her and she'd support us both financially. When I told her that was impossible, we argued bitterly. Sarcastically, I told her she should get a dog if she needed constant companionship."

As I thought back on the incident I started to laugh out loud.

"What's so funny?" Athena asked.

"Well, Artemis thought getting a dog was a great idea!" I said. "I couldn't tell if she was being serious or just trying to insult me by implying that I could be replaced by a dog. But the next day, she called to say she'd found a Malamute puppy and wanted me to help her go pick it up. I drove Artemis in her van down to a kennel that was in a small town about 100 miles away. When we got there, Artemis wheeled herself into a large fenced pen with the litter of Malamute puppies. The puppies took turns jumping up onto her lap. She was in seventh heaven. Artemis picked up one puppy she liked and handed to me.

'I think this is the one,' she said. I held the pup up in the air and nuzzled its belly.

'He's a beauty,' I said.

'I'm going to call him Midnight Sun,' she said.

"On the drive back home, Midnight Sun rode on her lap the whole way. The next two weeks were quite enjoyable. Artemis spent every waking moment with that dog and countless hours telling me why her new puppy was superior to every other dog in the world. Then one afternoon while I was out sailing, she left me an urgent message that Midnight Sun was trembling and having trouble walking. By the time I got to her house early that evening, the vet had already put the dog down. She lay on the couch with her head resting in my lap and sobbed hysterically. She blamed me for not being available when she needed me. A theme that was often repeated during our short relationship.

"I went on a business trip to Chicago and when I returned three days later, I went over to see Artemis. She had put framed pictures of Midnight Sun all over the house with candles burning next to them. It was like she'd turned her house into a shrine to the dog. She was moping around the house and had let herself go to hell. She'd always been meticulous about her looks, but now it looked like she hadn't bathed for days. She lay down on the couch in her bathrobe in a sullen mood. I brought her a cup of tea, but she didn't want it. I had found out that the stroke that killed Midnight Sun was a hereditary defect in Malamutes."

'The kennel has offered to give us a replacement puppy,' I said.

'I don't want another puppy,' she said, 'it could never replace Midnight Sun.'

'Nonsense,' I said. I was feed up with her self-pity. 'Tomorrow morning at 8 o'clock I'll be here to pick you up,' I said. 'We're going to go get the new puppy and you better be cleaned up and ready to go. If you're not, then it's over between us. I'm sick of being your nursemaid.' After I delivered my little ultimatum, Artemis just stared at the wall. 'See you tomorrow,' I said and left.

"The next morning at eight, when I pulled up in front of her house, Artemis was already sitting on the front porch in her

228

wheelchair. She was wearing a white cashmere sweater and fire red blouse. She looked gorgeous. As we drove out to the kennel, she sat stoically looking out the window. We didn't exchange a single word the whole trip and when we got to the kennel, Artemis didn't even get out of the van.

'Aren't you coming in to pick out the new puppy?' I said.

'No, I'll wait here,' she said. 'Pick whichever one you like.'

'Suit yourself,' I said. I found a frisky new Malamute puppy and thanked the kennel owners. When I got back into the van I set the puppy on Artemis's lap. On the drive home, she began to gently pet the little guy. I saw her smile for the first time in weeks. When we parked in her driveway, she handed the puppy to me.

'Let's call him, Midnight Sun 2,' she said.

I saw Athena smiling at me and paused.

"Father, you're such an animal lover," Athena said, "only you would insist on dog therapy."

"But it worked," I said, "it got Artemis out her funk and things improved between us somewhat."

"Somewhat?"

"Artemis still wanted me all to herself. It all came to a head one night when I dropped by her house after teaching an evening class at the university. She was in a foul mood and asked me if I could stay the night because she didn't want to be alone. I'd had never done that before and told her that I wasn't going to start.

'Then get the hell out of here,' she screamed at me. When I got

229

home your mother met me at the front door.

'Artemis just left a message on our answering machine,' she said. 'She claimed she's overdosed on her medication because she doesn't want to live anymore.' After I heard the message, I tried to call her back, but she didn't answer. I called Artemis again and this time she picked up. Her language was slurred and then she seemed like she dropped the phone.

'Artemis,' I said. 'Are you still there?' There was no response and I told your mother to call the ER at the hospital and tell them that I was bringing in a patient who'd just overdosed on her medication. I rushed over to her house and found the puppy outside on the front lawn and the front door wide open. Inside, her wheelchair was tipped over on the floor and Artemis was sprawled on the floor beside it. In the bathroom sink, I found a handful of empty medicine bottles and stuffed them in my coat pocket. I carried Artemis out to my truck, grabbed the dog, and sped off the hospital. At the emergency entrance, two medics were waiting and put Artemis on a gurney and rushed her into the hospital.

"I paced back and forth in the ER waiting room as they pumped her stomach, filled it with charcoal and put in an IV. The doctor came out and greeted me by name and I realized that he'd been one of my pre-med undergrad students years ago. He told me that Artemis was going to be fine. As a favor to his old professor, he said that even though her condition was life threatening, he wouldn't file a police report. I went in to her room and looked at

Artemis sleeping in the hospital bed. With her face blackened from the charcoal she looked just like Judy Garland when she sang "I'm a Tramp." I lay down on the floor beside her bed with the new puppy under my coat and went to sleep. The next morning, Artemis checked out of the hospital and I took back to her house and her assistant put her to bed. Then I went home and went to bed myself. I was exhausted."

I sipped my wine and looked at Athena. "That very night is the one you remember so well," I said. "Artemis got in her van and drove to our house."

"That's the night she showed up outside in her wheelchair and threw rocks at the house?" Athena said.

"Yes," I said. "After I managed to subdue her and bring her into the house, your mother made her some chicken soup to warm her up. Artemis seemed genuinely sorry for her behavior and after she calmed down, she apologized and went home."

"And the next morning, I answered the phone," Athena said, "and it was the police wanting to talk to you."

"Yes," I said, "Artemis had left a suicide note at her house saying that she'd gone off to kill herself. I didn't know what to tell the police since I had no idea where she might go. After three days of searching the police found her and the puppy in a motel up near Big Sur. They escorted her back to town and checked her into a psychiatric hospital."

"That's when her puppy moved in with us?" Athena asked.

"That's right," I said. "For those two weeks that Artemis was in the psychiatric ward, she underwent intensive therapy and I visited her every day. She seemed calm, almost happy. When they let her go home, I took her puppy back and we decided it might be best for her to work things out on her own for a while."

"And did she?" Athena asked.

"A week or so later, her assistant called," I said, "and told me that Artemis had filled her van with her essential belongings and left town. She had instructed her attorney to sell her house and the items remaining in the house. I never saw her again. Every few months or so, in the middle of the night, she would call and update me on her life and her health. After not hearing from her for almost a year, she called and said that she had married the mentor she had when she was in college. She was emailing me photographs of her wedding and, of course, Midnight Sun Two. She said that she was very happy and wished me the best.

'I hadn't heard from you for so long, I thought you were dead,' I said.

'No, still alive and kicking with one foot, my love,' she said, 'When I start to slide into the abyss, I let you be the first to know.'

'But I really don't want to know,' I said.

"How irrational and selfish on my part, but I couldn't help myself. I didn't want to go to a funeral, I didn't want to know that she had died or even that she was going to die. A month later, Stan

232

showed me an article in the *New York Times* headlined "Courageous Olympian Slips Away" and there was a picture of Artemis. The article claimed that the cause of death was an accidental overdose, just like Heath Ledger and Michael Jackson. Thankfully, she had done what I asked her to do and had not involved me in any aspect of her death. That was her last and biggest gift to me.

ATHENA

SAILING

The next morning I found Britta in the kitchen making a pot of oatmeal.

"Your father must have left early," she said. "When I came in the house at seven, I found a warm cup of coffee sitting on the table and no sign of him."

Father would often pour a cup of coffee and never get around to drinking it. I poured myself a cup of coffee and sat down.

"Father told me to let you know that he's gone off sailing for a week," I told Britta.

"Probably to Tibey Island," Britta said.

"His favorite getaway," I added.

"What are your plans," Britta asked me.

"I'm going to stay another week, see some old friends and help Arthur wrap up things at Mother's gallery."

"Wonderful," Britta said. "It will be good to have some company." I didn't tell Britta that I was considering moving back to Santa Cruz. I hadn't even discussed it with Father. I thought that I'd think it through and make up my mind by the time he got back. I saw an envelope on the table with my name handwritten on it. I took the envelope, poured another cup of coffee, and went out to the porch.

I sat down on the rocking chair and opened the envelope. Inside was a handwritten letter from father.

"Athena, my love, I want to thank you for taking the time to stay and talk with me. Your mother was the nucleus of my life. Whatever wild orbit I fell into, she always held me in place. Now that she's gone, I might just spin off into space. My only remaining concerns are for your welfare and that Britta be taken care of and someone tend the animals. I hope that our talk helped to resolve some things between us and will let us rebuild our relationship. I'm sorry if I hurt you in the past. You were and always will be my beloved precious daughter. Love, Father"

I sat in the rocking chair lost in thought. Deep down, I always felt that father loved me. I guess I'd become disillusioned with his lifestyle and closed my heart to him. Now I realized that he and Mother never had anything to hide from each other or from me. I'd just run off at an early age and shut them out of my life. Now it seemed like a new beginning was possible. And yet I felt a twinge of dread that Father's letter was somehow a goodbye. I read it again and felt better. Optimistic that when he returned, we could again be father and daughter.

I spent the week helping Arthur arrange mother's business affairs. Each afternoon I took Zeus for a ride and then spent the evening with Britta. She was planning a trip back home to Scotland and told me stories about how as a girl she trained border collies to herd the family sheep. By the end of the week there was no sign of Father. Britta said not to worry, that weather often delayed him on his sailing trips. But as the next week wore on, I began to fear that he would never return. And, indeed, he never did.

As the months past, there was no news. The Coast Guard searched and found nothing, not even a trace of his sailboat. I moved back to Santa Cruz and found a job at a small design firm. Britta stayed on and over time we became good friends. Finally, a year after Father had vanished, Arthur advised me that we should declare him dead. I was against the idea because I clung to some remote possibility that he would return. But Arthur insisted that we needed closure. He told me that I was going to inherit father's estate and that we needed make it all legal so that I could make decisions about his businesses and assets.

We arranged a wake at the house. Stan and Max were there along with a big group of Mother and Father's friends. It was a warm and loving affair and everyone stayed until past midnight telling stories about father. At one point in the evening, Arthur wanted a moment with me and we went into father's study.

"After your mother died," Arthur said, "your father called me and told me that he wanted everything he had to go to you, no matter how things worked out between you two. He had me draw up a new will immediately. 'Just in case things happen unexpectedly,' he said."

"Do you think he was planning to disappear after mother died?"

"We'll never know," Arthur said.

Then Arthur told me the size of Father's estate and I was stunned. I'd inherited a fortune.

By two in the morning, when everyone had finally left, Stan insisted on taking me out to the barn. He opened a cabinet that housed our film collection and rummaged through reels of film.

"Here it is," he said finally and pulled out a small film cannister. "Does the projector still work," he asked.

"Probably," I said.

"Load it up, my Angel," he said, "and let's take a look."

I threaded up the film, killed the lights and Stan and I got into the Porsche. Up on the screen, I was amazed to see footage of father and me sailing in his boat.

"Remember this?" Stan asked me.

"Sort of," I said. "It's like a dream, but I don't remember you filming us."

" I used to take the camera out a lot when I went sailing with your father," Stan said. "It was some of the most beautiful footage I ever shot."

There was no sound, just the silent film images on the screen. I must have been no more that five years old and I was sitting on Father's lap as he steered the boat. As we cut through the water, waves crashed over the deck and I held on to Father for dear life. Father was laughing and having a grand old time. I looked up at him and he kissed me on the forehead. I smiled.